A most anticipated book of 2020 from *The Millions*

A most anticipated book of 2020 from *Paste Magazine*

A most anticipated historical fiction book of 2020 from *Book Riot*

"A highly recommended literary page-turner worth a
second reading; fans of Gabriel García Márquez will delight in
this fantastical—and fantastic novel."
—*Library Journal, starred review*

"Impactful . . . Araghi's skillful combination of revolutionary politics
and magical realism will please fans of Alejo Carpentier."
—*Publishers Weekly*

"This superb debut follows an extended Iranian family
through feline curse, daily survival, unintended betrayals and the
transformative power of language."
—*Shelf Awareness*

"Ali Araghi's staggering debut is a book about time, about stories,
about what time and stories can and cannot do to save us.
It's a book about how wars, and nations, are made—not out of
violence, but out of the people upon whom the violence preys.
It's about family, inheritance, language, fate. It's a book about me.
It's a book about you, too."
—**Kaveh Akbar, author of** *Pilgrim Bell*

"What a joy to lose oneself in an Iranian magical realist
multi-generational family epic! Araghi's moving tale is unforgettable
in its twists and turns. The personal and the political are
perfectly intertwined in the way only Iranians know all too well. This
novel deserves its own rung on the Iranian fiction canon!"
—**Porochista Khakpour, author of** *Brown Album*

"Ali Araghi's stunning debut novel gives us what the so-called news can't provide, a portal into the heart of the place we think we know as Iran. Araghi's is the Iran of *One Thousand and One Nights* and he is our Scheherazade, the tale he's telling is magnificent, brutal, spellbinding, as well as being—like Scheherazade's —crucial to survival."
—Kathryn Davis, author of *The Thin Place*

"*The Immortals of Tehran* gives its readers hope and a feeling of transcendence, through incandescent language, and with the perspective of Ahmad, a truly unforgettable protagonist. A balm for the soul, and a book for a transforming world."
—Michael J. Seidlinger, author of *My Pet Serial Killer*

"Ali Araghi's debut novel is an impressive work of Middle Eastern historical fiction meeting magical realism. You are as likely to be mesmerized by the weight of historical events that animate the story's narrative as by the magical elements that create a pause. Araghi's work has been compared to Gabriel Garcia Marquez, Gunter Grass, Salman Rushdie and Junot Diaz. But more importantly, he is his own: an unmistakably original voice."
—Arash Azizi, author of *The Shadow Commander: Soleimani, the US, and Iran's Global Ambitions*

"Iran is a complicated country with a tumultuous history that defies linear narratives and simple explanations. A compelling literary portrait of Iran can only be drawn in a uniquely complex, ambitious, and vast novel. Very few books have fulfilled this goal as impressively as Ali Araghi's *The Immortals of Tehran*."
—Amir Ahmadi Arian, author of *Then the Fish Swallowed Him*

"Tinged with satire, Ali Araghi produces a cleverly fabled history of Iran, echoing a rich tradition of storytelling in a modern, original voice. Bold, unflappable and endearing characters will sweep readers along on an epic journey with political and social resonance today."
—Sahar Mustafah, author of *The Beauty of Your Face*

The IMMORTALS of TEHRAN

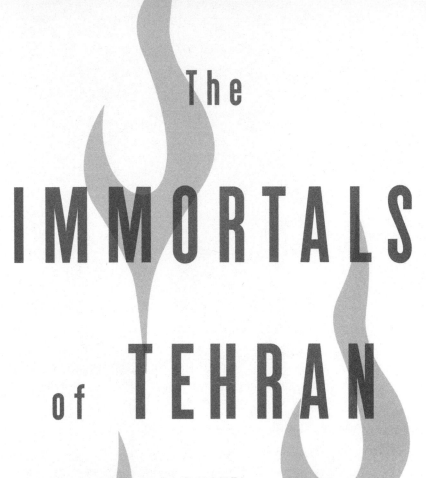

The
IMMORTALS
of TEHRAN

A NOVEL

ALI ARAGHI

MELVILLE HOUSE
BROOKLYN • LONDON

The Immortals of Tehran

Melville House Publishing
46 John Street
Brooklyn, NY 11201
and
Melville House UK
Suite 2000
16/18 Woodford Road
London E7 0HA

mhpbooks.com
@melvillehouse

ISBN: 978-1-61219-907-8
ISBN: 978-1-61219-819-4 (eBook)

Chapter 1 was previously published in slightly different form in *Fifth Wednesday Journal*.

LCCN: 2019957481

Designed by Richard Oriolo

Printed in the United States of America

1 3 5 7 9 10 8 6 4 2

Agha's Family Tree

The Torkash-Vand Branch

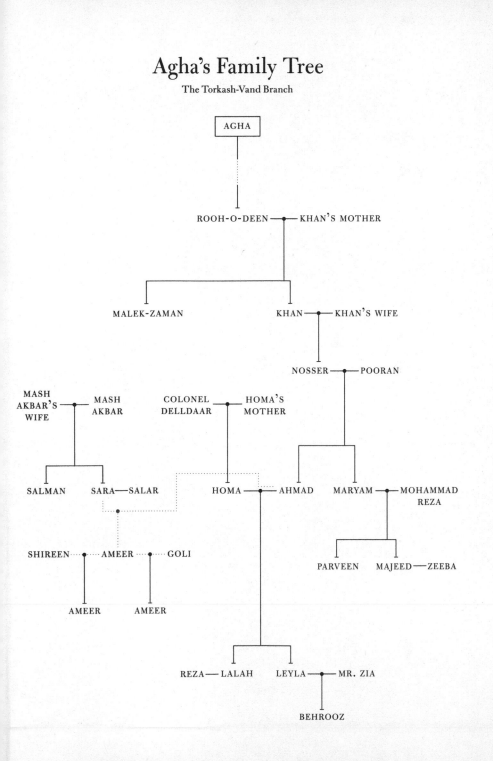

The IMMORTALS of TEHRAN

AHMAD WAS A TEN-YEAR-OLD BOY when he was a ten-year-old boy. Never would he have thought, as he played tag with his childhood friends in the village of Tajrish, that he would one day watch his best friend's father bite off a dead cat's ear. Ahmad could not have foreseen that he would one day work in a forge, pounding white-hot iron with a heavy hammer. His childhood imagination could never have pictured the trains that sped through tunnels under the big city, in which one grasped for a hanging strap. In short, Ahmad Torkash-Vand could not have fathomed that the fog that shrouded the village that early summer morning would change the course of their history.

On Ahmad's sister's wedding day, the morning fog descended the mountains as if some god had summoned it from the far seas. Many in the village had been in preparations since the marriage was announced by Ahmad's father one month before. On the Day of the Fog, as it would later be called by those who decided to stay, a knocking woke Ahmad from his sleep. The sound traveled, jerky and anxious, from the front door, across the yard, into the house, along the hallway, and into Ahmad's bedroom. For a few seconds he thought he had heard the rap in his dreams. His eyes were closing again when the repeated pounding yanked him out of sleep. He sat up remembering his sister's wedding. His mother had told him the night before that she would leave for the Orchard with the women from the neighboring houses shortly after dawn to prepare for the ceremony. She had asked him to let the chickens out of the coop, scatter some feed, and not forget to get them back in before leaving for the Orchard. That was his only chore for the morning.

The house was quiet. "Mom!" Ahmad called out toward his closed door. He sprang up from his sleeping pad on the floor to look out the window. Behind the white lace curtain, a fog had fallen so dense he could barely make out anything in the courtyard. With its chain-link fence lost in white, the coop was no more than the ghost of a large cage with blurry wooden posts. The blue hoez that reflected the overhanging elm branches in its calm water every morning had dimmed into an unidentifiable dark patch. Ahmad heard the nervous knocking again and this time Salman's voice came with it: "Ahmaaaad!" Ahmad was not unfamiliar with Salman's banging on the door, which often meant play time out in the dirt alleys or outside the village on the mountain trails, shooting pebbles at sparrows with slingshots. But his friend had never come so early in the morning, when it was time to prepare fresh meat for the customers and he had to lend a hand at the butchery. In response to Salman's shout, the rooster, Ahmad's favorite in the coop, cried out a hoarse *ghoo-ghooli-ghoo-ghoooooo.*

"Coming," Ahmad shouted as he stepped onto the wide veranda that overlooked the courtyard. The fog was the thickest Ahmad had ever walked into. If he had not already known where the hoez, the flower beds, the coop, and the cauldrons were, he would have lost his way in the limbo of the large yard. "Ahmad, hurry! It's your father." Suddenly the fog seeped into Ahmad's chest. From the pile of shoes and slippers, he threw on the first pair he could find, ran down the four steps into the courtyard, and sprinted to the front door. Salman was restlessly shifting his weight from one foot to the other. Worry shot from his eyes. Without a word, he started running. Ahmad ran after him, along alleys in which fog flowed like a river toward a white sea. In front of him, Salman was a ghost, only half-visible, partially dissolved. Ahmad had to exert himself to catch up with his swift-footed friend lest the fog eat him altogether. He kicked off his slippers. The only sounds were their steps on the ground, and their panting. The rest of the world had gone. Ahmad tried to think what might have happened to his father. He followed Salman around a corner and came to the open area in front of the mosque where a murmuring crowd had gathered. The people close to the entrance were more visible while the ones on the periphery blended into white.

"Here comes his son," someone shouted. The people Ahmad could see turned their heads toward him as the crowd parted to let him through. Both metal doors of the mosque were flung open. Usually only one door was used; the second was unlatched only for funerals, marriages, and ceremonies. Surrounded by the onlookers and standing taller than them all, Mulla Ali was waiting close to the door. It was the first time Ahmad had seen the mulla without his white turban. The man's sparse gray hair was in disarray, as if he had run his hand through it in different directions. He had draped his black cloak over his shoulders without changing out of his striped cream pajamas and white undershirt. Inside the mosque, a few men stood facing the small door in the corridor that opened into the stairwell inside the minaret. The turquoise tiles of the minaret faded into the milky haze before Ahmad could see what was happening up at the crown.

"Come down, Nosser," Nemat the Barber shouted up. "Don't do this to the House of God." Ahmad felt a hole open in his stomach down which his insides tumbled in an endless fall. It was his father Nemat was calling. The muffled sound of metal hitting something nonmetal was the only reply from the top of the minaret. "Step back! Step back!" shouted one of the men standing inside. Some ran out and others dashed farther into the mosque before something rumbled in the minaret and large chunks of broken brick shot out of the stairwell at the bottom. A flowerpot broke. Ahmad looked around at the faces he saw every day: the grocer; the bathhouse keeper; Mohammad the Carpenter; the baker; Salman's father, Mash Akbar—a short man with a big stomach—and everyone else. It was hard to make out the faces of the women who were sitting—mostly in white chadors, camouflaged by the fog—on the rooftops witnessing the incident. He could not tell if his mother was among them. Why would she be watching and doing nothing? Salman's father limped over to him and rested a hand on his shoulder. "What's my father doing, Mash Akbar?" Ahmad asked, but before Mash Akbar could answer, there was a gunshot from the top of the minaret: a shot into the fog. Everyone looked up in sudden agitation, although nothing could be seen. Ahmad was afraid. A second shot was fired. Salman covered his ears. Ahmad, too, put his hands on his ears and took shelter behind Mash Akbar.

Mulla Ali combed his black-and-white beard with his long, bony fingers and looked up at the top of the minaret. "Nosser Khan, come down!" he shouted. "There are no Russians in the sky." Another shot followed. A man stood next to Nemat the Barber with a sheet tied around his neck, half his head shaved clean and the other half covered in lather. Ahmad had seen him before, but did not know his name. Word had it he once loved a girl who broke his heart by running off with someone else. Now the man lived in a shack in the mountains and came down to Tajrish only to buy necessities, sell wild rhubarb, and shave his head. Nemat the Barber grabbed the man by the arm. "Let's go," he said, pulling gently. "Let's go finish you. The man's gone cuckoo again." This he said looking at Ahmad, as if the ballyhoo was the boy's fault. Ahmad kept his ears covered. There was another gunshot, and more brick came rolling down the spiral stairwell of the minaret.

"Nosser Khan," shouted Mulla Ali, "your son is here. Can you hear me? Ahmad is here."

Nosser was looking for trouble again; that was what Ahmad's grandfather, Amin-olla Khan, would have said. Khan had certainly not yet heard what was happening, or else he would already be at the mosque to right things.

"Khan" was what they called Ahmad's grandfather. He was not considered the chief of the village, but he had the village in his pocket. He was the owner of several apple orchards in Tajrish and the surrounding villages, in the foot of the Alborz mountain range, north of Tehran. In recent years he had purchased even more land and orchards in the eastern area of Damavand, and it was through his enterprises that years later, the Damavand apple became the most popular variety in the capital city of Tehran, synonymous with quality and taste.

Khan arrived in Tajrish a newborn in his mother's arms when his great-great-great-grandfather, Agha, moved the family from the western parts of the country with a scimitar and enough inheritance to buy a small orchard. Khan grew up with a keen sense of business. At the age of seven, when his father died, he took matters into his own hands, and he held the title deed to a new orchard shortly after he turned sixteen. In Tajrish, Khan was second to the village mulla. When the rumor had broken out that his orchards were haunted by jinns, Khan approached Mulla Ali, and it was with the help of the clergyman—who held a red apple in his hand and bit into it in front of everyone—that Khan shed his ominous reputation and persuaded the village people to work for him again.

Ahmad's father, Nosser, was Khan's only son. Khan's wife was in excruciating pain for weeks before Nosser was due. When the pangs started to throb, she first clenched her teeth, then bit her index finger. When she dropped to her knees clawing the carpet and calling out Khan's name, he would run to her room with opium. All the women in the house and many of the neighbors gathered in the main house when the due date arrived, saying prayers and reciting verses from the Quran. For five hours, as his wife's shrieks pierced the night, Khan sat motionless at the walnut desk in his room, twirling the tips of his black mustache and tapping his finger on the wood as if to tick off seconds that passed too slowly. When the screams stopped, he closed his eyes and listened first to the cries of the baby and then to the wailing of the women mourning the death of his wife. He got up from his desk and stood there for a while, tall, in his pressed suit and pants, not knowing what to do. With the back of his hand, he brushed off his lapel, which was not dusty. He straightened his suit, which stood as crinkle-free as black marble. He bent his head and closed his eyes listening to the sad sounds from downstairs. Finally, he took his Astrakhan hat from the hanger, and left his room to see the baby.

In the privacy of their homes, the people of the village said what they believed: that the sinister birth of the child had taken the life of the innocent beautiful woman. It was with a mixture of fear and reverence that the people of Tajrish regarded Khan and the young Nosser. Khan gave many work in his orchards and helped the poor. He orchestrated a movement to build a mosque in place of the old room where Mulla had laid rugs to use as the public praying room. The money that was collected allowed a dome, but ran out after the first minaret was erected. Hands locked behind his back, Mulla looked at the workers on the scaffolding installing the turquoise tiles halfway up the minaret and thought, *Who has seen a mosque with a single minaret?* After the mosque was built, Khan stood in the first row of the noon congregational prayer, right behind Mulla Ali. From that night on, that place of honor was established as his. Khan never remarried after the death of his wife, but he had two rooms built by the side of the main house in the Orchard and asked his sister, Malek-Zaman, to move in with her husband and her two little girls. "Malek, consider Nosser your son," Khan told her sister. He did this to save Nosser from the humiliation of having a stepmother and to give him the love of an aunt, the closest to that of a mother.

Nosser grew up to be a bully. Taller and stronger than the other boys his age, he ran the fastest and climbed the highest in the walnut trees until the village kids excluded him from their games altogether. Nosser, in turn, harassed his cousins and the others with sticks and slingshots and pinches and ruined their games. His aunt's husband punished him for his mischief when Khan was not around. One winter night he grabbed Nosser's arm and dragged him to the small stable at the end of the Orchard where Khan kept his two horses. He tied Nosser to a beam and filled his pants with horse manure before leaving him there for the night. He knew the boy would risk a beating from Khan for being a nuisance if he ever told anyone. But his stronger reassurance was that he knew Nosser was too proud to admit to the humiliation either to Khan or to anyone else. From that night on, every week or two, Nosser spent a night in the stable, his loose pants puffed with the soft, slimy mush.

Nosser seemed to be growing up much faster than the other kids. With a sparse, fine mustache under his nose, he looked fifteen at eleven. When he was fourteen, he vanished from Tajrish. He walked four hours to Tehran and volunteered to do his military service. "A goat chewed it," he said when they asked for his birth certificate.

"You have a big brother?" the officer asked. "Go get his. I need some papers here." Nosser shook his head. The officer eyed him over for a moment, then slipped him a piece of paper. "'I testify that I'm eighteen years of age,' write and sign."

After serving near the border of Turkey for two years, Nosser returned to Tajrish one day when men were loading a cart with apple crates. Without a word, he picked up a crate and joined in. A little boy dashed off to tell Khan. The cart was not yet half full when Khan came striding through the trees. Nosser stood straight, as if at attention, until Khan stopped in front of him inspecting his son's khaki uniform, his black boots caked with mud, and his face that looked more mature than he would have guessed: Nosser's beard, although trimmed, was full, his skin showed the tan that came with sweating work, and his nose had grown twice in size. He stepped forward and opened his arms, but before he could embrace his son, Nosser said, "Father, I have a wife now." Khan dropped his arms and squinted his eyes. "Her name is Pooran." Nosser's voice was starting to tremble. "And she's pregnant." Khan's eyebrows raised. Nosser welled up, but he still held his head high, casting down his eyes to avoid his father's, staring instead at his pressed suit and pants and sumac tie. Those moments when Khan twirled the tip of his mustache, a frown hovering above his inquisitive eyes, Nosser imagined himself ostracized from his paternal house, wandering the streets of the capital with his pregnant wife.

"I won't forgive you," Khan said, "the next time you leave your wife alone. Why aren't you with her?"

Although Iran was officially neutral when World War II broke out, Nosser enlisted in Reza Shah's army and went away again. This Ahmad remembered. He must have been eight, and his sister Maryam eleven. Before Nosser left, there was a ceremony in the mosque. Mulla Ali said prayers in a circle of villagers so Nosser would have a safe journey, shook Nosser's hand, and lowered his turbaned head to hug him goodbye. In their room Pooran pulled away from Nosser and averted his goodbye kiss. "They're waiting for you," she said picking up Nosser's bag from the floor. Looking into his surprised eyes, she relented. "I owe you a kiss." Out front in the Orchard, Nosser bent and kissed Khan's hand before getting into the Ford V8 his father had ordered for him for the occasion. Ahmad and a pack of neighborhood kids ran after the fern-green car in the cloud of dust that the tires stirred and stopped only after the vehicle distanced itself from them on the Shemiron Road, the road that snaked from the foot of the mountains to the capital. Ahmad's father was gone for a year and a half. He returned with a broken soul.

IT WAS SIX MONTHS NOW since Nosser returned. At first, he had locked himself in his room for ten days. Every day or two he would eat half of the food Pooran prepared and placed at his door in a tray. After the tenth day he opened the door and tried to resume his normal life. He talked less. He bought a hunting rifle and started trekking the mountains in his army boots and pants, coming back every other day with a rabbit that Pooran refused to touch. "Go ahead and do what you want," Pooran said, "but I'm not doing this and I'm not letting my daughter do this either." She believed hunting would bring misfortune to a household. It was big enough calamity that her husband killed animals that were meant to be killed by other animals only; she would not have them skinned and cooked in her house. This she announced with such determination that Nosser never again brought game home. Instead he fed his rabbits and quails to the pack of stray dogs that hurried to welcome him near the village, wary not to get too close to the houses and the children who threw stones at them.

Nosser followed the war news on the radio as if God had so commanded in his Holy Book. Not many people in the village were interested in the war or felt threatened by the blaze that was eating Europe or the fact that their northern neighbors, the Soviets, brought the war too close to their homes. Salman's father Mash Akbar, one of the two village butchers, was the only person who would discuss the war. Nosser spent many an evening with him going over the newspapers that came from Tehran every other day in the truck that brought provisions under a burlap cover.

It was in this situation that Pooran had to deal with Maryam's suitor. Three weeks after Nosser returned from the army, the Ford V8 chauffeur paid a visit to ask for their daughter's hand. He had seen Maryam on the day of Nosser's departure and he had fallen for the way a lock of hair hung over her forehead from underneath her chador. When the young man heard that the girl's father was back, he formally sought her hand in marriage. He was a chauffeur for one of Tehran's big merchants, a friend of Khan's. It was thanks to a mixture of politics and sincere affection for an old friend that the merchant had lent Khan his V8 and chauffeur for Nosser's special day. Pooran did not find her husband as interested in the matter as she expected. Given the suitor's good social status as a chauffeur, Nosser declared his approval with a nod of the head while listening to the radio and cleaning his rifle. Khan was the bigger supporter. He hosted the premarriage talks in his house in the Orchard with the boy's mother, father, uncles, and aunts. He liked that the suitor was named after the crown prince, Mohammad Reza, although, being lanky and carefree, he was not comparable to the son of the Shah in any other way.

On the day of the proposal, Khan was unnerved that Mohammad Reza talked too much, and Pooran found his ambitions to get into the import/export business or open a shop overly optimistic, as both enterprises would require a lump of money that Mohammad Reza did not have. Pooran had dreamed of a better groom for her daughter, perhaps a doctor who was also charming and handsome. Mohammad Reza was not even much taller than Maryam. But he seemed like a good boy and had a respectable job, and she liked the way his neat suit and tie looked on him. She would not be ashamed to show him to others and tell them he was her son-in-law. On top of that, Pooran was not brave enough to endure the fear of not finding Maryam a husband before she turned fifteen. After the groom's family had made a few trips to the Orchard, the wedding was announced.

In the following months Nosser began to think twice about the fact that his daughter was going to leave Tajrish to live in Tehran. The flames of the war that was devouring the world blazed too close. If anything happened, the capital would be the first to catch fire. Nested at the foot of mountains, in the shelter of rocks and boulders, Tajrish was safer. But, as they say, "A daughter belongs to others." He did not voice his concerns.

MULLA ALI PLACED HIS HANDS on Ahmad's shoulders and pushed him gently forward. "Nosser," he shouted into the white above, "can you see Ahmad? He's here, right here with me! Don't bring God's wrath upon the people. Don't do this to the House of God. For the sake of your son." A heavy silence fell upon the crowd who looked up into the fog listening for a reply. Crows cawed somewhere deep in the white murk from their perches atop plane trees. Sparrows chirped their morning songs. "Nosser Khan!" shouted Mash Akbar, Salman's father. "Nosser Khan, can you hear us?" Ahmad slowly removed his hands from his ears. "Nosser Khan!" The crows stopped their baleful shrieks and now it was only the song of the sparrows piercing the shroud of the fog that had enveloped Tajrish and its people. Ahmad turned at the sound of footsteps to see his mother rushing toward them. He wiggled out of Mulla's hands and ran to her.

"What's your father doing?" Pooran whispered as she approached the edge of the crowd.

"He's shooting flying Russians," Ahmad answered, squeezing his mother's chador in his fist.

"What?" she turned her eyes to the crowd as if, not believing Ahmad, she was looking to see what was really happening.

"I got up and I was going to feed the chickens and come help you. But Salman knocked and we ran here. Father is up there at the top of the minaret.

He's hunting the Russians, and Nemat said we are crazy. Father is fine, right?"

"God willing, son, God willing."

"Nosser Khan," shouted Salman's father, "your wife is here, too. Come down. Nosser, can you hear me?" But no human sound seemed able to descend from the invisible top. The sparrows had become silent too and now Ahmad could even hear the wheezy breathing of Mohammad the Carpenter, who had tilted his large head back and looked up into the fog with an open mouth. Sweat slid from his temple down his round, fleshy cheek. Time had stopped. The villagers had turned into stone figures in a hushed apocalypse. Then Nosser's voice blasted from the heart of the fog:

"Send the boy up."

Faces turned to Ahmad. He looked at his mother.

"God bless your father, Mr. Nosser," shouted Mulla Ali toward the minaret. "May your family live long. He's coming right up to you now. Just put the pickax down and don't throw any more bricks, Nosser Khan. All right? We don't want the boy hurt, do we?" Ahmad's mother gave him a soft tap on the back meaning, Go to your father. Everything is going to be all right. Mulla Ali accompanied him through the crowd. "He is at the foot of the stairs, Mr. Nosser." The door was open wide. It was a small, old, wooden door leading to a dark and narrow spiral stairwell that went up as if to a white hell in the sky. A broken lock lay on the floor. "Go, go." Mulla Ali pushed Ahmad in.

The jagged triangular steps curled around the inside of the minaret toward the crown. Ahmad wanted to hurry, but he had to place each foot carefully, avoiding the fallen chunks of brick. He ran, a groping hand on the wall, but the blackened plaster provided nothing to hold on to. Small openings in the wall allowed the softened morning light to penetrate the darkness. If the openings had been lower, Ahmad could at least peek down at the people, but all he could see now was the fog.

"Who is that?" his father barked from above. "Who's coming up? I have bricks. I'll throw. Who is there?"

"It's me."

"Ahmad?"

"Yes, Father."

"Come on up here, son," he snapped. "Quick."

As Ahmad hurried up, each step more covered by dust and pieces of brick, he began to hear his father's hoarse breathing. A few more steps and there he was, sitting on the stairs. Behind him on higher steps lay his leather boots and the pickax he had used to pry out bricks. Ahmad looked at the pockmarked wall, then at his father's rifle sticking out of the opening in the wall. The stock rested in his strong arms like a baby. The soft light from the opening lit the left side of his face. Deep wrinkles burrowed his dusty, sweaty forehead. He looked more like Grandfather. But Khan *was* old. Nosser was not.

"There you are," he said, his voice rasping, his eyes fixed on Ahmad with an unwavering intensity. "Where have you been?"

"I was down there," Ahmad replied, "with the others."

"Are you afraid?"

Ahmad was not sure what to answer.

"I said are you afraid?"

Ahmad shook his head.

"Then hold up your head and let me hear your voice. Are you afraid?"

"No, Father, no."

Nosser rolled over to look out the opening and a button popped off his shirt, bounced off the step where Ahmad was standing, and landed on the one below it. Ahmad fished the button from dust and debris. In the palm of his hand, it reflected the subdued white of the fog outside, as if it were pearl. Ahmad looked at his father's shirt. The dark-brown pinstripes cascaded and surged like waves. "Is your mother there, too?" Nosser asked, squinting down into the fog.

"Yes."

Nosser placed his cheek on the rifle and tilted it up. "They're there," he said with an eye closed. "Are you listening to me?"

"Yes, Father."

"Who's up there, if you are listening?"

Nosser had not said who was up there. Ahmad threw a furtive look out the opening from where he was standing: nothing was there but the milky sky. "Russians?" he mumbled.

"Yes!" Nosser roared with excitement as he turned to face his son. "Yes, boy, yes! They're up there spying on us. Of course. Why not? It's a war. Isn't it a war?" He paused for a second. "Is it not?"

"Yes, it is, Father," Ahmad said, slipping the button into his pants pocket.

"Listen, Ahmad," he lowered his voice as he leaned forward and grabbed the boy's shoulders in a firm grip. "Listen, Ahmad, they're going to come, put their filthy boots on our soil. From the North. Maybe others, too. They're here to make us a war country. I don't have much time left. But you have a lot of time. As much as you wish. You're still a little boy. I want you to be watchful. Keep an eye on land and sky. Do you understand?" Ahmad did not remember having seen white strands in his father's beard before. He had aged overnight. His cheeks were sunken and the black rings made the sparks in his eyes menacing. For an instant, Ahmad thought he was talking to a stranger. But the voice was familiar. "Do you understand what I'm saying?" Ahmad nodded, not sure what his father was talking about. "Good. Now there's one thing I need to tell you. Here." He lifted the rifle and nested it in Ahmad's arms. "This is like a baby. You have to hold it in your arms very carefully; tightly but gently. Like a baby. You have to take care of it." He took Ahmad's hand and placed it on the rifle. "And you know why?"

"Mr. Nosser, yo!" Mulla Ali's voice came from the foot of the stairwell. "How is the boy? Are you coming down? Can you send him down?"

Nosser looked around and picked up half a brick behind him. "Step aside," he ordered Ahmad and hurled it down the stairs. The brick ricocheted off the wall, tore a chunk off of the plaster, and disappeared into the darkness.

"You know why this is happening?" Nosser pulled Ahmad back in front of him. "Because the world is in a war. A big war. It isn't only us, it's the whole world, and the second time, too. It's been going on for years and now it's crawling toward us. I want you to hold onto your gun and promise to take care of your home and your mother and sister. If you see a sparrow in the air, don't shoot it, but if you see a Russian in the air, shoot it. Do you understand, Ahmad?"

He did not understand. He had chased chickens in the yard, hidden in the large copper cauldron in the basement while playing hide-and-seek, ridden on top of apple crates on the back of Khan's wagons, and even snuck into Rakhsh's stable without his grandfather's permission, but he had never held a gun in his hands. He had never shot anything except for crows, sparrows, and empty tins with a slingshot. His father was waiting for an answer. Ahmad nodded. With the nod came the slap in his face.

"Don't you lie to me! You don't understand. You have no clue what you are holding in your hands. You don't have the slightest idea your country is in danger and neither does anyone down there." Ahmad's ear was burning, but he did not dare let go of the gun to press it and soothe the pain. Tears welled up in his eyes. "Now listen to me: strangers will come, from the land and from the sky. There is a war going on. War is when strangers come to our village to take our things and kill our people, to turn us into a second Poland. They have guns and rifles like this one. So we need to have guns of our own to save our lives and protect our loved ones. Others can't see this now. But they will. You'll live a long life. Remember, you need to fulfill your responsibilities. Now repeat so I know you understand. You need to do what?"

"Fulfill my responsibilities," Ahmad answered, fighting back tears.

"Good boy, which is what?"

Against his will, a tear slid down Ahmad's cheek. "To protect my mother and sister and Khan and Agha."

"That's my boy." A smile flashed on Nosser's face. "It's not that bad. Collect yourself. All you have to do is accept them and cherish them and savor them as if you were drinking from a glass of cold barberry juice, as if you were sucking on a piece of ice in the summer." And with that he grabbed the barrel and put the tip in his mouth.

Ahmad's hands were drenched in cold sweat. It looked like he had shoved a gun in his father's mouth. Like he was going to kill him. But he was not. What he meant to do that day was to get up, feed the chickens, and go to the Orchard where everyone was preparing for the wedding: women of the village sailing around the steaming cauldrons, checking how much longer the stew needed to cook or if there was enough salt in the rice, others sitting on blankets and rugs, in front of heaps of herbs to be cleaned and crates of apples and cucumbers to be washed; men sweeping the ground and laying more rugs, carrying big bags of rice to the women and putting the watermelons in the narrow creek that ran through the Orchard. Ahmad had looked forward to the wedding tunes that the duo of musicians would blow into the sorna and beat on the dohol all through the evening and night. He had wanted to bet with Salman and the other boys who could keep his hands in the cold creek water the longest, watch the men dance, and maybe dance a little himself somewhere behind the crowd. He wanted to see if Agha would come out of his tree for Maryam's wedding. What he had never meant to do was put a rifle in his father's mouth.

At that moment Khan's strong voice echoed up the staircase. "Nosser, I'm coming up." It was not a request, nor was a trace of doubt in it. Khan was finally there to right the wrong. Ahmad watched his father's strong hand slide slowly along the barrel to rest peacefully over his frail fingers, as if to help him bear the burden. The hand's skin was darker and more wrinkled than Ahmad remembered, but its weight felt fatherly and familiar. Ahmad could hear Khan's footsteps. His father's hand was talking to him. Everything is going to be okay, it said. Ahmad's arms were tired from the weight of the rifle and his father's hand. He wished he could put it down for a second. But then it went off.

It was sudden. It was loud. Then it was silent. Not a caw from a distant crow, nor the faintest rustling of villagers' shoes on the dirt. There was no sound. But there was color. Red had splashed behind his father on the steps, on his boots and pickax, and on the bending walls that ascended still higher. Was his father's head there or had it disappeared? Had it bent back? It seemed that the fog had started to leak in through the opening to dissolve Nosser. And Ahmad too—until he felt his father's body, leaning heavily on the barrel of the rifle. He could not hold it anymore. He made no attempt at escape as his father tilted toward him, toppled, and everything went black.

2

HMAD'S MOTHER WAS ANXIOUS to hide the news, not from the villagers who must have already known everything there was to know, but from the groom's family who were due to arrive around noon and head for the Orchard. Tears streaming from her eyes, she pleaded with Khan and Mulla Ali and the people around the body in the mosque. Could they not postpone the funeral by one day and keep the wedding from falling apart? Otherwise they would have to wait for the Third night, then the Seventh night, the Fortieth, and the anniversary before anyone could even begin to think about a wedding again and by that time, who knew if the groom's family would still take Maryam, a year older and fatherless.

Khan sat cross-legged against the wall at a distance from the others, silent and pensive, his black Astrakhan hat on the floor by his side. Pooran got up from beside the body and walked over to him. "Khan, I swear to God,

I will make this wedding happen myself," Pooran threatened, "whatever it takes." She stood there looking down at Khan, oblivious to the fact that her chador had slipped off her head, showing the hazel mane cascading down the sides of her head in graceful disheveled waves, until some older women huddled over to fix it. They wiped her face and gave her a glass of cold water to calm her down so she could see the nonsense of what she was suggesting. Even if it was doable, even if all the village swore to keep their mouths shut, how could the absence of the bride's father be justified? The young girl's life would be doomed forever if her marriage began with such a ruse. Little by little, the sips of water sizzled on the raging flames that burned inside Pooran. Surrounded by women, some of whom had volunteered to weave the very rugs they were sitting on when Khan decided to build the mosque, Pooran despaired. She placed her forehead on the white sheet that covered the body of her husband.

Then Khan got to his feet. "We'll do as she said," he announced, fitting his black Astrakhan on his gray hair with three fingers. All they had to do was to surround the groom's family at all times with people who would not divulge the secret. Once inside the Orchard, they would be isolated from any outsiders. "Who will help my family?" he asked the people in the mosque. A hand went up in the front, then another, and then the rest. Khan sent some of the men to go door to door to the houses that flanked the path from the road to the Orchard. He ordered the women to continue with the preparations. "May God forgive our sins," Mulla Ali said loudly. "We need ice. Lots of ice to keep the body." Pooran hugged her husband's body and cried for a few minutes before she got up and drank the rest of the water in the glass. The ice had melted away.

SOME OF THE FOOD HAD burned over unattended fires. They emptied the cauldrons and washed them before starting anew. Pooran gave quick instructions to the men and women and hurried inside the house to her daughter. Maryam had locked herself in her room. Huddling behind the door, a few women were trying to draw her out. When all attempts failed, Pooran asked a girl to fetch a man from the garden. Mohammad the Carpenter threw some ineffectual kicks first. Then he took a few steps back and slammed his fat body through the door.

Maryam was sitting on the floor cutting her wedding dress into small pieces. White clippings were strewn all around her like snow. Apparently unperturbed by the intrusion, Maryam cut a strip off the skirt of the dress and flung it aside. Pooran closed the broken door and held her in her arms. Maryam said she would not marry with her father's body above the ground. Her mother reasoned that the wisest thing was not to cancel the wedding, that Khan was taking care of everything and many in the village were busy making sure that things would go well. In the end, she said that this was what Nosser would have wanted her to do. "That's a lie, that's just a lie," Maryam shouted, shaking her head, her cheeks rosy, her small nose red.

"Let me tell you something then." Pooran petted her daughter's hand. "Last night, in the middle of the night, I heard noises in my sleep. I opened my eyes. The room was dark and your father was not in the bed. I sat up and then I saw him. He was sitting on a chair in front of the wall where your wedding dress was hanging. When he heard me wake up, he turned around. He said all his life he had been waiting for this night."

Maryam put the scissors down and buried her face in her hands.

WHEN AHMAD FINALLY STIRRED THAT afternoon, he saw his mother sitting with her back to him, a silhouette against the huge, curtained window with panes of different colors. Ahmad heard his mother's stifled weeping above the other sounds that came through the half-open window: men and women talking, pots and pans clinking, the cries of children running around. He recognized some of the voices. His mother turned. "You're up at last!" Her eyes were red and puffy. She crawled to his bed and scooped him into her arms.

"My boy! My life! I was so worried. I'm happy you opened your eyes again." Tears streamed down her round cheeks. Her shuddering shoulders shook Ahmad's head. She put him down and wiped her tears with her sleeves. "But we can't tell anyone," she lowered her voice. "You have to keep everything to yourself for now. If anyone from the groom's family asks where your father is, say, 'I don't know', say, 'He must be in the Orchard somewhere.'" With her red headscarf that was now around her neck, she wiped a tear hanging from the tip of her nose. The room was hot. The feeble breeze only billowed the beige curtain. "Listen. Ahmad. Are you feeling all right?" Ahmad nodded. "Okay, listen. I have to go sort things out. Stay here in bed and rest. Do not speak a word about what happened today, all right, my boy?" Ahmad nodded again. His mother got to her feet. She hoisted her scarf and covered her head.

Before she stepped out of the room, she turned back to Ahmad. "You didn't kill your father," she said. It was not a question, but she waited as if for an answer, her hand frozen in the middle of a sweeping motion to tuck a fugitive lock of hair under the scarf. "Did you?" That was a question. "Tell me you didn't kill your father, Ahmad." Ahmad pulled the blanket over his face and buried himself in the hot, damp dark that was not quite pure: the light of day oozed in where the blanket had worn thin. He traced the irregular shapes of the patches of light with the tip of his finger. "This should have happened some other day, not today." She left and closed the door behind her.

Ahmad pushed the blanket away slowly and looked around. Apart from the mattress, pillow, and blanket, a big wooden wardrobe sat in one corner and a table with two chairs in another. He was in the small room next to his grandfather's which they often kept locked for guests. Khan's Astrakhan was hanging on the peg of the hatstand by the door; he had come to visit the patient in bed, but forgotten his hat. Ahmad got to his feet. His right knee hurt. He pulled up his pants leg, checked the bruises, and rubbed them. He walked to the window and swept aside the curtain with the back of his hand to look out through the red, triangular glass. Salman's father was skinning a red sheep that hung from a branch. Another red sheep was tied with a rope to an apple tree nearby, eating the red apples that had fallen on the ground. Soot from the red flames had blackened the bottoms and sides of three huge, steaming cauldrons. He shifted to the right and pressed his nose against the next triangular windowpane, this one green. His mother handed two green sugar cones to Ghasem who was sitting cross-legged in front of a big tray, hacking at a green cone and breaking it into small pieces to fill the sugar bowls. Salman and three other boys ran past. Ahmad's mother was now looking into one of the cauldrons while trying to keep her distance from the green flames that leapt out from under the vessel.

Ahmad wanted to go out. He shifted and looked through a blue pane. From among the distant trees, his blue grandfather walked hatless in front of Norooz the Gardener toward the wedding preparation scene. Ahmad did not know how old Khan was, but he knew he was younger than Norooz because he remembered the day he had sat on Khan's horse, Rakhsh, waiting for his grandfather to finish talking with Norooz and take him horseback riding. Norooz's white face had turned red with anger. "Sir, don't send me off," he said. "These trees are like my children. I have watered them and nursed them since you were younger than Mr. Ahmad here. Please, I will die if I go to another orchard." Ahmad remembered that day with clarity, not for anything specific that had happened, but because of his excitement on the back of the large horse. He had run his hand on her mane, trimmed and groomed, black from her head to the middle of her neck and white from there down. Khan was behind him. Ahmad held the reins in his hands. Norooz the Gardener looked up, too proud to beg the little child from years past who had grown up to become Khan. Khan must have nodded his agreement because Norooz nodded his head and put a grateful hand on his chest before he turned and left with his olive knit hat on his white hair. Those days Norooz could still walk without a cane and carry Ahmad on his shoulders when he was in the mood.

Ahmad stepped back from the window and went to a yellow pane. Khan and Norooz talked as they walked toward Agha's tree. When they reached its huge trunk, Norooz pulled the drape and held it for the yellow Khan to enter. Norooz followed and the drape swung back in place. That was where Ahmad wanted to be at that moment: in Agha's small house, with its two blankets, brass mug, and samovar. Agha had moved into the hollow guts of a thousand-year-old plane tree after he retired from the obligations of the orchards, and Khan fully inherited the business. The tree was Ahmad's haven. He sat on Agha's blanket and listened to his stories, the ones from when Agha was a little boy and the ones he said were from *One Thousand and One Nights* and Rumi.

The yellow sheep tied to the tree bit a piece off a dark yellow apple. Ahmad watched the bright flames a little until the tarp that was Agha's door moved again and Norooz stepped out of the tree. He called out to Mohammad the Carpenter who went around behind the tree and came back with the wheelbarrow. This meant they were going to move Agha. Soon they came out of the tree: the wheelbarrow, with Agha sitting cross-legged in it, and Mohammad pushing. Khan and Norooz followed. It must have been something more serious, or else why would Agha agree to come out of his tree in the first place? Maybe Khan had talked his great-great-great-grandfather out so he would be present at the ceremony. It would be a bad omen to sit in a corner and brood like an owl when someone in the family was getting married.

"Ahmad," a voice called. Salman was standing in the doorframe. Ahmad had not heard him open the door. Salman looked at him for a while without getting any closer. He started to play with the door handle. "Do you want to go out and play?" The door handle gave a squeak as Salman pushed it down and let it jump back up. Ahmad threw his head back as a no. "We're throwing apples at the watermelons," Salman went on. "We're going to play hide-and-seek next." Ahmad threw his head back again. "I will let you shoot sparrows." Salman pulled his slingshot out of his pants pocket. He waited for an answer, but Ahmad held still. Salman seemed to be out of suggestions. "I'm putting this here. Take it if you want to play." He set the slingshot on the floor at his feet without letting go of the handle. Then he left and closed the door behind him.

Ahmad turned back to the window and saw Salman run to his father and talk to him. Both turned their heads as Salman pointed to where Ahmad was standing behind the colored panes. Ahmad stepped back. He sat on the floor. With the tip of his finger, he traced the arabesques of stems winding up and down the rug, ending in flowers meticulously designed, but worn and pale. He got back in bed and pulled the blanket over his head to take shelter in the dark.

After a little while the door handle squeaked and Ahmad heard someone enter the room. "If you are not playing with it, can I take it?" Of course Salman wanted the slingshot back. He could not live without it. He was known for making the best slingshots. His specialty was shooting sparrows, the smallest and fastest of moving targets. Ahmad remembered the day Salman pulled two pebbles from his pocket, placed them in the rubber, and the next moment, two sparrows plummeted from the top of the wall, one into the flower bed, the other right through the wire netting, into the coop, in front of the surprised rooster who pecked at it but was not sure what else to do.

Something hit the blanket. Salman was shooting pebbles at him. One landed on his stomach, but not very hard. Ahmad stayed under the covers. A stone hit him on the shoulder, and another hit the tip of his nose and landed on his face. He could feel the weight of it on his lips. He slowly pushed off the blanket.

"Now look who's here to see little Ahmad!" Norooz the Gardener said with a smile. The four of them were there: Agha, Norooz, Mohammad, and Salman. "Now get up from that bed and come help." Norooz limped forward and threw the blanket back. He held Ahmad's wrist, helped him up, and took him to Agha's wheelbarrow. "Come. Sit," Agha said with that perpetual smile of his carved into the wrinkled folds of his cheeks, moving his head in the slightest of nods.

Norooz lifted Ahmad and put him in the wheelbarrow, in front of Agha. Mohammad the Carpenter gave a push and they headed out of the room into the corridor.

"So do you want to play hide-and-seek after?" Salman asked, striding by the wheelbarrow. At the end of the corridor were the stairs. Mohammad the Carpenter wheezed and pushed forward, strong as a bull. Ahmad was not sure what was going to happen at the stairs, though of course Norooz would manage as always. He felt Agha's consoling hand on his shoulder. He turned around and looked at him. Agha was smiling.

Down in the Orchard, Mohammad maneuvered the wheelbarrow past the cauldrons and the people, around the main house, to the back of the garden where the stable boy was holding Rakhsh's reins in his hand. Khan's favorite horse was ready for a ride, her white muzzle down, sniffing at the ground. "Khan wants you to ride her." Ahmad felt Agha's light hand again on his shoulder. They were pampering him and Ahmad did not know what to do the with their attention. If Khan had allowed him to ride Rakhsh any other day, he would have felt elation in his chest, he would have run to the stable and even helped the boy saddle the piebald. All he wanted now was to go back under his blanket. But he could not find a way to say that. Trapped in his head, "I don't want to" would not find a way to his tongue. Ahmad's only consolation was when Agha said, "I will take you with me when you're back from your ride." The stable boy hoisted Ahmad onto the saddle and walked the horse down the alleys until they were out of the village where the Shemiron Road began its journey from the foot of the mountains toward Tehran. The boy mounted behind Ahmad and the two of them rode through a sea of fog over the plains that had started to surrender their green to the yellow of the late summer heat. "Having fun?" the stable boy kept asking. Ahmad nodded, knowing the boy could not see the tears that dropped from his eyes onto the white shoulders of the horse.

When they returned to the Orchard, Agha was waiting by the stable. Ahmad sat in the wheelbarrow while the stable boy groomed Rakhsh. Then he wheeled them to Agha's tree.

AGHA STRUCK A MATCH AND turned on the samovar to make tea. Along with the muffled sounds of people working in the Orchard, some of the daylight came in around the edges of the tarp, which allowed Ahmad to see Agha's bent figure in his pistachio sweater, old, but light and alive as if attached to the roots of the tree that drew life from the depths of the earth. Above their heads, the hollow went up high into the trunk where light could not reach. It was an upside-down well in which Ahmad could not see a reflection, no matter how much he stared up.

"How many stories have I told you?" Agha asked Ahmad, who undid and redid his shirt collar button. "One hundred? Two? Three?" Ahmad did not answer. Agha placed the teapot on top of the samovar. I have a big one for you today. It's the best of my stories. It's about cats . . .

"Look at me, son."

3

A LONG LONG TIME AGO there was a boy who lived in a faraway village with his father, mother, brothers, and sisters. They grew wheat and barley on their small farm. Because of their hard work and the favorable rains, they harvested more crops every year. Little by little, they could have a few chickens, some sheep, an ass, and a cow. Things were going well until the boy's mother fell ill with a sickness that turned her yellow. After much futile treatment—and *futile* means it did not work—they were told that the only hope was a visit to the holy shrines in Karbala and Damascus. Long travels were very dangerous in those times, but the boy's father decided to take the risk, and the ass said he would help the man carry his wife on the journey.

Now those days people lived a harmonious life with animals—not all of them, but at least the farm animals. No one bought or sold them. The animals lived with people and worked for them in exchange for food and shelter. If someone could afford to build a stable, a barn, a pen, or a coop, they could get animals to live with them and the animals were happy to help with milk, eggs, wool, or farm work in return. That was before they became disgusted by the humans' greed and decided to stop talking. Of the animals that didn't belong on farms, some were wild. Others were not; they just didn't want to live and talk with humans—like giraffes, rhinos, mountain goats, and mice. Also cats. Cats were very territorial. They preferred to live alone and so they got together and formed their own country, somewhere in the deserts between Iraq and Syria. Now in those times there was no such country as Iraq. What we know as Iraq today was part of a big empire called the Ottoman Empire, which ruled for hundreds of years. Then the Ottomans were defeated in a war and the empire was partitioned into several countries. But before all that, the cats made their country in a large oasis saturated with well water in the middle of vast deserts far from any human settlement.

The boy's father gathered all the money he had saved and borrowed more from his brothers and the kind village people. The little boy said he wanted to go with his father and mother, too, but his father said no. It would be a dangerous trip for a boy of his age. The boy stopped eating and drinking and was soon so weak and thin that his father agreed to take him. To reduce the hazards of their journeys, such as getting lost and being attacked by bandits, people traveled in groups. Those groups were called caravans. A caravan of fifty people set off with the boy, his father, and his mother all on the ass. The boy and his father thanked the ass for carrying their heavy weight and took care to walk whenever they could. After a month, they reached the city of Karbala where the caravan sojourned—that means they stayed there—for three weeks to give everyone ample time to rest and visit the shrines.

Then they started the second part of their journey from Karbala to Damascus, crossing arid deserts from one caravansary to the next town, from one town to the next village, and from the village to the next caravansary. It was a few weeks into this second part when, one day, the animals started to feel uneasy. They asked the people to dismount them. The animals were panicking, but they weren't sure why. Some started running around on the sand when all of a sudden the sun went dark. The people told the animals it was just an eclipse and there was nothing to be worried about, but that was not very helpful. The animals kept running in panic until they saw the sun shining in the sky again. But shortly after they had resumed their journey, the animals started feeling uncomfortable again and asked the people to get off of them. Several started running around again. A mule traced and re-traced a circle without speaking a word to anyone. Before long, large clouds appeared on the horizon. The guides shouted, "Sandstorm!" and now it was the travelers who were taken by horror. They began running away from the clouds of sand that moved in their direction like plague, trying to escape the inevitable. Their fear blinded their eyes and deafened their ears and they didn't hear the cries of the guides and the camels who asked them to huddle and take shelter. By the folly of the ignorant, the wise too were afflicted. Co-lossal waves of sand washed over the desert and buried them all. Only the boy survived. He tried to dig his father and mother out, but no matter how hard he strained his eyes and worked his hands, he found nothing but sand. When he lost hope, he started to walk. He shuffled ahead in the desert with no food and water. On the second day, he fell down. He had no desire to get back to his feet again. He lay there and closed his eyes waiting for death to come. But as he had walked aimlessly, the boy had crossed the border of Gorbstan, the country of cats.

The patrols found him half-dead, licked his face, and took him to the city. He slept for two more days before he opened his eyes. The city was built around a large pond surrounded by low hills. The biggest of the houses was still shorter than the boy. They were mostly painted light rose interspersed with yellow, blue, or green. Palm trees had grown here and there among the well-tended verdure, all enormous compared to the small houses. Some of the roofs were domed, others were flat. He roamed around enchanted with the city and the cats who ignored him as they caught their daily fish from the pond and lay in the shade. The next day a young woman with long hair and a broad face appeared from behind the hill and wrapped the boy in a hug. She had lived there for some years since, like the boy, she had lost her way in the desert when she was very small and landed in Gorbstan by chance.

The cats gathered behind the woman in the plaza in front of their cat palace. She was their translator. As the boy recounted his story, she explained it to a large white cat with long hair and a flat face who sat on its hind legs in the gilt balcony, looking up at her sternly. When the woman was finished, the king of cats lowered his blue eyes to the boy whose clothes were torn and his face and neck red with sunburn. He was barely half as tall as the woman. The king of the cats opened his mouth in a long yawn, then let out a meow before he got to his feet and ambled slowly and graciously back into his chambers. The woman smiled at the boy and welcomed him to the city. The cats hailed him with celebratory meows and a kitten rubbed its hazel ear against the boy's bare ankle. The woman was glad to see a human being after so long. The boy was also happy to see the woman after an arduous trip—that just means hard.

Having no way to go back and no family to return to, the boy stayed with the young woman. She took care of him in her shack behind the hills. As the years passed and the boy grew into a stout young man, they started to feel bored of being alone with no one around them but cats. So they decided to make a baby. The baby boy made them so happy that they wanted another. The next year they had twin girls. They busied themselves with their children. The babies were never bored since they always had many kittens around to play with. When two years later, the man and the woman made another boy, their old home was no longer large enough for the six of them. Out of the wood from the trees, the man built a new, bigger house with seven rooms. Two years after that, another set of twins was added to the group. So it went on for some time: every year or two new members joined the family. With the help of the older boys, the man made another house for his growing family right beside the first. The older children resided the newer house—that means they lived in it—and the younger were divided between both houses so that in each house, either the parents or the older siblings would tend to the youngsters.

When they decided they had had enough of fish and date fruits, they started gathering the date seeds and grinding them to make flour and bake small discs of bread in a tandoor they dug outside. As the babies kept being born, they also had to add to the palm trees. They planted a grove near their houses. The girls brought water from the pond every day. Some of the cats began to worry about the humans who lived so close by, right beyond the hills, as the family grew even bigger. There were now five big houses and a well dug for their domestic use. Voices rose in protest asking for the humans to be banished from Gorbstan.

Two years passed. When the first house appeared at the crest of a hill, many said the humans had crossed the line. A group of cats went to the settlement to talk to the woman who was now in her forties. The number of fish in the pond had dwindled, the vegetation was growing sparse, and the level of water was going down fast because of the bucketfuls the big family drew for their date-palm farm. After she translated the cats' concerns for her husband, the man said there was nothing to do but to try to live in peace and harmony with one another, man and cat. The cats, though, said there indeed was something to do: they wanted the people to leave. The man said they didn't know the way out, but the cats had guides ready to show them the way across the desert to the first human town. The couple's children and grandchildren said this was their native home and they didn't want to go anywhere else. The woman, who was the only one able to speak cat tongue, tried to keep the conflict from escalating. She told her family that the cats in the end would be satisfied with them using a few less fish and buckets of water every day and that otherwise they had no problem with the family staying there. To the cats she said they needed some time to rectify things—that means to put things in order—and get ready for their exodus—that means for their big journey.

Another year passed, but not only was the family not showing any signs of pulling back, two more boys were added. Now in the streets of Gorbstan there were always a couple of small children roaming around, playing with the kittens, or going to the pond with a fishing pole, a bucket, or with empty hands just to swim and play in the water. The water had gone down and catching fish had become more difficult. One day, two little girls were playing at the pond. One of them splashed at a cat who was lapping at the water muddied by the girls. In a sudden fit of anger, the cat leapt at the girl and scratched her face.

Two of the girl's brothers took revenge by bagging a kitten that had strolled away from the others and beating it with thick sticks. The cats made it harder for the family to access the pond: they would attack the little ones and the bigger, stronger boys could get to the water only if they moved in groups and carried sticks. A boy lost an eye when a black cat sprang at his face from a rooftop. The boy's brothers got together and knocked down houses with their sticks and furious kicks. This intensified for another two years, by which time what was left of the cat city was no more than ruined houses, scorched walls blackened with soot, and littered streets.

One day, five cats laid ambush on a three-year-old boy who was playing on his own and scratched him until his cries died away and his blood dried on the sand. His brothers found his body and made a pact. That night, a group of young men raided the palace. They broke the gate and fought with the guards. They received scratches and wounds, lost eyes and ears, but when the sun rose, the body of the king of cats lay on the ground in the yellowed lawn, unmoving, with his blue eyes open as if looking on the destruction of his country. All of this would have been redeemable somehow if the pond hadn't gone almost dry. The little water left at the bottom of wells was murky and smelly. The place was no longer fit for living. The thousand-well oasis was lost.

Only a few days after the killing of the king, before the boys' wounds had healed or even stopped bleeding, the family got up at dawn and sensed a strange silence in the air. The cats were gone. The city looked as if no living creature had set foot in it in two hundred years. The family's only chance to leave that place and find their way across the deserts was right then before the winds erased the cats' footprints from the sands. They quickly packed the things they would need on the way: pots and pans, clothes, and some tools like spades, ropes, hammers, and axes. They took all the bread and dates they had and filled their water jugs with the yellowish, putrid water that came up in the pail from the bottom of the well. By late afternoon, they had placed all of their belongings on a cart and were ready to push ahead, following the cats' trails.

Of that large family only one survived. The children all died, one by one, after they drank from the well water, because the water was poisoned. The night before they left their country, the cats had gathered around the well and defiled the water with their urine. The father and mother hadn't drunk from the jugs so their children and grandchildren would have a few more drops to quell their thirst. Unable to believe how all of their children had fallen down into the sand almost at once, they ran from one body to the next. They shook them but didn't hear an answer. They wanted to cry, but their eyes were without a tear to drop for their loved ones. They had no idea why that had happened. Maybe the excessive heat? When they accepted there was nothing they could do, they buried their children in the desert and continued on their way, grief-stricken and exhausted. Sorrow clawed at the man's throat when a few hours later he saw a small village in the horizon. His children would have had food, water, and shelter if they had lasted only a little longer. Deep in his thoughts, the man pulled the cart on which his wife was sitting, since she was too tired and shocked to walk. Now that they were close to a village with people, now that she had no children to save the water for, maybe she could quench her own thirst with a few sips? The woman drank from a half-empty jug on the cart. When the village was so close and the man could make out the first houses, an invisible smile broke on his face. He called his wife to look at the view, asked if she believed they were saved. When he didn't hear an answer, he stopped and turned around. His wife wasn't on the cart. He looked about him, but couldn't see her. He squinted his tired eyes and saw her at a distance on the ground. He ran to her as fast as he could, but he was too late. She was already gone, lying on the sands with eyes and mouth wide open.

It was only much later, after the man reviewed the past events over and over again in his head, that he started wondering what terrible fortune had let the entirety of his family perish in such a way. He found the answer after he had made a new family. He married again and, being old and weak, had only one boy. As the years passed he saw what was happening: he wasn't dying. His son died young, but his grandson lived; his great-grandson died young, but his great-great-grandson lived. And he was still alive. With the wisdom that old age brings, he saw clear as day the price he and his lineage were paying for bagging and beating that kitten, for destroying the cats' country, for killing the king. Regicide is the deadliest of sins. Now they were doomed to see the deaths of their own sons. In the years to come, the man spent interminable hours pondering why he ended up living so long. He thought maybe eating dates for so many years was the secret, or the years he exerted his body to build houses, climb trees, dig the earth, and cut wood. Maybe it was the water from the pond. Could he have drunk from the Pond of Life, the pond that the early poets said Alexander was desperately seeking? But that day in the desert, as he cried tearlessly over his wife's pale body, all he wished for was to die right there. He saw himself years before: a child who had lost his parents. So many years had passed and he was still on the sand mourning his beloved who had departed forever. It was as if decades had vanished, his fruitless life passed in thirst and futile hope.

Farther ahead, the cats were on their way to Iran, resolute to take revenge, to turn the country the boy had come from into ruins just like he had done to their homes. They treaded mile after mile eastward, traversed deserts and climbed across the mountains that ran along western Iran, a land where no cat had ever set foot in before. They didn't mind. They were there to make a home of it, conquer it, and demolish it.

4

DESPITE THE SADNESS AT THE HEART OF THINGS, the festive face of the wedding distracted Ahmad from Agha's story as soon as he stepped out of the tree. Everything was happening in the large area in front of the main house. Like all the past village ceremonies, they had covered the hoez with broad planks to make a stage, the center of attention. The house was allocated to the women, where they took off their chadors and danced in their colorful dresses in the uncertain space between death and marriage. Some opened the curtains and watched from behind the windows and some, the younger ones, climbed a wooden ladder and sat on the gable roof.

Ahmad had never seen such a wonderful ceremony. Hanging from the trees surrounding the wedding area, lanterns shone subdued by the fog that had coated the Orchard with an ethereal enamel. A big crowd of men had gathered, some busy with last-minute tasks and some waiting for the groom to arrive. Calm and serious, Khan gave curt orders as he supervised with eyes sharp as an eagle's.

They took the groom to Nemat the Barber and then the bathhouse. When he arrived in the Orchard, the guests made a human corridor shouting out congratulations and showering him and his entourage with coins and sugar plums. Right hand resting on his chest as a sign of gratitude and humility, he greeted strangers on both sides of the aisle from the Orchard door all the way to the front of the house, with a smile some women in the crowd found inelegantly broad and others cheerfully open. Khan and Mulla Ali shook the groom's hand and hugged him. Behind the groom, his father looked around to find Maryam's father, but in vain. All that time, accompanied by percussive beats of the dohol, the sorna player blew into his instrument, his face red and his eyes shut. Women threw rose petals at the groom and trilled shrieks of joy as he was seated between his father and Khan. All in suits and ties, heads crowned in fedoras except for Khan whose Astrakhan was undetachable, they settled in their chairs and then there was a short pause. Everyone fell silent in anticipation. Khan glanced around and then nodded an approving head that marked the beginning of the wedding.

The first entertainers were a dancing group of men who waved colorful kerchiefs in harmonized movements. They whirled around and jumped and stomped on the planks. Next came a man who strode back and forth on the stage and blew a tree of fire from his mouth. He produced a dagger from the inside of his sleeve and drove it through his tongue without a drop of blood. With his tongue stuck out, he strode around for the applauding guests to get a good look. Then a young bony man stepped onto the covered hoez. He dropped a fruit crate down by his feet and announced that he would cram himself into it. He took off his shoes and sat in the crate, pulled one leg in first, then the other. Then he bent forward and folded his arms in. To prove that none of him was out, two men came and boarded up the crate with nails and hammers. One of them put the thin man's shoes under his arm and they took the crate away as if it was just another case of apples.

The guests clapped and whistled. The ones closer to the stage were sitting on the ground. Agha watched in his wheelbarrow from a corner. A two-actor troupe elicited loud bouts of laughter with a show about a master and his shrewd slave. Show after show followed. In between, servants walked about with big trays laden with cups of tea. Fruits and sweets were bountiful. Mouth-watering smells wafted from the pots and cauldrons. It was as if the wedding and its people were detached from the mundane pains and concerns, as if the thick fog protected them from whatever evil the stars might have in store for them. Long before, Khan had made the Orchard the place to hold village ceremonies: weddings, mourning, and religious gatherings. Free and for everyone. But compared to Maryam's wedding, the ones before were like fluttering lanterns in midday summer sun.

As Ahmad was watching the show, Salman walked up to him, patted him on the shoulder, and showed him his closed fist. The antennae of a cockroach waved like supple branches of a weeping willow. He motioned for Ahmad to follow him. The boys slipped out of the crowd. They went around the house and lurked under a window until Salman was sure no one was watching. Then he put his arm through the window and opened his fist. A few seconds later the women's shrieking began. Ahmad saw, through the fluttering lace curtain and behind a woman who flapped her skirt and hopped around like a scared rabbit, his mother keeping the company of the groom's mother, her hand on the woman's arm, her smiling red lips exposing white teeth. When Pooran's eyes, lined kohl black, turned toward the commotion, Ahmad ducked his head and walked back with Salman among the crowd around the hoez. Women went in and out of the house and the guests were fixated on the show. Nobody noticed Salman's sister, Sara, rushing out onto the veranda. Running down the stairs as fast as she could in her white chador wrapped loosely around her blue dress, she turned her head around, swinging a folded belt in her hand.

"I'm caught!" Salman said and ran away. Sara was three years older than the boys.

She saw Ahmad in the crowd and strode over to him. "I know it was him, I saw his little bald head." Ahmad knew Sara must have seen both of them. Ahmad had stood right by Salman when he set the cockroach free into the room and his own hair was no longer than Salman's. Nemat the Barber had run his manual hair clipper on both their heads only a few days before. Sara was furious. Her big, brown eyes shone with anger. "Poor woman, the thing flew right under her skirt. Do you know which way the rascal went?" she asked, her thin, curved eyebrows sloped into a frown. Ahmad shook his head as a no. Some of the men were taking furtive looks at them. "Come here," Sara said, pulling Ahmad by the arm away from the crowd. Behind a tree, far enough away to make the wedding a translucent apparition, she stopped. The frown had disappeared from her face. "Listen," she said, "there's this brat, I don't know who he is, maybe the groom's nephew or someone. He's running back and forth from the groom's mother to his father. I think they've set him up to find stuff out. He's a sneaky rat. Have you seen him? A little shorter than you with a ridiculous tie?" Again, Ahmad shook his head. "Okay, just keep your eyes peeled. I think they've started to suspect things. If he comes to you, don't let him get a word out of you, okay?" Ahmad nodded. Then Sara put her hand on Ahmad's cheek and looked at him. The men around the hoez laughed at something. The folded belt hung still from Sara's other hand. Her palm was hot; not the kind to add to the late summer heat, but a deeper warmth that had little to do with temperature, that had the ability to communicate even if in an indecipherable, arcane tongue.

"I know where he is," she said taking her hand from Ahmad's face, as if she suddenly remembered her brother's hideout. "Do you want to go with me?" She was not angry at Ahmad, as if he had not been an accomplice in the mischief. Ahmad cast his eyes down. Sara waited for him to make his decision. When she was sure Ahmad was not going, she smiled at him and turned around, but before she took the first step Ahmad had clutched her dress from behind. Sara turned back slowly but did not say a thing, as if what Ahmad had done was predictable. The look on her face said, "I know." She stepped closer. Ahmad bent his head down again. "Is there anything you want to tell me?" she asked. Ahmad shook his head. "Raise your head," she said firmly, but Ahmad kept his head down, then suddenly leaned forward and hugged Sara. Patting the back of his head, Sara looked around lest anyone saw them, but let Ahmad rest his face on her chest. "Listen, Ahmad," she whispered over his head, "I will always be your friend." Then she did not know what to say anymore. When Ahmad detached himself from her, she asked, "Are you sure you're not coming?" Ahmad's nod was almost imperceptible. Sara turned around and walked off, turned her head after a few steps with a look that said, It will be okay, and I'm really sorry, then hurried away with an elegance that was alien to the bounds of the dress.

The surprises of the night were yet to come. A mysterious-looking man with a beard and no mustache brought to the stage midget plants that were smaller than the palm of a hand. He walked around with a big tray and claimed what he had in the tiny flower pots were fully grown trees, fifteen years old at least. One even had a ripe tangerine hanging from its branches. Then two men rode bicycles with only one wheel and no handlebars. Then it came to the last, and most dazzling, show of the night. A lank, bony old man with disheveled hair and a long beard walked on shards of glass. They said all he ate was an almond a day. After he balanced himself cross-legged on the tip of his long walking stick, he asked for the planks that covered the hoez to be removed. Once the hoez was open again and the light from the lanterns shimmered off the surface of the water, the old man closed his eyes, dropped his stick and gingerly put a first step on the surface of the water. Everyone was dead quiet. He placed the second step in front of the first and started walking without sinking as if he was made of feather. It was so quiet Ahmad could hear the slight splashing the man's soles made against the water. He paced along the length of the hoez and back a number of times. After he stepped out, he dried his feet with the loincloth he had wrapped around his waist.

Time came for the paperwork to make the marriage official before God and Shah alike. The women took the groom and Mulla Ali inside. Khan, the father and brother of the groom, together with some closer male relatives, joined them. The bride and groom sat on chairs at the wedding spread in front of a mirror with everyone else behind them. Mulla Ali composed the marriage contract and handed it to the groom to sign, but before Mohammad Reza put the pen to paper, his mother said, "I think we should wait." The tip of the pen stopped midair. A hole opened up in Pooran's heart, sucking her blood into an abyss. The groom's mother no doubt suspected the lies Pooran had woven together with the earnestness that only truth could bring. The story she'd told—of the message that came two days before on a folded paper, stamped and signed by Colonel Doost, asking for Nosser's immediate departure to join the carabineers—cracked and collapsed at the woman's simple words. Pooran bent her head, closed her eyes, and accepted defeat. "We wish the bride's father could have been with us today," the woman went on. "But we appreciate his sacrifice and pray for his life and his safe return."

Pooran lifted her head and opened her eyes with a smile.

When the bride signed the contract, cries of happiness rose from those in the room. Mulla Ali recited what was necessary and showers of sugar plum rained on the couple as Pooran and the groom's mother took turns rubbing together two sugar cones over the bride and groom's heads.

Maryam left the next day, hugging her family and friends with a smile as she had promised her mother. No matter how much they insisted, Pooran did not walk with the others to the Shemiron Road to see off the newlyweds on their way to Tehran. Behind the wheel of the Aegean-blue Delahaye coupe, the groom waited for Maryam to say goodbye to her kith and kin. With his hands in his pockets, Ahmad stood at a distance and watched his sister hug the women and kiss Khan's hand.

"Now you're the man of the house," Maryam whispered in his ear. Ahmad locked his arms around her. "You take care of Mother. You promise?" Ahmad nodded his head against her chest. "I will miss you," Maryam whispered.

The groom revved the engine, stuck his arm out the window, and waved goodbye, then the fog devoured the coupe. In her room, Pooran hung up all of her colorful clothes in the wardrobe and put on black for her husband and daughter. She accepted Khan's offer to move from her house to the Orchard. The main house had more than enough rooms for Pooran and Ahmad. All through the packing, although he helped with the diligence of a boy who had been promised a treat in exchange for the task, Pooran wondered if Ahmad hated the idea of moving, because no matter what, he did not speak to her. Never even a word.

5

SOON CAME TIME FOR AHMAD to go back to school. The class was another one of Khan's gifts. Years before he had built a house at the edge of the village where the teacher would live. Students of different grades sat on the ground in a big room on mats they brought with them. To get Mulla Ali's support, Khan offered him the role of teacher. Mulla moved to the new, bigger house and was also given a mule for his daily commute to the mosque to lead the daily prayers. The mule was on top of the "gifts" each student had to bring in every now and then: two sugar cones, a tin of hydrogenated oil, a chicken, a packet of tobacco, and even an occasional small rug. As Khan's grandson, Ahmad was exempt from the punishments the other kids often received. If any boy other than Ahmad sat in the class without reading out loud from the book or dared not answer when called on, he would no doubt have had the soles of his feet lashed, the palms of his hands caned, or spent a few dreadful hours in the dark basement where, as word had it, jinns swarmed.

After a week of tolerating Ahmad's silence in the class, Mulla Ali complained to Khan. "What's wrong with you?" Ahmad's mother asked him. "You never had a problem with Mulla." Ahmad did not answer. Pooran made him clean the stable for three days in a row, promised him a bicycle, and then forbade him to go out of the house on the weekend until he broke his vow of silence. But not a sound came from the boy. One night, she sat by Ahmad's side and looked at him until the moonlight was no longer on his closed eyes. "You had a hard time," she whispered, holding her son's small hand in hers, "but you will talk to me. I know it. I'll wait for that day."

Ahmad walked to school with Salman every morning. Mulla Ali would pretend he did not exist, but it was difficult to ignore him. Ahmad was a keen learner. He had started to read long before anyone else in the class. His homework was always done in a flawless, beautiful hand: each letter curved meticulously into the next, the alephs stood all the same size, the dots were perfectly round, and the words formed such straight lines that even when tested against the spine of Saadi's *The Rose Garden*, they showed no bend.

One day, Salman had to help his father skin a sheep at the butchery and Ahmad did his homework for him; he copied the day's lesson five times in his own notebook, then in Salman's. The next day, Mulla Ali could easily recognize Ahmad's handwriting in Salman's notebook. Without delay, Salman was laid on the floor, his feet tied secure to the thick stick that two students held up. Strikes of the wet cherry branch landed on his soles with a sharp swish. After the punishment, Mulla Ali warned the class that from then on both the lazy student and the helper would get chastised. After the class was dismissed, Ahmad offered to help by slipping his hand under Salman's arm.

"I can walk all right," Salman said, brushing Ahmad's hand away. "I can even race you. Are you in?"

With his third step, Salman sank to the ground and curled like a snake in agony. They went home, Salman on Ahmad's back, arms locked around his friend's neck, feet throbbing with pain. "You know what," Salman said midway, "two plus two is all I need to learn. The rest is no use. I want to be a butcher." When Ahmad closed Salman's door behind him, he could hear him getting beaten by his father for having been punished at school. With those soles there was no running away for his friend.

That same afternoon, Ahmad returned to Mash Akbar's house. Lying on his stomach, Salman was doing the next day's homework. Without a word, Ahmad snatched Salman's notebook and pencil from him and started copying. "What are you doing?" Salman got to his feet, then sat back down on the floor. "What are you doing? He's going to beat me again. And you, too." Ahmad was not letting go. Salman crept ahead on his bottom and pulled at the notebook and the next moment, half of the notebook was in Ahmad's hand, the other half in Salman's. His lips puckered.

Do you have another? Ahmad wrote on the cover of the torn notebook. Salman shook his head and wiped tears from his cheeks. Ahmad motioned for Salman to wait. He ran to the Orchard and came back with a new notebook. Sara was bandaging Salman's feet with white cloth. Ahmad did Salman's homework until it was almost dark. Sara fixed dinner and the four of them, Mash Akbar, Sara, Salman, and Ahmad, ate in silence before Norooz the Gardener knocked on the door to take Ahmad home. Ahmad took the notebook with him.

The next day Salman could hardly sit still. The pupils went over to Mulla Ali's table one by one to have their assignments checked. Ahmad could see Salman shaking as he got to his sore feet on his turn. Mulla opened the new notebook and flipped through the pages. One look at Ahmad, who was sitting with his head bowed down, was enough for Mulla to realize what was happening. He had to tie them both to the stick, one after the other, as he had warned the day before, or lose face. He was silent for a few seconds. Leafing back and forth, he made as if he was inspecting Salman's assignment. "Next," he ordered and gave Salman back his notebook. Ahmad felt something inflate in his chest, making him lighter. From that day on, whenever Salman had to help his father at the butchery, Ahmad would do his homework and Mulla Ali would leaf through the beautifully written pages and call out, "Next."

WHAT AHMAD'S FATHER PREDICTED CAME true soon after his death: the Russians marched in from the north and the British attacked from the south, smashing and dismantling the Iranian army in a matter of hours. Soon after, the footsteps of the terrifying giant of famine could be heard across the country. Prices started to go up. Twelve miles away from the capital and in the shelter of generous fruit orchards, the village of Tajrish received the ripples of the crises with a delay. But they heard the news of how things were in Tehran, and with the winter came a shortage of wheat. The bakery opened four or five hours a day and the whole time, lines formed out front of men in thick coats and wool hats and women with sweaters under chadors. After the evening prayer one day the villagers in the mosque decided that the baker should not sell more than one disc to anyone, no exceptions. From the next day, every member of every family went to the bakery so as not to forfeit their share of the daily bread. Two serpentine lines rose and fell along Tajrish's alleys, the men's line in one direction, the women's in another. Women took their babies in their arms and asked for two discs. The baker counted the babies in at first, but when, in the middle of the winter, they threw back the tarpaulin and saw that the truck had brought half the number of bags of flour the village needed, they excluded children under four and reduced the quota to three discs a family.

The famine had come with the invasion of Iran, and few doubted that the foreigners had caused the plight. Ahmad was busy with school. He read voraciously and did his classmates' homework in exchange for an occasional book they might find in their homes and succeed in pilfering without their parents noticing. Little did he have to worry about the bread shortage as Khan received twice the quota, delivered to the Orchard every day by the baker himself because he did not trust the boy who worked for him not to spill the beans.

The winter came to an end, but the shortage did not, as people of Tajrish had hoped. They spent more time doing nothing because there was not much to do. Bread, oil, and sugar disappeared from the three village grocery stores. Salman's father, who killed and skinned six sheep and two lambs every morning, could hardly sell three small sheep a day. Meat was the first thing people cut from their meals, reserving it for special occasions only. Salman quit school before the others. He had not been able to afford gifts for Mulla and that did not make the teacher happy. He managed to find excuses to tie the boy's feet to the stick and leave welts on his soles. Salman was relieved when his father sent him to work at the carpenter's. At the same time, Mash Akbar looked for something his daughter could do beyond the usual housekeeping. When Pooran heard the news, she went to Khan and asked him to let her hire the girl. The house in the Orchard was big and there was always something Sara could do. Khan was reluctant to add to the people working for him. Pooran came back to his office and placed three pairs of earrings and an old silver tray on Khan's desk. "I'll pay for the girl myself." Khan looked at his daughter-in-law, clad in black mourning clothes. If he had known she wanted the girl to the extent that she would give up her belongings, he would not have rejected her. He put the earrings in the tray and pushed it back toward Pooran.

"Should I send someone to Mash Akbar?" he asked.

Pooran went in person and banged the door knocker. Sara was relieved to hear that she would be working in the Orchard that had been her second home since she had climbed trees and thrown apples at the boys when they were five. She was at first in charge of the laundry and anything else Pooran Khanum asked her to do. After her father left for the butchery in the morning, she would hasten through the chores, clear the breakfast spread, do the dishes, prepare the lunch, and tidy up the house, before hurrying to the Orchard. Shortly before noon, she would go back home to serve lunch and make her father's afternoon tea. Then she walked back to the Orchard to finish whatever had to be done before going back home again to prepare dinner. Pooran was easy on her, but she tried to conceal her feelings in front of the others, fearful that her affection for the girl might rouse others' jealousy.

She would have other people in the Orchard do the harder jobs. Many times, she would call Sara into her room to dust the furniture, sweep the rugs, or ask her opinion about the new curtain she was making. She gave Sara jars of pickles, jam, and tomato paste to take home. From a big, wooden chest in the corner of the room, she took out blouses, skirts, or long dresses that once belonged to Maryam and asked Sara to try them on. She watched the girl blush as she slipped out of her clothes and into the hand-me-down, twirling around so the older woman could admire her from all directions. "I'll find you a nice groom and sew you the most beautiful wedding dress myself," Pooran would say as she tilted her head and stared at Sara in Maryam's clothes.

When she had nothing to do, or when Pooran Khanum did not need her in her room, Sara looked for Ahmad. At times she found him silent, doing his homework in Agha's tree with the samovar boiling on the low table to heat up the place, and with Agha sitting cross-legged at the entrance looking at the Orchard that was starting to embrace spring. Ahmad would look at her and smile, and Sara wondered how he felt about her, then she told herself that he was still a child. When Ahmad was alone in his room in the house, Sara would go in, close the door behind her, and sit by his side and watch him do his homework. One spring afternoon sitting in the window frame, she turned her head from the Orchard toward Ahmad and said, "Teach me to read." Ahmad patted the rug and Sara sat right by him. "And to write," she added. Outside, the sparrows chirped their jovial afternoon songs in the naked trees. The rays of the sun were not warm enough to melt the snow yet. Ahmad walked to the window and knocked on the pane with his finger. "What?" Sara asked. Ahmad tapped again. "Do you want me to open the window?" Ahmad shook his head and, this time, pointed to the window instead of tapping on it. "The window . . . ?" A smile appeared on Ahmad's nodding face before he ran to his wooden case where he kept his new notebooks. He pointed to the window again, notebook in hand, and waited for Sara. "Window?" she repeated, uncertain what Ahmad meant. Sara watched him nod again. Back at her side, Ahmad opened the notebook with his small but long fingers and wrote the word *window* before passing the pencil to her. She rolled the pencil in her hand trying to get a good grip on it. The notebook smelled chic. The paper was crisp and smooth. The shaky lines she made bore only a distant resemblance to the shape Ahmad had put on the page.

Ahmad pointed to the door and put *door* on the next line. That was easier. Sara tried to duplicate the curves of the new word. Ahmad pointed to the rug. "Let me do this one," Sara said snatching the pencil out of Ahmad's hand. Below the *window* and the *door* she drew a rug with the center medallion, borders, and even the fringes. "Isn't this better?" she asked with an affected seriousness, turning the notebook for Ahmad to see. The teacher-like intensity in Ahmad's face relaxed into the open face of a ten-year-old. "Your turn."

Ahmad took the pencil Sara had held out to him and *rug* appeared next to the drawing. Tame and docile in Ahmad's hand, the pencil reared and panicked away to places Sara did not mean for it to go. "Help me with this." She took Ahmad's hand and placed it on her own. From the corner of her eyes, as her guided hand traced the right trajectory, Sara glanced at Ahmad, the tip of his tongue between his lips, focusing hard to make the word appear on the page. His long fingers lay warm on hers with the confidence of a leader who knew the way, who would not get lost, who would take you home safe. As they smiled at their success with the first three words, Ahmad looked at the gap between Sara's front teeth and wondered if she could whistle better than he could.

MULLA ALI CLOSED THE SCHOOL early that year, before the end of spring. Too few families could afford gifts anymore. The mulla told Khan he would open early in the fall when the dire situation would be behind them, God willing. But summer did not bring good news. The son of the bathhouse owner was the first to leave the village. He bundled a change of clothes in a piece of cloth and started the four-hour trek to Tehran, even though word had it that things were not any better in the capital. He had at least heard that the Russian soldiers gave away food in the streets sometimes. Salman replaced him in the bathhouse. The carpenter did not need help anymore.

There was barely enough work for one person. Salman had to tend to the fire and warm up the water two hours before the dawn. The bathhouse closed late in the afternoon; it was an ill omen to be in the bath when the sun was not in the sky. Fiery, ethereal hooved-feet jinns haunted the dark hallways after the sun went down, when only the dripping of water broke the silence. Everyone knew that. Terrified, Salman ran all the way to the bathhouse in the morning. He could only do his job because the furnace was accessed from outside and he did not have to go in the ghastly building. He copied the first chapter of the Quran on a piece of paper that he carried in his pants pocket and was always alert to utter the name of God if he found himself face-to-face with one of those creatures of fire because it was only the name of God, as Mulla Ali said, that could dispel those rebellious, satanic beings.

When hunger pierced deeper into stomachs, people turned to the mountains for wild rhubarbs, walnuts, and anything else edible that the rocks had to offer. With Khan's approval, Ahmad accompanied Salman to set snares and shoot, with a slingshot, an occasional quail whose neck Salman would wring as soon as he lay his hands on the struggling bird. In vain, the bird wiggled and squirmed for a short time before its head turned a whole circle and life departed its soft, feathery body. "You want to try?" Salman asked one day holding a quail by its feet. The bird flapped its wings in a desperate attempt to take flight toward the earth. Tucked under Ahmad's arm, the bird calmed down, its beak open as if gasping for breath, its heart pounding hard and fast like a miniature drummer was banging inside the downy ball. "Do it quickly," Salman said. "Hold tight, it'll fly away before you know it." It was a beautiful, soft creature. The color of the mountain. The color of dry earth from which grew all that was good. Ahmad parted the feathers until a trace of pink skin showed. It was not just a ball of down; it was a creature of flesh and blood. Under the late summer mountain sun Salman opened the canvas sack that hung from his shoulder. Ahmad wrung the quail's head and dropped it in.

IN THE FALL, AHMAD WAS the only student in Mulla Ali's class. So, the clergyman went door to door, sat in bare living rooms on folded blankets and threadbare rugs, asked how the family was holding up, and preached about the blessings of literacy in the new age to come while sipping at the tea he was offered. After the last rays of sun had departed from the western sky, Mulla shuffled in his sandals toward the mosque, nodding to the greetings of the people who walked in the same destination, and watched how the orange of the sky tinged the turquoise tiles of the single minaret. After the evening prayer, he climbed up the wooden minbar and sat on the third step down facing people. He pointed out the emphasis the Imams at the dawn of Islam put on the importance of education and specifically reading and writing. "Seek knowledge from cradle to grave," he bellowed at the congregation sitting cross-legged before him in rows, some nodding, some running prayer beads through their fingers, some playing with their beards. Separated from the men by a tarp curtain, the women, wound in their chadors, sat in rows that continued the men's. "*Read!*" the mulla howled at them all, "was the first word Gabriel had for the Prophet." The next day three new students showed up in the class, a number which compared to the twenty-three before the war was nothing short of shame and frustration, but what else could he do?

By then, Sara could read simple texts and write short sentences. She copied five lines of each new word in the notebook Ahmad gave her, carefully cramming the words on each line to save paper. When Sara had learned all the objects in the room, they set off on short journeys around the house and garden to find new things: kitchen, hallway, cauldron, soil, apple, fire. Back in Ahmad's small room, Sara would let her chador slip off her scarfed head and they practiced the words. Soon she started to read one of Ahmad's books. He marked the sounds of the words she stumbled over. With a satisfactory smile, Sara came to the periods: places where inanity gave way to meaning. With a period, words lost in confusion and whirling in the air like specs of dust convened and acceded; sap flowed up stems; flowers budded. When they came upon a word neither of them knew, Ahmad would run upstairs and knock on Khan's door. If he was at his desk working the abacus and penciling in his ledgers, he would explain the word to Ahmad while twirling the tips of his mustache. If he did not answer, Ahmad would knock again and wait. He never went in without permission. But one day, Khan did.

Without making any noise, he opened the door and stepped into Ahmad's room. Ahmad and Sara were lying on the floor on their stomachs, a book and a notebook open in front of them. Sara sprang to her feet, picked up her chador from the floor and covered herself. Khan's keen eyes darted around the room and landed back on the two kids. He did not like what he saw. Mash Akbar was a good man, a close friend of Nosser's, and his daughter, Sara, although at times inelegant and unrefined, was a well-natured girl. But his grandson's intimacy with the butcher's daughter was acceptable only to the extent that childhood gaiety would permit. Lying side by side behind closed doors was no such occasion. But Khan did not say anything. After a short while looking at the two children standing in the middle of the room, the door half-open behind him, his breathing the only sound audible, he turned around and left.

It was midfall when Khan summoned Ahmad to his room. He twirled his black mustache while the boy closed the door and stepped in front of the walnut desk. "As soon as the war is over and the fires are out," Khan said, "you're going to Paris." Ahmad was shocked, but he stayed still. "This war can't go on for much longer. You will go to lycée and then the Sorbonne. There are enough gardeners and apple pickers already. What this country needs is more lawyers. When you're back, you'll open your office in Tehran." He paused to check the boy's reaction. Ahmad's eyes welled up. His closed lips quivered. But Khan knew that once he saw the beauty of Paris which Khan had heard about from others and seen with his own eyes on postcards, the boy would be nothing but thankful to his grandfather; that years later, enjoying the privileges of his degree, he would see Khan's decision as pure wisdom. "Mr. Sergey will come soon to teach you French. You are a smart boy. I'm positive you'll learn to speak French fast." A tear slid down Ahmad's cheek. "Before you go, I want to make sure you heard me right; I want you to *speak* French. Do you understand, Ahmad?" Ahmad nodded and wiped his nose with his sleeve. "Now you can go."

6

ERGEY BLOKOV ARRIVED IN TAJRISH in a sparkling white
ZIS-110 with three bottles of Russian vodka stashed in his suitcase in
the trunk. Standing in front of their homes or with heads stuck out of
windows, the villagers watched the large car rumble up the streets muddied
in the drizzle. Children and dogs were sure the vehicle had no destination
other than the Orchard. They ran after it and stopped at a decent distance
as it screeched to a halt.

Khan's friend, Meer, had brought Sergey to the café one day. "If you
think you can find a better French teacher for your grandson than Mr.
Blokov, you're mistaken," Meer said to Khan, "given the current circum-
stances." Sergey was tall and had a gray ushanka on with hanging earflaps.
He spoke Persian with a Russian accent, but he said his French was indistinguishable from that of a Parisian and his English from that of a Brit. He

was on medical leave from the army for a disease for which he did not know the Persian name, but he looked healthy that first day in the café. As tall as Khan, but with broad shoulders, Sergey was a large blond who had a hard time fitting into the small wooden chair, but no difficulty polishing off his plate with the last piece of bread.

"You *could* go back to your country to rest and recover," Khan said to him as the waiter placed the three cups of tea on the table, "but you have decided to stay in this country?"

"Mr. Khan," Sergey said staring at him with his very blue eyes, "I have nobody in my home to go to."

"You don't miss your house?"

"Mr. Khan, that is not what I said."

Khan had first thought to make Sergey a small place on the lot behind the mosque, but he knew it would be impossible to get Mulla Ali's consent; as if it were not bold enough that Khan had invited an infidel to the village. Instead, Khan built him two rooms behind his own house: a small one with a wooden bed and wool mattress for sleeping and a larger one for everything else. Before Sergey entered his rooms, he asked for a ladder, placed his shiny patent-leather shoes on the creaking rungs, and climbed up with his suitcase in his hand. Once on the roof, he put down the suitcase, pulled out a short, thin pole, and secured it in place with rocks that he had also brought with him. Once the pole was upright, he tied a Russian flag to it, stepped back, and saluted the flaccid fabric.

"*Comment allez-vous, petit bonhomme?*" he said the first time he saw Ahmad in Khan's room. "Under my supervision," he turned to Khan, "this young gentleman will soon be more proficient in French than Persian."

"I expect nothing less," Khan said to the Russian man, but Ahmad knew his grandfather's comment was meant for him.

Ahmad's days were filled with Sergey. Every morning, he went to Mulla Ali and studied the Quran, classical Persian poetry, Arabic grammar, history, and geography. In the afternoon Sergey and his *dictionnaire* waited for him in the larger room. He saw the ragged book the first day on the table. Next to it was a plate of sweet-smelling candies. Sergey sat at the table and motioned for Ahmad to take a seat, too. "You can have a candy," he said, "after you say *bonjour*." He repeated the word three times, each time leaning forward more, urging Ahmad to utter the greeting. But in vain. A few days later a second plate appeared next to the first. Ahmad could take a fistful if he said only one of the words. Sergey read aloud a page from the *dictionnaire* in each class. The homework was to copy the page ten times. For Ahmad, it was an exercise in drawing. He traced the lines and curves of the foreign words as closely as he could, line by neat line. He could not fit the *dictionnaire* line onto a notebook line. He broke up the words at odd places and wrote from right to left as he did with Persian. One day, when Sergey was much too tired of trying to persuade Ahmad to speak a word, he got up and knocked back what was left at the bottom of a bottle. Soon his cheeks blushed and he continued the lesson with a happy smile. Then he laughed hard and spoke in a new language Ahmad did not understand. In two months, Sergey had not succeeded in eliciting so much as a syllable from Ahmad.

When he was not teaching, Sergey hiked in the mountains, rode Khan's horses, read books, or listened to the Russian radio. Out in the village, people avoided the foreigner they called "Blue Eyes." He had no one to talk to except for Khan with whom he walked in the garden before the burning cold made strolls joyless. Khan listened to Sergey chatter about the weather, the Orchard, and how Ahmad's classes were going. Sometimes he would repeat the story of his brother who had been drafted a year before him, after which no news ever came. Other times, he talked about girls. Sergey spent the weekends in Tehran. Every Thursday around noon, he got into his ZIS-110 in front of the Orchard and left for the city. Word had it that he spent sleepless nights in cabarets and paying occasional visits to underground brothels where Russian soldiers undressed Persian, Georgian, and Armenian girls. Sergey rode back to Tajrish on Friday evening, tired, disheveled, and unable to keep himself on his feet. He staggered straight up to his room and flopped down onto his bed.

With Sergey's classes, Ahmad barely saw Sara anymore and started to realize that he missed her. By the time French was over each day, she had gone back home. Sometimes he saw her walk past the windows of Sergey's room on her way to do chores in the Orchard. Ahmad felt like she was aware of him watching her from the angle at which she held her face: neither turned away, nor facing, just right to give the impression that she could see Ahmad in her peripheral vision. But she seemed reserved, as if it had been his fault that he had to sit in the French class all afternoon. Early evening in Salman's house, when Mash Akbar sat in the main room tuning the radio, the day's work past him and the steaming tea before him on the rug, when the village retired from its diurnal struggle to survive the famine, when there was time for a short game outdoors, Salman would take out his ball and ask Sara if she wanted to go with him to the Orchard. She shook her head and he went alone. "She says she's not in the mood," Salman said to Ahmad. "What's gotten into her?"

WHEN THE WINTER BEGAN DUMPING the first piles of snow on Tajrish, Khan went on his first weekend trip to Tehran with Sergey and became the Russian's inseparable companion. The Orchard felt strange to Ahmad when Khan was gone, even if it was for less than two days. Everyone else was there as always, napping, talking, complaining of pains in knees and backs, rolling cigarettes in the stable. But a void would open somewhere near Ahmad, as if the Orchard was on the edge of an abyss, as if everything was on the brink of crumbling. He tried to be close to his mother, but in the absence of Khan, it was she who was in charge. She would send Ahmad away with a few nice words and a pat on the head before hurrying to talk to Norooz, or to send the stable boy on errands. Ahmad would then go to Agha who was always in his tree, never going anywhere, never busy. When he heard footsteps approaching, Agha opened the tarpaulin curtain and stuck his bald head out, the long collar of his new turtle neck up to his chin. He greeted Ahmad with his permanent smile and complained about the itchy sweater as he emptied the teapot to put on a fresh pot for his young guest. As he sat in that tree with Agha constantly speaking in a hoarse voice that became shriller with each year, Ahmad felt the void shrink into a little dot, insignificant and harmless. Through the age-old plane tree, Ahmad's roots found solid ground to dig into.

Sergey seemed to have given up any hope of making Ahmad utter a word of French. By the end of the winter, all he did was read the next page from the *Dictionnaire Larousse* out loud and explain the words and some rules of grammar through the rare example sentences in the book. All the while he drank from his nice bottles that were replaced with new ones every Saturday after the trip to Tehran. One afternoon when Ahmad went to Sergey, he saw two glasses on the table next to the plate of Russian candies. Before he started the lesson, Sergey brought out three oranges, cut them in half, and squeezed them into Ahmad's glass. Then he took his bottle and poured some into the orange juice. "You have been a good boy," he said, "did your homework conscientiously and made it all the way to J in such a short time." He pointed to the book on the table and poured himself a little, too. Then he opened the window and broke off two of the icicles hanging from the underside of the window casing. He snapped the bigger one in half, and put it in his own glass. The shorter icicle he slipped in Ahmad's. Raising the glass to his lips, he motioned for Ahmad to do the same. It was bitter. It made Ahmad's mouth shrink. His face contorted as the acrid juice went down. He did not know what to do with the glass in his hand, to drink more or to put it back on the table. Luckily, Sergey took the glass from him. "Delightful," he said as he drank the bitter orange juice himself and chewed what was left of the icicle before putting the empty glass on the table. "You're such a big man. Now let's get to work. Open your notebook."

Ahmad felt a chilling ache shooting down his veins. Needles flowed in him. His stomach was smaller. There was not enough room inside him. He looked around. Sergey's bedroom door was closed as always. What was in there? He wanted to get down from his chair and go behind the curtain that partitioned off a strip of the larger room as a kitchen. But the chair was good, too. He had suddenly started to understand what Sergey was saying when he spoke his foreign language. He was not sure what the Russian exactly meant, but he knew he understood. He felt sick and well at the same time. He took one of the candies from the plate and twisted it out of the wrapper. Sergey said no, but Ahmad knew he did not mean it. All Sergey said was, "*Bonjour, no candy, repeat after me: bonjour.*" The heavenly taste of the candy was indescribable. He took it out, looked at it for a second, and then put it back in his mouth. Sergey said no, but that was a yes.

Unlike every other day, Sergey did not dismiss Ahmad after the class. He gave him food to eat and a garlic to chew on, which Ahmad did not. He then made some more food behind the curtain which was delicious and also tasted like garlic. He told Ahmad to stay with him for the night and they would play games, but Ahmad wanted to leave. He had a headache. He took the gum that Sergey offered him at the door, but spat it out right after he stepped into the Orchard.

Days later, as he helped shovel the snow from the roof, Ahmad told Salman about the drink. "How did it feel?" Salman asked. Ahmad fanned himself with his hand. "Warm?" Salman asked. Ahmad nodded. "Hot tea makes me warm." He threw a shovelful of snow over the edge of the roof down into the alley. Ahmad pointed to his stomach and his body. Salman did not understand. Ahmad wrote on the untouched snow with his forefinger: *from inside. all of my body. very warm.* It was then that Ahmad saw Sara step into the courtyard. He threw a snowball at her, but he missed. Sara turned around and looked at him on the roof. She smiled and packed a snowball to lob back. She was not avoiding him. Ahmad threw the next snowball at Salman and got him on the face. In the short moment that Salman stood frozen by Ahmad's surprise attack, a second snowball from the yard smashed to powder on the side of his face. The next moment, the shovel dropped and Salman bent over to scoop snow with a shout that rang from his wide-open mouth like a war cry. Things were back the way they had always been. The three of them were friends again, in a trilateral war.

But it did not last. The next day, Sergey and Khan left the Orchard for the weekend on two mules, the earflaps of Sergey's rabbit-skin ushanka dangling all the way, as the SIZ-110 could not make it up the sinuous alleyways of Tajrish in the snow. Ahmad found Sara alone in the kitchen. He held up his left palm flat and made as if he was writing on it. Sara shook her head and turned back to peeling cucumbers. Ahmad tapped her on the shoulder. *Why?* he mouthed.

"Go," she said, turning away from him again. In her were things she could not say. "You shouldn't be here."

WITH FIVE DRUNK OFFICERS SHOUTING at the table against the music, Khan's elementary Russian was of little use, so he drank his fill and hooked his arm around Sergey's neck. "You know, I'm going to send my grandson to Paris," Khan said out loud. Sergey spoke to the other officers. Some nodded. One snapped at a waiter. The other raised an eyebrow and said something from under his big mustache. Khan looked at Sergey, waiting for him to translate.

"What is he going to do?" Sergey asked.

"Is that what he said?" Khan asked.

"Who?"

"The one with the Stalin mustache." Sergey knocked back what was left in his glass. The other officers spoke through wide-mouthed laughter. Khan could only make out the name Stalin from the string of unintelligible Russian, which sounded like hammers pounding on nails. The officer pointed his finger at Khan and said something. A roar of laughter rose from the table. "What did he say?" Khan asked.

"Nothing," Sergey said still smiling, "some joke about Stalin. It's hard to put into Persian."

Khan looked at the officer for a while, then reached across the table for his glass. The uniformed man watched as the Iranian trickled his drink onto the wooden table. The smile evaporated from the officer's face. "My grandson," Khan said, "will be a lawyer, and maybe he'll go to the military school, and fuck a lot of European girls, and maybe he'll go to the military school, too, tell them Sergey"—he turned to Sergey, the liquid pooled on the table reflecting the yellow incandescent light from the ceiling—"and he'll fuck some French girls too, not the butcher's daughter, he deserves much better than a butcher's daughter. That's why I told her to keep away. 'Keep your nose to work!' Yes, that's what I told her, 'Keep your nose to your work!' My grandson will go to Paris, then he'll come back and sign up in the army of the young Shah and the young Shah will kick all the motherfuckers out of this country. All of them. How do you say motherfuckers in Russian?" He did not wait for Sergey's answer. "Then I said, 'Pooran,' and Pooran said, 'Yes, Khan,' and then I said, 'from now on I don't want no butcher girl flirting with my Ahmad, do you understand?' And then I told her, 'Do you understand?' And then he's going to go to Paris. Tell that Stalin-mustache motherfucker, Sergey, tell him."

IN THE MIDDLE OF THE next French class, two days later, Sergey excused himself and went out. He found Sara in the house and asked her to bring them two cups of tea because he was out of oil and could not use his samovar. But he did not go back to his room. When Sara went in, she found Ahmad alone at the table. He straightened himself against the back of the chair and shifted his weight from one side to the other as if he could not decide between getting up to go to her and staying where he was. On the verge of an unsure smile, he clasped his hands in his lap. She pitied Ahmad and thought of telling him about the warning Khan had given her through Pooran, so he would know the distance was something imposed on her. But she could not bring herself to taint his mother's image for him. "I'm sorry," she whispered and turned away. From his hiding place, Sergey watched Sara leave, then he went inside. That became the routine.

Three days of this had to pass before Sara felt safe enough to sit at the table, in front of Ahmad. Ahmad and Sara resumed their daily reading and writing, now condensed into flash lessons. Ahmad was even more enthusiastic than before. He did not sit down for the short time Sara could afford to be there. Outside Sergey's room, Ahmad would wink at her to catch her attention, as a playful acknowledgment of a shared secret that she did not want out. She turned away from him and he felt the change in her. She was becoming a grown-up. Now Ahmad never saw her out without a chador draping over her head. She seemed to have little time to play anymore. She worked harder and talked with girls of her own age. But in Sergey's room she turned back into the familiar girl that Ahmad had always known. She would hang her chador on the back of the seat and lean forward over her book and notebook and sometimes even smile a tooth-gapped smile at him when she dexterously found her way to the period at the end of a long, arduous sentence.

Sergey got tired of wandering in the snow-covered orchard while the children enjoyed their rendezvous and joined them in his room one day. "No, no, dear, I do not need that," he said to Sara, who had sprung from Sergey's chair. "I am going to sit in my rocking chair and listen to the radio. Never mean to intrude, but I don't want to freeze in the snow. You two go on with your work." Sara left earlier that day and Ahmad hated Sergey. She came back the next afternoon and stayed longer, but refused to sit and kept herself covered. It took her a week to get used to the presence of the Russian who, glass in hand, read a book, listened to the radio, or sometimes interjected a comment about what the two of them read. The day she finally sat down on the chair at the table, Sergey cooked for them. "Kasha is best with buckwheat," he said from behind his curtain. "My brother loved it with buckwheat. But wheat is good, too, you'll see. It won't be like my mother cooks it, but Sergey's kasha is first grade." Ahmad knew he had cooked the porridge not for him, but for Sara. He felt an even stronger hatred for Sergey in his heart when he insisted that Sara stay longer once the time came for Sara to leave.

The next morning, Ahmad decided to skip school to spy on Sergey. He banged the thick, wooden door of the Orchard behind him, but instead of going to Mulla, he hopped along in the knee-high snow until he got to the back side. Like a furrowing fox, he crawled through the water hole at the foot of the wall and squatted behind a thick tree and watched the puffed-up sparrows in the naked branches until Sergey came out of his room and walked to the stable with his hands in his long overcoat. His conversation with the stable boy froze over the blanket of snow and never reached Ahmad, but the clouds of fog the two men breathed out Ahmad saw and the wide Russian laughter he heard. After the dappled horse was groomed and saddled, Sergey left and came back when the sun had moved from the branches of one tree to the other, when Ahmad was hungry. The next day, he followed Sergey on his prelunch walk through the village and up a short trail. He saw the man sit on a rock, elbows resting on knees, and stare at the mountains for some time. There was a sadness in the occasional sips he took from a small canteen that he pulled from inside his coat. On his way back, Sergey tried to talk with the baker, the carpenter, a passerby, smiling and throwing accented hellos at them as if he were still a newcomer, ignorant of what was happening in the village and the country. The shops were almost empty. The shopkeepers, if they opened at all, idled inside, huddling in twos and threes around fires burning in emptied cooking oil tins. If an emaciated villager was out in the cold and snow, he walked listlessly as if to nowhere. Occasionally someone would approach Sergey to ask for money which he refused politely. Instead he gave them the gift of words: he asked them how they fared and what they thought was the solution to the famine. In reply, he received repeated solicitations for money. On the third day, Ahmad saw someone throw a stone at him. Sergey kept his composure, but hastened his pace back to the Orchard.

Ahmad got an earful when word reached Khan from Mulla Ali that he had not appeared in the class for three days. He had not caught Sergey committing any wrongdoing, but deep down he felt the stranger was not without malice and that was why he decided to sneak into his rooms the next weekend. The day before, when Sergey left his room to find Sara and ask for tea, Ahmad unlatched the window that Sergey never opened. On Thursday, right after Khan and Sergey had mounted their mules, Ahmad was in front of Sergey's window. He looked around, then gave the window a push and climbed in. His heart pounded in his ears as he turned the handle to Sergey's bedroom. The door screamed open to a small space with a bed under the window and a small desk right by its side. The nice wooden case under the desk was where Sergey stored his bottles of bitter water; Ahmad had seen him a few times, through the half-open door, squat in front of the case and then come back out of the room with a bottle in his hand.

Ahmad pulled the case out and opened it. The unparalleled bitterness of the first sip on his tongue distorted his face into a grimace. It was much worse without orange juice, but something inside him wanted to swallow it down anyway. He looked into Sergey's two suitcases and ran his hand over the sumac knit pullover. In the desk drawer was a wooden doll. Ahmad took it out. It was a painted woman without limbs, smiling in bright colors and intricate flowers as if in a summer garden. As he picked it up, Ahmad realized the doll was cut in half and something was inside it. He twisted the top and bottom apart and inside was another doll very similar to the first but smaller, also cut in half. Inside the second doll was a third doll and inside the third, yet another. Ahmad laid six of them on the desk. He did not know what they meant and why they were inside one another. When he did not find anything else interesting, he took one of the bottles and climbed out of the window. Before he went away, he made a snowball and threw it at the flag that hung listlessly from the pole. He hid the bottle in his room and wandered around in the garden only to come back for a second sip after a little while and then a third. Soon he was sitting cross-legged in the second-floor corridor, feeling the happiest and then the loneliest. He had to share that feeling with Salman.

Among the apple trees that were like wizened hands turned to the sky, and with the main building well out of sight, Salman sneered when Ahmad crinkled his nose and stuck out his tongue to signal bitterness. He could gulp down as much as Ahmad dished out. "In a single breath." Ahmad filled up half of the glass. Every swallow felt like hot nails scratching down his throat, but Salman was too proud not to force the liquid down. Afterward they shoveled a lot of snow into a big heap and Ahmad rode the wheelbarrow as Salman pushed it round and round until he dropped down panting on the snow. Salman took some of the magic water with him and drank it in the morning before heading for the bathhouse. Many a morning, as he worked the fire, he had heard the jinns' horrifying whispers calling him by name and mumbling other unclear things. No matter how many times he uttered the name of God, they would not leave the bathhouse. With the magic water in his blood, his mind was peaceful, impervious to any nonhuman creature.

Ahmad refilled the bottle with water and placed it back in the wooden case. Before even touching his bottles, Sergey saw that one had been opened. But he did not want word to get out, and from that week on, he would bring one extra back from Tehran: three for him and one for the little sneaker who came for it on the weekend. The addition of the extra bottle was a message for Ahmad: *I've got my eyes on you, little pilfering thing.* Although he still did not feel good when he saw Sergey beaming and radiant around Sara, Ahmad felt somewhat closer to the Russian man as an accomplice, someone with whom he shared a secret.

CONTRARY TO EXPECTATIONS, THE SPRING brought neither an end to the famine nor solace to the injured hearts of the wretched and famished. "The doors of heaven are closing," Mulla Ali said in his evening sermons in the mosque which was more crowded than ever before. It surprised him how people thronged to the mosque every day. Climbing up to his place on the third step of the minbar, he felt a fear of the impending moment when he had to turn around and look at the packed rows of faces waiting for him with growing expectation and uneasiness. Unlike the days of plenty when most left after the congregational prayer, now they stayed with haggard eyes fixed on Mulla, eager to hear about the famine and when it would end. Knitting his brows into a somber scowl, he taught them that every disaster to befall mankind was the consequence of sins committed in public or behind closed doors and curtained windows. They were only suffering what they had brought on themselves. He hollered at the hushed crowd, urging them to repent and return to God. The mosque should be crowded like that not only when calamity struck, but each morning, noon, and evening at every prayer. And the people who stayed in their homes, why were they not praying with the devout? Only by giving their hearts to God could they bring His compassion and mercy upon them and hope that the disasters that they had brought on themselves would soon come to an end. If there was not enough room for everyone in the mosque, as the praying area was almost brimful, they would expand the House of God to make everyone welcome, to extend their generosity and even make extra room for when guests visited. And if any man or woman was between them who harbored even so much as a hint of a doubt in their heart that the expansion could be done, that man or woman had to know that there were no limits to God's grace and power.

"If you take one step toward Him," Mulla said, pointing an index finger up toward the modest chandelier that hung from a plastered ceiling, "He will take ten steps toward you."

A few moments passed in silence before Mulla got to his feet and deliberately stepped down the minbar. Holding his hand up as a testimony to his true words, he pulled his only ring from his finger. "A gift from my late father, and my last worldly possession." He held the silver ring up, its red opal sparkling in the light from the chandelier. "May God accept it from his servant." He placed the ring on the minbar and hung his head in silence.

With the help of the people, a new wing was added to the mosque in just six months. The women's section, separated off with burlap curtains, was annexed to the men's and the entire new wing was dedicated to women. Khan managed to ameliorate his notoriety as someone who had brought a godless man to the village by sponsoring the building of a second minaret and announcing that as soon as the war came to an end, he would complete the mosque with a new, larger dome.

By the end of fall, the mosque was the jewel in the crown of Tajrish: new rugs were laid on the floors, fresh paint applied to the walls, and a new chandelier hung above the supplicants so brilliant that it hummed a barely audible hum of magnificence. More people attended the prayers than Mulla ever remembered. Even in the freezing cold of presunset winter, line after line formed behind him, and while he could not be happier at how his mosque had grown in size and glamor, he felt the pressure, as he spoke to them, of their expectant eyes inquiring why the war and famine had not come an end yet. It was as if he was responsible for the continuation of the scourge now that he had wheedled the last bits of their valuables out of them and exhorted them into such hard work, as if it was his responsibility to put an end to the war.

Mulla's first temporary solution was to show it was the people and not God who had to do more, that they were not doing enough. He suggested optional prayers between and after the regular ones that he felt sure people were too hungry and tired to attend. But contrary to his expectations the additional prayers were equally welcomed by all. Mulla breathed a few curse words every time he turned his back to that overzealous crowd to start a prayer. He bought a better radio and started listening diligently to the afternoon news.

"We need to do something about food," he told Khan one day when they were alone in the Orchard. "Does the Russian know how to stop the war?" Although Sergey was part of the army, Khan said, he was not much into the war. When he was a child, he had once met Monet in Paris and decided to become a painter. He was a no one in the big picture. But Mulla saw him somewhere in the picture anyway. If nothing else, he wore the uniform. With that smirk on his face, traipsing up and down the village, making fun of their misfortune, the man was undoubtedly up to something nasty. Soon Mulla came to the conclusion that the Russian's very presence was harmful for the village and that he had to be banished. Khan rejected the idea. Mulla Ali maintained his calm and mentioned Khan's trips to Tehran, inviting him to ponder what the villagers would think of him if they somehow got wind of how he really spent his weekends. To soften his threat, Mulla mentioned the pressure he was under from the people.

Khan suggested they go to Agha for advice. People revered the age-old man and would accept what he said as sagacious words. Mulla acquiesced. The two of them sat in the tree in front of Agha as he held his bony hands close to the samovar. "At my age, nothing can warm you." They told him how the war and famine were ravaging their village and the country and how miserable everyone's life had become. Sliding back to lean against a poshti, Agha listened in silence, his gnarled fingers resting on his knees. When they were done, he had nothing but a laconic answer for them:

"You want the truth?" his high-pitched voice broke. He cleared his throat and went on, "Kill the cats. Before it's too late."

In Khan's mind this evoked the story Agha had told him when he was only a child. He had thought the man would have forgotten his tall tale ages ago. He himself had never believed it. Or tried not to, even when his own father became so obsessed with cleanliness that he stopped touching food at the end of his short life, and even when Agha refused to die after his age was not determinable anymore. The day Khan's son, Nosser, shot himself at twenty-nine at the top of the minaret, Khan was closest to letting the shadows of the doubt that he and his family were under a wicked spell darken his soul. But he remained resolute to defy the myth and understand the incident in relation to reality. He had not turned every stone when his son left home at the age of fourteen to volunteer for military service. He had failed to make Nosser feel welcome when he came back and tried to be part of the family again. He had been negligent in his son's upbringing and promised himself he would make up for his shortcomings by doing whatever he could for his grandson, Ahmad. Sergey had to stay and teach the boy French.

"Agha is sometimes confused these days," Khan said to Mulla as they walked away from Agha's tree. Mulla looked at him waiting for more. "But I know he'd want us to remain patient and prayerful."

With his bushy eyebrows raised above his small eyes, Mulla threw a knowing glance at Khan and nodded his head, thinking he had to be cautious of the apple man's cunning. Someone who usurped the words of his own kin to smooth out his problems could stab him in the back if the situation became worse.

MULLA TRIED OVER THE NEXT couple of months to keep people hopeful, telling the rows of prayer-sayers stories Agha had not actually told about famines far worse than what they were experiencing. "Patience and prayers," his voice would ring in the mosque, "are the weapons with which Agha and his people fought with the famines of their time. Those two words. Gold. Gold." But when six families left Tajrish, he stood up in front of the congregation and said the main reason for their troubles were the foreigners in their country and that no wrong would turn right until they left. If those high up were not men enough to take a stand against the invaders, the people themselves had to rise and, hand in hand, banish every outsider from their land.

That was a declaration of war against Khan. In response, Khan struck a deal with one of the Russian commanders through Sergey at a party, and a week later the villagers ran to hide in their homes as two army trucks rumbled up the Shemiron Road. Khan and Sergey welcomed the drivers climbing down their vehicles at the end of the drivable road. Khan sent Norooz the Gardener to fetch men. Shortly after, the villagers were unloading the first truck, carrying sacks of flour up the trails like ants. The bakery was full of one month's supply for the whole village. The second truck was packed with oil, tea, rice, beans, sugar, and salt, which they stacked up in a storage room in the Orchard. The bakery fired up its tandoor after many months of disuse and once again the smell of hot bread wafted through the alleyways of Tajrish. Mulla stopped fomenting hatred against the Russians and Khan kept standing in prayer right behind him every night. He was sending his message: Mulla was wrong about the Russians; they had turned out to be the saviors, and Khan's generous heart was the one to support the people of God at all costs. The second convoy of food came in a month, and this time, everyone huddled at the end of the road as soon as they caught sight of the cloud of dust the vehicles stirred.

"If it comes to it," Khan said to Norooz as he watched the unloading, "I'll feed the whole village until the end of the war. Or after that."

NOT LONG AFTER THE WINTER came to an end, word spread that Sergey secretly took girls into his room. The families that had left the village only did so out of the embarrassment. Sara's father forbade her to go to the Orchard. Ahmad heard from one of the women in the building that she had seen the girl with a bruised face and a black eye. "The poor girl has done nothing wrong," Pooran said. She threw on her chador, like a warrior his cape, and went to Sara's house.

"I have been with her the whole time," she told a grim Mash Akbar who opened the door only halfway. "No one is more innocent than that girl."

"I know you for an honest woman, Pooran Khanum." Shame and grief bore on Mash Akbar; his head hung heavy with latent anger. He could barely look into her face. "You're like my sister. But people say things."

"Let me see her."

"With all due respect," Mash Akbar answered, "forget about my daughter."

With the door closing in Pooran's face, not only did Sara's days in the Orchard come to an end, but Salman, too, became a stranger to Ahmad. He avoided him in public and refused to talk to him even when Ahmad sought him out at the butchery. Ahmad ceased trying to win his friend back the evening he blocked Salman's way in the alley and grabbed his shoulders and shook them and mouthed *why? why?* Salman looked at him in the eyes for a few moments, then said, "You don't know what they say behind my sister's back, do you? You should have kicked her out of the Russian's room. You should have told me she went there." He jerked his shoulders out of Ahmad's hands. And with that he walked toward his home.

Khan strode into Sergey's room and yelled at him: "If you wanted girls, why didn't you tell me?"

"When I want girls," Sergey said turning his blue eyes back to the book on his table, "I go to Tehran with you. It's you who should come to me when you want girls." Khan pounded on the table. Sergey denied the rumors, only confessing to Sara's innocent visits which he said happened in the presence of Ahmad. Having witnessed the Russian's appetite for young, female bodies in Tehran, Khan could hardly believe him. But he was ready to feign it. A palpable tension hung over the village. Sergey stopped going out altogether and although no one dared direct any irreverence at Khan, he could feel their hatred behind the spurious appreciative looks.

Khan decided to stay home for a few days and put his thoughts together, but before he could do so, Mulla pulled a new trick out of his sleeve: after the evening prayer some days later he started talking about the Russians, this time specifically mentioning Sergey. He said he had proof of Sergey's otherworldly deception and evil. From a paper bag he pulled out a wooden doll on which a woman was painted in gay colors. He said some well-meaning person in the village had brought it to him from the Russian's very room to reveal his true nature to everyone. Brandishing the doll with a dramatic gesture so everyone could see well, Mulla twisted the doll in half to reveal a second one inside the first. He did the same thing four more times and every time more eyes opened wide in surprise. The row of six dolls standing in order of height on the minbar was evidence that Sergey was a womanizer, and that the six families who had left the village were victims of his lust. Fury welled up in the village.

Khan was in his room when he heard the angry mob break into the

Orchard holding up lanterns and waving sticks in the air. By the time he was out of the house, they had gathered in front of Sergey's rooms. The murmurs receded as Khan walked toward them with confident strides. He climbed up a rock at the foot of a tree and looked at the crowd, his face barely visible in the dark. With an unwavering voice, he announced that the man had done nothing wrong. Before the whispers snowballed into protesting words again, he said it was thanks to Sergey that they had bread to feed their wives and children, that if going back to misery was what they wanted, he would arrange for him to leave. But the man needed time to pack his belongings and prepare for his departure. Sensing the double thoughts brewing in the villagers' heads, Mulla accepted Khan's offer and said they would give Sergey three days, not a single day more; they wanted the Russian gone by Friday noon.

In the feeble lights from the lanterns Norooz and the stable boy held up near Khan, Ahmad did not see the whirlwind in Khan's heart, or the shaking of his hands that he hid in his pants pocket. The first thing Ahmad thought that night, as Khan stepped down from the rock and strode toward his house with the gardener and others following, was that more than anything he wanted to be like Khan: strong and resolute, a man of not too many words, but of exemplary determination, capable of anything.

Sergey had heard the commotion from his room but decided not to show his face. Khan opened his door and went in. The prudent thing would be for him to leave, even if temporarily.

"I understand, I understand," Sergey answered as he dragged at his cigarette. When Khan was gone, he sneaked across the garden to the stable boy's room. Through the small wooden window set in the cob wall, Sergey passed the boy a letter to take to Tehran, and before the boy had the chance to open his mouth, he stretched his hand through the window into the shadows of the room and slid a folded bill into the boy's breast pocket, promising there would be more when he made sure the job had been duly done.

Three hours after breakfast on Friday, Khan knocked and stepped into Sergey's room. The place was untouched, showing no sign of an imminent departure. Gently swaying back and forth in his wicker rocking chair,

Sergey was listening to Russian music wheezing from the radio that he had placed on a low table. A soft smile flashed on his wide, flushed face when he saw Khan. Without a drop of consternation in his blue eyes, he kept smiling and rocking to the beat of the song. If Sergey needed help with the packing, Khan offered, he could send for people.

"No," Sergey said and kept his ear to the speaker as if he had no interest in the conversation and would rather be left alone to engage with more pleasant themes. Khan suggested Sergey get to work sooner rather than later, since time was short. Mulla and his followers would be there any minute. "I haven't danced in a whole goddamn year." Sergey got up from his chair, took Khan's hand, and put it on his own shoulder. Khan saw the empty bottle on the floor by the runner. He sat the Russian back in his chair, but Sergey jumped to his feet and held out his hand. Khan did not take the hand. Sergey raised his arms sideways and started a little dance on his own. Unmoving as a cross from waist up, his legs crisscrossed like scissors cropping hair in a hasty cut. "You're old, Khan," he said. Khan turned the radio off and held Sergey by the shoulders. "Listen to me," he shouted into his face.

"It's all in here," Sergey tapped his index finger against his temple and danced on and on until Khan heard the sounds: the villagers were in the Orchard.

CROWDING IN FRONT OF HIS small house like three nights before, the villagers were offended at the audacity of the Russian. Khan came out, not knowing what exactly to tell them. He tried to keep things under control. He said the automobile had been late and as soon as it arrived their guest would be on his way, no later than an hour after noon. At that moment Sergey flung the door open and appeared with a pistol in one hand and a full bottle in the other. His large stature almost filled the frame. His round, white face was blushed even more than moments earlier when he was dancing. Ahmad watched from a distance and knew Sergey had drunk his magic water. The late afternoon breeze swayed a lock of the Russian's blond hair over his broad forehead and drifted through the supple branches of apple trees that flaunted their young shoots. "It's about time," Sergey shouted at the people with his accented Persian, "everyone went home. Enough of the farce. I don't want to hear a word about this anymore." Then he said something that no one understood. The sounds were familiar to Ahmad; he knew it was not French. "That flag up there, do you see that flag?" Sergey pointed to the Russian flag on the roof with the gun. "It says this is Russian territory and you don't get to decide about it."

Even Khan was taken by surprise. "Mr. Blokov," he said, "that flag, you put it there with your own hands. It doesn't mean . . ."

"Damn right," Sergey cut in. "Russian puts up Russian flag, Russian takes down Russian flag. Now away with you." He went in and slammed the door behind him.

Khan could only watch as the men broke the door and raided the rooms. Two shots were fired inside, but before Khan had time to wonder if Sergey had killed anyone, new sounds came from the other side of the Orchard. Russian soldiers had arrived in Tajrish in ten army vehicles, not unlike the trucks that brought food, and marched into the Orchard. Women shrieked and escaped inside. The men in Sergey's room poured out and ran for their lives. The villager on Sergey's roof was riddled with bullets before he could uproot the flagpole. By the time Sergey could open his bloody mouth against the shooting pains of his broken ribs, the soldiers had searched every inch of the Orchard and rounded up Khan and everyone else in front of the house. Norooz the Gardener raised his voice in protest. A soldier walked up to him, put his bayonet against his heart, and pushed the blade in. They put Sergey on a stretcher and sent him off to Tehran. Khan and his family were released. The soldiers spread out into the village. Sporadic gunshots echoed in the winding alleys of Tajrish for four hours. Before sundown, the drivers started their vehicles, the roar of which slowly faded out as the dust settled back down on the dirt road that, in the years to come, would be an asphalt street lined on both sides with overarching plane trees in the heart of a city so big that neither the dead nor the living residents of the village of Tajrish could ever fathom it.

7

AHMAD LOOKED BACK at the broken gate of the Orchard and tried to keep up with his mother's long steps. He heard a front door creak open behind them, halfway down one of the alleys, and a moment later a stone hit his mother in the back of the neck. She did not turn her head, but Ahmad saw Nemat the Barber's face looking through the half-open door in that unblinking way of his when he cut hair. Pooran hurried through the rest of the descent pressing on her neck, pulling Ahmad's hand, not saying a word, not even looking back at him, until she tripped over a rock and fell. That was the first time Ahmad helped his mother get to her feet and dust off her clothes. But even then, she would not look into Ahmad's eyes, as if embarrassed of the reversal of roles. She got to her feet and did not thank him.

A few hours after they mounted into the wagon, Ahmad and his mother entered the capital. He had not been to Tehran since his father died. One memory of the city alone lingered from before the Day of the Fog: the Smoky Machine, the two-car train that ran between Tehran and the city of Rey. Ahmad had ridden the machine twice on trips to the Abdol-Azīm Shrine that were less of a pilgrimage and more of a family outing. He thought he also remembered the turquoise dome and the flags flying at the top of the minarets, and his father refusing to go in with his mother, and games he played with other kids where someone screamed from excitement. On both trips, some children at the station had said the machine was alive. As if exhausted from hauling so much iron, the "horse" heaved black clouds of smoke from its chimney-like nose. Few people were on the cars; more huddled on the dirt area that was the platform to see their family and friends off or watch how the iron horse would come to life with a clatter and pull the two carriages on the shiny metallic roads. Ahmad had looked out of the open-air cars at the barren plains sprawling between the capital and the small town of Rey as they crawled southward. The rough ride and the demonic din of the metallic horse sounded sweet to him then, as it churned his insides with excitement.

Had it not been for the memory of the Smokey Machine, it would have seemed that Ahmad's life began the day he stopped speaking. The rest of his past had vanished. Now he watched with keen eyes and a heart pounding in uncertainty as he passed through the remains of the old gates of Tehran with his mother and the stable boy, with the pots and pans banging against the leather suitcases, toward the new apartment that Khan had rented for them, on the second floor of a two-story brick building in a row of similar houses with flat roofs. Each attached to its neighbors; the houses formed two unbroken walls along either side of the alley where, unlike in the village, people walked until late at night.

All the way from Tajrish to the city, images from the day before flashed in Ahmad's head: Sergey's broken door, the Russian soldiers raiding the Orchard like lightning, and the way the bedlam came to an end as abruptly as it had started. After the trucks left, Khan had stormed out of the house with his rifle in his hand. "My horse!" he roared, pacing the area between the hoez and the flower beds. He snatched the reins as soon as the stable boy returned with the piebald. Ahmad had run after him with the others, but they quickly lost him. Khan had ridden to Mulla's house and then to the mosque, but both were empty. He galloped up and down the tortuous alleys of Tajrish, under the tall, interweaving trees, and past the little green leaves that sprouted from the cob walls of orchards. He dashed along the brick walls that enveloped courtyards, past half-open doors where people stuck a head out to watch. He stopped when he came back to the open area in front of the mosque and shouted, "These bloods are on your hands, Mulla!" The last of the purplish orange was setting behind the western mountains. "These bloods are on your hands, Mulla!"

Years later Ahmad learned that not only had Khan's voice reached everyone in every corner of Tajrish, it had also traveled to villages as far as three hours away. That sentence never died. It lived in the Alborz mountains for years, going from gorge to summit, from peak to ravine. The inhabitants of Tajrish heard it every time it returned to their village, even after those who were children at the time of the Russian Invasion had children of their own, even when Tehran grew so large that the whole of Tajrish became no more than a neighborhood of the megacity, when the metal din buried every other voice except the sentence Khan had cried into the night.

WHEN AHMAD SAW THE CAPITAL that day, the orchards of Tajrish seemed to him to have been the promised paradise. The large city was a maze of narrow streets and alleys flanked by connecting buildings. Tehran lay close to the mountains, but had an open sky. There was nowhere to escape from the sun that blazed on the ground and walls. An occasional plane tree, elm, or cypress sprouted on the edges of sidewalks, but until he saw a bony, middle-aged man on a ladder picking leaves from a white mulberry tree and shoving them into his mouth, Ahmad could not imagine why the lower branches were all bare as winter. In the trees, only crows had nested. Other birds, even those that did not migrate, had flown away. Without birds, the city was as bizzare as a face without eyebrows. Tehran was a city of fading glory and growing horror. A combination of cars, buses, bicycles, passersby, and horse-drawn carriages wandered the streets in such a way that it seemed they had forgotten the goal of their movement. Where the streets crossed, four-faced lights stood in the middle changing from green to yellow to red. Glorious mansions of the royalty and rich and large government buildings stuck a head up here and there, but Tehran was a city of two-story buildings: lying low, dry, and warm. More straight lines everywhere, more cubes. Roofs were flat, some gable. There were many stores with wooden doors and windows, but food was scarce. Groceries were almost empty. Bakers sat on low wooden stools in front of their shops under the awning that flapped in the spring breeze. Hunger was visible on faces, like sadness.

As soon as a Russian truck roared in the distance, emaciated bodies swarmed onto the sides of the street, snatching anything edible a soldier might throw at them. Their shrunken bodies inside their loose clothes made Ahmad feel embarrassed of his full stomach. The first time he saw an apple tossed to a group of men, he immediately recognized the fruit: it came from Khan's orchards. If he had seen it in his hand, he could even have said which tree it came from. They were now called Russian apples instead of Damavand apples, as if they came from the country beyond the Caspian Sea, and not from the soil at the foot of the mountains he could see from the streets of Tehran. Later he would learn how Khan had managed to trade apples for food for the village before Sergey announced independence and people were killed in retaliation.

AT FIRST HIGH SCHOOLS WOULD not accept Ahmad since he did not have a formal education. But in the famine-stricken city there was no ceiling to what money could attain. Ahmad did not even want to go to school. In their apartment that felt no larger than a room of the Orchard house, he mouthed to his mother in the kitchen that he wanted to enter the army. But the next week Khan arrived from Tajrish and knocked on the door, and a few hours later, at the office of the principal, a clerk penned down Ahmad's name in the register.

Ahmad's first year was spent devising ways to avoid ridicule and practicing how to ignore the boys who walked up to him in the yard opening and

closing their mouths like fish. Just as he had in Mulla Ali's small village classroom, Ahmad shone as the best student in the class. He excelled in math,
physics, and chemistry as well as in history and geography. That made him
the object of more bullying from the start and the first day the teacher announced the math quiz grades out loud at the end of the class, Ahmad's A
made him more nervous than happy. A few hours later, wedged into the gutter outside school, fetid water seeping into his clothes, he promised Jamaal,
by a nod of his head, that from that day on, he would write Jamaal's name
on top of his math papers. Ahmad's math grades started to plummet. Jamaal
was so impressed with the results that he had to trample on Ahmad in the
gutter again to establish the same rule for the other classes whose teachers he
knew were not astute enough to suspect a thing.

Pooran was happy to be near her daughter, in the same city, if not in the
same house. After Ahmad left for school, she draped her chador over her
head and walked the length of the alley to the main street where she climbed
into the horse tram or bus and put a coin in the palm of the driver. By the
time she reached her daughter's house, Maryam's husband had left for work.
Maryam, too, would soon go out. She had made new friends: first Shamse,
the wife of another chauffeur, Maryam's husband's evening company at the
bar, and through Shamse three other young women. They were all from
families with high enough status to afford new shoes and food from the black
market: two wives of chauffeurs, a wife of a government high clerk, and two
daughters of merchants. When Pooran came over was the only time Maryam
could be with them without worrying about her son. The four would drink
tea and talk in Shamse's guest room. Shamse had finished high school, read
women's magazines, and believed women had to start an underground resistance movement; it could start in that same room. Four months had passed
since the end of the war, but the Russians had not left. Shamse asked why.
Maryam and the others listened to Shamse, but they did not think she was
serious.

Maryam was the youngest of the group and the only one with a child.
Being a mother gave her the confidence she had lost after her father and everything else in Tajrish had ceased to exist. Huddled around Shamse's sew-

ing machine, the girls learned from her how to sew. Maryam preferred to stay late, to see as little of her mother as possible, rather than bear to witness her mother's distress, the studious way she did the dishes. When no chores were left undone in Maryam's home, Pooran played with the boy, Majeed. She scooped her grandson into her arms before getting to work preparing lunch. Void of any trait of the Torkash-Vand family—the long fingers or the eyes that peered deep—Majeed had inherited all the features of his father: sparse hair, chubby fingers, and a face that looked baffled with amused wonder. But he was sweet. He would reach for Pooran's pocket to dig out his daily treat: raisins and roasted chickpeas.

FOR TWO MONTHS AFTER POORAN and Ahmad left for Tehran, Khan tried to set things right in Tajrish and bring his family back. But things continued changing. First Mash Akbar married Sara off to a man from the city who had already outlived two wives. Then the butcher and Salman left as well. One night some weeks later, when Khan's orchards burned in uncountable fires, he knew he had no place in Tajrish anymore. Walking among the charred skeletons of the trees, Khan patted the men who had come to help on the shoulder and whispered curses to Mulla. To keep the rest of what he had safe from the clergy man, he sold what he could, including the evergreen orchard that bore four times a year, and hid the money in Agha's tree.

"Keep this handy," he said holding out a hunting rifle. "Right by your bed." For weeks the small, old man leaned against gunnysacks jammed with paper money. Before he went to sleep, Agha would lift the edge of his mattress, load the rifle, lay it barrel down on the ground and sleep with his twiggy hand resting on the bump in his mattress. The night Khan came for the money, Agha was snoring. Khan's men took the bags out four at a time: one under each arm, one in each hand. Khan shook Agha awake.

"I'm here to say goodbye."

"Cats," Agha said sitting up, barely returned from the world of sleep. "Listen to me, Khan. Kill them."

"Are you ever going to let it go?"

"As many as you can. As soon as you can."

"Give me the rifle."

Outside, Khan took a last look at the Orchard in the moonlight: silver coated and serene, studded with a cornucopia of rubies. "Careful, my boy, it's loaded," he heard Agha say from within the tree. "And don't forget me. It's too empty here without the money."

It was the end of fall when Khan moved to Tehran. He stepped out of the automobile and told the driver, as he put on his Astrakhan, to wait by the side of the main street. He walked into the alley avoiding the looks of the passersby. In front of Pooran's apartment, he took off his hat and put his finger on the doorbell. It would be the first time he rang a bell to a home without himself having a better one. A car stuffed with money sacks in its trunk and back was his only possession: paper in bags and nothing more. He pulled his finger back, put his hat back on, and walked toward the street. Half an hour later, he rang another bell. "I need to buy a house," he said as soon as his old friend, Meer, opened the door. Meer invited Khan in to rest and spend the night; they would start the search early next morning. "No, Meer, today," Khan said. "The money is in the car." Meer looked at Khan for a few seconds, then put his hand on Khan's shoulder and said, "I'll go get ready."

The third house Meer took Khan to see had a large garden and a hoez. "Maybe there is one more we can look at," Meer had said, squeezed by Khan in the front seat as the chauffeur turned the wheel and the car slid into the street where the house was, "but not more than that." The street was wide and quiet, the houses flanking it wide and large, unlike Pooran's street where houses were crammed like two rows of matchboxes. It did not matter that the house was far from Pooran; they would all be together soon. Khan did not have to see the fourth house. He got to his feet and sent Meer away with three full sacks. Then he took the rest of the bags inside and laid his mattress in one of the two rooms that looked out on the garden. The smell of money was the last thing that went through his mind before he closed his eyes.

The next day he brought himself to ring Pooran's bell and stomp up the stairs. He took off his polished shoes and stepped in. Before he said anything, Khan stood at the door and looked at the living room, the bedroom, and the kitchen, all that was there to see. "When the time comes, you will move into my house," he said to Pooran.

"Not now?"

"I may move again. I can't keep you on your toes. It will be before long. As soon as I know what to do."

"Can I help?"

"You are helping, dear."

He paid them a visit from time to time, tended to what needed his attention, and left money behind the mirror on the sill on his way out.

As Ahmad's resolution to be like Khan strengthened, Khan's own faith wavered. Fear slithered into his soul like a snake and he wondered what would happen if Agha's story was more than a story. For the first time, Agha's age struck Khan as an ominous sign. Why was the old man still alive? He had spun yarns of the times of the Qajar dynasty kings, not only the latest one, but the one who had gone to Paris for the first time, and the one people called "King Eunuch" about two centuries before. After some deliberation, Khan came to a conclusion: for the spell to break, his lineage had to break. He had to keep a closer watch on his family. He had to protect Pooran and to make sure Ahmad never had a baby. But it was a determination not free of skepticism.

A FEW WEEKS LATER AHMAD came home from school to find Khan sitting on the floor, not sipping from his small tea glass, a bunch of papers in front of him on the rug. He motioned for Ahmad to sit down, then picked up a paper, perused it front and back and put it down to pick up another from the stack. Sitting on a china saucer, his tea was cooling, and Ahmad knew his grandfather liked his tea scalding.

"Who are you?" Khan asked.

Ahmad was taken by surprise. He mouthed his name.

"I know for a fact that you're not." Khan twirled his mustache. "The

Ahmad I knew was better than this." He pointed to the report card and quiz papers, amassed by the tray on which sat a China sugar bowl next to the tea glass. In Khan's eyes was not anger but a dreadful disappointment. For years Ahmad had compensated for his tied tongue with diligence and the prospect of a bright future. The red marks on the papers were proof otherwise; that he was in fact dumb and lazy. He wished Khan would shout at him, slap him in the face, but keep his faith in him. But Khan got to his feet, took a long look at Ahmad, shook his head, and left. Ahmad cried inaudibly. He felt the urge to run after Khan, stop him on the stairs, show him that those crooked lines on the papers were not his handwriting, make him see what was happening at school, but something within him made him feel embarrassed. He was not a child anymore. He was the man of the house, even if the house was a small apartment. Men solved their own problems, without help from their grandfathers or mothers.

WHEN THE APARTMENT DOOR HAD closed behind him, Khan paused for a few seconds. He searched his mind for an excuse to go back in, listened for Ahmad or Pooran's footsteps inside to approach the door, open it, and take him back. Leafing through those exam papers with Ahmad cowering in front of him like a beaten dog had been so difficult that he had left sooner than he had wanted to. Now there was no going back unless they came for him. When extending his pause lost its meaning, he stepped down the stairs. Seated on short stools by half-open front doors, their heads receded into the collars of coats or the folds of chadors and headscarves, a few old men and women followed Khan with their eyes along the alley, sometimes smiling, sometimes saying a warm hello. When he turned into the street, a Russian truck passed on carrying six soldiers and a load of barrels. Khan looked around and waved for a buggy that waited under a leafless plane tree.

The coachman had his Pahlavi hat on. Every once in a while, he lashed an unnecessary strike at the mule, whispering under his breath to himself or the beast. People, young and old, walked the sidewalks, men in loose suits and pants, some with sloppily hanging ties, others without. "Sons of bitches," the coachman said. "Excuse my language sir, but they're vultures." He turned his head halfway toward Khan. "That's what they are. Don't you agree?"

"It's a difficult situation," Khan said.

"Difficult?" The coachman reached under his seat and pulled out a machete. "I have to keep this with me. The other day, I was parked by the street just like today, two streets down, close to the mosque. I went inside to, excuse my language, I had to go. When I came back a fellow had unhitched her from the buggy and was passing right by me in the street. He was walking so calm that for an instant, I doubted if she was really my mule or not. I looked the other way and saw my buggy where I had parked it and of course, no mule. I ran to the man and punched him in the face and took my mule back. I bought the machete the same day. You see my mule here? You see how she's a sack of bones? The guy was even lankier than her. You know how much hay is? Swear to God, the animal eats more than me and my three kids. And you can count her ribs from your seat, you see there? But she's all I have."

The mule struggled, pulling the creaking buggy click-clacking into a roundabout. Behind one of the windows of a bus, a little boy stuck his tongue out at Khan. The pistachio green of the bus reflected the late-fall sun. They exited the roundabout. The city droned on.

"I have a grandson who can't speak," Khan said after some time.

"That's not good," the coachman said. "I found a man for my eldest daughter last month, sent her away at last. She doesn't speak much either. But one less mouth to feed. The other two are boys. They can take care of themselves. Worst comes worst, they can go back to the village with their uncle. He still has a herd of sheep left. As long as grass grows from the earth there will be a few drops of milk to drink."

"I can't send my grandson back to the village," Khan said. "He has to finish high school. Although he isn't doing well."

"I sent my boys to school for three, four years. They kept ganging up on the other kids. Until I had it up to here and one day I sat them down and said, you went to school, you for three years, you for four years, and you're not the school type. Tomorrow morning you're going to work at the kebab shop in the bazaar and you're going to help the ice seller. Just like that: off to work. You're lucky you have a grandson, sir. Boys are easy."

Back in his house, Khan brought a chair out into the yard and sat in front of the hoez wrapping himself tight in his wool coat. Twigs and dead leaves from the overarching persimmon tree sat on the surface of the water. He looked around at his house. It was still new and strange. His yard was large, but compared to the orchards he had lived and worked in, it was no more than a coop, a stable, a sheep pen with a house on one side and three walls on the other. Behind two of the walls were the neighbors' yards. The third had the alley behind it. It was just a house in a row of houses, in a good neighborhood, but one of many.

Two hours before midnight, Khan stuck his hand into one of the sacks and shoved a fistful of bills into his coat pocket. Half an hour later, he pulled one out, tossed it over the counter, and said, "Vodka." When at two in the morning he was told to leave, he pulled out another bill and slapped it on the counter. "Maybe," Khan said to the barman, "you think you can control this place, this table, this 'shop' of yours, but can you control the roaches that scurry in the corners of this 'shop' of yours, too? Can you keep them from climbing up your squat toilet and creeping everywhere? All you can do is open that door and shout, 'It's time,' and close that door behind you and leave and be happy that you're the master of your destiny and walk in the cold and be happy that you locked that door of yours. You hold your fate in your hand very well. Dexterously if you will. And the fate of others. Well done. Clap clap clap. Clap for him."

Khan was still clapping when the barman caught up with him outside and gave him his Astrakhan that he had left on the coatrack.

"The roaches," he said, "they come out in the summer, sir. I can't do anything about them." He patted Khan on the back and helped his hand find the sleeve of his coat.

"What's your name?" Khan asked but did not wait to hear the Armenian barman. He turned around and walked away, his hat in his hand, forgetting to put it on all the way to his house.

WHEN THE FAMINE WORSENED, MARYAM started paying her mother. The afternoon Pooran found the rolled bills in her purse, something crumbled inside her. She had fed that girl since she was a little wiggling bundle of blankets. As long as Pooran remembered, maids, gardeners, and servants had worked for her, both in the Orchard and in her father's house. All that was gone. She rerolled the bills in her hand and slipped them into her purse. Neither mother nor daughter ever mentioned it. Tacitly turned into her daughter's maid, Pooran went to Maryam's house every day and helped with the boy and the housework. But the happiness she found in her heart at being with her daughter and her grandson did not dwindle even when she felt less welcome than before in her daughter's house. There were days when no one answered the door. Pooran used her spare key and found Majeed in a room, playing on his own. She took his hand and walked to the kitchen, reminding herself that the boy had a roof over his head, food to pass down the gullet, and a grandmother who loved him.

Feeding Majeed reminded her of the time she nursed her own children, when Maryam burped only with a lullaby and when Ahmad would not get off her breast at the age of two. Now, a shade of hair had started to show above Ahmad's lips. In his big black eyes shone the same glow that was in Khan and Agha's; the same that had burned in Nosser's eyes. They all had the vortex in their pupils, that dreamy character that was capable of anything, good or evil. Majeed had simple eyes full of curiosity or the unfamiliar world. He would not be hard to raise. She had raised a boy who did not talk, whose thoughts and intentions were veiled even from his mother, the one who was supposed to know him completely.

When she got back to the apartment, Ahmad was not home. Where in the big city he was, she had no idea. She was afraid her days of protecting her children from the world were already behind her. Outside, hunger ate people; men drew their last breaths on sidewalks and their skeletal bodies were later heaped onto the dustman's handcart. She had to talk to Khan about Ahmad's future, about the apartment that was meant to be only temporary, and was feeling smaller every day. When were they going to move to an actual house? Maybe Ahmad would do better in school if he felt more settled. The next time Khan paid a visit she would talk to him.

BUT KHAN DID NOT SHOW up when she expected him. Since their exodus from Tajrish, Khan had acted erratically, and lived somewhat in hiding. He had bought a house, Pooran knew that, but even she did not know where. She waited a few days, suspecting some unforeseen incident had kept him busy elsewhere. By the end of the month, she could not sleep at night. She rolled around. She stared at the ceiling. She listened to the hum of the apartment. All the horrors of the night hovered above her, whispering. At breakfast one morning Ahmad looked pensive. He kept his gaze on his bread and cheese, but the few times he looked up at Pooran, she saw in his eyes the glimmer of that dreaminess that looked like madness, the same that she had seen in Nosser's a few days before he climbed up the mosque's minaret and started shooting flying Russians. Her fears found confirmation when Ahmad was not home from school at the usual time in the afternoon.

What Pooran waited for at home, Ahmad sought outside. With no idea where to begin or who to ask, he walked the streets hoping to find a trace of Khan. For over a month he had believed that his grandfather would knock on the door any day, take his Astrakhan from his head, and ask for a glass of tea. The rustling of the sheets as Pooran turned over in her bed in the living room was in Ahmad's head every day at school. On a windy afternoon, Ahmad walked to Bob Homayoon, the nicest street of the city, where the rich spent time in the famous café and took promenades on sidewalks. The wind shook the last leaves off the rows of trees that separated the wide sidewalk and the street. Ahmad walked past the shops taking looks inside each. Most were empty except for the owners and occasional customers. A woman was inspecting some cloth in the fabric shop. The kebab seller fanned six skewers of sheep liver over glowing coals for two Russian officers who whetted their appetite with hot bread and wedges of onion while waiting for their meat. Ahmad dared not go in; he would not be able to make himself understood with hand gestures and he was sure none of those shopkeepers could read. They would make a fuss and soon he would be the center of attention in the shop or even in the street, as the shopkeeper might call out to his neighbors to help decipher the dumb boy. Tehran was large, but just like Tajrish, word spread fast. If Khan had a reason to be in hiding, he must have had a good one.

"Do you really think he's at some shop," Pooran yelled at Ahmad at night, "twiddling his thumbs, waiting for you to waltz in?" She had been waiting for Ahmad at the door when he came walking back up the dark alley. She had run up to him, slapped him in the face, then hugged him and cried.

"You're not lying to your mother, are you?" Pooran asked when they were inside.

Ahmad shook his head.

"You were just looking for Khan?"

Ahmad nodded.

"Nothing else?"

Ahmad shook his head.

"Will you promise me you come home right after school from now on?"

Ahmad thought for a moment and then shook his head.

Walking around after school became his ritual.

Having lost hope of Khan's return, Pooran trusted her daughter with the secret, hoping her son-in-law could somehow help with the search. When weeks went by with no good news, Ahmad noticed his mother spent her time rearranging the furniture around the apartment and washing anything she could lay her hands on. She had started doing more chores at Maryam's, sweeping the rugs, mopping the floors and stairs with wet rags, and doing the laundry in a tin tub. Pooran came home exhausted, barely managing to cook dinner or do anything but rest and knit for the winter. But the more Khan's absence carried on, the brighter a fire burned within her. She would do the dishes and cook dinner, then pile the laundry in the tub and dust the furniture. Late in the evening, when everything in the apartment was clean, she would rewash the glasses and silverware. Before she laid her mattress on the floor, she would take out a piece of clothing from her wardrobe—a skirt, a dress, or a blouse kept for a large party, one she had not worn in a long time—wash it, and hang it carefully on the clothesline in her room. In the morning, she would iron and smooth it back on the hanger. In her chest, she kept cuts of fabric. She took them out and placed fresh mothballs in their folds. Her favorite was light cream with large crimson flowers among waves of green leaves. That was for a very special occasion.

Despite her concern about her son's meanderings, Pooran did not recognize, in the midst of her engagement with fabric and water, that Ahmad was smelling new smells, his insides churned by fresh feelings. In his daily street-walkings, his eyes lingered on the girls and women. Many were draped in chadors, black or white with floral motifs, with an edge fluttering in the breeze sometimes. But like a hawk, he spotted the others, in coats and skirts, blouses and pants, heels clicking on the sidewalk, the more well-off in cafés, those riding in horse-drawn carriages, those who ventured out in dresses if the weather was lenient. He roamed about Bob Homayoon Street's two cafés where many Russian soldiers brought their ladies. Officers and high-ranking government officials stepped out of their cars with their dates for the evening. In light-gray suit and pants with his blue tie tucked into his vest, a whiff of a mustache above his lips and hair combed to one side, Ahmad watched them all.

TOWARD THE BEGINNING OF WINTER, the last shriveled leaves detached themselves from branches and with that withered the hopes of the poorest of the poor who had survived the fall by chewing on what could be found of leaves and grass. But soon word came that a group in a neighborhood south of Tehran had found a way of fighting the famine by eating hats. Someone had devised a recipe to transform the wearable texture of a hat into edible fibers. The inventor was a woman who had lost a baby to hunger. After nine months of undernourished pregnancy, her breasts had stopped giving milk three weeks after her girl was born. For a short while she took the swaddled girl from door to door to nursing mothers, imploring for a drop which they barely had for their own babies. After she buried her daughter, she decided to save her other two children at any cost. She went to her mosque mulla, then to a soothsayer. What she received would fill many an ear, but no stomach. Back in her home, after she found her pigeon and cat and mouse traps empty, she put a pot on the stove and began cooking. Boiled tree trunk was not edible. A dirt soup never became anything other than muddy hot water. Her children had stopped crying from hunger. Sitting on the floor, they played with their marbles as if they had accepted the futility of their situation.

She ran back to the kitchen and refilled the pot with water. She opened the wardrobe and went through the clothes and finally pulled out a small brown suit she had set aside for when her boy would be big enough to fit in it. A pair of sharp scissors sliced the suit into the boiling water. Mixed with salt and whatever spice was left in the jars, the small pieces of fabric turned into a murky liquid. "Come, kids," she said as she went to her children with two steaming plates, "Eggplant stew." Later, before she threw out the reeking concoction, she realized that the few bites the children had managed to swallow were cuts from the collar. With that clue and with the help of other women, hats were being cooked and served all over the neighborhood within two weeks.

Before long and for reasons unknown to the people, the government denounced the practice as black art and a hoarse voice on the radio forbade any transformation of headgear into food. The hat cooks withdrew behind closed doors and into sealed basements. Ignoring orders from the authorities, the hungry bagged their hats and searched their houses for any threadbare dusty headwear that might have been lying forgotten at the bottom of a chest or wardrobe. Through "mediums," who circulated neighborhoods, the bags of hats were delivered to the clandestine cooks. For every five or six wearable hats, depending on the size, the mediums returned four edible ones, sometimes steaming hot, but more often cooled by the winds that howled along the streets.

Some said the ban had been the work of Russians; empty stomachs did not know the definition of resistance or see the occupiers' sparkling boots and rifles. Besides, those who sat in the big government chairs had no leverage or competence to detect or do anything about hats. When a door-to-door search for cookhouses began in the original neighborhood and some were arrested, the cooking went on a hiatus for weeks before the remaining cooks split up and resumed their work, now scattered around the city. For a little while there seemed to be a respite from the pangs of hunger, at least in certain parts. But soon people ran out of extra hats and were left with the one they wore outside which they could not afford to eat.

Boys and young men started filching hats from pedestrians' heads and disappearing into circuitous alleys fast as the wind. They first targeted the middle-aged and older men whom they were sure to outrun. Embarrassed and furious, the bare-headed man would rush home or to some closed place so he would not be seen hatless in public. To discourage theft, clothes shops moved their hats to the back. The hat shops got raided and robbed so often that the business was no longer safe. Hatters worked with their doors closed and the corrugated tin shutters drawn all the way down as if the shop were closed. Customers would have to pound on the shutters. The hatter interrogated them about the purpose of their visit, and only after the customer slipped the money in under the shutters would the hatter unlock them, lift them up only as much as necessary, and pass the new or repaired hat out.

Soon everyone was concerned about their hats. They became wary when they saw someone approaching them. Expecting a sudden attack from any passerby, people would put their hand on their hat while carefully eyeing the approaching person. Years later, after the Russians had long left Iran and the famine was over, when the account of the hat-eaters had joined the myriads of forgotten events in history, tipping one's hat had become a form of greeting, although few knew the gesture's origin in bitter suspicion and hunger.

This complicated Ahmad's searches for Khan. People looked at every teenage boy on the street as a possible flincher. As people avoided him, his daily walks were reduced to chasing girls on the street and in shops.

FOR MONTHS, KHAN WOULD GET dressed a few hours after the sun had set, shove his hand into a sack, and head for the rundown bar. Before the winter chills turned the water into a block of ice, he had the hoez drained. The drainer man collected all the floating twigs and leaves, but soon more fell from the tree into the bottom and turned into a dark, tangled mesh and that was what Khan thought of when he looked at his long-unshaved beard that had started to overshadow the twirls of his mustache.

"I'm going to see my grandson, tomorrow," he told the barman, "right after school."

"Good."

"Did I tell you he studied French?"

"With Sergey."

"Right, right." Khan took a sip from his glass. "But Ara, you never told me how you lost your earlobe."

On his way to Ahmad's school the next day, Khan heard two shopkeepers talking about hat-eaters. He did not understand what it was, but he had it in his mind when he waited for the school day to end. Ahmad stormed out through the gates smiling at something the other boys were laughing at. Bereft not only of words but also of laughter at the prime of his life, it was as if his grandson was shouting out Khan's failure. Khan had not done enough for his family. He had made mistakes. Ahmad walked away from school and Khan felt he was not ready to face his grandson and daughter-in-law. He was empty-handed and embarrassed. As he was deep in his thoughts, someone dashed past and snatched his Astrakhan hat from his head so nimbly that he barely noticed it.

"You don't have your hat, sir," Ara said when Khan sat down.

"It's my last night here, Ara."

Vodka trickled into the glass. Ara raised his bushy eyebrows.

"I'm returning to God."

Ara wiped the counter with a threadbare towel and placed the glass in front of Khan. "Good for you, sir."

"It's easy to blame the Russians for the famine. You see them in the streets in their sparkling uniforms and boots. No one even sees the British troops in the south. Do you?"

Ara shrugged.

"But that's all surface." Khan knocked back what was left in the glass.

When Khan left that night, Ara One Ear opened the door for him. "You will be all right," he said, extending his hand. "If you decide to come here again, your next drink is on me, sir."

8

N THE LAST DAY OF FALL, Ahmad saw a girl. Waiting for her turn in the women's line, she was looking anxiously inside the shop. If a bakery managed a few bags of flour, it would open its doors for several hours during which a horde of people huddled out front in two lines to get their hands on fresh bread. Fights had been fought, door hinges had been broken, windows had been smashed, and the stronger had trampled the weaker. All over the city, the bakeries had closed their doors and installed metal bars across their windows. Hands squeezing coins would go in through a small opening and come out with hot flat sangak that was often ripped to pieces before it reached a safe distance from the crowd.

The girl stood close to the front. Struggling to stand her ground and keep the women behind from cutting in, she kept her eyes on the inside of the bakery, oblivious of the fact that her chador had opened, exposing the clothes underneath. He walked past the bakery deaf to the commotion of the people in line, never taking his eyes off the brunette locks of hair encircling that angelic face. He could not go far though. He turned around the corner and waited. The girl left the bakery empty-handed. As she passed him, Ahmad found himself enchanted by the way she walked. He followed her at a safe distance, lest people suspect anything. His heart pounded in his temples and the winter around him suddenly melted and evaporated. He undid his suit buttons.

That night Ahmad and his mother were invited to Maryam's place for the celebration of Yalda, the longest night of the year. It became obvious that the invitation was a veiled babysitting request when Maryam and her husband left for a party, leaving the boy with Grandmother Pooran and Uncle Ahmad. As if burdened by a guilty conscience, Maryam had set the table with a cornucopia of the best she had at home: a small bowl of shriveled pistachios, stale walnuts and raisins, dull and dry seeded pomegranates, plates of sweets dripping with syrup, all on a pashmina tablecloth with paisley motif. She had even lit two candles. Deep down, Pooran was offended that her daughter had left her on that special night, but she told Ahmad they should thank God she had a husband who could put food on the table and a roof over her head. Soon after Maryam and her husband left, Pooran got to work washing the dishes and dusting the furniture. The memories of the past years' Yalda nights when all the family gathered together accentuated the loneliness of that night. Norooz the Gardener would wheelbarrow Agha into the large guest room where they would sit around big bowls of nuts and fruit, listening to stories until well after midnight. Those memories were reminders that without Khan, something big was missing.

Ahmad had found an image to substitute for all that was lost: protruding cheeks, thin lips, a small, marvelous ear that had flashed from under the chador for an instant. Words came bubbling inside him. He took out his notebook and started in the language of love. "It broke," Majeed said, teetering up to him, holding a photo frame snapped in two. Ahmad raised a hand to the boy, meaning not now, and turned back to the page. He was stuck at the first line when he could not find a rhyme for "turquoise," but by the time his mother had rinsed the pistachios, walnuts, raisins, and even some of the sweets, he had written four lines in broken rhythm and loose rhymes about an ethereal and nebulous beloved. The main metaphor was that of the candle and butterfly and how eagerly the love-smitten insect would burn himself up in the flame for a fleeting kiss. He hid the notebook in his bag when his mother stepped out of the kitchen. They celebrated the night with wet nuts and soggy sweets that Majeed stuffed in his mouth, asking, "When's my mom coming back?"

AHMAD WAS A CONSPICUOUS FIGURE in the snow that blanketed the city the next day as he lurked around the girl's house hoping to catch a glimpse of her again. He walked around the neighborhood passing by her door over and over again. He stood under the skeleton of a locust tree and sat on the single step of a house. People threw looks at him as they passed. After several days standing in the snow for hours, while trying not to be seen by many, Ahmad had found out that the girl had two older brothers, both big, hulking, and scary with small eyes and scarred faces; a protective mother; and a sickly father who rarely left the house. A week had passed and Ahmad had seen the girl only once when she left home in the company of her mother. A number of streets away, they had entered a house and stayed for at least three hours. Toward the evening, when it started to get dark, Ahmad could no longer feel his toes. At night, he wrote poems and spent long moments staring into the air imagining what her name might be. As if tasting an unfamiliar fruit for the first time, he tested name after name in his head, before vetoing each for a more beautiful one. Nothing sounded good enough. He ditched school to try his luck in the morning, but all he learned was that she did not go to school. That was a big disappointment. She would not be able to read his poems.

THE END-OF-TRIMESTER EXAMS PULLED AHMAD back into the classroom. At the first one—history—as soon as he put his pencil on the paper, the image of Khan shuffling out of the apartment in disappointment flashed before his eyes. He paused for a second and then wrote his own name on top of the page with such determination that he drove the tip of the pencil through the exam paper. He knew Jamaal would give him the beating of his life as soon as the exams week was over and the serial cheating was revealed, but he was not going to remain passive. The first day after the exams he strolled into a neighborhood infamous for its feisty residents and street brawls where it was not hard to entice someone into a fight; all it would take was a look longer than a glance and a defiant face when he was asked, "What are you looking at? Never seen a man in the hellhole you're from?"

The first two nights he mimed slipping on an icy street. "Again?" his mother asked the second night. The next time, he put up his fists with a grimace as Pooran poked a gentle finger on his swollen cheek. "With who? At school?" she asked. Ahmad nodded. "Why?" Ahmad stuck his tongue out and pointed to it. "They make fun of you?" Ahmad nodded. Pooran stepped into the kitchen and came back with the small cloth bag. "Did I ever teach you to lie?" she asked, rubbing ointment on his wounds and bruises and petting his head.

Inevitably, Ahmad and Jamaal each had to go to the principal's office separately for explanations. After handwritings were compared, it took little investigation to determine that Ahmad told the truth. Jamaal was not even allowed to finish that day of classes. He was expelled immediately. With his small gang, he was waiting for Ahmad outside the large metal school gates. Accepting his fate, Ahmad walked among the three of them who escorted him into a quiet alley. He did not run away. He held his head up. Rocking on a branch, a crow cawed from the top of a bare plane tree. It had gotten wind of things. Ahmad pictured the blows that would soon land on his face and body, the pain shooting up his limbs, the burning of skin breaking open, the sting of chipped teeth, and the sore of the bruised swellings on his face. He felt weak in the knees and was about to sink to the ground like a pile of snow in the sun, but Jamaal's aides held his arms and helped him to his feet, like trustworthy friends respecting bonds of camaraderie, never letting their brother down in times of need. Where are my friends? The thought reverberated in Ahmad's head. It was Salman he was thinking of at that moment.

Even with the bitterness that had gone between them after the rumors about Sergey and Sara spread in the village, Ahmad was sure Salman would stand up for him against Jamaal and his boys. If he had been there. For now, Ahmad resolved to hold up his head and his report card the next time he saw Khan—proud and bruised.

They had barely entered the alley when Ahmad turned around and punched Jamaal in the nose. The two boys, thin and undernourished from the famine but experienced in the ways of street fighting, jumped on him like an avalanche and pinned him down in the blink of an eye, but Jamaal raised his hand and ordered them to stop. His other hand covered his nose. The two boys stood Ahmad up, securing his arms behind his back. Jamaal eyed him up. "Nice, nice," he finally said, his voice echoing in his cupped hand, "Our dumb dumb has balls, too. Who would have thought?" Then he extended his hand and offered to be friends. They needed each other's support during the desperate famine. The two boys let go of Ahmad. Undecided and doubtful of Jamaal's honesty but feeling a wild happiness at the sight of blood running down the boy's nose, Ahmad reached and shook his hand.

As they walked back along the alley, Jamaal gave Ahmad his address and said he could count on him if he ever needed anything. He admired temerity especially when it came from somewhere unexpected. Ahmad felt a dizzying joy. He had triumphed. He had transcended his fear. He walked light, each step landing not on frozen mud, but on a coat of fresh snow. Then Jamaal landed a heavy punch in Ahmad's stomach. The pain was a vortex that churned his insides into a sore mess. The three of them kicked Ahmad for what seemed like a long time outside of time, where nothing could reach anything. After they were done, Jamaal said, still standing over Ahmad, that all he had said before was true; Ahmad could count on him, but he also had to remember not to mess with him ever again. Lying on the ground, Ahmad felt that his hot face was melting the ice, now dappled with red spots. Sounds came to him: cars in the street; a bus that clanked past; two light-footed kids running; then some softer footsteps.

"Get up." The order came from above him, but it was not Jamaal. A pair of women's shoes appeared before his eyes. "We should put some Mercurochrome on your eyebrow." Ahmad expected his mother to help him up, but she stood there with a faint smile on her face. "You could have gotten them all. Your punch was good."

AHMAD CANCELED HIS AFTER-SCHOOL PATROLS until the scabs fell off and the bruises had almost waned. Then one day as he walked past the same bakery, he saw the girl in the line again. Without hesitation, he walked over and stood in the men's line which was shorter than the women's. With little difficulty—though not without receiving a few suspicious looks—he let a couple of men slide past him. He threw furtive glances at the women's line, trying not to be caught gawking. She was covered in her black chador that revealed no more than her face, but Ahmad vaguely imagined a perfect body underneath. She was worthy of all the praise he had bejeweled his poems with. And myriads more. One thousand nights would be too few to extol her beauty in his verse. Thanks to his calculations, the two of them got to the bakery door almost at the same time: first Ahmad, and after the woman in front of the girl left, the girl herself. As luck was with him, the baker threw the hot bread on the wooden table in front of Ahmad and shouted, "Finished for the day." It was at that moment, when the smell of the last freshly baked sangak bread wafted between them, that Ahmad found himself eye to eye with the girl of his poems. Amid the shouts and grunts of frustrated people and arms extended to grab the bread, Ahmad offered it to the girl and felt a hollow opening inside of him as her eyes widened in amazement. She would not accept it at first, but when one woman's hand flew to grab the bread, she changed her mind. Ahmad did not take her money; he was chivalrous. The girl could not insist too much in public, talking to a strange boy.

Ahmad's mother had not seen him that happy in a long time. He smiled from time to time as he wrote poetry after dinner. When she asked what he was doing, he mouthed *homework*. She was not upset about him hiding something from her because whatever it was, it was a warm and bright secret that brought out the spark in Ahmad's eyes. There was no mistaking it. She had seen the same glow in Nosser's eyes long ago when for a short time she had felt light in her heart. In her son's eyes was the splendor of love: the immature, immaculate love of youth.

9

AHMAD KNEW THE GIRL wanted to see him when she appeared at the bakery line at the same time the next day, after school was dismissed in the afternoon. She did not say a word, but Ahmad caught a flitting smile flash on her lips. The day after, they ended up at the bakery window at the same time again, a feat that would have been impossible without some pushing and cutting in. As the girl leaned over to reach for the bread on the table, her head straight, her eyes not straying from the window, she whispered to Ahmad: she would be at the grocery store down the street the next day. Brief and low, so no one else might hear, the whisper made Ahmad shiver.

Store after store, they enjoyed being in the same place together for a few, short-lived minutes, the girl talking to the shopkeeper, Ahmad looking at her; Ahmad asking a silent question about a good he did not need as she stole a peek at him, sometimes even helping the man decipher the demand of the tongue-tied customer, laughing with their eyes at the show they put on, trying to prolong the theater to its realistic limit. Exploiting the shopkeepers' momentary distraction, the girl would get close enough to whisper the location of the next rendezvous.

One day Ahmad slipped a small piece of paper into her basket. He knew she did not go to school and guessed she could not read or write, but he hoped curiosity would make her find a way to decipher the writing. And he was right. Although the decorum dictated that she not express her feelings openly, Ahmad could read the eagerness in her eyes when at the dairy shop she turned from the counter—holding in her hand cheese wrapped in brown paper—and whispered, "I love poetry," as if it was a way of saying, *I love you.* That was when Ahmad realized his future was not in the army. Nor did he want to achieve greatness by sending cart after cart of his family's apples to cities near and far. Putting words to page, that was what he was good at.

Ahmad wrote a new poem for the girl every day. After a while he attached a second piece of paper to his poem and asked her if she could read. While examining a spigot, she shook her head. The day after, as the shopkeeper steadied his stool to grab from a top shelf a large china bowl, Ahmad passed his note: *How do you know what I write for you then?* The next day a woman asked the shopkeeper for sumac and dried shallot when the girl whispered she had a friend who read for her. The day after Ahmad asked her name. The next day she whispered: "Raana," and when she asked his name, Ahmad had the paper ready to attach to his poem of the day and slip into a bunch of basil in her arms as she left the shop.

They soon exhausted the meeting locations in the vicinity of Raana's home. She would rarely use the same shop more than once, only when she had heard that a certain shopkeeper was away, the store run by a temporary hand. Ahmad was becoming a known face in that neighborhood, and many prying eyes and eavesdropping ears were prepared to spread word about the suspicious visitor. Raana and Ahmad ventured out into other neighborhoods.

Eager to hear the new poem, Raana would rush after her meeting with Ahmad to her friend's house, two streets down from her own, where she would unfold the paper and wait for the hieroglyphs to be deciphered. Then she would talk about her day's adventure in detail and answer questions about Ahmad: what had happened during the meeting, what Raana had said, how Ahmad had reacted, what he had been wearing, how he had walked up to her, and the one strand of hair above his left ear that stood straight out like a spike. Raana was grateful for having found a friend, two years before, with whom she could share her secrets; a confidante who even helped her find the next rendezvous.

"I only wish Ahmad was older," Raana said to Sara, fearing the day a suitor would knock on her father's door asking for her hand. Her family would not only accept the request, but inwardly revel at having one fewer mouth to feed. At the same time, a consoling voice whispered in her head: no one in their right mind would marry in these times of famine and hardship. That was why her father and two brothers let her go out alone; they hoped someone might see her on the way and like her. That was why her mother took her to the public bathhouse every week—even though they had a shower at home for her father who could not walk anymore without a cane—so that other women might see her long black hair cascading down to her hips, go back to their homes, talk to their husbands, and take her for their sons. Sara dismissed her worries.

"Life's more complicated than you think," she said, brushing Raana's hair that hung as low as the seat of the chair. "Think about me," she said looking into the mirror, that flat world in front of them. "Who would have thought they would marry me to the first man to ask my father and I actually fall in love with him?" She studied Raana's elegant, slender face, her white teeth, her pointed chin, her small ears. Above Raana's face hovered Sara's own: gap toothed, cheeks protruded, eyebrows thick. She was even more anxious than Raana herself to hold the next note in her hand, to unfold it and discover the handwriting she was so familiar with. The nights before Raana's shop dates with Ahmad, Sara felt paralyzed. She wiped her sweaty palms on the mattress, trying to hide her feelings from her husband who nipped at her breasts before going to sleep. Writhing and panting, she repeated Ahmad's poems in her head. Images marched before her closed eyes of his hand curving letters on the paper one after another for her to copy, of him springing to his feet as the door flung open, of Khan looking at them in his heavy silence.

LIKE A LOST BOY SURRENDERING to the futility of his search, Khan retreated into his house, brooding and waiting for a sign to arrive, something to show him the way, tell him who he was and why he lived anymore, something to reassure him that there was something left of his life other than a roomful of money. What he should do with his life and his family in those times of uncertainty was something Khan did not know. When his beard was so long he could hold it in his fist, he decided his asceticism had not been enough. A sign would not come to those who sat. If there were ever going to be an omen, it was he who had to seek it. One gray morning when a sparrow swayed on the bare branch of the persimmon tree in the cold breeze, Khan stepped onto the veranda and put on his shoes. The walk to the bazaar was long, but he would not use anything other than his feet.

In the roofed corridors of the old market, the decline and destruction caused by the famine assailed his eyes: many stands and stalls were left broken and deserted. The number of stores whose bankrupt owners could not afford to replace the smashed panes seemed to double with each step Khan took farther into that maze. In the small mosque, built deep within the labyrinth of narrow and winding corridors, he took off his coat, rolled up his sleeves, and performed the ablutions. With cold water dripping from his face and arms, he joined the sparse rows of men standing behind the mulla, ready for noon prayer. It was his first prayer inside a mosque since his migration from Tajrish. He did not remember the last time he had stood not right behind the imam, but further back among the ordinary people with their old shoes—sole touching sole—in front of them on the rug, lest they get stolen. In unison with dozens of afflicted, Khan listened for God as he stood still with his arms hanging by his sides and his head bent down, as he bowed, dropped to his knees, and rested his forehead on the ground. With eyes and ears open, Khan waited for an answer from God. He listened to the mulla's speech after the noon prayer and the one after the afternoon prayer. But God did not speak to him. Khan returned for the sunset prayer. He stood perfectly still and listened intently but to no avail.

"I'll make you talk to me," he held up his face and said to God as he left the mosque that night. On his way back, he stepped into several groceries before he found one that had forty dates to sell: dried and shriveled, five times the fair price. With each step he took toward home, the dates rattled against one another like rocks.

"I'll start tomorrow," he said to himself, blowing a white cloud into the night.

It was the first time Khan climbed down the four steps into the house's basement. A rusty, broken padlock hung on the narrow metal door. Inside, light from the cloudy sky shone through the two high windows onto the junk: a big wooden table nicked around the edges and blanketed under a thick layer of dust; a broken spade and some wood in one corner; a ladder lying on the floor with three rungs missing. On a rugged ledge on the wall, a rusty mirror reflected almost nothing through black spots and its coat of dust. Khan blew at the ledge and set the bag of dates next to the mirror. He climbed up the four steps back into the yard, then the other three onto the veranda. In his room, he bent over and lifted a bag of money into his arms; it was lighter than a crate of apples. He walked back into the yard, stood at the edge of the drained hoez, and emptied the bag. Bills flew down circling and swaying like many leaves detaching themselves from trees in a wild wind. The second bag was slit open and shaken empty. Green, rectangular money twirled down and rested on the dark slime at the bottom. Water seeped through the precious fibers. When Khan threw aside the last bag, the hoez was half full.

Then he started his fasting.

On the first days he stared at the faded green walls and saw the faded green walls. During the day he recited the Quran and stood in prayer until he saw from his window an orange light in the sky and knew that somewhere behind the innumerable houses that sat between him and the horizon, the sun was going down. He broke his fast with a date after looking into the mirror at his face, then prayed at night until the first rays of the sun broke the darkness. The flesh melted off of his body. His bones jutted out from under his thin, cracked skin. But his head was light and his vision clear. He no longer felt the need to relieve himself. The bonds that had held him down for his whole life had vanished. Every date that came out of the bag reduced his dependence on the mundane. As his eyes began to sink back into their sockets, his vision became keener. His look penetrated through the flaking layers of paint and plaster to observe the bricks and mortar underneath. When only one date was left, he had obtained the faculty to see beyond solid objects.

He stepped out into the street on the forty-first day and witnessed that the curtain had been pulled. The contents of pockets, what happened behind closed doors, and what people tried to hide from others were all clear to him as day. His joints creaked as he placed one painful step after the other toward the small mosque in the bazaar, hands deep in his pockets. The water that slid down his arm seemed to freeze the blood in his bulging veins, but he saw the red fluid flowing up the dark tubes. He saw his beating heart. He saw that he was fine.

More people were waiting for the prayer than forty days before. Like in Tajrish, hunger and misery had made the rows in the mosque longer. Lank and haggard, too skinny for his raincoat, Khan no longer stood out from the rest of the congregation. Like them he dwelled in the proximity of death, but in a different manner: he resurrected from it, they very close to be devoured by it. Anxious in the head and serene at heart, Khan positioned himself right behind the imam in the first row just like he was used to, the closest person to the leader of the prayer, connected to God by the shortest possible link. His most prudent spot. From the moment the prayer began, Khan gave his heart and soul to it. He closed his eyes to see better, to not be distracted by the two men who walked and laughed in the street behind the walls of the mosque. His whole body became one large eye, his ears alert to hunt for the faintest sign from Him. Hunger had opened an inner void that buzzed with need. The first prayer ended. The second prayer followed. Both regular praises of the Creator, but without Him doing anything but listening, without sending down a message.

"There is no God," Khan muttered to himself as he shuffled out into the dark corridors of the bazaar that snaked out and away from the mosque.

Contrary to what he might have expected, that realization did not dishearten him. Not only were his hopes not extinguished, but a fire was kindled within him. Burning in oxymoronic feelings of despair of the heavens and zeal for life, he set up a banquet of scrumptious foods and sweet-smelling drinks and gorged on chicken and kebab and all the succulent fruits that money could buy in the times of famine. His vision shortened with every bite he forced down his gorged gullet into his contracted stomach. The last thing he saw beyond his walls was his neighbor's bedroom. Whistling to herself and combing her hair, the woman looked at something out the window from behind the curtain and smiled a calm smile. Then Khan was back in his room surrounded by unremitting walls, bare and insignificant, telling of nothing. And suddenly he realized it all, he found the answer he had been looking for: *there would be no sign*; that was the sign. If there was no God, no sign would ever come. If there was one, Him sending no message was His way of delegating the responsibility of Khan's life to him. Fate was put in his own hands. Either way, he had a lot to do and much to fight for; protecting his family, saving people from hunger, and liberating his vulnerable country suffering in the hands of the occupiers. Even if he could not do all of that single-handedly, he had to try.

He took the ladder from the basement and walked out to the hoez. Rain and cold had turned the bills into a frozen slab that cracked when he set foot on it. Squatting on top of his money, he hacked at it with the broken spade and thawed out the chunks in the house. For a week, the house was carpeted with dirty wet bills. Then he shaved his beard, oiled the tips of his mustache, and knocked on Pooran's door.

"Pack up," he said when she opened. "You're going to a real house."

She stared at the unfamiliar face of the stranger with the voice of Khan for a long while, studying the sunken cheeks, the dark circles under the eyes, and the unkempt eyebrows, before she let him in and threw herself in his arms.

10

T HE FIRST THING that caught Pooran's eye in Khan's house was the large yard. The hoez was drained, but there was no reason that come spring it would not be brimful with clear water in which the New Year goldfish would swim. Two flower beds flanked the hoez on each side. In one stood a young locust tree and two pines. The other housed a persimmon tree, a vine, and lantana shrubs. The next fall, orange persimmons would swing on branches. Some would fall into the water of the hoez and the sun would shine on the floating orange fruit. The house itself was a one-story red brick with a flat roof. The kitchen was as large as the apartment living room and bedroom combined. The warm water faucet even worked. She assigned the smaller room to Ahmad and directed him to heap up all their things there before she started the washing and dusting.

Ahmad scrubbed the floors for his mother and wiped all the windows until the only way to ascertain their existence was with a hesitant fingertip. One day he came home and found a desk in his room. It was light-brown wood and the top opened into a large space where he could keep his poems and pencils. The upholstery on the seat of the chair was simple, but new. Ahmad touched the velvet-like fabric and the wooden back. He ran into the yard to Khan and hugged him. Khan patted him on the back of the head.

Ahmad's school was far from the new house. Khan offered to hire a buggy to take him to and from school every day, but Ahmad shook his head. Khan asked if he wanted to change his school. Ahmad shook his head fervently. Perusing Ahmad's new report cards, the old man twirled his mustache. "This is good," he said running a hand on Ahmad's head, "but don't get attached. You're too good for this place. You're leaving for Paris at the end of spring. You'll finish high school there." But Ahmad knew this was impossible. Nowhere in his mind did he see a future without Raana. He went to his room, took out the small lacquered box in which he had kept the ivory-white button from his father's shirt since the day of Nosser's death, and put it in his desk, at the bottom, in the corner.

One afternoon Khan came home and brought four cauldrons with him in the interest of cooking hats. Pooran was skeptical, and she worried about the gendarmes breaking into the house any minute. Keeping the cooking secret would not be an easy endeavor. The smoke and smell were what had exposed most of the previous cookeries. Something in the recipe produced a thick cloud of yellow smoke and a tang of raw fish and iron. Oozing through brick-and-mortar within a radius of forty contiguous houses, the odor woke babies in their cradles into uncontrollable fits of crying.

In horrified anticipation of the arrival of Khan's appointed "cook," Pooran scrubbed each cauldron by the empty hoez every day until the cracked skin on her fingers bled in the cold. At night, she pictured the moment when the cook would knock on the door and end the few calm days she had had in her new house. In a competition with an unseen rival, she cooked her best foods for her son and father-in-law. She lay on the sofreh plates of stew and dishes of saffron rice, complemented with sides of shallot yogurt and Shirazi salad. The days when Maryam and her family came to visit,

Pooran would not let her daughter help with the cooking. Like an animal who saw a younger, fiercer beast closing in to dominate her tribe and territory, she expelled Maryam from the kitchen.

Finally, the day came. The cook walked slowly in and the first thing she did was pull out of her bodice a clean piece of rag. She took Pooran's hand and bandaged her bleeding fingers. She was an old woman whose fragile body was wrapped in a white chador with a pattern of small flowers. Her hennaed hair showed from under her pistachio head scarf. She could hardly stand straight, but she had a blazing light at the back of her light-brown eyes. Ahmad moved the cauldrons into the basement. Nana Shamsi picked up the rusty padlock hanging on the latch door. "A new one," she said, putting it gently down on one of the steps, "please."

No one was allowed in the basement except for Nana Shamsi. She would receive her ingredients at the door and disappear behind the thick curtain she had asked for. Khan did not like the arrangement. He suspected several of the items the woman ordered were not used in the recipe. She would probably sell them herself and keep the actual ingredients secret.

The ventilation problem had to be solved before the cooking could begin on a large scale. Word had it that the yellow smoke was emitted from the turmeric or orpiment in the concoction, depending on the recipe each cook used. Nana Shamsi promised an odorless cook with premium ingredients and a pinch of her special powder, a mixture of ground herbs and some unknown elements, but there was little she could do about the color of the smoke. Khan moved his furniture into the living room and repurposed his bedroom into an airtight smoke chamber. Trusted workers constructed a chimney system to direct the smoke directly from the lid of the cauldrons into the smoke chamber, sealed from ceiling to floor—except for the windowpanes—with tar. During the day, they would crack the window and let smoke out little by little, invisible against the bright sky.

Khan hired two hatters to make headgear out of wool, fabric, straw, and used paper. One shopping basket at a time, Pooran smuggled hats in every evening and passed them to Nana Shamsi in the basement. The cooking took the whole night. In the morning, Nana Shamsi removed the lids from the pots and squinted through the steam at the soft hats floating in the thick orange brew. She would then climb up with difficulty into the yard and leave the rest to the others.

Nana was a simple woman from a small village in the northwest who had come to the city after the wheat in her sons' field died overnight shortly before the beginning of the famine. After a night of cooking she went to bed and slept for three hours, then got up and helped around the house without anyone having asked her. Not working was a state she was not familiar with. She washed the herbs, winnowed the beans and chickpeas, or pickled vegetables as if she was in her own house. Sometimes she sat in a corner of the living room or in the yard and told Pooran about her past while smoking her long pipe. When the crows, by their shrill, ominous caws, announced the imminent sinking of the sun below the horizon, Nana Shamsi would stand up to descend into her basement and close the door and curtains behind her. Two hours into the dark, fluorescent greenish-yellow smoke billowed out behind the pitch-dark window of the smoke room. Some nights Ahmad would roll up the outside wicker shades of the smoke-room window to let a soft glow light the yard for a short while. Khan became suspicious of that smoke. Nana was either a fraud or much less than a great cook. He decided to hire another, but Pooran walked up to his bed in the living room with a suitcase in her hand. "I'll go if she goes."

AS SPRING CAME, AHMAD HELPED with the delivery of hats, hurrying out of the house with warm servings, and from his deliveries he rushed to Raana. For some time, Ahmad followed her at a distance, wary of prying eyes, not daring to approach, until he ran out of patience and stole one of his mother's chadors. Shrouded in the large piece of fabric, trying to keep it from slipping down from his head and struggling to cover as much of his face as possible, he set out for the bakery. The soft spring breeze blew the chador open treacherously. He thought he could smell Raana before he turned the corner. He stood in the women's line and covered his fine strands of mustache with the edge of the chador. His heart pumped hot blood into his face. He did not know how close he could stand to the girl in front of him. Four women separated him from Raana. He knew her from behind: her height, the curve of her shoulders, the way she held her head a little tilted to the side. The line grew longer. Unsuspecting bodies—all clad in chadors like him—pushed forward, rubbing against him. Squeezing past the women in front of him was not easy. Since the beginning of the famine, everyone was ready to fight. He stopped trying and left the line. He stood under a locust tree and watched those two squirming lines of hungry people. A Russian army truck snorted by in the street. Under the tarped back, soldiers were sitting, rifles in hand. The truck was still in sight when the baker came out and announced, "Out for the day." People started to disperse reluctantly.

Ahmad followed Raana and caught up with her in a quiet street. The perplexed look on her face did not go away until Ahmad revealed his identity. "You can't do this!" she said with eyes wide-open, a hint of a smile on the corner of her lips, looking around in apprehension. For a moment, she was going to walk away, but the excitement was stronger than the possible consequences. Awkward and nervous, with her heart racing and her eyes flitting from window to window, she walked by Ahmad's side for the first time. "You can't do this," she kept saying, but soon she was proved wrong. From that day on, a veiled Ahmad would appear out of nowhere, from around a corner, from a recess in the wall, and start walking by her side, passing her notes with no concern of getting picked out by inquisitive eyes. They walked not as lovers but as friends, unburdened and unfettered. During their promenades she would forget hunger and her father wheezing in his bed. She felt an unnatural freedom she was not used to.

One sunny afternoon, she extended her hand to take the long-awaited note but the hand that bore it would not let go. Grabbing at the folded paper, the two hands hovered in the air for a little while in a quiet alley. Then one hand slid onto the other. For a short second, two hearts raced in young chests. Neither knew what to do next. Ahmad could not stand being close to her any longer. He let her hand go and rushed out of the alley.

With time, the initial electricity subsided into a heartening warmth that handholding and surreptitious touching of the fingers in quiet streets kindled. Ahmad was burning inside. He wanted more. Instead he gave more. His poems grew longer and more feverish. His notes were warm and restless, his touch affectionate and lingering. Raana burned with a smaller fire. Freed from her initial shock, she often became the one to extend her hand first, but fear walked with her everywhere she went. Except when she went to Sara's house to talk about her adventures or listen to the verses of love that Sara read with such zeal, sometimes forgetting to say the words out loud, as if it had been written for her. The day Sara mentioned her husband's imminent trip out of town to see a new doctor, the girls looked at each other as if they had arrived at the same thought. But the longer Raana pictured herself with Ahmad, the more the illicit encounter seemed like a dream of the past than a possibility for the future. She followed Sara around the house, unable to stop thinking out loud.

"I can't," Raana said standing over Sara who sat on the rug and unscrewed her nail polish.

"I think it'd be a waste not to," Sara answered, running the brush on the nail of her thumb.

"You think so?" Raana asked, walking over to the radio and back to Sara. "He is a gentleman. But how do I leave my house? What should I tell my mother? What if something goes wrong?"

"You'll be spending the night with me. I'm afraid of the dark without my husband."

"You are?" Raana's eyes opened wide as if not only that was a good excuse for her mother, but it was also true.

"Yes, terrified."

Raana did not answer the sarcasm. "I don't know." She sat down by Sara. "I'm so nervous. What if he turns out to be a jerk?"

Sara raised her head from her hand. "A jerk who writes poems for you is not called a jerk." She waved the brush in her hand as she spoke. "There isn't much as good as this boy out there. Trust me." She paused a few moments then got back to painting her nails, so deep in thought that she did not realize when Raana left.

AHMAD COULD HARDLY HANDLE THE anticipation. He made twice as many hat deliveries than the other days. He could not concentrate in class. Sleep skipped him at night. When the evening came, he was near the house an hour early. He walked around so as not to attract attention. The moon was in the sky and the windows were dark when he tightened his chador around him and started for the door, and it was at that moment when he heard someone say, "Naa." The sound came from above him. Ahmad looked up and saw a cat sitting on the wall that separated the yard from the alley. Front paws neatly placed in front of it, head held up and ears cocked as if to hear the most covert steps taken in the dark, the cat stared at Ahmad. A cat on a wall was not a new spectacle in Tehran. He shooed it away and was soon in front of the door. Before he pushed open the door that was supposed to be left unlocked for him, it opened and Sara appeared in the moonlight. "Somehow her brothers found out about you," she said, throwing worried looks into the alley. They had not let Raana out of the house since five days before and they probably would not ever again; certainly not alone. "You should leave now," she said. "But come back when this is over. I'll be waiting for you."

Ahmad strode away looking at his shadow sliding in front of him, wondering how Sara had sprung from the village of years ago into the doorway of that house. What he thought was long forgotten came pulsating back with the sound of his shoes in the dark streets. He suddenly felt the same pangs he once had in front of Khan's desk as he pictured himself leaving Sara for Paris, unable to cry out, "Never!" His feelings for that girl, which he thought were buried in those apple orchards, rose inextricable from his fervor for Raana. Frustration made him walk faster. What he did not know was more than he could fathom. He had heard from his mother that Sara had gotten married, but he had never seen Salar, the thirty-six-year-old man, twice widower, who had done, and would do, anything anyone would suggest to cure his impotence. After the notoriety he gained, following the death of his second wife, as a wife-killer, the man withdrew into his despair until one day he went to Tajrish to spend a relaxing day in the mountains and heard word of a Sara whose name had been smeared by a certain Russian officer called Sergey. He sent his father to talk to Mash Akbar and ask for Sara's hand, which was given to him in a humble ceremony. It was a bout of luck Salar never thought he would have. With a revived hope, he took his bride's hand and went back to Tehran hoping the doctors would give him a son. Sara was the first wife he ever loved. He made sure there would always be plenty of food in the house, he turned the small yard into a lush garden, and he nipped at her breasts every night. He assured Sara that God the Compassionate would soon give them a rosy-cheeked baby and it was with a heart full of desire that he had gone to a new doctor in the northern city of Rasht and was now driving back toward his home.

Two hundred miles south, Ahmad was walking away from that house. What echoed in his head with each step he took, above the murmur of confronting memories, was the name of the person he knew was responsible for what had transpired that night: Khan, Khan, Khan, Khan.

WHY DID YOU DO THAT? Ahmad wrote, and Khan said, "You will thank me later." Who told you? Holding his notepad in his palm, Ahmad wrote more and tore piece after piece out, handing Khan each reverently, but burning with anger. Sitting in his chair in the veranda, Khan read each note, and looked at his grandson writing intently with a red face. "When I was your age," he said after reading the last note, "I didn't dare look at my father in the eye. A son talked to his elder with his head bent down. Now look at you all impudent. What do you think you were doing mingling with a family you don't know? Do you know those two ruffians have their own beds in prison? One brother comes out, the other goes in, sometimes they're both in. You will not have anything to do with a family of this sort as long as I'm around."

Ahmad stood still for a while. *Who told you?* he wrote, sinking his teeth hard into his lower lip to fight the tears in his eyes. He did not see Khan's hands clenched around the armrest. What he saw was a blurry, stone-hard Khan, cold and unaffected. "That's not relevant." *It is to me.* Khan kept the note in his hand as he spoke. "Listen, my son," he said, crossing his legs, "you're just a kid. You should focus on your studies. Consider this a favor from a friend. After you're back from Paris, you'll have lots of time for romance. Now go wash your face and get ready for school tomorrow. Nothing other than first in the whole school will be good enough for my Ahmad."

Shortly before midnight and after he made sure Khan and his mother were asleep, Ahmad stepped into the yard and rolled up the wicker shades behind which yellow vapors drifted in the smoke chamber. He took a rock from the garden and hurled it through the window. Puffs of cloud billowed out and expanded into the sky like a genie ready for his master's command. Before the first rays of the sun pierced the dark, a burly gendarme broke the door open. With flashlights in their hands, they ran to the broken window and then into the house. Khan came out in his pajamas, two soldiers clasping his arms and dragging him toward the front door. At the same time another soldier came up from the basement holding Nana Shamsi in his arms like a baby. "She refuses to walk, sir," said the soldier to the lieutenant in charge who gestured with his head for the soldier to carry Nana out. They heaped the cauldrons and the cooking utensils and instruments into the back of a truck. As the gendarmes dragged Khan out, Pooran was shouting, "Where's my son? Where's my son?"

11

UNABLE TO THINK CLEARLY or hear the threats directed at him from the front passenger seat, Khan sat silent during the drive along the streets of the dawn. The dark was about to yield to the sun. The shops were closed, the streets quiet except for a few sweepers and a handful of early risers.

The gendarmes locked him in a dark room with four other men who were there for different reasons, one for murder, two for street fights and stabbing, and the last for allowing his donkeys to demolish and defecate on the greenery in front of the palace. Khan did not know what awaited him. A trial or some sort of prosecution? Four days passed. Three of the four men left. Only the murderer remained and Khan was almost sure he would be there for a long while. But on the fifth day, a man in uniform opened the door and shouted, "Old man, out!" Khan was led into a room where a major leaned his elbows on a large desk. On one of the chairs in front of the desk sat someone in a different outfit, a Russian uniform. Khan was bewildered for a few seconds. It was only after he was seated directly across from the Russian officer that the blue eyes gave the man away.

It was Sergey. His sturdy nose was not straight anymore: distorted into a crooked beak, it bent to one side halfway down over the bridge. His lower jaw failed to align with the upper. The first thing Khan said to himself was, *So the Russians have been behind everything—the war, the famine.* All the time the major talked, Sergey refused to look Khan in the eye.

"If there's a next time, I'll make sure you won't see the light of day again," the major finished his speech and buzzed for his aide to let the old man out.

"I won't leave without the woman," Khan said to the major, resisting the lieutenant's pull at his arm. Finally, Sergey looked at him.

"Some of us haven't changed, I guess." The lopsided smile that appeared on Sergey's face gave him a menacing look. He got up from his chair; it was the same tall figure who always stood straight, broad chest pushed out. He stepped over and put a hand on Khan's shoulder. "I know this man well, Major. This man is okay. He will make no such mistakes again. He will go home, live his life, and give my regards to his grandson, too. He is okay."

ON THE FIRST DAY OF Khan and Nana's arrest, Pooran had spent the morning and afternoon in the gendarmerie until she was certain she could do nothing for the prisoners, and went back home. The door was still half open. Ahmad had not returned. She checked to see if anything had been stolen and sat down on the edge of her bed. The ticking of the clock out in the living room was the only sound in the house. When the room was dark blue and the night just beyond the walls, she went to the kitchen, ate some bread, and went back to lie in her bed, but she was too tired to sleep. The moon appeared in her window and snailed out of the frame. She stared at the shadows on the wall and when it felt very late into the night, she turned her head again and looked out the window at the silhouette of trees in the garden.

When she turned her head back, the dark figure of a man was standing in the door. Pooran sprang from her bed, shrieking so loud that she was certain she woke up neighbors three doors down. The man's face was concealed in the dark. The faintest light from the window revealed several days of stubble on his cheek. Involuntarily, another shrill scream rang out of Pooran's throat. Khan is back, was the first thought that passed through her mind when she found herself thinking clearly again, but the man was of a smaller stature than Khan. Then she saw, in a patch of light, the man's left foot in an old, crinkled boot caked with dried mud. He had not moved since she had seen him, apparently undisturbed by her cries and unstimulated by malice.

"Who are you?" Pooran asked, her voice weak and out of her control. The man shifted weight and the boot withdrew into the shadows.

"I'm tired."

Pooran recognized that voice.

"Nosser?"

"I'm tired," the man said and for a few seconds the ticking of the clock was deafening. "I scared you. I shouldn't have come." He shifted again, withdrawing further back, taking with him his stubbled cheek into the gloom of the living room. "I should go," he said and turned away.

"No," Pooran almost shouted hurrying around her bed toward the door to grab his arm. She dragged him into her room and it was in the vague light that came from the window that she first noticed he had a rifle slung over the back of his right shoulder, nozzle pointing up. It was Nosser, dusty and thin, his cheekbones jutting out, his head crowned with a gray buzz cut. In his eyes was a recognition void of emotion, a dead look that seemed to spear past Pooran. "Why did you leave?" she asked, leading her husband toward the edge of the bed facing the window and reaching to take the rifle from his shoulder, but Nosser turned away, clasping the strap with both hands as he stared into her eyes. Pooran sat herself beside him.

"They needed me," he said looking out the window, "when the letter came."

Pooran was confused. "What letter?"

Nosser turned to her with a bewildered look. "The letter," he repeated as if only one letter had ever existed and then he told her about the letter that came shortly before Maryam's wedding, demanding his immediate departure to join the carabineers.

"But there was no letter," Pooran said, confounded at hearing Nosser repeat the lies she had told Maryam's mother-in-law. "You died."

"There was a letter." Nosser turned back to look out the window, his voice still cold. "I didn't fight all these years in the war without a letter."

"What war?"

Nosser was silent for a few seconds, then shrugged his shoulders.

Pooran reached across Nosser's chest and placed her hand on his hand, clasped firmly around the rifle's strap. She was not bothered by how he sat straight, void of emotions like a marble statue. She leaned her head on his shoulder. Closing her eyes, she breathed the dusty smell of sweat for a long time before she asked: "Are you hungry?"

Nosser was not hungry, but his thirst was unquenchable. He drank two pitchers of water before the sun went up. In the morning, Pooran unbuttoned his uniform and knelt to undo his shoelaces. All the time that she stripped and washed him, Nosser did not separate himself from his gun. Tilting his head back, he opened his mouth and drank from the shower until Pooran turned the taps off and wound a towel around his waist. In Khan's shirt and striped pajama bottoms, Nosser sat in the veranda, his rifle in his lap and a glass pitcher by the leg of the chair, barely noticing Pooran, rarely turning his head to acknowledge what she said. When time came for sleep, Pooran took him by the arm to her room where she had put an extra pillow on the bed. "I can't lie down," Nosser said. "Why?" Pooran asked. "I'm the guard." All night he stood by the door, rifle in his arms, leaning against the frame, and when Pooran woke up shortly after the break of dawn, he said, "I had missed the way you snore," then he took his empty pitcher and went to the kitchen for water.

Pooran swept the yard and had the windowpane replaced. Whether or not Nosser turned a head toward her did not matter. She told him how she missed Nana Shamsi as if she had lost her mother a second time. She told him how Ahmad had grown up and how the past years that he was not with them had rolled by and how she felt there was no stopping her life from falling apart. Squatting by the flower bed, she shouted to Nosser that in a week or two, the lantanas would bloom, the clusters of color would appear in white, yellow, and pink turning later into orange and red and purple. All through summer bees and butterflies would flit from flower to flower. The vine needed better support. Pooran brought the broken ladder from the corner of the yard, leaned it against the wall, and wound the supple stems and tendrils around the rails and rungs.

"What do you think?" she asked Nosser. Nosser turned his head but did not say anything.

On the fourth night, Pooran filled up Nosser's pitcher and went to bed with a foreboding in her chest. She woke several times, each time worriedly sitting up and looking toward the door, each time finding him where he was, in the doorframe. The last time, Nosser turned his head and said, "When I was the guard, no eye opened even a crack." He said it with such reassurance that the next time Pooran opened her eyes was when she felt a hand on her shoulder. Nosser was standing by her side, back in his uniform. It was still dark but the kind of darkness that preceded the morning.

"I must go."

Even though Pooran knew all along that the moment would come, she locked her arms around him and cried until the uniform was wet against her cheek. "My job is done here," Nosser said. "Khan will be back today." Pooran felt the weight of his hand on her head. "I must go back."

"Where?" She looked up at him.

"To the war."

"The war is over, Nosser." The war had ended in early fall the previous year, around the time Khan had succeeded at enrolling Ahmad in high school. The grocer had put an extra egg in Pooran's bag and congratulated her. Then everyone was talking about it. But the Russians had not left. They stalked the streets as if nothing had changed.

"I will miss you," Nosser said and bent over to kiss her. As he left the room, Nosser took the pitcher from the floor. Pooran jumped out of the bed and walked behind him into the living room, through the short corridor, out onto the veranda, down into the garden, and across to the front door. All the way, and even when he was closing the door behind him with a metallic clank, Nosser did not turn around to throw a last look at her. Pooran cried until the sun was up. Then she brushed the dried mud from the carpets with her hands and put the dirt in a vial.

KHAN CAME BACK THAT DAY. Pooran rushed past him to Nana Shamsi and sank herself in her arms. Nana patted Pooran on the back and assured her with a smile that she had had a good long chat with the prison ladies. The fresh, soft putty around the windowpane and the absence of Ahmad revealed the story to Khan. Pooran saw his anger in the way he pressed his lips together under his large mustache. Then Khan turned away from the window and asked Pooran if anything important had happened when he was gone. "Ahmad's not back yet," Pooran said as she followed Khan to his desk. "I said anything important." He sat at his desk. Pooran shook her head, but from his intense look, she knew Khan was not finished, that something else was coming. She was nervous. She thought maybe she should not have fixed the window, that the broken pane might have been useful evidence for something. "I want you to know," he said, "that you are what keeps this house together." Pooran smiled. "And thank you for taking care of the vine."

THE MORNING THE NEW CAULDRONS and utensils arrived, Pooran bolted the door and would not let the worker in. "No more hat cooking in this house," she said loudly as if to herself as she crossed the yard back to the house. The boy sat on his low cart by the door in the street, waiting for them to let him in so he could make the delivery and collect the money, until Nana Shamsi convinced Pooran that in hard times it was everybody's responsibility to extend a hand and pull others out of the bog. "Okay," Pooran said as she got up from beside Nana Shamsi for the door, "but be careful with all this. I won't lose you again. I have said enough goodbyes already." Soon the yellow cloud warmed the smoke chamber once more and hungry people in the neighborhood took lids off of pots, fished out fedoras, berets, beanies, Pahlavis, and cloche hats, soft and dripping with juice, and sunk their teeth into them in exchange for whatever they had to offer, which many times was just a profusion of gratitude and benedictions for the kind heart of the one who fed them.

But not long had passed when almost overnight people stopped buying hat dishes or even accepting them free. Their ravenous eyes longed for a bite, but even the regular customers began turning away the delivery boys. Word arrived soon after. The clergy had issued a decree: consummation of any apparel was deadly sin. Relieved, Pooran washed the cauldrons by the hoez and tidied up the defunct cookery. She placed pots of geraniums on the edges of the hoez and weeded the flower beds. The cooking was put on a hiatus and Nana Shamsi started helping with the housework.

With an unfaltering determination, Khan started looking for new ways of defeating the famine. For months he tried in vain. The day the Russians left, he was squeezing key lime to attempt a dirt marinade. He heard the news on the radio and froze with a half lime in his hand, a drop of juice hanging from his forefinger. In a matter of days, the streets were empty of the uniformed men that for the past five years were such a common sight. People used pots as percussion and danced in the public. The famine seemed to follow the Russians' trail and soon Khan emptied his bowls of dirt back in the garden. In the coming weeks, a certain calm started to seep into the house. The weather grew warmer, the whole yard bloomed, and one day Nana Shamsi stepped into the kitchen and said, "Birds are back." She held Pooran's hand and took her into the yard. A mourning dove perched on a low branch of one of the pines. Pooran welled up. "Don't distress yourself, my dear." Nana put her frail arms around her. "He will be back, too. This is his nest." Nana meant Ahmad, but Pooran saw Nosser in her head, leaving with the half-empty jar in his hand. Soon the sparrows followed and Khan saw a cat dash out of the half-open door of a house with a piece of meat in its mouth. People could buy meat again.

NOT LONG AFTER, NANA SHAMSI had a dream in which a dilapidated old man stepped out from inside a big tree, looked at her for a while, then tilted his head and grinned. Hovering in the dark, the head wailed in a way that sounded like *tell Khan, tell Khan.* As the head withdrew into the darkness of the tree, it said, "Tell Khan. It wasn't the Russians."

Leaning against the spade and running the tip of his finger on the sapling he had planted, Khan listened as the cook recounted her dream. Nana went back into the house, and Agha's cat story came to life in Khan's head once again as he stamped on the soil at the foot of the young tree. With the tapping of his foot in that early afternoon sun, Khan remembered news from the past year, before the Soviet withdrawal, of an uprising in the Azerbaijan Province: a local government had announced independence, a conflict that had resolved shortly after the end of the occupation. He leaned the spade against the wall and left for the store.

Before paying for the map, Khan unfolded it on the shop counter and traced the closest path from the borders of Syria and Iraq to Iran. If there had been any truth to Agha's story, the cats would have entered Iran from the northwest corner, and that was the Azerbaijan Province.

The next afternoon, Pooran drew the curtain to the loud voice of the worker talking to Khan as he hauled the cauldrons, ovens, and copper ladles out of the basement and replaced them with a vice and piles of newspapers and magazines.

What is he up to now? Pooran sighed and closed the curtain. Khan nailed the map to the basement wall right across from the door and began his investigations.

12

WITH JAMAAL'S HELP Ahmad found work with Oos Abbas, a forty-year-old blacksmith who sized Ahmad up with arms crossed over his chest, like he was buying a mule, before motioning him to step forward.

"Are they after you?" he asked.

Ahmad raised his eyebrows.

"The gendarmes, the police? Anyone?"

Ahmad shook his head.

"With these muscles you'll last a day here," he said, "no more than two for sure." He paused. "And you have a long face." Then he turned to Jamaal. "Long face is not cut for this work, but he can stay a day or two."

Soon Oos Abbas was surprised at Ahmad's zeal in pumping the bellows, making the crimson fire roar. "This doesn't come from those spindly arms."

Ahmad slept at the back of the forge on a threadbare kilim. After Oos Abbas left the first day, Ahmad locked the door and lay down on his carpet. The sun set and the orange light crept in through the windows. All evening and night, he saw images of Raana in his head. Raana tearing a piece off the fresh bread, Raana walking, Raana holding her basket open for the shopkeeper to put the bunch of herbs in, Raana pulling glowing-red iron out of the fire, Raana sitting on the short, blackened stool in front of him, Raana working the bellows. He wiped his tears and joined Jamaal's gang the next day.

The fights took place in the Pit, a circular depression in the ground at the brickyard. Not too far away, the long chimneys of the brick kilns were silhouetted against the setting sun breathing out clouds of smoke into the sky. Spectators stood around cheering and making bets. "Do you have a name or something?" someone from the crowd called at Ahmad the first day he walked to the Pit with Jamaal. "I'm talking to you. Cat got your tongue?" The next moment, Ahmad was straddling the boy, rubbing his face into the dry dirt, and punching him in the ribs. When they jumped into the Pit— Ahmad, Jamaal, and the two boys—their rivals were waiting for them. Four against five. Jamaal was accusing the rivals of being cowards for having appeared with one extra when Ahmad's silent punch sent one of the boys flying. Amid ecstatic cheering, the brawl ended just after it began. Soon no one in the neighborhood dared to mock or pick on Ahmad, and if a stranger did so, boys readied themselves to watch a fight in the Pit, where Jamaal's knife had scarred faces and Ahmad's fist had broken ribs. One fourth of every bet in the crowd would go to Jamaal and his boys; Jamaal would get half of the money himself, Ahmad half of the other half, and what remained would go to the other two boys. Dead tired of the day's work and evening fights, Ahmad would lay down on his kilim and fall asleep before he had time to mope or mull. With every day that passed, the flames flared a tad shorter and Oos Abbas knew that an unseen fire was being extinguished. When the summer was almost over, Ahmad took the money he had saved and signed up for night school. He walked two hours every day and punched extra people for Jamaal when he needed books.

Within a month there was no one who could beat him at arm wrestling.

At night, after he returned from the Pit and rubbed Mercurochrome on his wounds and scratches and pressed on his bruises to assess the damage, he took the newspaper, shook the dirt out of it, and read. So it was with pain that he learned about Mosaddegh, a member of the parliament and one of the founders of the National Front Party, who in some years would become Prime Minister. With his big ears, a head bald on top and gray on the sides, and a long nose on his horse-like face, the politician looked like a kind, old father in the photos. Reading Mosaddegh's speeches on the nationalization of oil gave Ahmad's poems a taste of the political. Ahmad debated with Oos Abbas by gesticulating and fervently shaking his head as he landed the sledgehammer on glowing spades. At that time, Oos Abbas was one of the few people around Ahmad who cared enough to voice an opinion about the political issues that seemed immaterial to many. When Ahmad broached a topic they had not talked about before, though, Oos Abbas would reduce their debates to a simple mantra: "Leave empty talk to empty people. We have bread to win. Those, up there, they don't. They have their games to play. We have a fight. We fight iron. They don't have a fight."

Ahmad did not agree. The day he spoke of oil for the first time, Oos Abbas did not seem to understand him. Ahmad brought the lamp from a corner of the forge and pointed to its oil storage. Then he sat on a number of imaginary seats arranged in concentric semicircles and made a heated but silent speech to the nonexistent members. "Parliament is where they talk about things that don't exist," Oos Abbas said in response. His father had told him the story of the first parliament: how the cossacks rolled in mule-drawn cannons, shelled the building, and hanged a dozen members before the dust settled over the rubble. After a long hiatus, the next parliament decided to only discuss things that did not have material existence so as not to offend anyone in power. "Even you could be a member," he told Ahmad, "because it doesn't matter what anyone says or not. It's an assembly of mouths, with no ears." Ahmad would not swallow the myth. He unscrewed the cap and tilted the lamp. Oil trickled down on the hardened dirt floor of the forge. Oos Abbas sat on his armchair and scratched his chest through his undershirt that was his work attire, too. Ahmad pointed to the iridescent puddle that reflected the light of the sunny day outside. "It's not lamp oil, but this black goo that comes out of the earth, that's what they're talking about." His itching not satisfied, Oos Abbas pulled down the collar of his undershirt and scratched his hairy chest more with his forefinger. "There, take a shovel, be my guest, take a dig. When you reach the black juice, I'll believe you and your parliament." In the near future, Oos Abbas would find himself in the minority. People would believe in the viscous black fluid and see it as the reason for the election of a Prime Minister who had succeeded in nationalizing the industry, as well as the Coup that toppled him, and much more of the history to follow. No one ever saw the oil with their own eyes, but the bludgeons and blood were real.

"You know what you're doing?" Oos Abbas said one day as he laid the sofreh on the small table in the back of the shop for second breakfast. "Escape." Ahmad kept his face down to his work. Sparks leapt from the grinding wheel. Oos Abbas put the fresh bread on the table and unwrapped the cheese. "You write about politics, because all you really do is try to forget that girl." Ahmad raised his eyebrows, his head still down. "What, you think a year is long? How long has it been? A year? Two years? Whatever. You think two years is enough to forget someone? What if I told you twenty? How about twenty?" Strong tea trickled from the spout of the teapot into small, glass cups. Ahmad held the knife up and looked at the reflection of light in the blade, then gave the handle a few turns and put the knife back to the wheel. "I want you to know what's going to happen: you'll try to jam all of that love into the hammer and bang it away, look close into the fire until all of it burns off of your face. You read all that gibberish in the paper to feel you're big, that you're dealing with important things, that you don't have time to think about her. But what's going to happen is you'll write crappy poems and no one will ever read them and all of a sudden you look in the mirror and see a forty-year-old man who still thinks about that one stolen kiss on a night that refuses to leave your memory." He broke a lump of the cheese and rubbed it on a piece of bread with his stubby thumb. "Now come eat."

Three weeks later, Ahmad's first poem was published, proving Oos Abbas wrong. On a Thursday, after he was done at the forge, Ahmad started for the Pit and, as he did every week, bought the *Young Iran* magazine on his way. He leafed through and suddenly stopped walking. His ghazal was somewhere in the middle of the magazine below an ad for the Westinghouse fridge. He read it from top to bottom over and over again, tasting each word and letter. People passed by him looking over at what he had in his hand. By the time he got to the Pit panting, the fight had already started. He elbowed his way through the crowd and jumped in, but before he could stop thinking about his poem, someone heavy was sitting on his chest.

"What's this?" Oos Abbas asked the next day, refusing to take the trampled magazine, ripped across the middle, that Ahmad held out to him. Ahmad turned the pages and wiped some dirt off of his poem. "That's yours?" Ahmad nodded. Oos Abbas took the magazine and lowered his big round head as he looked at the page. "Well, I can't read," he said giving the magazine back, "but even if it is, you know one swallow doesn't summer make, does it?"

BY THE TIME HE FINISHED high school, Ahmad had published fifteen poems in newspapers and journals under the pen name Silent Fist, which Oos Abbas found "as interesting as this horseshoe." The poems became popular among an offshoot of the Tudeh Party that worked in favor of the nationalization of oil. In a letter that came to the forge, they asked him for poems to publish in the special issue of their magazine, *Rebel*, for the anniversary of Marx's birth. His hidden identity added appeal to his sophistication as well as intensity to the denunciations. But a critique of *Rebel* soon called the proponents of the oil movement "ignoramus traitors," and Silent Fist a "vacuous voice of vanity whose ideology fails to surpass the communism of the Tudeh Party high school brochures, a dimwit whose discordant words enjoy no more than the mystery of anonymity."

Although he never joined the party, Ahmad had read the pamphlets and was aware of its growing influence in schools and universities as well as in factories. He believed his path to the heights of greatness went through politics, that he would not create lasting poetry worthy of attention if he did not engage himself with the same issues that busied men in the royal palace, government, and parliament. He devised metaphors in his poems that were read as references to the oil movement and the party. The summer after he graduated, his first political essay came out in which he lamented what he called the prevalent ignorance of ordinary people—those who worked the lands and those who worked the machines—that had caused the suffocating atmosphere, general poverty, and the corruption of those in power:

In a society where the labor is rendered impotent by superstition and ignorance, how can we expect to succeed in severing the hands of those who loot our God-given treasures?

The essay was published in *Rebel* and was read and referred to in some political circles. Lying on his sleeping mat at night, with his hands locked behind his head, Ahmad asked himself if he was a vacuous voice of vanity. The sound of someone practicing the violin came from the apartment upstairs. It was a man in his thirties. He always started an hour before midnight. The discordant notes inspired Ahmad to sit at his small desk. He opened the magazine and turned the pages to his essay. He looked at it for a few moments, then closed it and started to write another.

FALL CAME CALM AND TENDER. It dissipated the unbearable heat and brought Mosaddegh and the National Front a season closer to victory. Composed and charismatic, the old man who had gotten into parliament as Tehran's number one representative walked with a cane—a souvenir of his time in prison and a necessary accessory for rheumatoid joints—and made speeches that brought cheering and applause from his listeners. With his characteristic bald head, the tall, thin nationalist had become a vanguard in oil battles and the hero of many.

The leaves of plane trees withered yellow and fell like hands about to clench into fists. There was an aroma of romance in the cool breeze. Fall was Ahmad's favorite season, when the city showed itself off like no other time, with the intolerable heat already gone and the penetrating cold not yet on the horizon, with greens turned into yellows and oranges, with falling rain and leaves. He watched the old people who sat by their doors in alleyways, the passersby, men in suits and hats, women in chadors, in blouses, skirts, and dresses walking on sidewalks and across the streets in which an incongruous mixture of cars, buggies, carts, and buses started and stopped, and among all of that, the weaving bicycles. The wounds the famine had inflicted on the city had healed. People streamed into and out of the repaired and repainted shops. New trees had been planted along the sidewalks and shopkeepers kept flowerpots out front. Walking in the alleys Ahmad could see the tops of trees from behind the walls that enclosed yards; vines and ivies snaked on top of walls; on crowded sidewalks, the street vendors sold steaming boiled beet and fava beans. The city had survived. Life had seeped back in. In the distance, the ever-snow-covered cone of Mount Damavand towered in the Alborz range. Fine and fragile, fall reminded Ahmad of his family: his mother, his sister, and the little boy, Majeed. He had not seen them in years. The hatred that boiled inside him when he left home had abated. Fire had purged his soul.

NANA SHAMSI HAD THE DREAM a week before. "The boy's coming back," she told Pooran at breakfast. "What boy?" Pooran asked after a moment of pause. "He's grown taller than the door," Nana Shamsi answered. The following Friday, when the neighborhood fruit seller had brought out the first persimmon of the season, Ahmad hopped onto the horse tram and knocked on Khan's door. Nana Shamsi opened it, held up her small face framed in a pink headscarf, and looked at him for a few moments with a smile. "The boy's here," she called out toward Pooran across the yard. When Nana stepped aside for Ahmad to bow his head and walk in, Pooran did not turn to look at her son. The yard was a lush little garden in warm colors, a minuscule Eden in spite of all the leaves that fall had claimed. Pooran was picking grapes from the vine that crawled up the ladder and along the top of the wall before scaling three ropes onto the corner of the roof. Ahmad stepped forward, took the basket from his mother, and held her hand in his. Although still free of wrinkles, her skin had lost its bright freshness. Strands of white waved inside her hazel mane like fish in a stream. He pointed to his chest and mouthed, *I'm Ahmad, your son.* But Pooran did not turn her eyes away from the yellow bunch that dangled in front of her. Ahmad placed his mother's hand on his chest. She would not budge. Finally he kissed her fingers and let them go. She picked up the basket and went inside.

"Four years and six months and eighteen days,"—the voice was as strong as before, though slightly gravelly, as if he had a sorrow stuck in his throat—"that's how long she waited for you." Ahmad turned around. Khan's eyes and cheeks had sunk in. His skin was darker than Ahmad remembered. His hair was thinner. His bushy eyebrows cast his face in a constant effortless frown. But a narrow smile appeared on his face, the tops of his salt-and-pepper mustache moved. "This will always be your home," he said opening his arms. Ahmad looked at his grandfather for a while. His legs wanted to go forward to accept the invitation of the man he had revered most, and to feel at home again, but Ahmad's memories of him—all from when he was taller and walked as if he took each step with a plan—had a bitter taste behind them. A cool breeze rustled through the leaves. Khan dropped his arms. The smile shrunk away. "You're still mad." Ahmad nodded. "Do you have children?" Ahmad shook his head. "Can I speak to you about something?" Ahmad did not answer. "It's important."

The large basement table was strewn with books, papers, and magazines, pens and pencils, rulers, a knife, and an abacus. Against the wall stood two short bookcases. Old, yellowed volumes sat on the two top shelves, brittle and about to collapse. To the left, a curtain partitioned off a section of the basement. After he had furnished the basement with new equipment, Khan had sat and written down Agha's tale and read it word for word for a week. Then he started studying the uprising in the Azerbaijan Province. The harder he explored the printed and oral news and rumors, the farther he found himself from piecing together the puzzle. What had been called the *People's Republic of Azerbaijan* had many gaps in its short, one-year history. People's names had been inconsistent or untraceable; a small local government had formed, but it was not certain how; the man who had drafted and later read the declaration of independence had been called two different names; there was never a photo of the appointed minister of war who had warned the farmer resistance. Soon after the threat, the farmers' crops wilted as if the water that ran in the fields had stopped being water. And that was the beginning of the famine. Khan had not at first given much significance to the people who had reported hearing a purr in the background on their radio when the independence announcement was being read. "But then"— Khan got up from his chair—"I saw this." From his bookshelf, he pulled a hefty tome with faded black leather covers and gingerly put it down on the table. He turned the brittle pages with dextrous movements of his aging fingers and stopped on a page that, from the other side of the table, seemed to Ahmad like the drawing of a flower. "Listen to this." Khan began reading:

> *That the petals and leaves of the regret flower are of poisonous nature and that the bane is most murderous to the cat is knowledge that passed down to us from the times of our forefathers and a matter I disserted on in the preceding pages of the present treatise, but what I, after years of examination, have found which since its discovery has not failed to astonish me, is the fact that the feline, itself, knows this. One ought not to confound this knowledge with the instinctual refrainment of the beast from eating plants in general. Many years of observation have shown me that the death in the regret flower passes through a cat and leaves the body in the beast's last urine and the cat knows this.*

Here Khan stopped and looked up at Ahmad as if waiting for the excitement of the discovery to come from his grandson. "Now do you see this? This is how the famine started. It was the cats." Ahmad found the story intriguing. Even if bleak and foreboding, cats sacrificing themselves by chewing the purple gossamer of the regret flower petals and urinating annihilation and ruin before drawing their last breath had something of a poetic nature to it. "You must be wondering what the Russians' role was in all this," Khan went on, excited to have prepared answers for Ahmad's unasked questions. From the pile on the table, he pulled a page from a newspaper and handed it to Ahmad. It was almost four years old. Ahmad perused the page, but did not find anything extraordinary. "Above the caricature," Khan said. A short piece of news set in a small block of text talked about a rodent infestation in Azerbaijan. "The Russians leave, the Shah sends in the army, Azerbaijan is back, then what happens? Rat issues. Cats had the whole region, they killed the crops, they influenced the party and the local government. And the Russians protected them."

Ahmad got up from his chair and put the paper on the table.

"Wait. Have you seen the map?" On the wall facing Ahmad, the map was marked by small arrows and X's. Khan showed him the routes from the deserts in Iraq, into Azerbaijan, and ending at last in Tehran. "There are words about the Tudeh Party, too." Ahmad started for the door. "I don't know if I believe this myself yet," Khan said, "but cats roam the buildings of the party. Go and see for yourself." Ahmad turned back, took a pen from the table, and wrote on a piece of paper.

"Yes," Khan said after he read the note, "a few cats around doesn't necessarily mean anything but I'm talking about cats waltzing into the door where they print their things in the morning. I have seen it with my own eyes. Come with me and see for yourself. A printer is not the street or a house now, is it? What are the cats doing there? Who do you think runs the place? Or should I say what?"

Neither spoke for a few moments.

"I'm running experiments."

Khan was trying to understand what the cats wanted. He thought going back to the primitive stages of man-beast communication in Agha's tale might be possible. The few books he found on weird creatures and history of sorcery seemed at first promising. He read about the cats' feeding and behavioral routines and anomalies. He repeated mantras and performed acts of austerity and penitence and at one point divined significance and received a renewed encouragement from the cry of a street cat. Then in an obscure passage in the margins of one of the books, he found a slanted handwritten note about the link between the souls of a cat and a man who look alike. Khan walked behind the curtain. "The first step is to talk." Ahmad heard him move things around. Khan came back with a cage. "Recognize him?" The wooden cage dangled in his hand. With ears flat against its head, a blue-gray sat in a corner looking at Ahmad with eyes wide-open. Its mouth was twisted and half of its nose seemed to have been burned. The cat looked weak and ill, but its eyes were so alive they could rain blue sparkles. "Say hi to Sergey," Khan announced. "He will help me with languages."

POORAN BUSIED HERSELF IN THE garden and refused to talk to Ahmad the whole day.

At night, Ahmad sat on a chair by the hoez, the collar of his coat turned up, his hands warm in his coat pockets. The moon was reflected in the still water on which a few leaves floated. Soon they would drain the hoez for the winter. Khan snored in his room. Like crystal chandeliers, the grapes glistened in the silver light. Ahmad heard the door creak open behind him and the darkened figure of Nana Shamsi shuffled out of the house, her back bent from the weight of her age. "I have dreamed," she said in her slow manner. "You will leave and you will do many foolish things. The next time I see you, you will be in a bloody fever. The next time you see me, I won't be breathing." She shifted and stood right before Ahmad. Against the moonlit black sky, she was a silhouette not much taller than the seated young man. "My husband never kissed me," she said. She smelled raw like the New Year's goldfish. "Will you?" she asked, but did not wait for a reply. Leaning forward, she put her lips on Ahmad's. The touch was soft and rosy as if her lips had preserved the freshness they must have had when she was a teenage village girl. Ahmad felt Nana's hand on the back of his neck. Then she went back into the house. When the first rooster cawed somewhere in the neighborhood, Ahmad stepped out the front door and clicked it shut behind him.

13

FTER LIVING IN THE FORGE FOR A YEAR, Ahmad had rented a moldy basement room nearby that became his first home. That night, the kiss from Nana Shamsi unsettled him so much that Ahmad slept not in his basement room, but in the forge again. He lay out the old kilim and, staring at the dark ceiling like five years before, fell into reveries of his courtship with Raana. With fingers knotted around the handle of the sledgehammer, he had pounded the frustration and confusion out of himself. He had flattened metal. He had cracked noses and ribs until he had found no trace of love within him for that girl anymore, but now it rose up again, a distant memory in the dark.

All night, Ahmad stayed awake. Then he got up in the morning, folded his kilim, and bought a razor. In front of the mirror over the wash basin, he shaved the soft hair on his cheeks and upper lip for the first time and washed the blood from the cuts. Once again, he hid a chador under his suit and waited around the corner from Raana's door. The door was the same, five years older, with more paint chipped off here and there. The streets were more crowded now than when he first did his trick, but he managed the donning of the chador without being noticed. On Ahmad's seventh day of watching, the wind blew in stray flakes from the snow that was falling in the mountains. He saw one of Raana's brothers with a wife and two children going in the house, but never the father, in spite of his old habit of going for a morning walk with someone holding his arm. And never Raana. Ahmad turned up his collar and decided he would wait for her for no matter how long. Once again, after years, he had to rock his toes in his shoes buried ankle-deep in the snow. The winter was hard. One day he had to dig through the chest-high snow for an hour before he could get out of his house.

Toward the end of the season, the postman handed Oos Abbas an envelope. "You're becoming famous," he said holding the envelope out to Ahmad. "A new poem?"

It was a short note from Raana. She had been aware of him the whole time, seen him from behind the curtains, but she could not leave the house unattended. Her brothers would kill her if they got wind of her walking out alone again. But she could not stand to see him waiting for her in the cold anymore. She would soon make the arrangements.

Several days later, as years before, Ahmad snuck up to Sara's house, this time on a moonless winter night, pushed the door open gently, and passed through a short corridor into a small yard.

It was as if that distant night had been put on hold for Ahmad to resume five years later; as if nothing had happened in the interval except that he had lived one alternative of how things might have gone. This time, it was the same night and it would go some other way, as planned. Ahmad took off his shoes and stepped on the rugs. The place felt empty, but before he had time to figure out where he was, before he even smelled the scent of jasmine, two arms locked around his waist from behind. His chador had fallen from his head at some point. He turned around and held her in his arms. He wanted to see her face, but the curtains had been closed tight. His groping hands slid up her back and framed her face before he glued his lips on hers. The room vanished into a kaleidoscopic whirling darkness. His restless legs started moving; he took a first step and then a second, and then it was Raana who took the lead, pulled him and then pushed him until they were dancing a silent dance around the room, her head on his shoulder, the soft carpet caressing their soles, her warm breath eddying around his neck in quick, excited gasps that diced the dark. He slammed his shin against the edge of something. Raana pulled him away from another corner. She must have had better eyes than him to see the furniture through the obscurity. Short breaths cleft the night. After some time, at some unknown spot in the house, Ahmad took a step backward onto a puffy softness on the ground: a mattress, sprawling cool, expecting. Never before in his life had Ahmad wanted more to have a voice, to utter terms of endearment, to say even the smallest of words to Raana, the girl who straddled his chest and leaned forward to join lips with him. If only she could read, he could at least make a note and ask her to talk, to whisper his name, to say something, anything. She wanted to be one with him maybe, he thought, two bodies united without the interruption of sounds. But he wanted sounds. He rolled over and sat up. A phantom in the dark, Raana's body sat in front of him: like him, cross-legged; like him, expecting. Extending his hand, he placed his palm on her chest, gave a push and now the silent girl was on the mattress. The night flowed through them.

Cherry blossoms.

THE NEXT MORNING THE OIL industry was nationalized. It was a big victory for Mosaddegh and the National Front Party. They celebrated at noon by firing three shots at Cannon Square. Majeed, who was playing tag in the alley with some other boys, looked at the sky and ran inside to ask his mother and grandmother where the sound had come from. Neither Maryam nor Pooran knew. They were busy with housework and Majeed's younger sister, Parveen. The boy climbed down to the basement. Khan did not know either. "But let's find out," he said to the boy, smiling playfully and pushing on the armrests to raise himself from the chair. Majeed's large eyes sparkled.

Out in the streets Khan soon learned about what had happened from the first shopkeeper who was standing out front chatting with a customer. Half an hour later he followed the seven-year-old around a corner and the vast expanse of the Cannon Square opened up in front of them, surrounded on four sides with government establishments. Gathering in the middle, in the large rectangular area with patches of greens and a few lonely trees, a great number of people cheered around the Marble Cannon.

"It's something like that they're firing," Khan said to the boy, "farther out of the city." A small group shouted half-hearted slogans against Mosaddegh in a corner where three nosed buses waited for passengers. From the windows of the long two-story building of the Ministry of Telegraph and Telephone, men looked down at the square. Many stood around watching on the sidewalks and many walked along indifferent to the news. Then Khan had an idea. "You want to play a game?" he asked Majeed. "It's called count the kitties." Excited, the boy listened to Khan's careful instructions and watched his papa crouch down to tie his undone shoelace. "You should learn to tie your own shoes. You're going to school soon." Majeed looked down with hands in his small pants pockets. "Thanks, Papa," he said and ran off out of sight. Khan sat on a doorstep and talked to a grocer. An hour or two later, the boy came back to report the number and Khan bought him some dried sour cherries and a rooster candy. On a hand-drawn map of the city, Khan marked the number of cats in each district as he and his great-grandson walked street by street, then back again to the same areas for new counts. The women of the house were happy about the changes they witnessed: Khan had come out of his obsessive illusions and become outgoing. He took the kid out for walks whenever Maryam paid a visit, which gave them more time for her younger girl.

Every passing day added a few more dots to Khan's maps. "You see this?" he would show the map to Sergey. "These are your friends, see? Now you want to tell me what they're up to?" The cat cowered in the corner of the cage not taking his eyes from Khan. But Khan could not sit idly until Sergey acknowledged the question. He studied his charts and drawings at night to find the pattern of the cats spreading across the city. Soon a problem presented itself: he could count the cats, but he had no knowledge of the way the felines moved from one point to another. If he could gain that knowledge, he would be able to test his hypothesis that shortly after the cats migrated to an area, things would go wrong there—that there was a relation between the cats' activities and havoc.

One night he made a trap by balancing the rim of a heavy pot upside down on a short Y-shaped stick to which he tied a string. He placed some lamb fat under the pot and waited in his basement, holding the other end of the thread in his hand, squinting through a window into the night. Two hours later he pulled. The pot dropped with a loud clatter. Inside, the cat growled and hissed and clawed at the copper vessel. With a foot on the pot, Khan wound some rags around his hand and forearm before he lifted the rim and reached for the frightened animal. By the time he managed to throw the cat into a gunnysack, his sleeve was torn and his wrist was bleeding. All night the sack swung on a peg on the wall behind the curtain, jerking back and forth from time to time.

"I need your iron," Khan told Pooran after breakfast the next morning. Back in his basement, he tonged glowing-red coal into the iron, then from behind the curtain, he took the squirming sack off the peg and put it on the table. With heavy books from his bookcase he tried to pin the restless cat's legs. In its gunnysack, the cat squirmed free, toppling the stacks. Khan took out his hefty tomes and dumped them all over the animal until the sound that came from underneath was of total surrender. Then he pulled the cat's tail out. The books wobbled. He spat on his finger and tapped the iron. The spit sizzled into vapor. When he pressed the iron on the tip of the tail, the cat sprang with such a force that it sent the books flying in the air. Smoke wafted from the scorched tail as the gunnysack rolled back and forth. It knocked over Sergey's cage and then stopped squirming. Khan picked it up and let the cat out of the bag in the yard. The animal dashed up a tree, leapt onto the top of the wall, and was gone faster than death. "Keep your eyes peeled for Scorch Tail," Khan told Majeed. Three days later Majeed saw the cat in an alley with a fish head in its mouth. Khan had expected it to move elsewhere to conduct whatever plot it was supposed to carry on, but the cat had stayed in the neighborhood. When the summer was over, Majeed's father bought a new house on the other side of the city and Khan lost his full-time aide.

FOR A WEEK, AHMAD STOOD out front of the forge two hours before noon when the postman pedaled by raising a greeting hand and smiling to Ahmad without ever applying the brakes. Ahmad would go back in and hope a note would come the next morning. Trying to find a relief for his frustration in words, he wrote poems every night. He devoured newspapers and magazines. Then he wrote more. The next morning, he would clean up the forge, get the fire going, step outside, and wave to the postman who rang his bell twice, flashed him a smile, and rolled past. At night, Ahmad stared at his words and said them in his head as they formed on the paper. He ran his fingers over them. Ink smeared.

One night, when he was starting a new poem, Ahmad sensed the presence of something behind the words he formed on the paper, something underneath the curves. He could almost see a faint gleam, each letter adding to whatever was behind the array of letters. He turned the light off and held his face close to the paper, and saw a very weak aura. The words emitted a glimmer in which he saw with clarity a mosquito circling. The bug had buzzed around his ears for the past hour. He fanned it away, but it came back spiraling in toward the poem, until it was swatted to a bloody splotch on the paper.

TWO MONTHS PASSED AND THE postman did not come to the forge. Ahmad realized that somewhere in that time he had stopped waiting outside. His heart was empty of that unbearable craze that once made him storm out of the forge for Raana. He was optimistic and hopeful about the changes in the society. Mosaddegh, having succeeded in unifying the parliament into a unanimous vote for the nationalization of oil, was appointed Prime Minister and announced a policy of tolerance in which free speech and free press were everyone's right. He wrote a letter to the chief of the police stating that no man should be prosecuted for what they wrote about him in print, no matter what. The strands of Ahmad's feelings for a beloved in the dark, unseeable in her nakedness, were impossible to untangle from his political interpretations. His politics were romantic, his lyrics political. But his love had migrated from his heart to his papers. He wrote unspecifically and equivocally. A critic of the Prime Minister and a supporter of the Shah quoted one of Ahmad's poems in a newspaper editorial. A range of accusations had been brought against the man who was officially the second highest-ranking official of the country. Ahmad was furious about the misappropriation. "What's with you now?" Oos Abbas asked him. The fires he was making at the forge were raging again.

Shortly before the Coup flashed through the streets like a knife from the pocket of a thug, Salman showed up at Oos Abbas's forge in gray wide-leg pants, a black suit, and a striped gray tie. He doffed his fedora and stepped in. "If you think you can hide behind your alias forever, you can't be more wrong." Salman and Ahmad hugged a long time, rocking back and forth and patting each other on the back. The many stories they had, they exchanged at Café Lalahzar. After Sara had married and left the house, Mash Akbar, Salman's father, moved to Tehran too, to start a new life. On the night Sergey announced independence, the Russians had rounded up the suspect attackers in the open square in front of the mosque. Like Khan, they looked for Mulla Ali, too, but he was nowhere to be found, so they took the men away in the backs of their trucks. Tajrish was not a place to live in anymore. Mash Akbar closed down his butchery. Scarcely anyone could afford to buy meat anyway. The memories of his long-deceased wife and the absence of Sara lurked in every corner of the house, leaping at him at night until finally one day, Salman came home to find two big bundles in the middle of the large room, one of which his father straddled, tightening the knot that held it together. "We're leaving," he had told Salman between clenched teeth, his bad leg dangling on one side of the bundle, his knuckles white, his eyes not moving from the knot, "this damned house." Before the sun went down, they entered Tehran through the defunct Shemiron Gate, a half-torn monument that marked the old borders of the city, the father limping, holding his son's hand and pulling the rein of the donkey that barely kept its knees from bending under the load. They had their things stolen from them within the first three days. They slept on the streets for a week before someone came with a moving job for the donkey. It took Mash Akbar five years before he could afford to rent a place and open his small butchery in a cheap neighborhood.

"I admire your hand, my friend," Salman said. "It fights well and it writes well." Ahmad wrote on his notepad, tore the page out, and slipped it over to Salman.

"I know," Salman said, "they misused your poem. But it's not your best, is it?"

Ahmad took the paper back and wrote some more.

"That's easy to fix." Salman pushed the paper back to Ahmad. "Write another and start it like 'My PM, I love him!' And everyone will know you are not against Mosaddegh." He laughed and waved down the servant for a second tea.

Ahmad wrote.

"Oo," Salman raised his eyebrows, "That's the party's official publication. I don't know if they'll publish you."

Ahmad flipped the paper and wrote.

"I don't know much about that, Ahmad, but I'll ask. I can't promise. It's big. They take it seriously. Some say it comes directly from Moscow. I don't even know who runs the journal."

The page was almost full. Ahmad wrote three words on the edge.

"*Some say tabbies?* What does that mean? Who says what?"

Ahmad laughed the matter off with a silent wave of his hand.

"Too many punches in the head in that pit, my friend?" Salman said and leaned back.

They drank more tea and Salman smoked a cigarette. Before Salman left, Ahmad tore another page out of his notepad and wrote on it.

They will publish my poems.

NOT THE MAJOR JOURNAL, BUT the Youth Organization of the Tudeh Party accepted Ahmad's work. The editor's essay that accompanied the poem posited that it was long past the time for literature to migrate from the courts and the ivory towers into factories, workshops, and farms where it belonged.

"Congratulations, Anonymous!" Salman yelled when Ahmad walked through the door at Café Lalahzar. "The left likes you. Happy now?" Ahmad shook his head. *It's not the real thing. But thank you*, he wrote on the copy Salman laid on the table and hung his arm around his friend's shoulder. At Café Lalahzar Ahmad found a lost brother. Salman would go up to the café owner's desk, say hi, pat him on the shoulder, and then put on his own favorite record. He would walk back to Ahmad and read his drafts with a concentrated frown. He underlined the lines he liked best. They were the same ones that shone the brightest at night. Salman could not write one line of poetry, but he could tell good from sloppy.

In politics, Salman was the poet. He had joined the Tudeh Party a few years back, soon after he moved to Tehran. Ahmad's politics pulled from the space between the communism of the Tudeh and Khan's belief in the royal family, especially the young Shah. He saw himself in the middle, free to pick what was right. "But you want to get published with the lefties," Salman said. *Because the ass-kissers of the Shah stole my poem.* "I know." Salman tapped him on the shoulder. "But listen, Ahmad." He leaned forward and laid his hand on Ahmad's arm. "To me you're like a brother I never had. No, no, that's not true; you are my brother. So when I say this, you know I say it because I love you, right?" He did not wait for Ahmad to answer. His thick eyebrows knotted into a stern frown above his brown eyes. "You don't know mule manure when you write politics. You're an awesome poet. I'd bet my head over your lines. Stick to it. You put whatever you want in your poems. You want to write political epic, I'm with you. You want to get published with the party, I'll try to help. But stick to your rhyme. Essay schmessay. Let go of all that stuff. Your home is poetry. Do you hear me? Does any of this get into that head of yours?" Ahmad smiled and thanked Salman for his concern. Salman was not sure how much he had convinced Ahmad, and Ahmad, certain of his friend's good heart, became resolute to show himself and his friend that he could achieve anything he set his heart on.

The young men's visits in the café continued as before, filled with poetry and companionship. When the two were not discussing the young Shah, new to the throne, or oil or Mosaddegh's opening the society up, they smoked hookah and played backgammon as they poured hot tea from small glasses into saucers and drank with sugar cubes in their mouths. "What did you buy that elephant of a gramophone for in the first place?" Salman would shout at the owner when the song finished and he had not had time to change the record yet. Lalahzar Street had transformed since the first time Ahmad set foot on it, when he strolled the city looking for Khan. The old pavement had been replaced by a layer of fresh asphalt; more cars were on the road, and the rugged cobblestone had become a sign of older times of backwardness and slowness. A second café had opened a few doors down. Stores were built on the lots that had been left empty between buildings like missing teeth. At one of those stores Majeed had his first ice cream.

ROM HIS DINGY BASEMENT, Ahmad moved into the second floor of a two-story building. Now he had two separate, facing rooms that opened onto a small corridor. On the first floor lived the landlady who sat in her rocking chair in the yard and held her radio to her ear. A flimsy metal staircase climbed to the roof from Ahmad's balcony, and the only way to reach it was through the window. On hot summer nights Ahmad bundled up his mattress, blankets, and pillows, and stepped out of the window and up the staircase. With his arms behind his head, he lay looking into the stars before he set up his mosquito net.

In the evenings, after the sun went down, he sat at his desk and took out his pencil to put words on paper, trying to make them glow. He erased the dimmer words and tried new ones until the draft gave off a good glimmer.

When he could read whole lines by the light they emitted alone, Ahmad knew a poem had been born.

"Do you sleep early, Mr. Ahmad?" the landlady asked him one morning. "I don't see your lights on very often." He saved on electricity money by lighting the newspapers he read with his poems, which he put on top of a stack of books on his desk as a reading light. He also wrote essays for small papers on social and political issues. When he called the Prime Minister a "national hero" after Mosaddegh tried to annul the Shah's legal control on the armed forces, some pro-Shah publications published denunciatory editorials and put Ahmad on a list of condemnable names in contemporary literature, some big, some "fledgling like a certain Silent Fist."

We search the light no matter what, he wrote after he saw his published name. That sentence did not glow hard enough. The dim light died away as he crossed out the words. *We search the light in the heart of darkness.* Stronger, but not satisfactory. *I seek the light in the heart of the dark.* His hand was lit brighter with each word, but he crossed out the line for the third time. *Sunk in the dark, I seek the light.* A soft spotlight shone from the paper on his desk to the ceiling. That was a keeper.

When he read that line the next day, Salman got to his feet and motioned for the waiter to shut the gramophone up. Then he read it out loud again and finished the poem blushing from the intensity of feelings. Sporadic clapping and whistling rose in the café. Someone shouted, "Encore!" and Salman read the lines again, gesticulating with his free hand, enunciating the words. Ahmad and Salman received more applause and two free teas from the café owner.

That was the poem that the Tudeh Party magazine published.

"You got what you wanted," Salman said at the café, "but be careful, Ahmad. It's not hard to draw the line from 'Anonymous' to 'Silent Fist.' You're playing with fire."

Ahmad nodded his head and smiled.

"Also there's going to be a protest," Salman said after the waiter put the hookah on the table. "Want to come?"

Ahmad traced with his finger on the table: *When?*

WALKING HOME FROM SCHOOL, MAJEED spotted Scorch Tail up
an elm tree in a sidewalk on Shah-Abad Street. Ignoring his mother's for-
bidding him to touch the telephone, he made his first phone call to Khan.
Finally, the cat had moved to another neighborhood. Khan had long awaited
that migration. He zeroed in on the area and began to lunch at the chai house
on Shah-Abad Street every day. The workers got to know him. They would
start him off with two cups of "lip-burning" tea followed by a bowl of deezee
with extra fat floating in the broth that covered a large piece of lamb and op-
timum amounts of potatoes and beans. They were swift to bring another two
cups of saffron tea and a hookah before the plate and bowl were taken away
from Khan. From the first day he entered the chai house, the workers were
struck by the aura of greatness that the old man exuded, the way he twirled
the tips of his mustache and sat cross-legged with his back straight, occupy-
ing more space than he needed. Word circulated behind his back that he had
been a tribal khan who had fought in the south against the British during
the World War II occupation. The waiters looked with awe and suspicion at
the maps that he spread in front of him after he smoked the hookah. They
noticed his visible restlessness with each passing day.

After two weeks his maps started to show unusually high cat traffic. Every dot he had made with the tip of his pencil was a cat he had seen as he
walked around the neighborhood: one dot was a kitten trying hard to climb
a plane tree, one a cat dozing off in the shadows of vine leaves on a wall,
two were the ones dashing away from the untimely kick of a butcher, and
another was a tricolor that rode in a wooden crate tied to the cargo rack of a
bicycle with head held high, as if proud of having shrewdly hitched a lift with
the unsuspecting dolt of a pedaler who, pants legs tucked into his socks,
zoomed toward destinations the cat was uninterested in. Khan's calculations
predicted that something would occur in the Shah-Abad Street area in the
first month of summer. Theft, robbery, street brawl, or something bigger;
Khan was not yet sure.

Summer came. Khan was wary for a month. Every uneventful day
added to his disappointment and doubt that his theory on the cats might
be disproven. The chai house workers kept bringing him fresh hookahs

and hot tea. One, grown especially fond of Khan, would stride to the door greeting him loudly and leading him to the special place he had set aside for the man and his maps. Finally, on a hot afternoon, when Khan was blowing out smoke, he saw two boys running after a cat in a mischievous game. Stray cats and dogs were often chased by boys who had nothing better to play with. Khan put the mouthpiece to his lips when a second cat dashed past the chai house on the sidewalk. He got up and went out into the street and saw them everywhere: in the trees, by the wheel of a parked bike, in the street and alleys. A white cat looked at him from among the fetid trash in the gutter. Two lurked on the wall like commanders of an army overlooking the operation from their vantage point. People glanced at them, raised eyebrows, and passed with more indifference than Khan could comprehend. Soon the felines dashed out of sight, leapt up walls, sprinted away into the unknown recesses of the city. In a matter of hours, Mosaddegh resigned and the new Prime Minister was inaugurated with a harsh admonitory speech that threatened to confront any unrest with force. A fleeting smile appeared on Khan's lips. He took Sergey's cage out to the edge of the hoez in the yard. "I think I got you beasts pegged," he said as he cupped water and sprinkled it playfully on the cat that took shelter in the corner of the cage. Then he lifted the cage and started dipping it slowly into the water. As if accepting its fate, the cat did not move as the water rose from its paws to its stomach and then its shoulders. The cage swung and jerked with the smoothness that water gives to things when Khan plunged it all the way down to his wrist. The ripples distorted the reflection of the moon. The cage came out dripping. Sergey hissed and clawed at the wooden bars.

"That was for what you did in my orchard," Khan whispered.

It was with unbearable exhilaration that Khan stood in front of the chai house the next day and watched with the workers and the other customers the shouting protesters sweep Shah-Abad Street. People wanted Mosaddegh back in office. When warning shots were fired by the police, the crowd surged back, only to drift forward again, excited and stimulated. Khan tasted success in his mouth. He could not spot any cats under the unruly stampede of legs, but he was sure they were somewhere nearby. They had completed their job; now they were watching it unfold. How they had succeeded in wreaking such havoc was something Khan thought deeply about as he walked back home against the waves of people who marched toward their hopes. For a brief moment, Khan thought he picked out Ahmad's face in the crowd among the many other insignificant shapes, punching the air as he mouthed the slogans. It seemed as if the chorus of voices was coming out of his throat only. Three consecutive gunshots dispersed the protesters and the next moment the doppelgänger of Ahmad was gone.

Before the week came to an end, Mosaddegh came back in what Salman called a "historic victory for the people." Ahmad eulogized the fallen protesters in a long poem that Salman recited at Café Lalahzar. "This calls for a necktie," he told Ahmad the day before reading the five pages. In his blue tie and suit, with waxed hair combed back, Ahmad sat beside Salman, his arms crossed on his chest, his legs crossed. Eyes flitted from Salman to Ahmad and back. Among the people at the café was a young woman in a light-gray jacket and skirt, her black hair fastened in a bun, casting long looks at Ahmad as she drank her coffee from a white cup. The young man in front of her wiped his broad forehead with a handkerchief from time to time. Full of young zest, the woman was composed and elegant.

After the applause and as the server placed the free cups of tea on the table, the young woman rose from her seat and approached them. "I follow your work in the papers. Your poems have a certain je ne sais quoi that's lacking from other poets' works. Please never give up on writing." She smiled and went back to her table. Ahmad watched her take deliberate steps in her black heels back to her table.

The daughter of an army colonel and a lover of poetry, Homa had first read Ahmad's pen name in the papers her father brought home for inspection. Silent Fist was the first poet she had seen in real life. The young man had defied her stereotypical image of a poet as a laid-back, shy creature whose efforts at mental acrobatics had taken a toll on his physique. The strength mixed with the joie de vivre that she found in his poems paralleled Ahmad's hefty blacksmith's arms and fine posture. He had no voice of his own and yet, it seemed to her, the words that came out of his silence could be the voice of many. Café Lalahzar became Homa's haunt the nights of Ahmad's readings, which had become a weekly event. When Ahmad glanced over at her, she would lock black eyes with him for a short moment before reverting them down to her coffee or back at the man with the broad forehead. There was grace in her gaze and in her turning away.

On a Friday, amid the heated applause and whistling for the new poem, Homa rose from her wooden chair and traipsed over to Ahmad's table. "I think we're doing this the wrong way," she said to the two young men. At her suggestion, Ahmad got to his feet and Salman sat back down. It was the first time Ahmad stood in front of an audience who leaned back, sipped from their teas and coffees, and blinked their eyes waiting to hear his poem. He could feel the weight of the looks on him. "Ready?" Salman asked and began the poem. Ahmad mouthed the words. Halfway through, Salman slid his chair behind Ahmad. Now it was only him. For the first time in many years, Ahmad felt what it would be like to speak. Even though the words did not come out at the same time as he had made his mouth look like them, it was a marvelous feeling. He received a standing ovation from half of the café who followed Homa's lead.

I'll marry that woman, Ahmad wrote with his nicest hand on the edge of the day's newspaper and slid it to Salman.

"What about that other girl?" Salman asked. "What was her name?"

Ahmad did not remember the last time he had thought about Raana. The image of her face had been replaced in his head by that of the woman sitting at the table by the wall, her hair in a flawless bun. The only person who might have known about Raana was Sara, who had shrewdly and generously accommodated Ahmad on his tryst. He could not talk about that night with Salman. He wrote on the edge of the paper: *There was once an apparition called Raana. It disappeared in the dark.*

"What about that man she's always with?"

He's a nobody.

New love was a fresh breath of life into Ahmad's writing. When reading the love lines in the café, Ahmad would not look at the young woman, and that was how Homa realized it was her he was writing about.

KHAN KNEW IF HE TALKED about how he had predicted the unrest after Mosaddegh's resignation, not only would no one believe him, they would
suspect he was out of his mind. If there was something to be done, he had
to do it alone. Some weeks after Mosaddegh was reinstated, Khan saw new
movements. Cats were congregating in a different part of the city. He saw
timid kittens trying to get acquainted with the bustle of the new world without allowing too much space between themselves and their mothers. Scorch
Tail was gone from his neighborhood. Khan trapped another cat and pushed
a screwdriver into its eye. Cats moved around like boiling magma in the cone
of a volcano and Khan could see that on his maps. Verbal attacks against the
Prime Minister were rising in number. His climb back to power was chal-
lenged as illegal. Among those who wanted the old man with the walking
stick gone was the Shah. "It's because of the oil," Salman said. "There's no
such thing as oil," Oos Abbas said, "that's why they nationalized it." At the
same time, the Tudeh Party, although pronounced illegal by the Shah, was
the target of more denunciations as evil God-denying communists. But with
Mosaddegh's free-press policy, articles were also published in defense of the
ambitions and the utopia that the party, if allowed, would pursue.

One Friday in the middle of Ahmad's silent reading, the large café window behind him was shattered with a terrifying sound. Large as a brick, the
rock landed on the floor. When a few months later a group of thugs stormed
in and turned the café tables over, the owner had to put Ahmad's readings
on a hiatus which ended up being permanent. Although he triumphantly
mouthed many more poems and long speeches in the coming years, none
ever had the sweetness that those Café Lalahzar readings did, when Homa's
hands clasped under her chin, her eyes fixed on him.

The first thing Ahmad did after Salman gave him the news of the cancellation was to write hurriedly on his notepad: *Where do I find Homa now?*
"At the café!" Salman said.

15

COLONEL DELLDAAR PRESSED HIS LIPS together when a major, who was new to the department and tried hard to be friendly with everyone, leaned forward and congratulated him. He had no idea what the wisecracker was talking about. "Your son-in-law, the poet." The major held that the relations between the Colonel's daughter and a certain young man were common knowledge among the regulars at Café Lalahzar. The Colonel called up his nephew and berated him for slacking on his supervision. The young man denied the situation. He confessed to his uncle that there had been something going on between Homa and Ahmad, but it had never gone past a few sentences decent enough to have been uttered in front of the whole café. There was nothing there to gossip about. "Then how come I hear gossip?" The nephew had no answer. He bent his head and apologized.

Two days later, when the time came to leave the café, he followed Homa out past Ahmad and Salman's table. The broken pane had been replaced, CAFÉ LALAHZAR written on it in large calligraphy in red paint with yellow shadow lines, and the owner had taken the opportunity to replace some of the older chairs and tables. It was at one of those new tables that Ahmad and Salman sat that day. When Homa was in the automobile, her cousin closed the door and ran back inside. He leaned forward and slapped his palms on the table to hold his face close to Ahmad. "If you want your head to remain on your neck, don't even think about her," he whispered to Ahmad, pushing the words through clenched teeth. Homa saw her cousin through the window, his fist, his involuntarily knotted brow.

"I'm going to dinner with someone you have heard of, Colonel," Homa told her father at the table after the servant had put the steaming platter of rice on the table and left the dining room, closing the door behind her.

"There's your daughter for you," said Homa's mother, turning away from Homa and shaking her head at Colonel Delldaar, pressing her lips together and putting her fork and spoon down in a way that made it unmistakable that their daughter's affront was somehow the Colonel's mistake.

Ignoring her mother, Homa put some rice and chicken on her father's plate, then picked up her own. The ceiling fan blew free a lock from Homa's mother's hair which she tucked behind her ear with her fingers, fury darting from her eyes toward Homa in sideways glances. "Don't put pressure on the poor boy either," Homa said, composed, keeping her head down to her plate, "he has been as good a chaperone as one could ever be."

Under the scrutinizing gaze of his wife, the Colonel looked at his daughter, not knowing what to do. Homa was the only one of the three eating. "Okay, let's not get carried away," he said. "Let's talk after dinner. Everybody, eat."

The next Friday, Ahmad was already seated at a table when Homa arrived. His shiny patent-leather shoes were the first thing that caught her eyes. Ahmad got to his feet and fastened his suit button as she walked toward the table in a pistachio-green dress and light-rose heels. A smile broke on Ahmad's shaved face. The waiter pulled the chair out for her, took their orders, and rearranged the table fan by the wall toward them.

"I thought I was early," she said, hanging her purse over the back of her chair. "I hate to keep people waiting." She looked at her watch, a small rectangle on the inside of her right wrist fastened with a narrow brown band. "I guess our date begins in four minutes, then." She looked up at Ahmad. "I say let's be punctual?" Ahmad nodded with a smile. Homa leaned back and locked her hands in her lap. Her thin, painted lips were like ruby cut to good curves. Deep calm of the forests of the North in her eyes. Her fastidiously cut bangs swung ever so gently in the breeze from the fan. The murmur of the diners clanking their silverware on china plates and softly speaking to one another washed through the restaurant. Homa's eyes flit to and away from Ahmad. Outside, the late summer evening was yielding to the night. Lights were on in windows. Homa extended her hand and gave the pepper shaker on the table a turn. She smiled at Ahmad. Ahmad smiled back. Shaped like a vague pear, the steel pepper shaker had five holes at the top. That was how Ahmad knew it was not its twin salt shaker which had more. Homa looked at her watch. It was not time yet. The waiter placed two plates on the table next to theirs. Steam rose from rice topped with chunks of grilled lamb and halves of tomato. The man moved the small crystal vase from the middle of his table to make room for more food the waiter was bringing. Ahmad looked at the vase on his own table. The roses were beginning to wither. He touched a petal. Homa was looking at him, a play in her eyes, a restlessness in her heart. She looked at her watch for a few more seconds. "Okay, hi," she said, looking up with a smile. "Not the best way to kill four minutes, right?" Ahmad reached into his inside pocket, but before he had opened his notepad, Homa had slapped a notebook on the table. "Do you mind?" she asked. She pushed it in front of Ahmad. "I mean, I was thinking of keeping it. Just our first conversations?" Ahmad found that a nice surprise and slipped his notepad back into his pocket.

What of yours do I get to keep? was the first thing he wrote in Homa's notebook.

Homa sat back and squinted her eyes as she thought. "How about something I've never told anyone?" Ahmad leaned forward and rested his crossed arms on the table as a gesture of enthusiasm. She told him that when she was seven, her mother made her a rag doll with unmatching buttons for eyes. The day before she went to school, she asked her mother to go with her, but she said Homa had to go alone, because all the other girls went alone. She asked if she could take her doll with her and her mother said no. At night in her bed, she took out her eraser from her pencil case and sat her doll in front of her by the eraser. She told her doll that she could not take her to school, but she would take that pink eraser in her stead, so she would not be away from Homa in spirit. Miss Buttons said, Okay. That was the reason she had two erasers in her pencil case in first grade: one to use, one not to.

Tell me another story of when you were little, Ahmad wrote the next time they sat in the restaurant and Homa told him about the time her cousin, the same Ahmad had seen at the café, had pulled her hair in a hide-and-seek fight, and Ahmad wrote about the time he did Salman's homework and Mulla did not dare punish them in the classroom.

Homa read the pages once in the restaurant and again at home. Even though she had not seen Ahmad yet, Homa's mother did not like him. "How am I supposed to tell others that my son-in-law is dumb?" she said out loud in the kitchen so Homa would hear. "Oh, the things they will say behind my back!" Colonel Delldaar was nervous. He knew how hardheaded Homa could get. Rained with reproaches from his wife to show some backbone, he did what he thought was best: try to gently talk Homa out of her immature infatuation with the poet.

"You're good for nothing," said Homa's mother to Colonel Delldaar in their bedroom.

TWO MONTHS LATER, NANA SHAMSI walked into the kitchen. Pooran was chopping herbs. "The boy's coming again," she said, "but I won't be here to see him." The day Pooran opened the door for Ahmad, Nana Shamsi was in her village, tending to her sick granddaughter, putting wet towels on her forehead that burned with fever. Pooran would not look at Ahmad. With her head cast down, she turned around and started for the house. Ahmad ran into the yard and blocked her way. He held her face in his big hands. It was the second time he looked straight into his mother's face since the teenager in him broke the window and left the house. Tiny wrinkles appeared in the corners of her eyes. *Will you ask a girl's hand for me?* Ahmad mouthed. Pooran was not looking at Ahmad yet, but she could still read her son. A few moments passed. A cool breeze blew into Pooran's hair. Then she looked up at him. And smiled. "Is she beautiful?"

KHAN WOULD NOT GO.

"I've been waiting for this moment since he was born," Pooran told him.

"Some things should not happen," Khan said, "and this marriage is one of them. I can't give my consent to this."

"But why?"

"Because I don't want another Nosser in my family."

Pooran remained silent for a short moment. "There will never be another Nosser."

Khan was drawing sectors on his map the next day when Ahmad bowed his head and stepped in through the short basement door. The passion and embarrassment of the youth had painted his face a soft rose. Khan knew what Ahmad was there for, but he put the needle of his protractor on a new point to make a full circle while the boy struggled with his pencil and notepad. Ahmad bent over the desk, writing and sliding papers over before Khan. Khan took a passing look and brushed them off his map. Ahmad wrote more. At last Khan put down the protractor.

"This notepad of yours, you're going to have it in your pocket for the rest of your life," Khan said, "because of your father's folly." In silence, he looked at Ahmad for a while. "Have I told you the story of my father?

"Rooh-o-Deen was a kind man, the nicest father I have ever seen. True, he did not talk much; he would not express his feelings openly, but you could see his emotions as if his whole being was transparent. He would treat his family with respect. In those times that a son feared his father's belt and heavy slaps like a beaten dog, he never so much as shouted at me or my mother. He was the only man I knew who helped with housework, although he would not let it be known. It was a fact that Rooh-o-Deen did not have the ambition to expand on what was handed down to him from his own father, but he worked hard on both of the orchards. He was a god-fearing man. He took care of us.

"Then one day, he packed his clothes to go to the bathhouse. My mother reminded him that he had been to the bathhouse only three days before. He said he needed to clean himself anyway. Three days later, he bundled his clothes under his arms and shuffled to the bathhouse again. When he came back home, he sat and drank the tea that my mother brought him. Before he finished the tea, he sniffed at his armpits and said he needed a bath. He patted me on the head on his way out. Soon the bathhouse keeper would find him sitting at the door every morning before daybreak. He would stay there all morning and come home for lunch. He wouldn't touch the spade any more. So I had to start to run the orchards at the age of seven. The mulla came with some of the village whitebeards. They talked and talked, but the next morning, my father was standing outside of the bathhouse even earlier, before the morning prayer was called.

"He stopped eating because he found food itself filthy. Meat was rotten flesh and blood of carcasses and greens came from under dirt. After two weeks, four men held his arms and legs and force-fed him roasted lamb and broth. He stuck a finger down his throat and threw it all up. Then he ate soap and went back to the bathhouse. He scrubbed his skin away with a coarse loofah. Soon he fell sick. Yellow pus oozed from his skin. He shrieked from his bed for four days, stopping only to catch a breath. So loud he howled that no one in the village slept a wink in four nights. I saw my mother in the kitchen pressing her hands over her ears.

"When the last night was coming to an end, his cries stopped. The whole village was immersed in a soft silence. A few minutes later, a cock crowed. When I opened the door, I saw my mother sitting on my father's chest, her hands locked around his frail throat like two pincers. He had been dead for a good while, but my mother was still sitting there, her tears dropping onto my father's face. His eyes were open, almost popping out of their sockets, staring up; his hands clutched her wrists. She sat there for a long time until she heard the knocking on the door. People had come. Then she asked me, 'Help me with the fingers.' They were so stiff she could not free her own fingers from his.

"My father and your father, that's been enough. I don't want to see a third. Do you understand me, Ahmad? They were good people and what they did was not their fault. I'm not saying it was the cats for certain, but it might have been. I think we are the family in Agha's story. Think about it, your father died so young. So did mine. Agha is still alive. Why is he not dying? Because he's not going to. I'll be like him. And so will you. If you ever have a baby boy, you will certainly see his demise. You are the only person I'm telling this." He lowered his voice to a whisper. "I may have found a way to prove to you what the cats are doing in the recesses of this city."

He walked over to Ahmad's side. "I predicted the uprising after Mosaddegh's resignation. Before it happened. All from how the cats moved between neighborhoods. It's all on this table. Wherever they go, catastrophe hits. It is all in these numbers and lines. Those creatures are on to us." He pulled the papers closer. But Ahmad shook his head.

I'm not here for anything cat, he wrote. He fell down to his knees as Khan read his note. He would never ask Khan for anything again. He did not care if his son would go mad or not. He would even promise not to have a child if Khan attended the proposal ceremony. Homa was all he wanted.

"What do you see in her anyway?"

Ahmad held out his arm. Khan gave him his notepad. *She gave me as much of a voice as I ever had.* He kissed Khan's hand. The old man tried to pull away, but Ahmad held it hard like a drowning man whose life depended on that hand only. The plea in his eyes was honest, the supplication in his grip was warm. Khan looked at him for a few minutes. Then he shook his head.

Ahmad got to his feet and snatched some paper from the table.

She has the courage to want me

In spite of her family
And I'll be no less
I'll imagine I don't have a grandfather
It's not harder than publishing in Tudeh Magazine anyway

Khan read the last sentence and kept Ahmad from writing more. "They published you?" There was a pride in Ahmad's nod. "Of course they would. Did you forget what I said? The Tudeh Party is under the influence of the cats."

Ahmad started for the door. Khan held him by the arm.

"Listen. I have proof the cats were behind the rebellion in Azerbaijan. The Soviets protected them. That's why the Shah couldn't send in the army to take the province back before the Russians left. Then the cats started the Tudeh Party which is against the Shah and against what keeps this country in order. Of course they will support Mosaddegh and of course they will publish you."

Ahmad ripped a page out of his notepad, wrote on it, and slapped it on Khan's chest.

I loathe you.

Khan fell silent. He listened to Ahmad panting and watched his red face. Sergey moved in his cage behind the curtain. Khan looked at the note and read the sentence again. "I think you're wrong," he said, "and I can't condone this, my son." Ahmad opened the door. "But if you get married," he said before Ahmad was out, "I'll throw you a wedding they write about in books."

AT THE PROPOSAL CEREMONY, AHMAD, Pooran, Maryam, and her husband sat in a room where twelve of Homa's relatives had gathered. The awkwardness caused by the absence of a father or an elder male member of Ahmad's was palpable. Great Uncle, Colonel Delldaar's uncle and eldest in the family, found no one to talk to, the closest person to him in age being Pooran, a woman who did not even seem to be in her forties yet. Resting one palm on the other, both hands on the curve of his erect walking stick, he sat in a big chair, in the good part of the room, farthest from the door, looking at the gathering with a frown. His silence was a sign he was offended. The Colonel kept the ceremony from falling apart by maintaining a conversation with Pooran, turning his eyes to the groom with a smile or a nod every now and then. He began by talking about how the prices of eggs had gone up. He said, and Pooran agreed, that it had gotten so warm in the past couple of years, to the point that the ceiling fan was not enough anymore and they had to add the floor fan to the guest room—he pointed to the fan that scanned the room near the Great Uncle. Then he added how the house itself grew unusually hot in the summer and cold in the winter and he thought there was something wrong with the design and then he asked Pooran where she lived and was surprised when he found out that Ahmad did not live with her, but rather in his own place. He was not impressed when Pooran named the neighborhoods where she and Ahmad lived. Then he asked what the groom did for a living and nodded his head with a forced smile when Pooran said he worked at a forge and was also a poet. "Very good, very good," he said, faking interest, nervous about what his wife was thinking and what Great Uncle would say later, hoping that by some improbable miracle Homa would change her mind.

"It was a disaster," Colonel Delldaar cried out after the door clicked shut behind the suitor and his family.

When the phone rang a week later, Homa's mother looked at the clock. She knew Pooran was on the other end of the line calling to hear the bride's answer. She had called right on time, as she had promised. Homa's door flew open and out she ran, book in hand, her index finger bookmarking the page she was on. Standing close by, an expecting smile on her lips, she waited for her mother to answer the ringing phone. Homa's mother placed her hand on the handset. The phone rang again. Homa's mother looked at her with raised eyebrows, her inquisitive eyes fixed on her daughter as if questioning for the last time if she was certain of her decision. Homa breathed a frustrated sigh that her mother read as her not wanting to discuss the issue anymore. The phone rang again. Homa's mother shook her head and picked up the headset, an affected smile involuntarily appearing on her lips as she said hi to Pooran. Yes.

FROM THE CHEST IN HER room Pooran took out the fabric she had set aside years ago for the dress she would wear to Ahmad's wedding. Large, red flowers sat on a background of light cream among lavish green leaves that grew from waving branches. Folded into a square and carefully bundled in a piece of brown canvas, the fabric had lain there since Ahmad was five, the year Pooran's mother brought it from the hajj pilgrimage. When Pooran closed the chest and unwrapped the canvas, a cloud of green moths flew out like water sprouting from a fountain, some fluttering out the open windows, some pinning themselves on the curtains, others alighting on the cream walls, wings slowly opening and closing. She pinched the edges of the fabric and held it up in front of her and saw the holes. All that was green had gone, the leaves no longer attached to the branches. For the first time she went to Seyf Zarrabi's fabric shop. In a clean and pressed suit and tie, the man hastened from one shelf to the other behind the counter and took long looks at Pooran's face as she evaluated the fabrics. She sewed dresses for herself, Nana, Maryam, and Maryam's baby girl, Parveen. Mohammad Reza, Maryam's husband, became Khan's right hand. He rented chairs, dishes, and cutlery for the wedding dinner and found a proper orchard for the wedding day. Khan hugged Salman when he came in with the cauldrons and ladles. What was broken to pieces in Pooran was being fused back together with the happiness her son's marriage brought to her heart. The only thing she regretted was that the festive event had not happened sooner. If she had told Nosser that his son would have a wedding, he may have stayed longer, at least until after the ceremony, or come back to be there.

One day when Pooran was threading the needle at her sewing machine, there was a knock on the half-open door. Khan walked in with two sacks of money in his arms. His gray hair had started to recede to show the dome of his head and accentuate his large ears.

"Should you need more," he said putting them down on the rug, "there is more." He left the room whistling a happy tune. No matter how hard she thought, Pooran could not remember the last time the old man had whistled.

A WEEK BEFORE THE WEDDING, Ahmad took off his fedora and followed Homa on board a long-nosed bus that coughed out black clouds as it clanked its way toward the village of Tajrish. He watched from the dusty window the dirt road he had taken to Tehran eight years before with his mother. Buildings had sprouted where there used to be trees, walled-off orchards with overhanging branches, or sprawling, barren land. Midway there, Ahmad tapped Homa on the shoulder and pointed toward the front of the bus. Through the windshield, Agha's tree was visible in the distance, on the lower mountainside, towering high over the greenery and roofs. They got off at a wooden bench and a sign marking a bus stop where there used to be nothing. They started toward the village, Homa panting as she caught up with Ahmad who strode quickly up the steep alleys to avoid familiar faces that had put on eight years of wrinkles. He raised a hand in response to the occasional greeting.

With half of its leaves fallen, the other half brown and orange and yellow, but still consoling and strong, gently swaying in the breeze, the giant plane tree stood taller than everything in the village, a beacon that showed them the way. The wooden door to the Orchard was ajar. Ahmad pushed it open. Homa was catching her breath, but she was fascinated to see where Ahmad had grown up, walking past dead trees and trying to bring them back to life in her head, to bring out imaginary fruit from their branches and to shrink Ahmad in front of her to a five-year-old boy—let him play to see what he did, where he went, and what his voice sounded like. They made their way through waist-high weeds, Ahmad agile, as if his feet instinctively found the right place to land, and Homa pushing through behind him. Ahmad knew nothing would grow on those trees ever again, but the only tree that mattered to him then was the one that never bore anything to eat.

The same drape covered the opening to Agha's tree, the same worn and weathered tarp. "Who's there?" called Agha's voice. He had heard footsteps. "Mulla, is it you?" At that moment the drape was pushed aside and Agha's head emerged from inside the tree, jutting out of his old but clean, red turtleneck. He had not changed; the same perpetual smile was on his lips, but beneath that facade Ahmad could see irritation. On all fours, his eyes darted from Ahmad to Homa for some time. "You don't live here anymore," he said with an affected petulance and pulled back in. The tarp swung back to its place, stiff from years of exposure to sun and rain.

Before he jumped on his horse for Tehran, Khan had made arrangements with his stable boy: he was to stay and look after Agha, and in return, he would receive rights to use the Orchard. Three days after Khan's departure, the boy had rolled up five of the finest rugs in the house, tied them tight on the back of a mule, and before anyone got wind of it, he had sold out all he could in Tehran and vanished from the village. When the villagers went to Agha's tree, they pinched their noses first, then saw the small piles of feces right at the entrance. Mohammad the Carpenter had dripped water into the old man's mouth and Mullah Ali took up the responsibilities of taking care of Agha.

Ahmad went in. It took his eyes a few seconds to adjust to the relative dark and see the jumble of things. Without a family to tend to Agha, Mulla Ali had moved all the old man needed inside the tree. Inevitable as a mast on a boat, the samovar stood on the low, wooden table, under which Agha's shaving box sat by some china plates and bowls and the tea tray. A jacket and a coat hung on separate nails on the tree walls, the rest of the clothes piled on the pegs of a short hatstand and by the foot of it, his chamber pot. In his constricted tree room, Agha sat on the mattress that was his bed at night. "We are here to invite you to our wedding," Homa called from outside of the tree. "I have heard a lot of good things about you." She cracked the tarp and stuck her head in. "Will you come, please?"

Agha looked at Ahmad and the girl for some time as if contemplating the invitation. "Festive news," he finally said, his face opening like spring, "this calls for the light." He produced from behind the samovar a lightbulb and a socket attached to a yellowish, white cable that reached into the tree through a small hole. "Mullah turns this on when he comes after the dark." Ahmad went out to look.

Swallows circled the sky, gay in their erratic embrace of the dusk.

"Plug it in, boy," Agha said from inside.

At the other end of the cable was a plug. High on the tree a half-broken outlet was screwed to the trunk. A thick black cable snaked out of the outlet up the tree, then away toward the wooden power pole behind the cob walls of the Orchard.

"Plug it in already."

It was a rickety assemblage to transfer stolen power, primitive and unsafe.

"You go check on him," Homa told Ahmad, taking the end of the cable from him. Ahmad went back inside, but he froze when he brushed aside the tarp. The old man had unscrewed the bulb and was waiting with his finger stuck in the socket. He looked at Ahmad with the pleading eyes of a kid who desires nothing more than for his mother to buy him the toy. The next morning, Ahmad wheelbarrowed Agha down the alleys and took him to Tehran on the first bus. Ahmad sat by Agha, who refused to talk or turn his head away from the window.

HE SAID HE WOULD NOT go to the wedding either, but when the day was near, Agha made Ahmad go back to Tajrish to fetch his purple tie from the hatstand. In Ahmad's old room at Khan's house, Agha sat on the edge of the bed, a short stool under his feet, as Pooran tied and retied his tie, holding the mirror in front of him until after the fourth try he was satisfied. "Can you ask Khan," Agha whispered leaning forward, "to get me a wheelbarrow?" Pooran smiled and assured him she would. "Can I paint it purple, too?" he asked.

The ceremony was in midfall in an orchard west of Tehran where city services had not reached yet. Toward the back walls—where the well was—two mules trotted on a conveyor belt attached to a generator that produced the electricity for the wedding. The central building was decked with colored light bulbs like flickering fruit grown out of brick and mortar. Ensembles of musicians performed one after the other. With the Azeri music, Colonel Delldaar hit the floor and danced in his cap and uniform. Small and crumpled, but in his pressed, cream suit, Agha waved a cheerful handkerchief. Sitting cross-legged on an armchair next to the Great Uncle, with his wide tie coming down his neck and resting on his lap, he was too small for an adult and too wrinkled for a child. After a while watching the youths dance, Agha turned to the Great Uncle. "I want to get married, too," he said, shouting to make his squeaky voice heard. The Great Uncle nodded as if only to be polite. "There's a girl in the house," Agha said, "I like her." "Good," the Great Uncle said, then turned his head back toward the circle of dancers. "Her name is Nana," Agha said nodding to himself, as if approving his own decision.

Khan would not sit in his chair. He paced so much to make sure everything was carried out as planned that he would rest for three days after the wedding. The music excited the cantankerous Great Uncle, too. To the applause and gay whistles of the youth who stood clapping in a circle, he took his walking stick hanging from the back of his armchair and joined the Colonel in the Azeri dance. Holding his arms straight out to his sides, like a cross, his legs sprang up and down with slow moves that showed remnants of a harmonious dexterity of years long gone. He snatched Colonel Delldaar's hat and donned it on his bald scalp with a soft whirl. "Now the groom!" Great Uncle called after a while. Cheers went up to the sky from the orchard when Ahmad entered the circle. The women watched—some in the orchard from the peripheries of the dance circle, some in the house from behind the windows. Their own dance floor—the large salon, decked with white lace and ribbon and flanked with two rows of chairs in front of which sat small tables laden with fruit and sweets—was a gaudy scene of jubilance and jitter, where Homa's best friend was dancing with Shamse, a friend of her sister-in-law. The bond between the two, though distant and flimsy, barely there at all, brought solace to Homa, whose mother's heart was not with the wedding. Behind her made-up face that smiled at Pooran, Homa could read her mother's dissatisfaction, except that this time she tried not to show her usual disapproval outwardly and Homa was at least grateful for that.

In her white wedding dress, she watched Ahmad from behind the lace curtain, in his black suit in the circle of men, holding his arms up, swinging to the sides to the rhythm of music, and she did not feel a doubt about the decision she had made. Music slipped out of vibrating strings and throbbing percussive skin, from under restless picks and hands. Great Uncle reached into his breast pocket and threw a fistful of bills into the air, then a second. Children dived to collect the money from under the stomping feet. Seeing this, Khan left the circle and strode away from the celebration. Outside, he motioned for the chauffeur to open the trunk of the white Jaguar. Back at the dance the crowd split open to let in Khan and his driver boy who carried two sacks under his arms. Khan dug his hand into one and the bills flew into the air. Children ran around trying to catch them as they spun like raining pinwheels. The Great Uncle emptied his pockets and then motioned at Colonel Delldaar for more. As the evening proceeded, more nimble-fingered musicians performed. The cool, fall breeze could not dry sweat off the dancing bodies. Until the last one dropped down panting, Khan and Great Uncle showered bills on the dancers. So much money was dispensed that after the wedding was over and the last of the guests had left, the owner of the orchard spent a sunset to sundown excavating bills from under mud and dirt.

The last player of the night was Maestro Shahnaz. After the dinner tables were cleared, a humble wooden chair was placed for him in the middle of the open space. The night was calm except for the murmur of those outside and the chatter of those inside and the chirping of the creatures of the night. The maestro approached his chair with slow, calm steps and sat himself, eyes cast down. He crossed his legs and balanced his taar on his thigh. A silence fell over the wedding as he turned the pick in his hand and took a deep breath, his head bent toward his instrument. With the first strum of his pick on the strings, the dead branches of the trees turned soft and before the end of the overture, green shoots had sprouted on them. A few scales into the rhythmic piece, blossoms opened on the leafless trees. The music was almost visible, floating in the breeze, weaving in and out of the plum trees, billowing the curtains into the house, scaling up the women's legs and wafting around their bosoms. Suddenly happy cries rose from the bride and groom's room. The bride's dress had bloomed. Homa's mother kept picking the blossoms from her veil so she could see. Ahmad smiled at Homa and got up from beside her to look at the maestro through the window. The orchard was carpeted with orange and plum blossoms that grew and fell from the trees. A pinkish-white petal sat on the maestro's bald head.

"We'll be happy together," Homa whispered in Ahmad's ear when he sat back by her. Ahmad took her hand and gave it a gentle but firm squeeze. "This is a sign."

After the wedding, the newlyweds boarded the automobile that Mohammad Reza had, with Khan's directions, rented for the wedding ride. Parked right outside the orchard, the Jaguar, too, like all the other cars, had grown little flowers on its handles, trunk, and hood. Sitting in the backseat, one ringed hand locked into a ringless one, smiling and calm, Ahmad and Homa circled the streets of the city in the mirth of their unity. Years later, after the Revolution and the Eight-Year War had already become history, when Ahmad walked the streets of the megalopolis of Tehran and saw how people decorated their wedding cars by taping gladioli to the hoods, trunks, and door handles, he felt an urge to write on a piece of paper and show the person nearest him, *That's the doing of Maestro Shahnaz. You should have seen the orchard that night.*

16

THE COMING MONTHS saw an escalation of speeches made by several members of the parliament arguing that Mosaddegh, the Prime Minister, had caused the uprisings of the past summer with his childish resignation. He was a traitor and his office was illegal. One small paper even claimed that he had meant to take over the army and orchestrate a coup against the royal family. Those were grave accusations that, although not picked up by the mainstream papers, showed what measures the opponents of the Prime Minister were prepared to take to topple him. "Bullshit," Khan said out loud in his basement, "Isn't it bullshit, Sergey? We both know who was behind what happened. Don't we, Sergey?" The cat was silent on the other side of the curtain.

Toward the end of winter, Khan was surprised by what his figures and charts showed. Something new seemed to be brewing. A large number of cats had been mobilized as if by well-thought orders from some headquarters. He put Sergey's cage on the table. "I know you have been in here for long," he said. The cat sat still in the corner. "And I'd believe you if you told me you did not know what this is all about. But you can still help me." Sergey did not move, never taking his blue eyes away from Khan. "If you do," Khan said, "I will let you go." He paused for a second. "I will open the cage and out you can go; anywhere you want." He looked at Sergey for a moment longer. The cat did not show a sign that he would cooperate with Khan or even that he understood what the man had said. "Anywhere. Even back to Russia." A few days later, Khan came down to the basement with a small cat in a bag. He wound rags around his hand and forearm, took the cat out, and shoved him into Sergey's cage. Then he left.

He came back after two days and put the cage on the table, wrapped his arm again with deliberation, looking at the two cats. The new cat hissed and meowed. Khan grabbed him by the neck and put him out on the stairs. The cat leapt up and was gone into the night like he was escaping hell. Khan closed and bolted the door. "I hope you two had a good talk, Sergey." He unrolled a map of Tehran on the table and held it in place with four books from his bookcase. Then he took Sergey out of the cage and put him on the map.

"Now is your chance."

Sitting on the map with his head lowered and his paws pressed together, Sergey stared at Khan for some time. "I know you know what I am talking about," Khan petted the cat's ears flattened back against its head. The blue-gray fur reminded Khan of the rabbit-fur hat Sergey used to wear in the Orchard. "We have done each other harm," he kept petting Sergey's head, "but we have helped each other, too. You ruined all I had, remember? Yes, you did. Yes, you did. My Orchard, my orchards, yes, they're all gone. How long I spent building all that, planting tree after tree for so many years. You ruined the life of that poor girl, Sara, too, and the whole village. What havoc!" The cat was motionless, but Khan could feel his heart racing within his body. "You helped me, too, no I have not forgotten. I admit, I was scared in there. When they took me to that boor of a major, I was happy to see you there, although I was sorry for your face, too. I was. I still am. But you did me more harm than me you. We had fun, too. Remember that night in Tehran? You were howling my name. The poor girl I was with was afraid. I was afraid. Your girl had already taken off. Of course she would; you had alcohol in your veins, damn it, and who knows what you were doing to her. You don't remember, but you said, 'Khan, I can't find my underwear. It's important that I find my underwear,' like they were the only thing that could save your life. And I pointed to them on the floor and you looked really long, and then turned your head back, with those bloodshot eyes of yours, and said, 'Khan, I think you're drunk. That's my pocket towel.' Yes, that's what you said, 'pocket towel.' And no matter how much you deny it, I saw your thing too. Now get up." Khan stopped petting the cat. Sergey looked at Khan for a short moment, then got to his feet. "There you go, there you go." Sergey walked to the edge of the table and looked down, then came back to the map. He sniffed at the paper and looked at Khan some more. "What I want is for you to tell me what the cats are up to. Where are they going to strike this time?" Khan sat down on his chair and crossed his arms. Sergey watched. For half an hour, he walked on the table, jumped down and went behind the curtain, came out, jumped back up on the table, until finally he lowered his head, as if studying the map. Then he lifted his paw and gently scratched at the paper. Khan got up and looked at the marks. "The Prime Minister's house! They have aimed high this time," he said petting the cat on the head, "Now that's cooperation. We'll soon see how you did," he said as he put Sergey back into the cage. "You'll be very sorry if you've lied to me."

It took Khan two more months to come with his most accurate estimate for the big happening: two thirds into the summer, the next year. He compared his calculations with Sergey's scratchings with a smile of satisfaction: he had the time and the place.

"Now we'll have to wait and see, Sergey. We'll have to wait and see, my friend."

AHMAD'S APARTMENT, BOTH ROOMS COMBINED, was smaller than the smallest of the rooms in Colonel Delldaar's large house, but Homa saw it as the modest start of a quest to build a better future. Homa's mother refused to visit her daughter in "that rat hole." Homa swept both rooms and dusted everything from ceiling to floor. She rearranged things to her liking and replaced some old furniture with new pieces. She tried to converse with the landlady in her spare time, when Ahmad was at the forge, or when she used the kitchen in the yard. Meek and reserved, the old woman was afraid of an imminent imaginary war. She refused to touch onions since the day two messengers from the army had brought back the remains of her son in an onion sack. When the home was spotless, and she had prepared for dinner, Homa would walk down the alley to the main street to grab a buggy or a taxi, if she could find one. Most of the time, she would take the horse tram and go over to her father's house, trying to ignore her mother's self-righteous pity for her miserable new life. Homa would come back home in time to make the dinner, all ears for when Ahmad would open the door and step in with shopping bags in his arms. She bought a few balls of yarn and stole a pair of needles from her mother's basket and knocked on the landlady's door.

"Will you teach me?"

For a couple of weeks, Homa sat with the landlady knitting and talking to her and making tea for the two of them until she was tired of the meaningless repetition. Then she went to Ahmad's bookcase and started reading until the smell of fresh bread wafted into the apartment. Homa went to the window and watched Ahmad cross the yard. She took the bread and bags from him and hurried to get clean cloth. "We can spend less, if we have to," she said wiping blood off of his face, "if it's what it takes for the fights to stop." Ahmad shook his head. Homa unscrewed the Mercurochrome bottle. "My father can pull some strings. I'm sure he would find you a job somewhere if I asked him." Ahmad shook his head, smiled at her, and went to the forge the next day.

It wasn't the fights but the silence that Homa had underestimated. Having soon lost its novelty, Ahmad's quiet grew louder every day until Homa could hear it clear and boisterous. She plugged the radio in and turned the knob until every corner of both rooms were filled with human voice. Ahmad turned the volume down when he came home. He motioned to remind her the landlady had warned them, albeit timidly, that the sound was troubling. Homa then became garrulous. She told him the minutest details of her day. Her shopping, her knitting, her preparing the food, all she had heard on the radio, the book she had read, and her visits to her father's house. She went as often as she could, seeking her premarriage life in which things were familiar. The silence and loneliness exhausted her to the extent that her mother's snides became tolerable. The family trip to her father's villa by the sea in the North was what Homa looked forward to the most, the two-week trip the family took every summer.

A week before the trip, Homa could talk of nothing else. She described the villa in detail. A two-story white house with a gable roof and working fireplace, and a view of the sea. She would sit Ahmad down on the narrow mats they had spread on the rug at the foot of the wall and plan how they would build a fire on the beach, put potatoes in it, and watch the waves wash over the sand. She brought a leather suitcase from her parents' and started carefully folding her clothes, unfolding to straighten out a few last creases and refolding before putting them in. She pulled three books from the bookcase and placed them on the clothes, topping them all with her sandals. Two days before the trip, she closed the lid and buckled the straps.

One evening Khan knocked on the door. "Give me one last chance to prove the cat story is true," he told Ahmad when Homa was down in the yard washing tea glasses in the kitchen. Khan leaned forward to put a hand on his grandson's knee with a gentleness that revealed a humility coming from earnestness. "Something big is happening. I know the exact streets. Come with me and I'll show you. It should be any day now. My maps match what Sergey says." It was the ardor with which Khan had thrown the wedding, the meticulousness with which he had bought himself the new black suit and a pair of patent leather shoes, and the fastidious way in which he had folded his square pocket that had left no doubt in Ahmad's heart that Khan loved him beyond what he believed in or objected to. That was why on that evening, he decided to give his grandfather another chance.

When Ahmad handed her the paper, Homa fell silent for a long while. She read the note and pouted the way she did when she was deep in thought.

"You can't tell me why?"

Ahmad shook his head and saw disappointment in her eyes. *I'm sorry*, he mouthed.

Sitting cross-legged on the ground playing with the edge of her skirt, Homa was silent for a long time. "You know my mother will say so many things about you," she said, raising her eyes to Ahmad, "but if you can't even tell me why you can't come with me, you must have a good reason." She was not angry. She got to her feet and straightened her skirt. "But I'm going without you."

A FEW DAYS AFTER HOMA had gone, Oos Abbas was drinking tea in his chair when Salman walked into the forge holding a little boy's hand. It was Sara's boy. Salman had promised to take care of him for a few days while she was away with her husband in another city to meet a doctor, but an emergency Tudeh Party meeting had been called. "Things are touch and go," Salman said in a hushed voice. "They couldn't have waited a day; they set the meeting for tonight. I have to be there." With his wavy, brown hair, the boy looked up at Ahmad, a lively glint in his eyes. Once again Sara had come out of the blue into Ahmad's life—this time through that little boy—from a past still alive in memory: from the days of simple words and childhood games; from that confused night when Raana did not come; from that other night when Raana did come, when Sara was absent, but her presence was gossamer over the surface of the painted walls, light as air, gliding as shadow. Ahmad shook his head. "It's important, Ahmad," Salman said. "Just for tonight. I'll make arrangements tomorrow. I'll pick him up first thing in the morning. He's a sweet boy."

Ameer was not two yet. He amused himself at the forge with a top and a few rocks Oos Abbas gave him to play one ghoal, two ghoal with. "Let him run around and play," he said, "and he'll drop as soon as you take him home, sleep all night, and they'll pick him up tomorrow. Easy." The boy had his mother's eyes, deep and penetrating. After he became bored in the forge, he went out and ran after the grocer's three chickens that pecked at the dirt in the flower bed. Ahmad wondered if the boy had his mother's cunning, her exuberance and audacity, too. Sara had been the one to read Ahmad's correspondence aloud to Raana. She knew all that had passed in the deep recesses of Ahmad's heart, and she had risked ignominy and disgrace by letting the sinful encounter unfold in her house.

"The boy's a spitting image of you," Oos Abbas said to Ahmad as he left the forge in the evening holding Ameer's hand. Ahmad smiled at the joke. At night he played with Ameer, gave him a chickpea to turn in a copper mug. Ameer climbed the mattresses and blankets folded and piled in a corner of the room. Perched on top of the wobbly stack, swinging it back and forth, he made as if he was riding a horse. Then he climbed down and teetered to the window. "Can I go out?" Ahmad lifted him into his arms, took a long and high step through the window and onto the balcony, and climbed up the metal stairs. In the yellow light of a bare incandescent bulb, Ameer ran around the roof laughing loud, then tried to look over the parapet. Ahmad hoisted him and held the mesmerized boy in front of the flickering lights of the city at night. As the night dragged on, Ahmad watched Ameer play and get tired. The realization came to him when Ameer was drawing in a notebook, fighting sleep. The similarities between the boy and himself were more than a joke: high forehead, long fingers, oblong face, little earlobes one wanted to flick at for hours. How could Ahmad not have seen those big black eyes in Ameer's little face at first glance? He got up, took the notebook from Ameer, and put him to bed.

Salman did not come to pick Ameer up the next morning. Homa came back in the afternoon and fell in love with the boy at first sight. I think I have something to tell you, Ahmad wrote on his notepad. Homa played with the boy in the yard and reprimanded Ahmad for not having ever invited Salman, Sara, and her family over. Ahmad crumpled the note in his hand.

KHAN HAD BEEN MISTAKEN BY about ten days. The two men roamed around where Khan was expecting things to happen. They drank tea in a coffeehouse. Ahmad bought a newspaper from the stand and leafed through as they waited. They smoked a hookah, but nothing disrupted the calm of that beautiful day.

"These things cannot be predicted to the date," Khan turned to Ahmad on the bus to explain the failure of his prophecy. He threw sidelong glances at the other riders and leaned in to whisper into his grandson's ear. "Those animals are shrewd. They can change plans like that." Ahmad smiled at him and put his large hand on his thigh as if he, and not the older man, was the consoling grandfather who reassured him that everything was all right. Khan was not surprised when ten days later he could not convince Ahmad to go with him again.

This time, Khan witnessed his predictions come true. Holding his maps in his hand, ebullient, he was present at the exact streets where a coup unfurled: a coup that those ignorant of the ways of the felines would later claim was backed by that far-off country by the name of America. Contrary to what the Prime Minister's opposition claimed, Mosaddegh had not organized the Coup, but was the victim of it.

On that day, before Ahmad left home for the forge, there came a banging on the door, the type that announced trouble was waiting outside. Ahmad climbed down the stairs and opened the door. Salman sprang in. It was Mash Akbar, his father. A crowd of thugs and laats had attacked his butchery. Ahmad bounded up the stairs two at a time, briefly explained the situation to Homa in a note, and ran out of the house after Salman.

As they got closer to the main street, the din of the demonstrators reached him. Before they turned onto Lalahzar Street, Ahmad could make out the *Death to Mosaddegh!* and *Long live the Shah!* slogans from the confusion of shouts and cries. Thugs streamed along Lalahzar Street waving clubs and machetes. Most of the stores were closed. The ones open, either caught by surprise or underestimating the gravity of the situation, had their windows smashed. Fruit rolled on the sidewalk and got squished under leather soles. A car rode alongside the demonstrators laden with men riding inside and on the roof, like a metal porcupine with human spines. One man held a framed portrait of a decorated young Shah in a uniform. Negligibly small groups of Mosaddegh supporters were being beaten as the sticks and clubs rose in the sky and paused for a short moment at their apex before swoosh-ing back down. Many escaped and many watched from behind windows, cracked doors, or farther away on the sidewalks.

Ahmad ran past Café Lalahzar and saw in a glance the broken chairs and tables, and the shards. Many a nervous evening he had sat in those chairs trying to look confident when the young woman two tables away turned her eyes on him. Following Salman, he darted through the crowd on the sidewalks and, after a few turns into narrower streets and alleys, slowed to a stride. A small group of people were gathered in front of Mash Akbar's butchery watching the laat Asghar Rostam and his three novices drag Sal-man's father out. Asghar Rostam was one of the most feared laats, who wore his long scars across his face as his badge of honor and boasted how he had stabbed the One-Eyed Reza in the left eye. They had thrown Salman's fa-ther on the ground out front and circled him in their black suits and fedoras like three crows. Asghar Rostam accused him of lying, of fraud, and of sell-ing meat that would send the eater to hell. Two of his novices went inside the shop and came back out grinning, carrying two dead cats each on their shoulders as proof of the man's culpability. Their eyes closed, the cats lay as if peaceful and content on the shoulders of the novices.

Among the crowd, as the novices dropped the cats on the ground in front of Mash Akbar, Ahmad was wondering how the dead cats had ended up in the butchery. "You are a godless piece of shit just like your commu-nist son," Asghar Rostam shouted at Mash Akbar. Ahmad looked around. Salman was gone. Saliva drooled from the lips of tongue-tied Mash Akbar kneeling at the foot of the laat. Asghar Rostam picked up a rock and hurled it through the window. "Feed him the cat," cried someone in the crowd. The grin that appeared on his face showed the laat had liked the idea. He picked one of the dead cats from the ground. Two of his novices held Mash Akbar as Asghar Rostam shoved the lifeless animal in the butcher's face. Mash Akbar sobbed with clenched teeth. In vain Ahmad looked around for Salman. The thugs in the crowd whistled and waved their sticks and fists. Asghar Ros-tam's jackknife flashed open. "Someone's losing an ear today," he shouted, pointing the knife in Mash Akbar's face. "Is it going to be the cat or you?"

Then suddenly, with the ferocity of a ravenous wolf, Salman's father tore off the cat's ear in one bite. He chewed with saliva dribbling from his mouth onto his shirt. The thugs roared.

The shots were fired at that moment.

Asghar Rostam's pierced body dropped on the street and the panicked crowd dispersed. The bullets that Salman fired from the roof of the house across from his father's butchery marked the beginning of a long period during which the Tudeh Party saw its demise. The Shah's intelligence service cracked down on the party, hunting out its members in clandestine branches of the army and top government positions. The prisons, with the passing years, became places of savage torture of the sort that engendered dread and rage. The bullets that pierced the laat's body that day blazed at their core with flames of a revolution.

In the confusion that ensued, Ahmad rushed to Mash Akbar, put his strong arms under his unconscious body, and lifted him. Panting as he swerved among men running in different directions, he half-ran, half-walked to the nearest hospital while the demonstrators converged upon the Prime Minister's house. Soon the doors broke open and the mob poured in. The traitor was arrested, his house turned to ruin. As Sergey had shown. As Khan had predicted.

AHMAD GRABBED A FOLDING CHAIR and sat by the hoez beside Khan. The night was warm and heavy with low, sparse clouds that veiled the half-moon from time to time. The city was closing its eyes with the hope of forgetting what it had seen that day. The Prime Minister had been put in prison. Soon he would be sent away to his hometown, locked in his house until the last day of his life. *I believe you*, Ahmad wrote, *today I saw how they worked, even when dead.* Khan waited for a wandering cloud to float past the moon before he read the paper. He turned to Ahmad and put a serene hand on his grandson's shoulder and gave a gentle squeeze. *But there's no winning this. I can't spend my life tracking cats. I need to believe in life.*

Lying by Homa under the mosquito net on the roof, Ahmad wrote what he saw as a poem of hope for the future. He rolled over and brushed Homa's hair from her face before he kissed her on the cheek. Her face was bright with the light from the paper. The crickets chirped. He wanted to wake her up and tell her all about Ameer. He touched her on the shoulder, brushed away hair from her closed eyes, and shook her gently. "No," she said and turned her back to him. Ahmad could not sleep the whole night. He perfected the poem to an arrangement of words that shone even after the first rays of the sun smote the sky.

In the wake of the Coup, a number of papers, supporters of the fallen Prime Minister, were shut down. Among the journals were those that had published Ahmad's works. Now the explicit references to oppression and injustice in Ahmad's writing frightened editors into rejecting his work. Faced with obstacles and closed doors in the outer world, Ahmad redirected his search to the world of words. He deliberated on his poetry and saw, as if for the first time, the form of his writing, the classical: lines of the same length, the same number of syllables, each line divided into two equal half lines. For over a thousand years, high literature had been constricted by those laws, the slightest divergence from which would not be fathomable. It came from an age-old system of deep-rooted oppression and control. Poetry was in rigid blocks, circumscribed in rectangles: prisons for words that translated into prisons for people. Why did poetry have to be forced into predetermined rhythms? The rhyme diverted speech from the freedom that natural conversation and thought enjoyed. His attention was drawn to the poet Nima of Yoosh who for the first time had broken the law of equal lines a few decades before. But even Nima of Yoosh was still confined with rhythm and rhyme. Was there a way, Ahmad asked himself, grandiosely, to break free?

Seeing Ahmad's struggles at his desk, Homa tried patiently to create a calm atmosphere at home. After dinner and tea, when Ahmad opened his books and grabbed his pen, Homa picked up her yarn and needles and went downstairs. Having heard the young woman's footsteps, the landlady opened the door before Homa knocked. Sitting in armchairs, the two women knitted and talked while the radio played music from the top of a low wooden table in the corner of the room. The old woman would make herself coffee on a low gas stove and then brew some tea for her guest. "The sooner, the better, honey," she would tell Homa from time to time. "You should have as many children as you can while you are young." Under the mosquito net on the roof, Homa would read Ahmad her favorite poems before sleep, some of which were Ahmad's. When she did so, Ahmad threw a tightly muscled arm across her chest. Listening to the sound of crickets, Ahmad thought night after night whether he should tell Homa about Ameer, that lovely boy who looked too much like him, but then he consoled himself by remembering that Homa had seen Ameer, and was not struck with the similarity between the man and the boy. Then he would fall asleep.

17

ALTHOUGH HE HAD JOINED JAMAAL'S GANG for mercenary reasons, Ahmad now realized that he had continued not for money alone, but for the bonds that fighting abreast of one another had tied between the four of them—and also for the fight itself, the thrill of dodging a kick and then landing a punch, the panting, the racing of his heart. *One last time*, he wrote to Homa at night.

Jamaal understood. "You're becoming a father soon." At his last fight, Ahmad attacked with a religious devotion and single-handedly took four men, one with a machete. *It's okay, it's over*, he mouthed to Homa who looked at the wound on his arm with horror. But it was not okay. The open wound would not close. In a few days infection built up like a small painful pillow and Ahmad could not leave the bed. Homa called a cab. The driver slung Ahmad onto his shoulder like a sack of wheat and lay him on the back seat, then pulled him onto his shoulder again at Khan's door and, with the guidance of Pooran, took him inside and put him on the bed in his old room. Agha had crouched as far into the corner of the bed as he could before the driver dropped Ahmad down. He looked at Ahmad's pale face as if he could not believe the young, healthy man who had wheelbarrowed him down the Tajrish alleys was lying there with eyes closed and mouth half-open, panting as if his body anticipated a fever. The doctor came to the house, but was unable to treat the wound. The next week, he recommended amputation. "Or it will kill him." Ahmad was losing weight by the hour. His eyes sunk into his tired, sweaty face. He was so pale it was as if blood had congealed in his veins. Colonel Delldaar suggested they take him to France, to knowledgeable physicians who were also equipped with the latest developments in medicine.

The first thing Pooran did when she heard the word amputation was write a letter to Nana Shamsi who was out of town. *Come soon, Mother, I need you.* She went to the Abdol-Azīm Shrine in Rey. The Smoky Machine she had taken with her children and husband years before had been put out of service; instead there were buses. After kissing the old wooden doors, she entered the big courtyard and bowed toward the domed building. Inside, she inched ahead through the many chador-clad women to touch the gold- and silver-plated shrine. "I want you to give me my boy back," she whispered. But she was too distressed to wait for the dead saint to grant her wish. She took the bus back from the shrine to an herbal physician some neighbors had told her about. She boiled crushed lavender, saffron, and rotten turnips and poured the foul-smelling elixir into Ahmad's half-open mouth.

Agha had panicked from the first day they brought Ahmad in. He evacuated Ahmad's room, which he had settled in since they brought him to the capital, and moved to the living room, shouting with alarm from time to time so someone would take him to check on Ahmad, although he could not bear to be taken into the room. In Pooran's arms or on Khan's back, he would cover his face with his hands and steal a look at his favorite boy through his fingers and soon turn his face away. He could not sleep at night. As if stricken by the sheer weight of an imminent death for the first time, Agha, who had seen countless people die during his innumerable years, would cry out Khan's name in the middle of the night. "Go check on the kid," he instructed an exhausted Khan, with bloodshot eyes wide-open, gesticulating toward Ahmad's room, "I can't hear him breathe." Khan assured Agha that Ahmad would survive. "Do something," Pooran begged Khan. Like a maniac, she went from one neighbor to the next, from one acquaintance to the other, and asked if anyone knew of any cure.

Seyf Zarrabi, the owner of the neighborhood fabric shop, sent word that his father once had an infectious leg when he was young. A doctor from a neighboring village had cured the infection with an ointment, the recipe of which he had given Seyf. "I'd go far for my dear customers," Seyf told Pooran in his shop, "miles more for an esteemed lady such as yourself." He ran his palm on the few waxed strands that crossed his bald scalp. "My pen and paper are in there if you don't mind." He locked the shop from inside and lead Pooran to the small room in the back. "Are we ready for the recipe?" he asked, running a gentle hand along Pooran's back. Closing her eyes and listening to the buzz of the teal Westinghouse refrigerator in the corner, Pooran memorized the recipe as a passionless vertigo swept across her.

But the shopkeeper's prescription proved ineffective. When fever and delirium seized Ahmad, Homa locked herself in the bathroom and sobbed for an hour. Then she came out and said, "Let's do this. From now on I'll be his right arm." The night before they planned to take him to the hospital, a knock on the front door echoed across the yard and into the house. Without saying a word, Nana Shamsi walked, taking one short, deliberate step after another, across the yard and straight to Ahmad's room, where he lay in his bed, his face streaked with sweat, his undershirt stuck to his chest. "The next time I see you," Nana bent over and whispered in Ahmad's ear, "you will have both your arms. The next time you see me, I won't be breathing." Then she put her hand on Ahmad's forehead for a short time and left the room. Within a week, the wound stopped secreting pus and healed. When Ahmad swallowed his first spoon of soup, Pooran hid her face in her scarf and left the room. Moved by joy, and by contrition about what she had done at the fabric seller's, she cried in the kitchen.

No longer willing to be without Nana for even a day, Pooran wrote to her, and a few days later, the old woman arrived holding her granddaughter's hand. The girl's other hand groped along the door and the walls as she walked in. "I like this house," she said with blue eyes that looked at no one. Zeeba had lost her sight after she ate an herb in the wheat fields outside of her village when she was little. Her golden hair shone in the fall sun. Khan had a room built for Nana Shamsi and the girl on the roof of the house. The workers wheelbarrowed in brick-and-mortar and soon a rug was spread across the floor. Khan designed an elevator that worked with ropes and pulleys to take Nana Shamsi from the yard to the roof. The wooden platform could be lowered and elevated by turning a handle that was set on the elevator itself. Zeeba soon learned to operate the elevator and help her grandmother up and down. She felt her way around the house for a few days, but by the end of the second week she was playing hide-and-seek with Majeed and helping Maryam take care of Parveen. With the permanent addition of Nana Shamsi and her granddaughter to the house, Maryam brought her kids over more often. Zeeba knew each member of the household by their footsteps and maneuvered through the halls with such ease that the only sign of her blindness was the fixed gaze that lanced past everyone.

Khan would not listen to Agha's pleading to take him back to his tree. "It's my home," he said, "I miss it." But Khan said no. "Then make me a room on the roof," he said. Khan rejected his request. Ascending to the roof to tend to Agha would be too much trouble for Pooran. "Nana has a room," Agha said. "I want a new room." Khan heaved a sigh, and the next day workers wheelbarrowed in bricks and built a small room with a big window in the corner of the garden. They asked the old man what color he wanted his room painted and he picked light green. "Can I have a swing?" Agha asked. Khan made holes in a big bronze tray, passed ropes through them, and hung it from the ceiling. When they sat him in the tray, the smile on Agha's face took on a calming depth as it sank into the creases of his skin.

AS HE WALKED THE STREETS now to keep an eye on the cats, Khan felt that his legs were not as dependable as before. He had to stop from time to time, sit on the steps of a building, and give his knees some rest. Once he almost fell when he stepped into a hole in the sidewalk. He avoided another fall by holding onto a young tree. When the third time, he managed to land on his hands and brush off the dust from his trousers unhurt, he made up his mind.

"Shaft, beech, single piece. Handle, oak," he ordered, "carved."

Three days later at the carpenter's, he turned his cane in his hand and examined it from the brass tip and the thin rubber at the very end up the varnished, simple but elegant shaft, to the derby handle that at the end morphed into the head of a roaring lion, mouth wide-open, fangs intimidating in their miniscule, wooden ferocity. Cane under his arm, Khan strode toward the tailor. He tried on his new suit and pants and squinted into the mirror. Then he marched toward the hat shop, donned an Astrakhan, and examined his reflection to see if the hat could replace the old one that the hatsnatcher took years before. Clad in all new clothes, with a light-blue pocket square tucked in his breast pocket, Khan held the handle of his cane tight, thumb resting on the head of the lion, and put the tip on the ground for the first time. From that day, he took his cane with him on his walks for cats, as an assurance that when the time came, he could lean on it. But he walked faster and with longer steps as if to prove to the passersby that he did not need the cane. As a result, he walked more and spotted more cats in the streets. "Kill them," was all Agha said rocking in his tray. But even if he did that, how many could Khan kill single-handedly?

"By the way," Agha added one afternoon when Khan came back home and knocked on Agha's door to see if he wanted anything, "you look good."

"Thank you," Khan said standing outside at the door.

"And your cane," Agha said eyeing Khan as if with admiration, "it has made you look younger."

"Thanks. I'm going in now," Khan said and started to turn around.

"I want to marry Nana," Agha shouted before Khan had time to take his first step. Khan turned around and looked at him lightly swinging.

"No, you can't," Khan said surprised.

"Why? I have my own place and a purple wheelbarrow."

"You just can't."

"Are you saying I'm old?"

"No," Khan said, but did not know how to complete his sentence. "Wait a minute, have you talked to her already?"

Agha shook his head, then said in a drawn-out, child's voice, "Will you?"

"No, Agha," Khan said, his initial surprise turning into irritation. "This cannot happen. It is not customary and it is not right. This story ends here."

He closed the door behind him and went in.

SERGEY DIED IN THE WINTER. Khan went down to the basement but did not hear the cat move in his cage like he always did when he heard Khan's footsteps. He opened the curtain and found the cat lifeless in his cage. Khan buried Sergey under the pine tree in the yard. "Goodbye, my friend," he said as he covered the body with dark, wet soil. "Please forgive me."

That night, Khan could not sleep. From his window, he looked at the small mound under which Sergey's body lay, a brown spot in the snow-covered flower bed that glistened in the night. He ruminated over the memories of the past all night, and so it was that when the first rays of the sun shot into the sky, he was awake to hear the noises from Agha's room. Khan got up from the edge of his bed, hastily put on his sandals at the veranda, crossed the yard on the paths the kids had stamped into the snow, knocked gently, and went in. In the dim light he saw Agha was swaying, but he was not sitting in his tray. He was hanging from his neck. Somehow the old man had dismantled the swing. Khan dropped his cane, hurried to Agha, and hugged him hard, taking his weight off of the rope. He did not know what to do. "Help!" he shouted. "Help!" He could not cut the rope on his own without letting the old man dangle. "Help!" he shouted louder and as he waited for someone to come, he buried his face in Agha's frail body and cried.

"It's okay," Agha said, stroking Khan's white hair, his high-pitched voice consoling. "It's not working. I'm too light now."

SALMAN MANAGED TO DODGE THE Shah's intelligence system for more than nine years. He showed up at Oos Abbas's forge one late spring afternoon, hugged Ahmad, and gave him a letter for Sara. He could not risk a second visit anywhere and had already been to Sara's house two weeks before. Oos Abbas made tea and the three of them sipped as the young men exchanged the latest. Salman stuck to the personal. His father had closed the butchery after his recovery and stayed home until Salman could not continue to support him any longer. Sara wanted to go to work, but her husband did not allow her, so Salman worked longer hours—he was an electrician. Then Sara went to Mash Akbar and said he was too young to retire or mope, not too old to remarry, and honestly that was unviable. Mash Akbar went out and became a hand in a grocery store. Ahmad knew Salman's not talking about politics or the Tudeh Party meant something, but could not help asking, *How are things?* and by that both of them knew what Ahmad meant. Salman had met a girl, a petite woman whose energy was inexhaustible "and her tongue unstoppable," he joked. Ahmad concluded that the girl must have been a fellow party member, or someone Salman shared political beliefs with, someone Salman walked the streets with. Perhaps they worked or even lived together. *Do you live in a commune?* Ahmad meant to ask, but he did not. The furnace ticked cool. Salman told Ahmad agents might come to him. Ahmad could, and should, tell them the truth, that Salman had been here. He left without saying where he was going and when Ahmad might hear from him again.

The letter was the perfect excuse for Ahmad to see Sara. Ahmad had long wished for the encounter, although he did not dare arrange it himself, for fear of finding out to be true that which he hoped was impossible. That, he told himself, was the reason he had not divulged the secret of Ameer to Homa. He hoped against hope that when he faced Sara, her incredulous looks would say, Are you crazy? Of course this is not your son. He hoped that Ameer would leave his life as unexpectedly as he had entered it. He hoped to see the boy again and find him as similar to his father and mother as nature could make manifest. Sara's husband, Salar, a middle-aged man, although rather reserved and reluctant on political issues, seemed happy to meet Sara's childhood friend. They sat in the living room, leaning against poshtis, tea glasses steaming in front of them on saucers. "This is Ahmad," Sara said with a smile, playfully introducing and reminiscing. "He ripped my shirt open once when playing tag." Salar tried to banter away the boldness in Sara's recollections. She did not shy away from Ahmad. Were those knowing eyes revealing a shared secret to Ahmad or was this just an old friend delighted to relive innocent memories?

Ameer walked out of his room and without looking at the guest took his short steps to his father, where he sat cross-legged and bent his head. "Kids these days grow fast," Salar said, "like weed." The boy had grown. More than Ahmad would have thought. Nestled in his father's lap, Ameer was a boy of three in the body of a five-year-old. While Sara told her husband how Ahmad had taught her to read and write, Ahmad's eyes flitted from Salar to Ameer, and the fewer similarities he could find between the two, the more distracted he became. How he wished to be alone with Sara and put a definite end to his doubts once and for all! But even then, how could he bring himself to ask Sara if her son was a bastard, if she had tricked Ahmad into sleeping with her on a dark night, passing herself off as another woman? When Ahmad was leaving, more doubtful than when he arrived, Salar did not offer the common formality of inviting Ahmad to visit again. Something in his face showed a hatred for the silent man, as if he knew the secret, as if he knew he was raising Ahmad's boy.

18

OMA GAVE BIRTH TO A GIRL. They called her Leyla. She was a perfect mix of Homa and Ahmad and worked miracles. With her first cry, she expelled the silence from the two cursed rooms. Colonel Delldaar ironed his uniform, polished his shoes, and welcomed his granddaughter while standing at attention with a stern face, but welled-up eyes. When he saw the newborn, Homa's Great Uncle abandoned his idea that a man had to earn what he possessed and gave Ahmad and Homa the present of a small house. Before the baby was a month old, Homa had rejected the landlady's offer of a decreased rent five times. When the moving day came, she had to talk her away from the door with the promise of weekly visits.

"What about no rent?" the old woman whispered in Homa's ear as they hugged.

The new house was not grand, but it was located in a calm neighborhood. The front door opened into a short corridor that led to a large living room. The kitchen could house a six-seat dining table and still leave Homa enough room to freely walk from the cabinet to the sink and the stove. The windows in the larger bedroom opened to the small but cozy yard. Homa bought all new pots and pans for the kitchen. She did not protest when her mother made the final decisions about where the furniture would go, or when she shook her head and decreed that the curtains Pooran had sewed for the new house would not go with the armchairs in the living room. With the baby so little and fragile, Homa could not bring herself to lose the little of her mother's affection and interest that she had won after the birth of Leyla. Pooran was offended when she saw the orange curtains draping over the windows, but said nothing. The new house, the baby, and the constant visits from both her family and Ahmad's brought a healthy rose to Homa's cheeks within two months. Even the baby seemed to like the new house. Lying on her back in her bed, she gurgled and smiled at everyone.

One late night, at a time when visitors were not expected, the sound of a stifled knock wound through the house. Ahmad opened the door to Salman, who slipped in silently and gently closed the latch bolt behind him. He had a present in his hands. Homa opened the box and took out a pair of small red girl shoes. The three of them sat with the tacit agreement not to discuss the fugitive in the living room, but the friend who slapped his thigh and laughed when Homa told him how, when Ahmad had his fedora on, Leyla would cry in his arms, not recognizing him as her father, but broke into a hesitant smile when Ahmad took the hat off, only to pout again when the hat was back on.

Homa brought fruit in a basket and put on the kettle to make tea. Ten minutes later, before the tea was quite ready yet, a short high-pitched whistle sounded in the street. Salman sprang to his feet. "Goodbye ladybug," he said to the sleeping baby in her room. "Grow up soon." With a confident calm in his movements, Salman rose from by the crib, hugged Ahmad, congratulated Homa again, and climbed the stairs up to the roof of the house. That was the first time Ahmad and Homa had Salman in their home and the last time anyone called Leyla "ladybug."

Khan was enamored with the baby. Even when no one was busy, he volunteered to look after her. He had a room built specifically for her on the roof next to Nana Shamsi's. The baby and whoever looked after her would rest in those quarters, and when she grew up, she would know she always had her own private shelter no matter what. Parveen was so excited to have a cousin that when they told her she was too small to let the baby sleep on her legs, she offered to wash her dirty diapers.

Parveen would climb up an empty tin bin to reach the clothesline. After she was done, and when no one was in sight, her brother, Majeed, took the pins off and left the wet diapers to the mercy of the breeze. Later, Parveen picked the white pieces of cloth from the ground and branches of the trees, shook them, then washed them again.

"Do you want to play count the kitties?" Majeed asked Khan. Patting baby Leyla on the back while rocking her in the garden, the old man tousled the boy's hair and sent him away.

"Some other time maybe. Have you done your homework?"

MAJEED BECAME A WANDERER. WHEN he found the opportunity, he would skip school and run to the movies to be mesmerized by the bright rectangle. Before he could gather the money for a ticket, he would squat for days on the sidewalk across from Cinema Royale and stare at the large painted poster above the entrance. In the foreground, the likeness of the lead actress revealed ample legs from under a miniskirt in a coquettish pose. In sizes proportionate to their fame, the mustachioed actors occupied the rest of the painting touching the brim of their fedoras with a thumb or looking off into the distance. Street vendors sold food and drinks in front of the theater to the stream of people that came and went. When he ran out of patience, Majeed waited for his father's loud snores at night, stole out of the bed, tiptoed to the coatrack, and pinched coins out of his father's pants pockets. Amidst the loud cries of men rising from their seats to swear at the characters they did not like and the crackling of roasted sunflower seeds breaking open between teeth, Majeed sat rooted in his seat, hugging his school bag, swinging his short legs, enchanted by the black-and-white images that danced before him: the love scenes, the flirting scenes, scenes of cheating, scenes of fighting.

THE NEW BABY HAD CHANGED Majeed's park excursions into crusades for his mother's attention. Maryam, Homa, and Pooran gathered with the children in Khan's house every Friday and set off for the horse tram station with baskets and bundles. Once in City Park, Majeed walked, hugging his ball and watching his sister circle around Homa and Leyla, trying to take the baby's hand or hold her in her arms. Majeed kicked the ball as high as he could and tried to catch it before it hit the ground. One day a man came to the park pushing a Ferris wheel. The rickety structure wobbled and squeaked along the paved paths, slow like an ambivalent proof of divine presence, before coming to a stop by the side of the playground. Once it was secured in place with rocks that the man wedged under the wiggly wheels, Majeed approached. Painted red, green, and yellow, the thing was an assemblage of four metal seats, shaped like simple rockets, attached to two circular rings that formed the main frame of the wheel. The wheel man lifted the kids and sat them two per rocket seat—to earn more per round—then he turned them round and round by holding the frame rings with both hands and using his thin body's weight as the motor, pulling down, springing back up to grab the frame and pull down again, like a well-designed, clockwork power system. Before long, a line of eager kids formed. Majeed ran to the blanket where his mother sat leaning against a tree, talking with Grandma and Aunt Homa, rocking baby Leyla on a pillow she had put on her outstretched legs. He asked if he could go on a ride.

"You said you wouldn't want anything again if I bought you the ball," Maryam said, "remember?"

"But I don't want the ball," Majeed said, stamping a foot on the ground. "I want to ride."

"With Mom's permission," Homa got to her feet, "I can take the kids."

Maryam fixed her reproaching eyes on Majeed for a little while. "What do you say?" she asked the boy.

"Thanks, Aunt Homa," he said and ran toward the line. "I want my own rocket," Majeed told Homa once their turn came. "Me, too," Parveen said. But Majeed would not ride if Parveen also had a separate seat. In the end, Parveen agreed to share a rocket with Zeeba and let Majeed have his own.

With her eyes pinned to the unseeable in the distance, Zeeba gasped as she went up and swooped down. One hand holding tight at the side of the metal thing and the other clutching Parveen's arm, she could hear the happy laughs of the children around her and the ecstatic cries of Majeed that came now from above now from below. She could not hear Parveen, and had to call out her name to check on her. Parveen did not answer. She wanted to get off, but something in her stomach kept falling and churning. If she opened her mouth, her heart and stomach would spill out. Majeed was ecstatic. Waving a hand in his mother's direction, he called out from the zenith of his climb like he was coming back from a years-long journey across foreign waters and soils. Maryam turned an acknowledging head but soon reverted her attention to Pooran and the baby who flapped her tiny arms and legs on the blanket. Intoxicated with a sense of flying, Majeed would from then on grab any opportunity to get himself to the park and drop a coin into the palm of the man who ran the Ferris wheel. Every coin he pulled out of his father's trousers was laden with the weight of an imminent decision: the movies or the wheel?

AHMAD'S FIRST BOOK WAS A success for a young poet. Half of the two thousand copies were sold in three months and by the end of the year, a second printing was in order. Soon after the book was out, he was invited onto the editorial board of the weekly magazine *Our Times*. The first evening he came back home from work, Homa was ready, dressed in blouse and skirt. "We're celebrating," she responded to Ahmad's questioning look. "Finally out of that forge." They rode a cab to the restaurant where Homa had made reservations. In the post-Mosaddegh time of caution, when certain things could not be told, Ahmad published his political essays in *Our Times* with such audacity that if it had not been for his growing, but controversial, fame as the inventor of a new poetry form, the owner of the magazine would have shown him the door after his first editorial. With the increase in the regime's intolerance for critical opinions had come a time of disappointment. Defeat and despair dominated literature. Ahmad's essays were his way of expressing his rage, though diluted so as to be printable. Anxious, Homa would ask if he was being too risky. They were parents now. Ahmad would shake his head and write that he knew what he was doing. "But I will not read them anymore, okay?" Homa said one night. "I don't know why you can't stick to your poems. You're not even good at this." She went to the baby's room thankful that Ahmad could not continue the conversation.

One spring morning two agents came for him. Surprised and nervous, Ahmad half-stood, not sure whether or not to extend his hand. They closed the door behind them and started politely. The first man asked about Ahmad's writing, the references in his poetry, and the true meaning of some of his symbolism. He recited excerpts of Ahmad's poems and essays from memory, asking for clarification. Trying to remember everything he had written, and to be consistent, Ahmad made up explanations, hoping the vagueness he had put into his verse would help him get away with what he truly meant. When the first was done, the second agent changed the subject to Salman. Salman was a killer, a fugitive, and the member of an illegal communist party, but guided by Salman himself, Ahmad knew there was one route to go: the truth, and of that he did not know much. "Are you sure?" was all the man asked when Ahmad wrote he did not know where Salman lived and that he had not seen him since shortly after his baby was born.

When Ahmad went to work the next day, someone else was sitting at his desk and the editor was not in his room. *I understand your trepidations,* Ahmad wrote, *but I regret having worked for a coward.* He slapped the note on the desk and left.

"Once a blacksmith, always a blacksmith," Oos Abbas said when Ahmad walked back into the forge, yanked the sledgehammer out of his hand, and began such pounding that the little mirror on the wall rattled. A few weeks later a flatbed trailer squeaked to a halt in front of the forge and Ahmad had the workers unload a number of new hacksaws, a heavy red welder, and an electric sander. "Progress, ha?" Oos Abbas said and plugged in the welder. From that day, they started making doors and windows. With the growing number of cars in the streets, demand for horseshoes had already fallen to almost nothing. In the coming years, orders for spades, axes, and pegs also vanished; it was doors, windows, and banisters that kept the forge going. The day Ahmad bought the tools for the forge, he did not think he would one day call Oos Abbas to fit his window with bars to put his mind at ease, and that the old blacksmith would arrive with that same welder.

With wrath still brewing deep within him, and immensely affected by the beauty of the small human being in his arms that was his daughter, Ahmad finished his second collection of poems in a year. He was invited to read at the University of Tehran by some students interested in contemporary poetry. The event was denounced by many of the professors of literature as profane. Few, if any, were inclined to recognize the arrhythmic, unrhymed havoc that called for the abolition of the classical form. Ahmad sat in front of the audience as a junior in literature read the poems out loud to the students and those who had come from outside the university and found not only a poet who wanted change, but also a tender, fatherly voice who saw the world as if with the eyes of a newcomer, innocent, incredulous, and curious. They liked Ahmad.

WHEN LEYLA TOOK HER FIRST steps, there was purity and daring in the immensity of the effort she used in placing one foot in front of the other and the magnitude of joy she received from the fulfillment of her endeavors. Ahmad and Homa followed her closely, ready to catch her if she were to run into furniture. After Leyla dropped back onto her hands and knees, Ahmad wanted to witness that majestic moment again. Nothing in the world could rival the ambition with which life survived and thrived. *I want another*, he mouthed to Homa. Their second daughter would be born two years later. They would call her Lalah.

Soon Leyla was zooming out of one room and into another, stopping and pointing at the furniture. She would look up at her mother and make a sweet sound. "Table," Homa would say. "Yes, it's a table . . . That's a shoe-horn . . . No, no, no touching. It's dirty." Then one day a bolt of panic struck Homa when she realized Leyla was not speaking. Ahmad tried to console her, writing that his affliction had not come down to him from his father, but had been the result of an incident. But all Homa saw was her husband writing with his head down and a daughter who, when Homa called her, would look up at her mom—her brown, wavy hair curling up around her head—but would not make a sound. "Say Ma," Homa urged the girl, "Say Daddy." Homa's mother fed her granddaughter raw pigeon eggs three times a week. Pooran boiled sheep's tongue, which Leyla ate with a healthy appetite, looking at her grandmother for more, but never saying a meaningful syllable. The noises she made, with which she had broken the house's piercing silence, were now so painful to Homa that she had to leave the room when Leyla babbled as she played with her dolls or drew on the walls with her crayons. Homa took her to a doctor who did not find any abnormalities or disabilities. Once again, the apartment was becoming a void from which there was no refuge. When Ahmad came home from the forge, Homa not only found no solace in his presence, but felt helpless in the face of the horrifying duplication. "Say, Mama," she shouted at the girl, holding Leyla's tiny shoulders in her hands, her face red with anger, frustration, and fear. "I said say, Mama." When Ahmad was around, Leyla followed him like a duckling, as if scared of her mother. A second doctor did not see a problem either. "Don't worry," said the third, "she'll talk your ears off soon."

Visiting new doctors became a weekly ritual. When she had seen them all, Homa started over again and after a few months she resorted to the physicians who had found healing in ways not known to the world of science. Boiled herbs and concoctions proved ineffective. Leyla refused to drink from a vial with an olive fluid that reeked of rotten fish. Homa clamped her between her knees and force-fed her the viscous remedy. Leyla ran a burning fever for four days straight. *You shouldn't have given her so much trash,* Ahmad wrote on his pad sitting by the side of Leyla's bed. *Look what you did to her!* Homa crumpled the note and threw it into Ahmad's face. For the next four days Ahmad tried to mouth an apology or write her a note. Homa would either turn away or drop the unread notes into the trash can. Finally Leyla's fevers subsided and she sat in her bed smiling, opening her arms for her father. When Ahmad walked out of the room with Leyla in his arms, Homa looked at him long enough for him to mouth his silent *sorry!* Then Homa went and bought a prayer.

A few days before, she heard the name of Haji. "You've never heard of Haji?" a woman in the neighborhood asked with a hint of condescending surprise. Haji was a prayerwright. His name began circulating around the city after two incidents. To a merchant who was almost bankrupt with cockroaches that had infested his rice he prescribed a combination of four short prayers to intone in the warehouse and blow in the direction of the grains. After two days, word had it, no matter how deep he dug into the bags, nothing came out in the merchant's cupped hands but, grade A, clean, pure rice—almost pearls. A few years later, he had built himself a mansion that was only second in magnificence to the Shah's palace due to a purposeful demonstration of humility. As the story of his great fortune made the rounds in the city, so did fame and deference for Haji. One day a young man asked him to prove the power of his prayers. Haji said that well-spoken words could even make someone invulnerable against bullets. "I'll try it," said the young man. Haji penned a two-line prayer. "Say this and God willing no harm will come to you."

On a crisp morning some days later, whispering under his breath, the man stood in front of a crowd. They had heard the news and come out to witness the test in the barren lands outside of the city. Close to some unfinished buildings, someone pulled out of a gunnysack a rifle he had inherited from his grandfather. The hum of the crowd standing a short distance behind the shooter subsided when the rifle rested on his shoulder. For a few seconds everything lapsed into a delirious stillness. One man on one side, and facing him, a crowd of people and a loaded gun. The gun went off. The man collapsed to the ground as if his strings had been cut by an unforgiving slash. They buried the body and walked back to the city whispering about what had happened. In response to someone who questioned the prayer, a woman said maybe the man did not say the words right. By the time the sun set on the city, there was almost no doubt in the hearts of the witnesses. Only a handful expressed their cynicism. "Well, we'll never know," they said. In fact, the faithful were right. The man never got to utter the prayer. Tongue-tied by the horror that loomed before him, he could not move, he could not open his locked jaws. No matter how much he tried, he could neither re-member a word of what the turbaned man had given him, nor could he move his lips to cry that he had changed his mind, that he no longer wanted to take bullets in his heart. The whole city heard about Haji overnight, not as a phony, but bona fide.

Homa whispered the prescribed prayers with meticulous attention and blew at her daughter, waiting for the unspecified day when, as Haji had said, she would say her first sweet word. One morning when Ahmad was in the yard and Homa was chopping herbs for lunch, Leyla walked into the kitchen, looked up at Homa, and asked, "Mother, what is SAVAK?" The night before, Homa had been talking to Ahmad about the new intelligence department the Shah had established to improve national security, wonder-ing how important it would be in the long run. Ahmad was worried, but Homa was hopeful this would be an insignificant addition to the structure of the government. Years later, before the Revolution shook the grounds on which palaces stood upright, SAVAK would become the name that sent shiv-ers down the spines of most, except for the dauntless for whom *down with the Shah* was not just a slogan, but an effervescent desire bubbling up from the rarely plumbed depths. But the day Leyla asked about SAVAK, Ahmad and Homa did nothing but revel, one blushing in hushed joy, the other in fits of ecstatic laughter and tears.

From that day on, Leyla talked with the fluency and accuracy of an adult and the sweetness of the child she was. When in Khan's house, she spent long hours in Agha's room, chin resting in her palms, listening to the old man's unending stories. But when Ahmad learned about it, his breathing quickened. *Don't leave her with Agha alone EVER again*, he wrote in his notepad with such force that Homa suppressed her questions into a hesitant nod. Agha kept calling Leyla's name when she played with the other kids in the garden. Leyla would look in his direction, not sure whether to listen to her heart or obey her mother's new rule.

I don't want you to ruin her with your stories, Ahmad mouthed to Agha one day. "But she reminds me of you and Khan," Agha said, "when you were her age." His voice trembled as he talked. *And you ruined us both. I won't let your stories haunt my daughter for the rest of her life.*

THAT NIGHT AGAIN SLEEP WOULD not come to Khan. He lay still in his bed, the blanket up to his chin, staring at the tarred ceiling. He uttered maledictions to the devil and closed his eyes, but an awareness in him flung his eyelids back open. He took his cane and got to his feet to look around the house, tearing through the fragile texture of the night, peeping at those sleeping in their rooms, lingering to make sure he heard them breathe. Wobbly and shaky, the elevator squealed as Khan worked the handle. He checked on Zeeba and Nana Shamsi from behind the window. They were lying in their beds in the moonlight. Khan turned back and stood there on the roof for a while looking up at the sky. Hands locked on his cane, he walked back and forth and thought. After a few minutes, he went toward the edge to take the elevator and it was then that he glanced down at the yard and saw something. It was floating in the hoez, still as a log and not much larger. It was Agha. Through the leaves of the persimmon tree, Khan could see moonlight shining on his unmoving body, a halo of glistening water surrounding him. He hurried onto the elevator and cranked his way down. Agha's back and haunch were above the water, but not his head. Khan knelt by the hoez and rested one hand on the edge. The body was too far from his reach. He used his cane and tried to bring Agha closer to him, but the body only seesawed gently in its place without gliding any closer. Khan turned his cane around. He could barely breathe. Holding the wet tip in his hand, he reached the handle out for Agha. Khan inched forward, stretched his arm as far as he could, and finally the lion caught Agha's pants. He pulled and heaved the cold body out of the water. He rolled the old man over on the edge of the hoez. Agha's wet face gleamed in the moonlight, his permanent smile beaming at Khan. "Agha! Agha!" Khan called, panting for air. His throat burned. He could not believe that Agha would never open his eyes again to ask for something in his high-pitched voice. "Agha! Agha!" he called, his eyes starting to tear. But the old man opened his eyes. "Are you okay?" Khan asked. Agha blinked, but said nothing. "Can you see me? Can you hear me?" Agha's lips parted. "Who would have thought, son." Water dripped from his wrinkled lips. "I've become a fish."

From that night on, Khan locked Agha's room himself every night. "This madness has to stop," he said to Agha before closing the door.

"Nothing can be stopped," Agha said, "I have been around long enough to know that much."

19

ETERMINED TO NOT ONLY PREDICT and spot the next turbulence the cats would cause, but also to prevent it, once again Khan descended to the basement, and to the maps that he had left untouched after Leyla had been born. More diligent than ever, braving a weariness that crept up the marrow of his bones, he set out recording what he witnessed. So determined was he in those days that he spent nights out sitting on doorsteps. He came back in the morning, with bloodshot eyes, to Agha pounding on the locked door.

"Give me the key," Pooran said, "or I will have that door smashed open the next time he needs to relieve himself."

Pooran spoke with such boldness that Khan handed over the key and walked to his room like a sleepless apparition whose only occupation was to keep a close eye on the streets so that in the course of the next years, he would witness the signs of something even graver than the Coup he had predicted before.

THE THIRD BOOK OF POETRY sold more copies than the first two combined. Controversy arose more and more in literary circles. For the first time, someone hailed Ahmad "the Rumi of our times," because of the rebellion in his poetry, "an iconoclast who shattered the idol of a thousand-year tyranny of predetermined poetic forms." The critics who previously deemed him not worthy of wasting ink on decried his work as a blind copy of the contemporary French poetry, which had "nothing to do with our people and their poetic palate." One paper called him "the Dumb Poet whose nose is long enough to poke into politics."

"You should do what you used to in the café," Homa said one night. "I think it was beautiful. I miss those days."

Like the first time, it took Homa's charms to bring Ahmad before an audience. From that day on, he would stand in front of his listeners at his readings with his papers in his hand, mouthing his poems. Sitting on a chair behind him someone would read the words out loud and those who went to the events would soon forget the lag between the sound and Ahmad's lip movements. At a reading organized by *Dust and Blood*, a magazine with thinly veiled leftist proclivities, Ahmad mouthed a short but fiery piece. He had placed the narrator of the poem in a dark and cold prison with no hope of ever being freed.

After the reading, a young man, almost as old as Ahmad, in a fedora and a suit, pressed to perfection, rose from his seat and walked up to him. The man's thin eyebrows above a pair of round glasses gave his shaved face a vaguely feminine radiance. "Zia," he introduced himself as he shook Ahmad's hand. "Can I have the pleasure of inviting you to coffee?" He was the nephew of a former member of the parliament, Great Zia, and the central figure of a small group of moderate critics who, although retired from the legislation, had kept his leading role and planned to have someone in the next parliament. "Poetry is what holds this world together, in my humble opinion," Mr. Zia said. "And good poetry"—he took a sip of his coffee—"we should feed on it." From then on, he was present at all the readings, and when Ahmad started to preface his poetry with short introductions that revolved around the issues of the country, Mr. Zia offered to look at them beforehand. "When you grow up with an uncle whose least important guest is a parliament member or a minister"—he touched the bridge of his glasses with his forefinger—"you have no choice but to develop a sense for these things."

Three years later, at the dinner table, Mr. Zia would ask Ahmad if he had ever thought of running for parliament. Ahmad would pour himself a glass of yogurt drink and slowly nod his head.

NEWS OF AN UNSUCCESSFUL ATTACK against the Shah ricocheted across the country. The gunman had missed his royal target but left two holes in the door and a small spiderweb crack in the windshield of the automobile that carried His Majesty out of the gates of his palace. Most peculiar was the fact that, though the guards opened fire at the men in the car, they had managed to escape unharmed. Before long, word began to circulate that the car had been made impenetrable to bullets because of a spell the shooter used. Haji the prayerwright's name came up on every mouth again. More people than ever sought him out at home.

To every client who mentioned the incident, Haji would say, "That was not me. But these things are all in the books." He would finger the Bic pen hanging around his neck with a thick string and repeat: "One reads with one's heart and these things are all in the books." There was no initial government reaction to the rumor, but a week later, Haji disappeared. The government blamed the assassination attempt on the dissidents, specifically clandestine offshoots of the communist parties that, as the radio announced, were changing strategy to resort to acts of armed violence.

"SAVAK is flexing its muscles," Salman said to Abdoo over tea. Abdoo was a dark-skinned medical student at the University of Tehran who came from a poor family in a small village on the coast of the Persian Gulf where "you put fish in the pan and the pan in the sun, and voilà!" Abdoo was a friend and a member of the Tudeh Party who had devoted himself to teaching kids in poverty. He traveled to the farthest villages of the South and taught multiple grades in the same room or tent. With the harvest season beginning and the kids becoming busy in the fields, Abdoo had come back to Tehran.

"If you ask me," Salman said, "they'll kill the prayer man."

Abdoo disagreed. "True, there's no punishment for regicide but execution, blah blah, but the Shah has enough trouble as is, my friend. They'll keep him nice and warm, maybe for a long time. That Haji man has made himself some reputation. They can't kill him, and that, in my humble opinion, is a sign of atrophy. If they meant to, his body would be rotting in the ground by now."

It came to pass more quickly than Abdoo expected. Within a month the radio announced that His Majesty had granted clemency to the offender. The grandeur of the country and well-being of the people of this land were the only things nonnegotiable and uncompromisable in his royal opinion. Everyone who walked on this soil had to be ready to make sacrifices for a better future, including His Majesty.

Salman picked up the phone and called Abdoo, his first sentence ready on the tip of his tongue: *Damn you, Abdoo, you were right!* If the announcement was actually true, the Shah's atrophy was more critical than what Salman had thought. He sensed a change in Abdoo's tone, an almost imperceptible trembling. It was as if he was talking not with the words he said aloud, but with a second set that Salman did not hear, but should have. As soon as he hung up, Salman took his wallet, packed his documents in a brown attaché case, and left his apartment. He called Abdoo a few more times from public phones, but Abdoo did not answer, and Salman decided it would not be prudent to keep calling.

IN WEEKLY MEETINGS WITH AHMAD, Mr. Zia talked about the logistics of approaching his candidacy. They met in Mr. Zia's large rose garden where he walked with his hands clasped behind his back and admired the flowers. Every now and then he would bend over and pat one on the side, a strange thing to do, Ahmad thought, as if to gauge how healthy the flower was by how fast it swung back and forth in response to his tap. "My wife gets the credit for the palette." Cordoned off in patches of the same color, the roses blushed from white toward red. Mr. Zia spent longer among the whites. One day, after the attempt on the Shah, he pulled a sheet of paper from the pocket of his suit and handed it to Ahmad. "I have reserved columns for tomorrow," he said. Ahmad unfolded the paper. The note said that in a public notice, Ahmad Torkash-Vand, scholar, poet, and public speaker, had condemned the attack and expressed hope that the law would bring the culprit to justice. Ahmad lifted his head with a questioning look.

"The editors are waiting for my call," Mr. Zia said.

Ahmad raised his eyebrows. He would not endorse taking up arms against what he deemed wrong, like Salman did, but Ahmad did not find any urge in him to condemn that attack either. Violence had to be castigated, but so did the rule of the Shah, which had grown more autocratic after the Coup. Joining and forming armed militia was the wrong solution for the right cause. He had not thought Mr. Zia would stoop to aligning himself with the pro-Shah majority.

"How far do you think you'll go if you hold your head up too high?" Mr. Zia asked. "Here's your first lesson, Ahmad: always find the right ass to kiss."

Ahmad thought for a few moments and convinced himself that if he succeeded to reach the parliament, he could work to make things right in the right way. But the road there would not be free of obstacles. Mr. Zia's strategy was another wrong way to achieve the right thing. He nodded his head.

"The big ass," Mr. Zia said, "always the safest. We should play a game of chess someday." He patted Ahmad on the shoulder. "I bet you're a tough one."

To shift his public image from poet to politician, Ahmad wrote speeches to accompany the readings that Mr. Zia arranged. In the course of six months, poetry waned from the events altogether. "Want their votes?" Mr. Zia said. "Tell them about sacks of potatoes. You know what I mean." *That's economy*, Ahmad wrote. "Politics and economy sleep in the same bed." With over half a year until the elections, the rehearsing began. The dinner with Mr. Zia's uncle and a group of merchants from the Tehran Bazaar was boisterous and interspersed with laughter. Lamb and chicken kebab were served. Haj Mohammad, who had the monopoly of hydrogenated oil, questioned the likelihood of a rookie getting in. "We'll work on it," the uncle replied. "You enjoy the thigh." Not convinced, the merchant turned to Ahmad. "Tell me, why should I spend my money on you?" Ahmad took his pen and wrote on the merchant's hand: *Because you don't want to regret missing your opportunity to help a future member of the parliament.*

Great Zia leaned over, looked at the merchant's palm, and let out a hearty laugh. "Convincing, ain't he?"

When the next weekend Ahmad and Mr. Zia stepped out onto the veranda to talk in the garden, a man in threadbare clothes was standing uncomfortably at the beginning of the path into the rose patches. His long face had borne innumerable lashes of sunshine and his worn shoes were caked with mud.

"Look who's finally here," Mr. Zia said with a smile. "Say hi to your voice, Ahmad."

In response to Ahmad's questioning look, Mr. Zia threw an arm around his shoulders and called out to the man, "Say something, Hushem."

With nervous uncertainty, the man answered, "What should I say, sir?"

The words came out of his mouth so sonorous and strong that the yellowing leaves trembled and fell from the trees above their heads. A dog started to bark in the distance.

"What do you say to that?" Mr. Zia squeezed Ahmad's shoulder. "Have we done well or not?"

MAN WITHOUT VOICE
WILL SPEAK FOR THE PEOPLE

Pooran saw Ahmad's picture in an open newspaper in Khan's room. A small picture for a small politician. She took the newspaper from the desk and clipped the picture out with scissors. Sitting straight in a suit, the knot of his tie tight and neat, his hair slicked back, and his head turned to look at the reader, her black-and-white Ahmad was now a big man. "Thursday, 6:00 p.m., Danesh Sports Club," said the text in the newspaper under the empty rectangle.

After lunch on Thursday, Pooran got ready, threw her chador on her head, and took the bus. In a small arena with high, narrow windows and a few rows of concrete platforms for seats, chairs had been arranged to face a low stage. More than half of the seats were taken and a noisy traffic of organizers and guests—men clad in pants and suits and women in dresses and high heels—walked around, their confused chatter echoing down from the high ceiling. She sat herself in the back row as a bout of applause and whistling rose. She looked around and saw Ahmad walking toward the stage. Ahmad stepped up and raised his hand as a sign of greeting and gratitude. After the last isolated clapping subsided, Ahmad started: "My dear brothers and sisters, we are gathered here today because we all love our country." The voice boomed around and rattled the windows. Pooran saw the man who talked instead of her son and soon lost interest in the voice of the stranger. She did not hear Ahmad's words, but watched him speak with one hand clasping his lapel like a pin. She could see a few strands of white hair on his temple. Nostalgia enveloped her like a blanket on a snowy night and murmured in her ear reminiscences of her baby Ahmad as he played hide-and-seek in the Orchard with the other kids, as he climbed the short trees and reached for the apples on the higher branches. Nosser was with her then, if distracted and not there in spirit most of the time. Ahmad's holding of the lapel, his looking directly into the eyes of his listeners, and his speaking with a borrowed voice, was nothing that had come from Nosser. That was Khan.

After the speech, Pooran approached the group that had gathered around Ahmad. Mr. Zia was the first to see her. "Can I help you, madam?" he asked stepping forward. Pooran walked past him. The group of men and women split to make way for the chador-clad woman who stopped right in front of Ahmad.

What are you doing here? Ahmad mouthed with a hesitant half smile.

"Why?" she asked. "Are you ashamed of me?" Before Ahmad opened his mouth, she continued. "I don't want you to do this, Ahmad. This is not you and I hope you won't get elected. I wouldn't vote for you if they let me vote, and I will tell everyone I know not to vote for you."

Back in her house, Pooran brought a chair and sat by Khan and Agha in the yard in the evening breeze that swung the branches and fresh leaves. Like the two old men, she stared at nothing specific, but what surrounded her: the orange tree, the rosy tendrils of the grapevine reaching for something to twist around, the goldfish swimming in the hoez now twice as large since when they swirled in the bowl on the New Year table. This family and their silences, she thought. They were impossible. She got to her feet and cranked her way up to the roof where Zeeba stopped working at the loom to greet her without turning her head. Halfway done, the rug boasted arabesques and floral motifs in brilliant colors. Staring through the loom at the soul of the rug, the girl picked the right hue by rolling the twines between her thumb and forefinger. "It's time I find you a good husband," Pooran told her. Standing by the girl's side, Pooran looked at her golden hair gleam in the last of the daylight that the lace curtain sifted into the room.

"No one takes a blind girl," Zeeba said tying a knot around the warp.

Pooran stroked the girl on the head and said, "Any man will be lucky to have you." But she sensed disbelief oozing out of her wounded words, wafting through the air to the girl who was now already a year or two past the age she could have become a wife. She was barely recognizable from the little girl who had run her fingers on the knocker and said she liked the house. What was Pooran doing with her life all those years as this girl's breasts grew so full?

Back in her room, Pooran sat at her dresser and brushed her hair. She pulled her dark blue dress out of the plastic cover and rubbed on her neck a touch of the French perfume she kept in her wardrobe. In that uncertain time after the sunset and before the dark, she threw her chador on her head and walked to Seyf Zarrabi's shop and bought meters and meters of fabric, testing, with a slow deliberate touch of her fingers, each bolt that Seyf pulled from the shelf. Breathing audibly, Seyf Zarrabi excused himself and disappeared into the back room. He returned behind the counter a few minutes later walking in a thick cloud of strong cologne, a red tie hanging from his neck, his freshly waxed hair combed over his crown. At least he had the discretion not to make a suggestive comment. He pulled another bolt from a top shelf and unrolled it on the counter. Pooran felt the fabric between her thumb and forefinger and saw the gray that tainted the pink of her nails and the tiny but numerous creases on her fingers. They looked sad. "Four meters of this," she said, and before Seyf put the scissors to the fabric, she stepped over to the back of the shop and, without a word or a circumspect look, walked behind the counter and slipped through the narrow entrance, into the back room where the teal Westinghouse fridge buzzed in the corner.

"YOU'RE NOT CUT OUT FOR politics..."

. . .

"When was the last time you wrote a poem?"

. . .

Ahmad was sitting in a chair. Homa walked up to him and snatched the letter he was reading out of his hand. "I miss your poems." She sat on his lap and put her arms around his neck. Ahmad locked his arms behind her back and kissed her. He motioned for her to bring him paper. By the time Homa got back to the living room with the notepad and pen, Ahmad had picked the letter up from the floor. He took the pad and wrote:

I'm a man of anything I desire.

The smile that lingered on Ahmad's face did not diminish the horror Homa suddenly felt at that sentence. She wondered for an instant who it was that had her tight in his arms, like a snare around a rabbit's foot, but before the angst became intolerable, the phone rang. It was Mr. Zia. She watched Ahmad listen carefully to the man before knocking on the receiver with his fingernail: one knock for *yes*, two for *no*. The more complex codes, the combinations of knocks and silences, she had not been able to decipher. Nor had she made a great effort to do so. After the phone call, like always, Ahmad went to his room and wrote a note to Mr. Zia.

As the elections drew closer, Ahmad worked on his speeches until well after the girls were asleep in their beds. He held up the first draft and read it with proper gesticulation and facial expressions. He scrapped the draft and wrote anew until he had a satisfying version. In a matter of a few weeks, Ahmad had reached such a harmony with Hushem that even his presence right beside the podium or stage or stool attracted little attention. Some would notice the scrawny man with the sun-baked skin who opened and closed his mouth in concert with Ahmad's like a fish out of water. They would point him out to one another, but after a few moments, eyes would drift back to the candidate. No one directed their cheerful applause to Hushem and no one shook hands with him after the speech.

Two months before the elections, the New Iran Party proposed a coalition. They were not as right-wing as most of the parliament, but kept themselves somewhere near the center. "Conservative sycophants!" Ahmad's voice thundered in the rose garden through Hushem. The two had attained such unity of thought and movement that Hushem could anticipate Ahmad's words by looking at the back of his head. "And Great Zia said no, right?"

Mr. Zia patted his white roses on the side. "They'll have more seats than us anyhow, if we get any that is."

"So you're in this for the seats," Hushem's voice said.

Mr. Zia looked at Ahmad and smiled. "There's nothing in there but seats," he said. "What are you in this for?"

"A strong parliament is a must if anything's to change. And strong means at least a few who are not just puppets."

Mr. Zia turned around and dismissed Hushem. After he heard the metal gates of the garden bang closed behind the villager, he turned to Ahmad. "New Iran is a party. You may not like them, but this is as far away from yes-man as you can get without getting your ass kicked out of the seat. Great Zia is going to give them only one name: it's down to you and the other two. I need an answer now: Are you in or out? You're young, you're a poet, and you have your alluring silence; people like you. Great Zia knows that. And he's willing to throw all his weight behind you, but you're going to have to work both with him and the New Iran. If this is not acceptable, we'll shake hands right now and part ways. But if you still want to do this, the party is next Thursday."

As Mr. Zia said those words, Ahmad looked into his brown eyes behind his round glasses and thought he was a good, honest man. But Ahmad doubted his uncle. That day, he decided that while he could not count on Great Zia, he would use the old fox's power to get to where he wanted to be.

THE ANNOUNCEMENT CAME THE FOLLOWING Thursday in the rose garden. Seventy men from the New Iran Party sat around large tables as maids came out of the kitchen carrying heavy trays laden with cups of hot tea and glasses of sweet rose water drinks with ice. The Great Zia greeted the notable guests and then the food came out. Plates of stews and platters of rice were arranged like petals around broiled lamb at the center of tables. Bowls of yogurt, pickled garlic, and herbs were set within everyone's reach. Big chunks of ice floated in jars of water. A layer of crushed dried mint had formed on top of the yogurt drinks. Hushem had changed into a blue suit and a pistachio tie. Sitting beside Ahmad, he was careful to speak when, and only when, Ahmad opened his mouth. He took small bites and devoured hastily in anticipation.

In response to the few questions he was asked at the table, Hushem shook or nodded his head or shrugged his shoulders. Night had set in and the smell from the roses wafted through the windows into the laughter and clinks of spoons and forks on china plates that rose from the table and swirled back down by the blades of the ceiling fan. Ahmad turned to him at one point and Hushem read his lips out loud: "Hushem, relax," Hushem said to himself with Ahmad's face smiling at him and Ahmad's arm patting his shoulder. "I'm not going to say another word until the dinner's over." Everyone laughed.

Over tea and hookah after dinner, some of the New Iran candidates made speeches. Ahmad's handpicked words synchronized with Hushem's voice cracked the lens of someone's eyeglasses and received a standing ovation. At the end of the night, the guests shook hands and left the garden for their automobiles that idled outside. Dr. Taash, vice president of the New Iran Party, extended his hand and said in a hushed voice, "You want my advice, son? Get a doctorate first. Or go back to your forge and your poems. You speak well, but this is not child's play." In the dim light that came from the incandescent bulb screwed to the wall by the garden door, Hushem squinted for a twitch in Ahmad's facial muscles. But Ahmad did not speak a word. He smiled and squeezed the older man's hand hard, looking straight into the doctor's eyes as they grew wide-open from the pressure. After Ahmad loosened his grip, Dr. Taash hurried out rubbing his hand.

Back home, Ahmad opened the bedroom door as though he was tiptoeing to catch a fat pigeon. He changed into his pajamas, slipped into the bed, and breathed out a long breath. He was now Great Zia's official nominee. The night was silent and heavy. On the other side of the bed, Homa lay awake, her back to Ahmad. With closed eyes, she wondered about the details of Ahmad's night, where he had been, who he had talked to, what he had done and ate. She was tempted to reach for the flashlight on the nightstand but decided against it. Ahmad would fall asleep soon. She would ask him tomorrow. A few minutes passed. Sleep would not come to her, and Ahmad's breathing had not yet lapsed into the telltale calm rhythm she knew well. He was still awake. In a sudden movement, she grabbed the flashlight, flicked the switch on, and shone it on Ahmad's lips.

"So how was your night?"

I'm the candidate, he mouthed with a smile.

"You're what?" Homa asked.

The candidate, Ahmad repeated slower, opening his mouth wide to make the mime readable. *Turn the lights on and I'll tell you.*

"No," Homa said. "That's okay." In the yellow beam that lit Ahmad's face, Homa looked at his five o'clock shadow, at the few hairs that stuck out of his nostrils and at his eyes squinting against the flashlight and hoped that everything would go well. Although she still loved him, she did not want him to see her. She turned the flashlight off and lay on her side with her back to Ahmad, and although Ahmad turned toward her and stroked her hair, she felt, at least that night, that she was sleeping alone.

20

TWO WEEKS BEFORE THE NEXT SUMMER, Majeed was at the theater as the streets were being beaten under the shoes of the people who marched ahead and the boots of the soldiers and officers who would not retreat. The lover on the screen was walking in quiet sidewalks, struggling with the question in his heart: should one leave one's beloved if one is certain that another man will give her a better life? With every step of the lover on the carpet of the dry, orange, and red leaves, a calm, crunching sound reverberated in the theater. It was at that moment when Majeed felt his seat was shaking, and before he had the time to complain in his head that someone was kicking from behind again, the whole theater trembled. The wall behind the screen fell with a loud rumble, a tank came in through the screen, and Majeed found himself in the middle of the uprising. The tank stopped on top of the debris with a hiss, coughing up a puff of smoke. Somehow the screen was not detached from what kept it in place; ripped and crumpled, the white sheet was still hanging behind the tank. Outside in the daylight, people ran back and forth across the street. The hatch opened and the tank driver, a young soldier in a khaki army uniform, scrambled out and jumped down. In shock, he looked around at his tank in the cloud of dust and smoke, the fallen wall, the moviegoers who were running away in panic, and the persistent screen that now displayed a vague shadow show of the commotion outside overlaid by a pale picture of the lover in the leaves. The driver ran toward the back exits where those previously watching the movie were now pushing one another. Majeed, who had sprung up onto his seat at some point, ran and joined the fleeing crowd.

Resting his palms on the back of the man in front of him for support, while being shoved ahead by scared bodies, Majeed made his way out of the hall and ran up the stairs. The door to the projection booth was left half open. He looked around. The room was empty. He jumped in, turned the projector off, took the reels out, and snapped them into the rewinder. While the rewinder whirred, he collected the other five reels of the movie. From the little window through which the projector shot its beam at the screen, Majeed looked down. Except for some curious people from the street who climbed the rubble to get close to the tank, there was no one in the theatre. Outside the projection room someone ran past the door. When he heard the slapping of the end of the film on the body of the rewinder, Majeed turned the machine off, fitted the last reel into a case, and snapped the lid closed. Without trying to hide his armful of cases, he walked out of the door and down the stairs. "Hey, hey," said the box office ticket seller bending over to put his mouth to the opening, "what are those?"

"I've got to see the end," Majeed said before running away awkwardly, a stack of six-reel cases in his arms. The ticket seller went back to staring at what was unravelling in the street outside his cubicle. Even if he had stepped out, he would soon have given in to exhaustion and lost the young man among the bodies that strove to change history.

Majeed hid the film under his bed and went back to the cinema. The soldiers had dispersed the people from the neighborhood and guards with G3s hanging from their shoulders were posted around the tank. It took him four hours to walk to three other theaters in search of more film. The buildings stood intact without a cracked window, but they were all closed after the actions of the day had heated up. He walked back home hands shoved into his pants pockets as the day began losing color and the demonstrations and occasional shots abated. On his way, he walked toward a grocery to buy eggs for his dinner, but before he went in, he saw the hand.

Severed from the wrist, it was stuck in the lower branches of a young plane tree. The blood had congealed to a dark substance that looked sticky. The owner of the grocery store stepped out of his shop and swatted the hand off the branch with a long broom. "I should have closed today like the rest," he said, half to himself, half to the stranger that was Majeed, and went on complaining as if he was talking to the person in charge of all that. "This is how you run a country. Nice, nice." The hand landed in the sidewalk flower bed, at the feet of a brown striped cat. After a moment's pause, the cat sniffed and pawed at the hand, then turned around and walked away. Majeed remembered playing count the kitties with Khan, a game he loved because it allowed him to walk the streets without worrying that his mother would scold him for wandering. He remembered the nights he crawled out of bed to press his ear to his parents' door, anxious to know whether he would hear his father's harsh shout, a slap on his mother's face and then a stifled cry, or tender smooching sounds that acted like a soporific on him. On the nebulous nights when Majeed heard his father work open one of his gallons of homemade vodka, when he heard both the stifled cries and the tender smooches, Majeed had heard his father talk about his mother's side of the family, the "cuckoos." It was only on those nights, when his father's legs became too erratic to keep him in one place, that Majeed heard his father call Khan "Mr. Meow."

In that June dusk, as the cat looked at the hand with suspicious curiosity, Majeed thought maybe Khan had not been such a cuckoo after all, although he did not exactly know how the old man had spent his life. On his count-the-kitties outings, Khan too would search the nooks and crannies of the streets for cats. Majeed only knew how to count up to eighty. Twice he came to the limit of his knowledge and asked God to take all cats away from his path, and both times God did not listen to him. Stressed what to report to Khan, he ran back and gave him the number: eighty. From then on, when he got to seventy-five, he would run back, keeping his head down to the sidewalk for fear of seeing more. The day Khan buried a cat in the garden, Majeed was watching from behind the window in Pooran's room. But whatever cat passion was in the old man seemed to vanish at a point, sometime before Ahmad ran for parliament, during a period in which something vital in Khan seemed to have died. He sat long hours in one spot in the yard. Pooran brought Agha out and sat him on a chair by Khan. Like statues carved out of marble, the two old men sat motionless. They dissolved into the air. Agha would crawl out of his stupor soon, cry out that he wanted to go to the park. If no one was free to take him, Zeeba would wheelbarrow him out front into the alley, right by the metal door. Khan's absence was bigger and longer. Pooran would bring him tea, or a sour-cherry drink from which he would take no more than a few sips. Having finished his share, Agha would glance at Khan's full glass. "You don't want it, right?" He took the glass from Khan smiling as if he had won a prize. "If you don't drink," he said smacking his lips after the first sip, "you will dry up and wither away."

"What's eating you, Khan?" Pooran asked even though she, too, knew that Khan would not divulge the secrets of his heart even to those closest to him. "It'll pass," he answered with a forced smile. The day the results of the election were to be announced, Khan was already seated by the hoez when Zeeba woke up with the first rays of the sun. At breakfast, Pooran turned up the radio that sent wheezy, shaky waves throughout the house. The night before, she had lit an extra candle praying that her son would not get elected. At noon the announcer began to read the list of the new members of the twenty-first parliament. Except for Agha who sat in his purple house wheelbarrow—one that Pooran had asked Khan to buy for moving Agha around inside the house—everyone was standing around the radio that sat on a low shelf in the living room. Khan had a hand resting on his lion and another on Agha's shoulder. Zeeba held Nana Shamsi's hand. Name after name rang out of the speaker. "Please, let it not be Ahmad," Pooran entreated with her eyes closed before the next name rang out. "Ahmad Torkash-Vand" was the twenty-fifth name out of thirty. "I always knew it," Agha said, excited, hitting the sides of his wheelbarrow. "That boy will do things. I knew it."

By late afternoon, when the family had gathered in the house for the occasion, Khan rose from his chair, determined that it was a time to celebrate, not worry, and by the time Ahmad stepped into the yard, followed by Homa, their two daughters, and Mr. Zia, the house was decorated with colored string lights from the yard up to Lalah's room that Khan had built on top of Leyla's after she was born. "You see that room on top of mine?" Leyla told a four-year-old Lalah. "That's yours."

When the guests were gone, when the night was playing its tricks dexterously, Pooran found Ahmad alone. "I hope you know what you are doing, Ahmad. Right and wrong are not always easy to see." Ahmad reached for his notepad in his pocket, but Pooran put her hands on his cheeks and held his face up. She held his hands in hers, looking up into Ahmad's eyes. "You know I didn't want you to do this." Small insects fluttered around the hanging bulbs. "I love your poems. Sometimes I don't understand them, but I love them. I read them when I miss you. You're in them. But when I listen to you speak about this and that thing in politics, you're not there. Do you think you can prove me wrong?" Ahmad nodded. "Ahmad," Pooran said after a few seconds of silence, "can I sleep tonight knowing that my son will not be on the side of the wrong?" Ahmad nodded, this time more confidently.

Over a year after Ahmad assured his mother of his intentions, the tank ran into the theater. News of the new protests and arrests reminded Ahmad of the Coup ten years before when he himself was on the street hauling Salman's father to the clinic, the Coup that had put Prime Minister Mosaddegh in house arrest in exile. If everyone stuck to the law, be it the government or those who criticized it or the ones who wanted the Shah gone, none of that would have happened, neither on that day, nor a decade before. The next day, Ahmad stepped to the podium in parliament and made a speech, as always without using the microphone, calling out those who resorted to violence, who demolished public and private property, who gave in to the temptations of illogical wrath in place of embracing the path of reason. Because he could not say anything against the Shah, his speech was understood to be for him. There was enthusiastic applause from the conservative majority, surprised to agree for once with the youngest person ever elected to the parliament. They unanimously condemned the perpetrators and thanked the police and the army for their continued efforts to restore peace and order in those tumultuous times. A widespread crackdown on dissidents began the next day.

THE DAY AFTER AHMAD MADE his speech, Mr. Zia visited him in his house. That meant one thing: the Great Zia did not want to have Ahmad in the rose garden. The girls were at school, and the two men sat in the new armchairs Homa had ordered a few months back. She brought two cups of tea in a tray and read the message in Ahmad's eyes that said, *Confidential.* She took her red plastic shopping basket and left the house.

Ahmad wrote in his notepad.

The summer had come soon that year. The pedestal fan in the corner scanned the room like a traveler lost in a new city.

"No one knows what you really meant. There's nothing out there but your recorded words. And they're not making Great Zia or even the New Iran happy with the current orientations. And they're the ones you called sycophants once."

Ahmad wrote.

Hung on the wall that separated the kitchen from the living room were framed photos. In one of them Homa smiled in a boat with her fists closed around the oars. Another was a portrait of a stolid, decorated colonel standing at attention. Mr. Zia flicked a white flake of something off his pants.

"Yes, a peaceful protest is preferable, and yes, there might have been misunderstandings. But the bottom line is that you suddenly positioned yourself as an advocate of suppression and a supporter of the government and the Shah."

The fan was trying to help the air cooler that sent air in from the top of the roof through vents close to the ceiling.

"You can't just say you are not this or that, Ahmad. You should have listened and waited. Words mean things. This is not poetry, this is politics. You . . . "

Ahmad cut him short by raising a palm.

I know what Im doing I know what Im saying and the last thing I need is for someone to tell me what poetry is. He held the note before Mr. Zia's face.

"Listen Ahmad." Mr. Zia leaned in. "I know you as a nice man. I know you have a good heart and I know you want things to be better. All I'm saying is that we need to do a little adjustment of our path. You'll go see them, Great Zia and the others, and things will be okay." He pulled some folded paper out of his suit pocket. "You say the right thing the next time and everything will be set right, I assure you."

Ahmad opened the papers. It was the text of his next speech. He looked at it for a few minutes. Mr. Zia picked up one of the tea cups from the tray and handed it to Ahmad, then held the sugar bowl in front of him. Ahmad set the papers on his lap and took a piece.

Before Mr. Zia left, the bell rang. Ahmad rose from his armchair and buzzed the door open. Lalah's high-pitched voice telling her mother and sister how she taught her friend to whistle echoed in the short corridor before she opened the door and ran into Ahmad's arms. He picked the young one up and kissed her. Leyla said hi to Mr. Zia who had also stood to greet the ladies. "It's nice to see you again after so long," she said shaking hands with him.

"It certainly is," Mr. Zia answered with a smile, looking at Leyla standing straight in front of him, her light-brown hair pouring over her shoulders on her chest.

"You don't remember when it was," Leyla said, her eyebrows raised as if to say, *I knew you wouldn't remember.*

"Of course, I do." Mr. Zia put the tip of his forefinger on the bridge of his glasses and pushed up. "A few months ago, at the slopes."

"Over a year ago," Leyla said slightly shaking her head, "the day Dad got the election, in Khan's house." Then as if to absolve Mr. Zia of his negligence, she added, "Of course you were too busy for details."

The way she talked made Mr. Zia feel he was very close to failing a test. He put his hands in his pants pockets. "Did you have a good day at school?"

"We sang the 'Iran the prosperous land' song," the younger girl said, still in her father's arms.

Leyla said, "I presume you know the education system offers little more than rote." Mr. Zia nodded with raised eyebrows. Sporadically, on a few occasions before, he had talked to Leyla and he knew she was not an average kid, but he had never had a conversation this impressive with the girl who now spoke twenty years more mature than her age, and seemed to flatter him. He felt his palms sweat in his pockets. "Next week is exams week anyway. It means we should have learned a lot by now."

Mr. Zia sensed that this was a hint for him not to keep her too long. "I'll let you go then and study," he said, extending his hand. "It was nice to see you again."

She put her delicate hand in his. Mr. Zia smiled. Leyla smiled back at him and the green cherries on the tree in the yard ripened into sparkling rubies.

"I'm bringing another round of tea," Homa said from the kitchen.

"That's not necessary, Mrs. Delldaar," he called out, "I'm leaving." Then he turned to Ahmad. "I can't believe she's ten?"

"Nine, nine," Lalah said still in her father's arms. "And I'm six."

Two days later, Ahmad stood in the parliament and read his dictated speech. In a change of position, he said that the dissatisfaction of people was the result of negligence of those in power in their duties. Forgoing his emphasis on both sides having to refrain from violence and focusing on the regime was not as upsetting for Ahmad as the fact that now he was a mindless, voiceless puppet, who was not even allowed to think. It was to no one's surprise that the confusion of protesting cries, denunciatory comments, and booing drowned the feeble applause like rumbling waves. At home, Ahmad paced the yard and tapped out phone calls in his room. His plate on the table stopped steaming. Homa warmed the food up and it stopped steaming again, but Ahmad would not go to the table.

THE DISAPPEARANCE OF ABDOO WAS the event that made Salman realize for the first time, and deep in the marrow of his bones, that he was not playing a game. After he left his apartment, he went to a friend's for the night and called his node, Hooshang. Hooshang had already heard the news and confirmed: Abdoo had been arrested. They arranged to meet near the entrance to Cyrus Park, under the plane trees that clung to their last dried leaves, on a wooden bench by the newspaper stand. In the autumn sun that did not warm anything, Hooshang drew on his short, cheap cigarettes and told Salman it was imprudent of Abdoo to give Salman his real name. "Your phone was tapped," Hooshang said. "They were coming for you, too." Both Hooshang and Salman would change their apartments and numbers. Salman would have a new contact node. Salman shook hands with Hooshang and thought, as the short man walked away, his hands in his jacket pockets on the sidewalk that was strewn with shriveled leaves, whether or not he should have told him that Abdoo had known Salman's real name, too.

His new node was Mashdee, a sickly, middle-aged grocer with a knit hat on his head and an Azeri accent on his tongue. "Four kilos of rice, please," Salman said to the man. "Guests are pouring in left and right." Behind the counter, the grocer recognized the code words, and waited for the final part. "In a burlap bag, if you have one." The man threw a glance at Salman, pushed the revolver into the grains of rice, and handed the bag to him. In a note tucked inside a folded bill, Salman passed him his address and new telephone number. Back in his apartment, Salman kicked off his shoes and put the bag on the floor in the living room. Then he sank his hand into the rice and took out the revolver. As soon as he held the gun in his hand to weigh it and aim at the lamp and the framed photo and the shoehorn, he felt something against his fingers. Turning the gun over he found his cyanide capsule taped to the grip. Salman detached the blue pill and rolled it in the palm of his hand for a few minutes: light in life and heavy with undefinable possibilities of relief; not a painkiller but a pain-preventer. He sewed inside pouches in his pants pockets and never distanced himself more than an arm's reach of the pill. He smuggled guns and ammo that came to the grocery shop in gunnysacks of rice. Each time the truck arrived, the second bag was the one with the stash.

Salman read the news of Ahmad's controversial speech in the afternoon newspaper. The day before, he had been among the protesters himself. A tea and cigarette after he woke up, he was dressed and ready. The usual fifteen-minute walk to the bus stop took him only eight minutes. He hopped on the red double-decker bus, and two hours later, he was walking within a river of men who punched the air and walked in a slow but constant flow chanting slogans, some holding up placards. Those who did not participate watched from windows and half-open front doors. Soon the crowd got to where the police and army soldiers had blocked the streets ahead, a scene that angered the protestors. They tried to push forward, but dispersed with the warning shots that were fired into the air.

Salman too ran away and took shelter behind a green Vauxhall Victor parked in a narrow street where a young boy, perhaps still in high school, crouched too. In the short moment when the two waited for things to calm, the boy touched Salman's arm and pointed under the car. By the tire, sitting on its haunch, holding something between its teeth, was a black-and-white cat. Salman expected the animal to look at them for a few seconds and run away, but instead it got to its feet, turned its back to them, and dragged the thing it was holding in its mouth. There was a sound of metal grating on asphalt. The high schooler lowered his body to look under the car. "What on earth," he called and, reaching out his hand, brought out a G3. "Let me see," Salman took the weapon and examined it. It was an army-grade rifle, the kind the soldiers had in their hands on the other side of the demonstrations. "What on actual earth," the boy said, squatting before Salman, not taking his eyes away from the dark, polished metal of the G3. Salman clicked the magazine out and weighed it in his hand; it was still full. "What do we do with it?" the high-school boy asked, excited. "Who would believe this?

Maybe there's more." He lowered his body again to check under the car. The cat took a few steps back toward the tire, looked at the two men for a few seconds, then turned and dashed away. "Okay, can I have it back?" the boy asked, getting back to his squatting position, putting his hand on the rifle. "If they catch you with it, you're done," Salman said, gently pulling the rifle into his arms. "You think I don't know?" Now the boy was standing straight.

"Do you even know how to use it?"

"I'll learn." The boy yanked the G3 from Salman's arm. "Plus I was here first." Holding the rifle in his hands, the boy ran toward the other end of the street, away from the demonstration, and out of sight. Salman walked back to the main street, and having heard word that the gendarmes had opened fire a few streets away, hurried in that direction, but by the time he arrived, the wounded had been carried away. He had not witnessed the shooting firsthand that day, but he did see the bending of street signs and breaking of phone booths. He did see a young bearded man, mad with rage, hurl a rock through a sweets shop window and he was there when some men set fire to a school, and so he tried to understand what it was that Ahmad had talked about in his speech. For a few days after the incident, Salman thought about whether the brutality of the regime warranted violent reactions, but when a week later, dissidents were arrested in scores, he came home, pulled from under a pile of newspapers and magazines the paper with the news of Ahmad's speech, and held a lit match to Ahmad's photo.

In Mashdee's grocery, Salman asked for rice. "Good rice is hard to find these days. I hope, I'll have some soon."

Stories circulated about the SAVAK's tortures: bleeding welts on soles, metal beds with arm and ankle straps, electric shocks, and specially designed pliers to pull out nails. Salman now obsessively kept his hand on the pill in his pocket as he walked. Soon he even went to bed and woke up feeling for it through the fabric of the pouch as if his life depended on that little, blue capsule.

The day he was arrested, he had just stepped out of Mashdee's store with eggs and tomatoes for dinner. They had talked about this and that as Salman fixed Mashdee's fan that sat on the counter and refused to work faster than a windmill. Salman had his phase tester screwdriver clipped to his shirt pocket. That little screwdriver won 80 percent of his daily bread. He could cut wire with any knife and strip it with matchstick flame, but the phase-tester screwdriver was as indispensable as his thumb. Salman had known, since Mashdee never talked about rice, that the time to fight back had not come. When Salman was done with the fan, Mashdee plugged it in and turned it on—speed one—and the air blew away a newspaper from the counter. Salman did not accept the money Mashdee slid on the counter, and Mashdee said, in return, "Don't even think about it," when Salman fished coins out of his suit pocket to pay for the eggs and tomatoes. A bond more personal than that of a shared goal had started to form between him and the aged man.

Right outside of the shop a car pulled over. Holding a piece of paper in his hand, a man stuck his head out of the window and asked Salman if he could help him with the address. Salman had barely read the first words on the paper when he heard the back doors of the car open and felt someone grab his collar from behind. In a burst of force that erupted deep within, Salman managed to yank himself free and dodge the hands of the agent who had opened the front door and sprung out of the seat. Salman caught a glimpse of the holstered pistol under the agent's flapping jacket. He sprinted away on the sidewalk as fast as his legs could take him. He knew he could outrun them. At the same time, he was making the plan of his escape: he would dart across to the opposite sidewalk and run against the traffic. He could lose them in the serpentine streets and alleys he had come to know like the back of his hand. For a fraction of a second before he had crossed the street, Salman's mind wandered back to another sprinting years before through a thick fog toward his friend's house. Now he was running to save his own life exactly because of the friend he had dearly loved. He pitied himself.

Then Salman was rolling on the ground. For the rest of his life, and no matter how he tried to remember, he never learned that he had simply tripped on a piece of rock on the sidewalk. If there was a right time for the pill, it was then. First he did not realize what kept him from putting his hand into his pocket, but when he lifted his hand, he saw his forearm had snapped in the middle, as if he had grown an extra elbow. Where was the pain of the broken bones then? Why hadn't he heard the cracking of the radius? He tried to slide his left hand into his right pocket. The pill slipped out of his pinch a few times. Rolling onto his side to reach deeper, he saw the agents closing in. Sounds mixed in his head. His own panting, the approaching footsteps, the indistinguishable murmur of people crowding to watch the scene. The pill was between his thumb and forefinger. He paused for half a second. Less than that. Could he endure the pain and still live? Spend two, five, ten years behind the bars, but come out one day and walk in the fall again. He would eat ice cream. He would jump in the water. How painful could pain be? But they would not let him off the hook until he had given them all the information to arrest the others: Mashdee, Hooshang, Sara, even though she was not an active member anymore, others who he had never even met. Young boys and girls like him, who might have children of their own. What would happen to Ameer?

They would not let Salman off the hook. That was what he was most afraid of. The literal hook. Word was around about the hook house, a concrete room with no windows, down in the horrid mazes of some unknown building, where meat hooks dangled from the ceiling, reserved for the tight-lipped to contemplate on the upside down of the world with impaled ankles. That was it. He popped the pill into his mouth, but before he could swallow, they were on top of him. They turned him over. Two hands jerked his jaws open. A third reached into his mouth. Salman tried to swallow, but the fingers that slid down his throat made him retch. He tasted dust and iron and the pill came back out with greenish-yellow bile.

Once in the back of the car, Salman was blindfolded. He screamed as handcuffs made broken bone grate against broken bone. All along the ride, which seemed never-ending though he later found was very short, Salman repeated: "Not the hook, not the hook. His name is Mashdee. Not the hook."

KHAN HAD BEEN THERE, TOO, seen it all. With the accuracy of a mathematician, he had predicted the exact day the streets were going to explode. Pooran had blocked his way at the door the night before the tank went through the wall of the theater. The weight of the years was visible in the old man's face. Despite his efforts to shave his cheeks smooth, wax and twirl the ends of his gray mustache, and dress in a clean, pressed suit every day with his new Astrakhan, despite his evident hope to fight time, Khan had become what he had resisted his entire life: an old man. He walked slower and put more of his weight on his cane. The dull pains in his knees were now as real as the leaves of the trees in his garden, as certain as the dirt in the flower bed.

"You must get some rest sometime," Pooran said with a disappointed concern, knowing Khan would do what he had dressed up for. She stepped aside when Khan reached for the door with a smile for an answer. Like the rest of them, like Agha and Nosser, like her own Ahmad, in Khan's veins ran the secretive blood. But he had something the others lacked. An elegant charm that demanded respect, an equanimity that seeped even through anxiety and fear, even through absurdity. Sometimes Pooran felt that she had looked at Khan more as her own father than Nosser's, not just after she became a widow, but since the very day she met her father-in-law.

That night Khan positioned himself on the street that his charts showed would see the opening scene. The patrol Jeeps passed, but either did not see him or were not threatened by an old man dozing off on the steps of a red brick building, his cane across his lap. The stores opened like every day: first the bakeries, then the coffeehouses and lamb-brains shops. The grocers whispered the name of God as they drove their keys into the padlocks. A few hours after the sun was in the morning sky, people started gathering, first as passersby. A military bus arrived. Conscript soldiers jumped down and blocked traffic. The chanting began. Behind Khan, an old woman stepped out of the building and spread a piece of cloth on the step before she sat down.

"Is your grandson there, too?"

Khan shook his head.

"Mine is," she said, "God save him. God save them all."

Fists started to pump the air and the shop owners pulled down the blinds and put the padlocks back on. With the help of two other men, the woman's grandson held the ankle of a teenage boy and carried him, running, to an ambulance. On his way back, the grandson picked a rock from a sidewalk flower bed and hurled it through the window of the Iran National Bank branch on a corner. A Molotov cocktail followed and flames flew out like a genie. With their expected shrewdness, the street cats nimbly avoided stampeding crowds, crouching in the heart of things, the nooks and crannies that the city offered, not to men, but to them only. The when and where of these animals Khan had been able to answer for long now, but he could not yet solve the problem of how. It was then that a tank arrived. Khan and the old woman could not see it. They only heard the people running away, warning others with grating cries. Later that day, it would run through the wall of the theater.

The reinforcement had succeeded in dispersing the protesters, but Khan knew the second act was about to unfurl and he knew where. He had seen enough though. He clutched his lion and went back home. He did not hear Ahmad's speech the next day, but the grocer, the butcher, and the neighbors had things to say about it. The Prime Minister was changed in five days and the new cabinet was introduced to the parliament for a vote of confidence. All the sixteen ministers were voted in by a landslide majority. Among the hands that shot up was Ahmad's. The paper had arrived at his house from Great Zia the night before. The messenger boy had rung the bell and waited on his moped for Ahmad to nod his approval before throttling away. It was a simple list of the names of the ministers, and in front of each, a yes or a no.

The house was dark when Ahmad went home that night. Homa and the girls were already in bed. He did not turn the lights on, but sat in the low telephone bench and, as usual, called Mr. Zia, waiting for him to start. "The Great Zia thanks you for your vote today," he said after some pause. There was not much else to say. They had gotten what they wanted. "How is your family by the way?" Mr. Zia asked. That was not a question Ahmad could answer on the phone, and both men knew it, but Mr. Zia could not help asking. His question was not a real one, but a camouflage for another he meant to ask: "How is Leyla?"

Ahmad hung up. That night was the tenth in a row his mother had not called. Since Ahmad had been elected, Pooran listened to the live broadcast of the parliament sessions from beginning to end. In the evening, she would call to ask what he had voted. "The bill on the salary raise for nurses?" Ahmad would tap once on the receiver for a *yes*. "The one about the budget, the second one?" Ahmad would tap twice for a *no*. She had become a mother worrying about her boy's homework, just like those first nights in Tehran when she came back from being a maid in her own daughter's house and checked that Ahmad was sitting on the floor with his books and notebooks open before him.

Ahmad was at first relieved when she stopped calling, then saddened. The night after he voted the new cabinet in, he remained in the low chair after Mr. Zia said goodbye. He wiped the receiver with a piece of cloth. He untangled the twists of the cord and, with the same rag, dusted the table that did not need dusting. He flicked small pieces of things off of his pants. His mother did not call. The night was calm and warm. Light from the half-moon came in through the French door spreading over the rugs. His mother was the last person he thought could stop believing in him, and yet it had happened. Somewhere in the dark of that house, though, there were three people who were still with him. He still had them.

The ceiling fan lashed the air around the bedroom. In the faint light of the night lamp Homa sprawled on her back, head turned to one side, each limb flung out in its own direction. Ahmad crawled in and coiled himself as close to Homa as he could, and listened to her breathing until he fell asleep.

THE NEXT MORNING, HOMA WOKE up with a strange feeling that it was late. The clock showed twenty past eight, over an hour after she usually woke. Maybe she had forgotten to unlock the alarm. Then she realized that Ahmad was not at work, but lying beside her. His alarm had not gone off either; both had overslept on the same day. "Up, up, honey, it's late!" She shook Ahmad on the shoulder and sprang out of the bed to check on the girls. Ready in their school uniforms, Leyla sat in an armchair in the living room, hugging her bag, while Lalah hopscotched on an imaginary court on the rug. Leyla had prepared breakfast for both of them, dressed her sister, and sat down to wait. Homa was hurriedly getting ready when Ahmad stepped out of the room and motioned for them to stop, announcing that Wednesday was off. "What do you mean?" Homa asked, baffled, already standing at the door in her navy-blue dress and black pumps, with puffy eyes and barely combed hair. "The kids have school." But Ahmad was serious in his jovial good mood. They would later call the principal and explain, but they were going to spend the day together. Once the bewilderment of Ahmad's strange proposal turned into the acceptance of an unexpected holiday, it was not easy to make an excited Lalah wait. She quickly changed out of her school uniform into her favorite green dress and kept calling, "Is it time yet," while standing ready at the door.

Two hours later, the taxi pulled over by the side of the road and the family stepped out. To their left were high rocky hills and to their right trees spotting a green strip of land that stretched along a riverbank. Ahmad paid the driver and asked him to return late in the afternoon. They laid the blanket in the shade of the tree. Ahmad tied a strong rope to a bough. Homa folded a sheet into a seat and sat on the swing first. The girls took turns pushing her. They played tag. Lalah found a turtle and loaded its shell with three rocks. In the changing room Homa devised—holding up the sheet against her body—the girls changed into their swimming suits and ran for the stream. Leyla splashed Lalah and Ahmad. Lalah cut her toe and cried. They dried up as they ate lunch. Homa climbed a walnut tree, sat on a branch, and as she swung her legs, dared anyone to climb as high. The girls tried and failed to get a foothold on the tree. "Come on, girls!" she called down at them and then teased them more: "I thought you'd beat me. Oh, it's so beautiful up here." Ahmad sprang up and sat by Homa's side. The branch bent dangerously under the weight of the two adults who had arms around each other's shoulders. The girls looked up at the soles of their parents' dirty feet. In the afternoon, they waited by the roadside for the taxi. Cars zoomed past in both directions. Ahmad's glance shifted from his watch to the end of the road. Tired and bad-tempered, Lalah rested her head on her sister's chest. Leyla threw an arm around her. "We can try the passing cars," Homa said to Ahmad, touching him on the arm. She was tired, but happy. "Someone's bound to take us."

But then their taxi appeared far away in the bend of the road.

THE RIPS IN AHMAD'S RELATIONSHIP with the Great Zia's circle were mended. Before every parliamentary session, the messenger boy rode his moped to Ahmad's, rang the bell, and handed Ahmad the papers from the Great Zia. *They tell me what to say*, Ahmad wrote to Homa after dinner one night. *They tell me what to think. That's what they wanted from the beginning, a puppet who would raise his hand when they pull the string.* He threw the papers to the floor.

"This is their condition for their continued support," Mr. Zia said on the other end of the line each time they spoke. "I say we meet at your place this evening and talk about a few things," he suggested over and over again. Ahmad thought the reconciliation between himself and the uncle had been the doing of Mr. Zia. He also had noticed the shadow of the involuntary smile on the man's face when he had talked to Leyla that day in the hallway, and the way he touched his glasses as he did when he was nervous. Ahmad knew he could have been wrong, that he might have mistaken the shining astonishment Leyla kindled when she talked for a deeper passion. But he made sure they would not see each other again. With the pretext of confidentiality, he would ask Homa to take the kids to her mother's or Khan's house before Mr. Zia arrived. Meeting after meeting, Mr. Zia sat in his leather armchair waiting for that door to open. The common question of "how's your family?" brought forth a flash in Ahmad's eyes that told him *I suspect*. The first time he brought a box of candies, Mr. Zia placed it on the coffee table. "For the kids," he said. "A friend brought it from abroad. Best chocolate in the world. Well, I don't have children. This will be put to better use here."

A silence fell. Mr. Zia felt Ahmad's quiet spiraling up his throat and pressing on his windpipe.

On the next visit, Mr. Zia put his papers down on the table and bent his head low.

"I know you know," he said.

He took his glasses off and buried his face in his hands. It did not take long before a tear dropped from between his fingers. "I'm ashamed of it, but I can't help it." Mr. Zia did not know what to expect at that moment. He was ready for rage. If Ahmad beat him, he would take the blows and be kicked out of the house. He would not raise a hand. Deep down, he was even asking for it. For something. Silence and uncertainty weighed on his head as if his brain had turned into lead. The night coalesced behind the curtained French doors. At Ahmad's touch on his shoulders, Mr. Zia raised his head to the writing on the notepad: *Wait ten years.*

Mr. Zia sprang to his feet and straightened his suit and tie. "I will," he said as if standing at attention.

Ahmad wrote on the pad and held it before Mr. Zia. *Then if she wants you, you will have my blessings.*

Mr. Zia was not thinking how far in the future ten years was. The path had disappeared from before his eyes, leaving only the shiny end, the delicate, brilliant Leyla.

"Can I see her sometime? Once a month only?"

Ahmad shook his head. Something crumbled in Mr. Zia.

"What if she finds someone else? What if she forgets me?"

The few moments that it took Ahmad to pen down his sentence on his notepad was the longest period of Mr. Zia's life. He went back to his childhood, to his old age, to his happiness and despair, before he arrived in the living room in Tehran to the words, *I won't force anything on my daughter. This is your bet. Are you ready to wager?*

His eyes welled up and he nodded his head. Before he left, Mr. Zia wiped his face on the sleeve of his suit and put on his glasses.

21

NANA SHAMSI DIED a little into the winter that lasted for fifteen years. After the tank rode into the theater, a journalist was audacious enough to write—and the editor-in-chief too radical a critic of the regime not to publish—an article with a trenchant political bent against the regime that ended with a bleak paragraph:

> *The land that has seen the age-old hero, Rostam, defeat demons and enchain monsters in the heart of the mountains, the land that witnessed our today's national hero, our exiled Prime Minister, Mosaddegh, shackle the Brits and sever the hands of the Anglo-Persian Oil Company from our God-given natural resources, how can this land bear to witness so much oppression and injustice? I*

don't know. Will this soil ever bloom again? I don't know. Will the
life-giving warmth of spring thaw our frozen hearts one more time? I
doubt it. My heart testifies to the opposite: that it is worsening by the
day. I can feel it in my ancient joints: a long winter is on its way.

Nana Shamsi caught the pearl eyes and her sight declined rapidly. Pooran would take her to the doctor, but Nana said, "I have seen more than I would have wanted to." When the world became too blurry, she relied on the guidance of her granddaughter. With her trembling hand on Zeeba's shoulder, Nana walked across the yard and sat on a low stool by the front door to listen to the sounds of the world without seeing the faces that greeted her. When all light left her eyes, Pooran called in a doctor. Lying in her mattress, Nana Shamsi listened to the sound of the stranger and felt the fingers that pried open her eyelids. After a short pause, she heard the man's voice. "God giveth life and He taketh it away." She did not hear the rest of what the doctor said to Pooran before he stepped from the edge of the roof onto the planks that formed the floor of the elevator: "It's not just her eyes. She has no more life in her."

Shortly after the doctor's visit, the sounds began to go. She had thought she would fight to the very end. Now she was calm. Her skin was still there. The pressure of caresses, the weight of the quilt, the soft of the water going down her throat, she still had those. Warmth and cold, she had those. The weak vibrations in her throat when she said something, she had that. And the pain. She wished the pain would go, but then how else would she know she was still alive? That went on for some time. How long? Some time. Nana! Nana! Do you remember, Nana? What was your name? Raindrops on dry soil. What was your name, Nana? Do you remember the rocks? Where is my son? I knew Ahmad would not come. Name. Someone is waiting at the door. I want another kiss. Clouds, white and fluffy. I knew he would not come. Rain . . .

THE GAPING HOLE IN THE snow-covered graveyard—a dark rectangle in the flat sheet of whiteness—devoured the small, shrouded body. Dressed in heavy coats under black umbrellas, the family Nana Shamsi had lived with for so many years watched the shovelfuls of moist dirt spread over the white cloth. Two circles formed around the grave; Pooran, Zeeba, Khan, and Ahmad were the smaller one; the rest of the family together with a few of the neighbors stood behind them around Nana. Squatting in the snow and with a lantern by his feet, the Quran-reciter intoned in a sad, husky voice. Homa and Maryam consoled Pooran, keeping close to her, rubbing her shoulders and arms. Like a child, Agha clung onto the back of Majeed, his frail arms around the young man's neck. His blue coat flapped in the wind like a cape. Behind Majeed, Leyla and Lalah could see the tip of Agha's black tie hanging out from between his legs. Fall had only recently left them and they did not know the winter was there to stay.

Until the day they bulldozed the cemetery flat, Pooran visited Nana's grave every Thursday night. For fifteen years, she could not do the traditional washing with water and dousing of the gravestone with rose water because the water would freeze. She could only brush the snow aside to reveal the words in the stone:

Zinat ol-Moluk Shams-Abadi
Born 1254
Departed 1342

She would gouge the snow out of the carved words with the tip of her fingers, then dig a pebble from under the snow and knock on Nana's gravestone with it, as if on her door. Then she would whisper chapters from the Quran.

In the small backroom of the fabric shop, she sat on the thin mattress Seyf Zarrabi laid on the floor. He opened the fridge and gave her a bottle of Coca-Cola. She took a swig. "Tonight, you'll have to talk to me, Seyf." She lay down. "Talk Seyf, talk."

In the next hours, Pooran began to see some beauty in the way light reflected off of Seyf's bald scalp and in his awkwardly telling her stories of his childhood, not quite sure what Pooran wanted to hear. The sternness that Khan and all of his family had in their blood was absent from him. Seyf's days were full only of colorful bolts of fabric, of measuring, and cutting;

like fabric, he was see-through. Unlike Nosser. Nosser was an impenetrable soul. On the other side of Khan there was nothing to be seen with certainty. Pooran liked the way Seyf was not sure how to please her that night, bringing her a pillow, then a second, then deciding it was too high, a third thinner one. She liked the way he made tea and sour-cherry drink at the same time. It felt good to have a man struggling to make her happy. "Do you have another?" Pooran asked. Seyf wrapped his arms around her from behind and Pooran shivered as she held the cold bottle of Coca-Cola in her hands. "My boy came today," she said. "I didn't think he would." She could feel Seyf's breaths glide over her ear. "I don't know my boy anymore."

An hour before the call for morning prayer, Seyf pushed up the blinds from inside his shop and stepped out. Even at three in the morning, no matter how much Seyf insisted, Pooran would not let him walk her back home. "Not even a dog is out in this snow," Seyf would say. "You never know who's peeking behind the curtains," she answered. From the orange sky, flakes of snow drifted down softly onto the white blanket. In the assurance of snow, Pooran left the fabric shop. When she got home, she could not feel her toes.

BY THAT TIME AHMAD HAD built friendships with a number of influential figures in the government and parliament, the power near the center. He began to learn about the familial connections of the people in the sensitive positions and when toward the end of the calendar winter Ahmad's sister asked him to find Majeed a job, he was in a situation to help.

He is what, twenty-five?

"Just twenty, brother," Maryam said.

Just? . . .

As Lalah and Leyla circled around their aunt, Ahmad made a phone call, then sent a message. His condescending behavior, if not new to Maryam, was more evident, but she was always certain there was a heart in him more sympathetic than he showed. She wondered what was in his head. No doubt he was comparing her boy with himself when he was twenty. By that time, he had published a number of poems and worked in that forge. He was only thirty-two and he was in the parliament and all that he had done without speaking a word. Maryam's son had not even finished high school. He had wasted his life working in this and that shop, every time leaving after a few months until his father found him another. Maryam felt ashamed.

"He wants to really work this time," she said. "If he can find some clerical position, he will stick to it. He has promised me."

What does he want to be?

"Anything. He will stick to it. He will make his life with the money. And he wants to do poems, too. Just like you, brother."

The next day Majeed went to work at the Railways Company. They sent him to the support and maintenance department, office of evaluations. Although the trains were still running across the country, they had put work in the headquarters and administrative offices on a hiatus because of the snow. From the second week on, Majeed went to his office an hour before noon until two hours after lunch. At the cafeteria, and after complaining about the quality of the food, one of the people at his table asked him what his "line" was. Soon Majeed learned that a job at the Railways Company meant connections to the top brass. He found himself surrounded by a number of ambitious writers and poets, and one painter by the name of Shaapoor who said he had got there through his father's acquaintance with an army general, but behind his back, they said he was connected to SAVAK. The Railways Company was the place to make decent and steady money for little to no work.

With his first salary, Majeed rented a house with a large basement and put his reels in a corner against the wall. He had never gotten to finish the movie that the tank had interrupted. But first, there was much work to do. He dusted, wiped the floor and walls, and had the whole place painted. A few days later, he descended to the basement and tested the paint with the tip of his finger. It was dry. All that was left was the projection system. He found one secondhand at a shop near the Cannon Square. With the help of the lorry driver, he moved the projector and table in. He could not wait for that magical moment when he would flick the switch on and see the 5, 4, 3, 2, 1 on the white sheet. The machine whizzed to life and the bright rectangle appeared on the wall. The image was nothing compared to those in the real cinema; it was blurry and pale and there was no sound of course, but he sat in his short metal chair and watched from the beginning again reel after reel. Pinned to the thin sheet, Majeed's eyes followed the young man falling in love with the girl at the café and despairing at finding out that she already had a suitor of high financial and class standing. The young lover wandered the streets moping. Who was he? A nobody, just a nobody in love. What love added to him was not good for anything. And who was he to deprive the girl he loved of a bright future with another man? The man said goodbye to his love in the brisk dusk after a ride in a pedal boat shaped like a white swan.

"I need sound," Majeed said to the Railways guild of artists, as Shaapoor called the group of six that dined together at noon every day, "and a video camera. Maybe I'll make a film myself."

"Phenomenal!" said Shaapoor, the painter. He kept a trimmed beard and left his top two shirt buttons undone no matter how many jokes the other guys made about his chest hair curling out, which they called "wool." "Do you know photography? I have a camera. I'll bring it tomorrow. Cinema starts with photos just like literature starts with words."

"Just like painting starts with strokes," Short Poet said. He had received his nickname not because of his height, but because he wrote short poetry. "Just like every felt hat starts with strands of wool."

They laughed.

"No, of course not," Shaapoor objected, not minding the joke, "that's different. Painting is a continuum. It can't be broken up. I didn't expect to hear this from such an intellectual mind as yours."

"Watch out for that rat," Short Poet said to Majeed later after Shaapoor left.

The first thing Majeed recorded with the camera was the snowy New Year. White spring was not without precedent in the memory of parents and grandparents. Majeed's own father remembered the year in his childhood village when an unexpected cold froze the water in the hoez and the goldfish in the bowl out on the veranda. His mother remembered Uncle Ahmad digging tunnels in the snow with his friends, shortly before one New Year. Khan had a handful of cold spring memories in his mind and Agha was not surprised at all. One year the cold had not left until one month into the spring. He did not remember when it was, except that the king had traveled to Europe for the first time.

"And I still had some hair then," Agha said smiling.

TOWARD THE MIDDLE OF THE last summer before the snow, the gofer brought Mr. Zia a message. He opened the envelope right at the door as usual. While the red moped idled on its centerstand, the boy waited for a reply. Trying not to look at Mr. Zia too brazenly in the face, he played with his cap in his hands and threw furtive glances at the man so he would be ready when spoken to. He knew the letter contained something important when Mr. Zia's eyes opened in surprise behind his glasses. The man suddenly felt a confusing urgency. For a few seconds, he did not know what to do. He read the note again, then put it in his breast pocket and closed the door. The gofer shrugged to himself with raised eyebrows, then pushed his moped off of the centerstand and got on, but Mr. Zia opened the door again. "Thanks," he said, handing the boy his tip. The boy shoved the bill into his pocket without looking at it out of reverence, then throttled away. When he turned onto the main street, he took out the money. It was the biggest tip Mr. Zia had ever given him. The bluish bill fluttered in the wind. The boy kissed it and shoved it into his pants pocket.

Mr. Zia shaved and took a shower, then got as close to the mirror as he could with a fine pair of scissors and made sure there was not a single extra hair sticking out of his nose or ears. He combed his hair and eyebrows and decided on brown for his suit and cream for his shirt. He paced his room for an hour until he could not stand the wait anymore.

He arrived at the park half an hour early. All the way he had thought of the day he had cried in front of Ahmad. Sitting on a bench, he craned nervously lest he miss them. Off of his temples he wiped sweat that was not from the summer heat. When he saw them coming, he sprang to his feet and hid behind a tree. Hand in hand with her father, Leyla traipsed in the dappled shade of the trees that lined the pathway, a dead ringer for her father and a completely different person at the same time. If there was anything childlike in her, it was her stature and the bright yellow of her skirt and the small red bows on her hair. The father and daughter walked slowly to the empty playground. Leyla touched the slide and swing and withdrew her hand quickly. They sat on a bench in the shade and talked, one gesticulating, mouthing, and writing in his damn notepad, the other serene, saying things that Mr. Zia knew would be nothing but perfect words of intelligence and sweetness at the same time. Later, after they were gone, after he had followed them for only a few steps and watched her saunter away, almost hovering as if on clouds, Mr. Zia looked at his watch and could not believe an hour and a half had passed.

From then on, Leyla would ask her father to take her to the park on the weekend and look for an opportunity to call the message boy and give him the message. She would spot Mr. Zia at a distance, at times with sunglasses, at others with a hat, coat, and scarf, and on other days with wool gloves, his breath clouding before him. She would throw him an acknowledging look and a fleeting smile, then turn to her father and prolong the stay as long as she could.

When the two men met, Ahmad could feel the tension under Mr. Zia's skin, the surge of words blocked at the last moment before leaving his mouth, congealing on his lips. In his head, Ahmad lauded the man's composure. The facade of indifference Mr. Zia raised, in spite of the ten years Ahmad had put in front of him, was impenetrable except to Ahmad who saw the thousands of entreaties quivering in his eyes. Those, he decided, were the signs of true love. Unaware of his own daughter's plots behind his back, he thought he had protected Leyla by leaving Mr. Zia to the vulnerability of love.

"Is there anything else I can do but wait?" was all Mr. Zia could muster the courage to ask, and he felt the authority that Ahmad exuded when he shook his head no. Among the naked bushes of rose, they walked for some time without a word. "We're diverging," Mr. Zia said. "We had the illusion we were going to the same place, but I got sidetracked by a nine-year-old girl and you by your own hubris. This is a slippery road, Ahmad. Don't run so fast you can't keep yourself upright." Ahmad stopped and wrote in his pad.

Are you threatening me? Mr. Zia put his hand on Ahmad's shoulder. "I'm bound to you. There is nothing I can do and you know that. If there is one person who wants you well, it's me." Ahmad took Mr. Zia's hand from his shoulder. *I think we should end our relations,* Ahmad wrote. *It's in everyone's interest.*

That evening Ahmad pulled open the top desk drawer in which Homa had put his poetry. All of it was there: copies of his three books, his poems clipped out of magazines, as well as all the drafts of unfinished works. She had wrapped them in thick, brown paper. Light shot out from the stack when he unwrapped the bundle. He flipped through those early writings and saw himself young and raw, his poems dull and dark. He still remembered the first one that had faintly shone. As he leafed through, the poems brightened. Then, with a sweep of his hand, he brushed everything back into the drawer, took out a pen, turned off the light, and started to write poetry again. The words he put on the paper glowed, though faintly, still as reassuringly real as the paper they appeared on. He had not lost it. He crossed out the lines that faded for new ones that made the poem shine until he had to squint at the paper. It was a game of light and dark. At that moment the door opened and Homa came in with the girls. Standing by the desk, the kids watched, mesmerized by the light that shot from the paper onto their father's face. Homa jumped up and down on the bed before she let herself flop down. She spoke nonstop for an hour. "Are you starting a new book? This one will be even better than the other ones." Lying on her side, she propped up her head on her palm. "When the New Year comes, we should take a trip. No, two trips: one with the four of us, and one with my family. And this time you're coming too." She said they had to go skiing before the winter ended. And she told Ahmad what she had planned to do in a few years when the girls would be a little older. "I'm going to go to university." She had contemplated it through and penned down her long-term plan. "I can't be a housewife my whole life." In the course of two or three years, she would decide what she wanted to study and prepare to take the entrance exam. Ahmad smiled and nodded. "And I can't wait to read your new poems to my parents."

In the middle of the night, Homa woke up feeling the sun had come up too early, then she saw Ahmad hunching over his desk, working, the shadow of his head stretching across the ceiling like a dark ghoul looming behind him. Ahmad turned his head, eyes half-closed, smiled at her, and turned back to his work. For five days and nights, Ahmad did not leave his desk and Homa slept in the girls' room. He slipped each full sheet into the drawer, rubbed his eyes, and took out a new piece. The first day, Homa brought in food and water and took back the cold, untouched plate from Ahmad's desk. He would not answer, as if he could not hear her. "You'll go blind," she said shaking him on the shoulder. She tried to pull him out of his chair, but with a swing of his strong, blacksmith's arm Ahmad brushed her off like a bull's tail a fly.

On the fifth day Ahmad was writing around dark-red spots on the page that, to his eyes, were ink black. When she opened the door and saw the red streaks on Ahmad's cheeks, Homa screamed and ran to the phone.

The two days Ahmad spent at the hospital were filled with visits, short and unidirectional, from politicians of both sides, the progovernment and the factions critiquing the Shah. Mr. Zia came the first day.

"Listen to me, Ahmad," Mr. Zia said, "I have some bad news for you. The New Iran Party will withdraw their support for you. My uncle won't do much either. I don't know why. Either they think they can't get what they want or something else is going on." He looked at Ahmad's long face, a week-long beard on his cheeks, still on the white pillow, tilted up toward the ceiling with the white squares of bandage over his eyes. "Do you hear me?" Ahmad's light nod was free of consternation. "I keep trying to get to the bottom of this. I promise I'll do whatever I can for you. Even if you don't want it, you can always count on my friendship. I promise you won't see me anymore."

In the dark, Ahmad listened to ten or fifteen voices one by one, on his left and right. To some he could not attach a face. One such voice was the deputy of the Ministry of Publications and Information who offered him a position. Ahmad listened in silence. "I am familiar with your literary endeavors. This is government, Mr. Torkash-Vand. This is where you can fly, if you already have wings that is, and I know for a fact that you do." A sad, white light shone into the room from the blanket of snow that covered the flat roofs and the tops of walls outside. On a parked car, cat footprints drew a line from the roof to the hood, continued on the ground, and faded out in the snow over a flower bed. The deputy minister left his number on Ahmad's bed. Some time passed in silence. Ahmad wished he could see the snow. He listened to the sounds of the hospital: the clicking of shoes on the hard floors echoing along corridors, indistinct words spoken by indistinguishable people, and the irregular moans of someone in pain. He created the world of the hospital in his head: the nurses in white uniforms with white hats; doctors with longer uniforms and polished shoes; metal beds with clean, white sheets; a medicine cabinet somewhere full of bottles and vials; a little girl in the waiting area whose high fever was melting the metal chair she was sitting on; the smell of formaldehyde; a faint whiff of stale flowers somewhere; and suddenly a familiar smell that was alien for a second. It was the smell of apples and fresh soil and new shoes. It was the smell of his mother, then the smell of her hands that ran on his face and in his hair and shortly after, another smell: Khan's. But Agha's smell was absent. *Where is Agha?* Ahmad mouthed. Is he okay?

Pooran looked at Khan, not sure what to answer. "He's home, son," Khan said, laying a hand on Ahmad's hand. "They don't allow wheelbarrows in here."

At the end of the visiting hours, all the sounds and smells left but Pooran's, which stayed through the night.

IN THE MIDST OF HIS darkness on the second day, Ahmad heard high-heeled footsteps enter the room. Then came the rustle of a bouquet of flowers before he felt the weight of it beside him on the bed. Their smell camouflaged the strangely familiar scent of the woman barely recognizable under the perfume she wore. Ahmad turned his anticipating head toward her. "I haven't heard from my brother in eight months." It was Sara. "I fear they might have caught him. I wouldn't have come to you if I had anywhere else to go. Ahmad, you know Salman, he's not as strong as he makes himself seem. Can you put in a word? Ahmad, my father can't take it anymore." Ahmad groped for his pen and pad on the table by his bed, scribbled blindly, and handed the pad to Sara. The disarray of crooked words still had some beauty to it. *How is Ameer?*

"He's good."

Just good?

"He's taken after his uncle. We've got to make sure he won't do anything stupid, me and his father. He does things, I guess, that he hides from me."

Ahmad wrote on the pad with force. *Who's his father?* He waited for an answer. None came. He waved the pad in the air where he thought Sara's face was, but she stayed silent. He scribbled again.

I want to see him. When they open my eyes.

"I'll try to manage it." Ahmad heard the rustling of a tissue. "I should go now. He's waiting. Will you help me?"

Ahmad sat up in his bed. He wrote.

Ameer is here?

"Yes. He drove me."

Ahmad gesticulated to Sara before he realized he had to write. *Bring him in.*

When Sara went out, Ahmad combed his hair with his hand and pulled at what he had on to straighten any crinkles that might be there. His mind traveled back to the night in Sara's house where he went for Raana, that faraway girl. He heard the footsteps and Sara's voice almost at the same time. "This is Mr. Torkash-Vand, your uncle's friend." The emphasis on "your uncle's friend" was without a delay and unmistakable. Ahmad turned his face toward the sound. He could feel the presence of two people; the rustling of clothes was audible, their mere gravity palpable. "They were friends since childhood."

She did not say "we." She hid from her son what she had boldly talked about in front of her husband that day in her house. Ahmad heard what might have been a shifting of weight from one foot to the other.

"It's good to meet you, sir." The first time Ahmad had seen him, Ameer was the calm little boy who had held his Uncle Salman's hand at the door while shooting curious looks into the forge. Ahmad touched his temples, picked at the edge of the tape that held the white gauze over his eyes, and ripped them off. Sara stifled a faint cry. Ahmad's skin burned. Light invaded his closed eyes. The back of his head throbbed. He pressed his eyelids together and squinted to blurry patches of color. Two figures stood before him. One was a woman, but the other was not a boy. He was almost as tall as Sara. That could not be Ameer. "This is bad for your eyes," Sara said. "Close your eyes." Sara, that baffling woman, had thrown him off again. That could not have been Ameer. Within a short moment, the nebulous picture evolved into detailed reality. The boy was not a boy. He was a man, with a beard and a black mustache in sharp contrast with his white, soft skin, standing with one hand in his pocket, the other nonchalantly swinging a blue cap. "Close your eyes, please." When he could make out the details of the faces, Ahmad saw consternation on Sara's and disinterest in the young man's. He looked for his pen and pad, but Sara intervened. "Mr. Torkash-Vand, this *is* Ameer." She looked at Ahmad as if secretly confessing to a wrong they both shared the blame for. The twelve-year-old boy looked twenty and Sara knew that.

"What's wrong?" Ameer asked, turning to Sara, a suspicious look on his face.

"Nothing," Sara said.

"He knows me?"

"No, honey," Sara said, "that's not what this is about."

"It's about the beard again?"

"No, Mr. Torkash-Vand's eyes aren't used to the light yet."

Ahmad looked at them for a little while.

"I know what this is all about," Ameer said. "Yes, I have a beard, so what?" He stormed out of the room and left the door half-open.

Ahmad picked up the gauze and put it back on his eyes—rolled at the edges, the tape would not stick well—and ran his fingers over them with extra pressure as he turned his back to Sara, lying on his side and pulling the blanket over him.

"He's just a bit precocious, but nothing's wrong with him." Sara took a step toward the bed. "Please help me find Salman. He always looked up to you." Ahmad did not move. He felt the bed depress under the weight of Sara. "Remember that Russian officer, Sergey?" Sara said, her voice near now. "You remember how my father dragged me out of the Orchard after people started gossiping about me and the Russian, don't you? I don't know if you know, but they talked about Khan and you, too. People talked about me and you alone in your room. But even then, when Salman was mad at you, he never spoke ill of you." Ahmad listened in his darkness.

"Please help me find him, Ahmad." He heard her get up from the bed, put her coat back on, and slide the strap of her bag over her shoulder. "And the boy is really okay, Ahmad," she said after a little pause. "He's just tired of the stares. He's all I have." Ahmad heard her heels tick away toward the door. Then the hinges squeaked, and, behind the closed door, the clicking receded into silence.

Homa came after visiting hours with a bowl of Ahmad's favorite soup. *Have my phonebook with you?* Ahmad wrote. "No. Why?" *Can you get it tomorrow? And messenger boy?* "I'm not letting you open your eyes," Homa said. "Work can wait." *It can't. Short messages. Will write eyes closed.*

In the dead of night, while Homa snored in her chair, Ahmad lay awake with his bandaged eyes closed thinking about Ameer.

22

NO ONE KNEW HOW THE REVOLUTION BEGAN. Years later, long after the Shah had flown away and throngs of revolutionaries celebrated in the streets of Tehran, everyone searched their minds to find an event that marked the beginning. To the many religious, the day the tank rode into the cinema, Black Thursday, was the tipping point. The leftists went back to the incident a few years earlier when a group of armed Fadaee Guerillas attacked the Siahkal post by the Caspian Sea and killed three gendarmes with machine guns and hand grenades to free an arrested comrade. To Khan, it was always the cats.

By Black Thursday, Khan no longer harbored any doubt that the people in the streets, the leftists, the parliament, the government, the army, were all being driven by feline plots, but were gullible enough to believe themselves effective players in the game. He had improved his techniques when he found medieval mystic literature on the behaviors of animals and animates, and the calculations regarding good and evil. After Sergey's death, he removed the partitioning curtain, emptied the basement of the cages, the vice, and the trash and turned the space into a small library. Shuffling heavily, he would bend one painful knee after the other down the four steps to the door that he no longer kept locked. With a shaky hand he leafed through the yellowed pages as he wheezed in the musty air.

In the afternoon, he took his agate worry beads and walked the neighborhood, said hi to the baker, the grocer, the butcher, and the fabric seller, Seyf Zarrabi. He would chat with the shop owners for as long as they could, until a customer walked in or the phone rang, or until Khan felt he had stayed too long. On his way, he passed a bead under his thumb whenever he saw a cat, and when back in his basement, penciled down the headcount in his tables. His calculations reached perfection with Avicenna's *Remarks and Admonitions*. By fusing empirical methods with the philosophies of the tenth-century thinker, he drew new maps and made projections and eventually took his pencil in his old hand and wrote on his paper: February 11, 1979.

He grabbed his walking stick and stepped out of the basement. The hoez that they had drained for the winter was now full of snow. Majeed had stopped by in the morning to shovel open walkways in the yard: one from the front door to the house, one to Agha's room, another to the basement. In spite of Pooran's concern that he might be late for work, Majeed cranked his way up the elevator and shoveled the portion of the roof in front of Zeeba's room where she now lived alone. He had piled the snow in the hoez and taken pictures of it with his camera before he left.

The snow had stopped now. Sitting on his chair, Agha was looking out of his window. Inside his room, a gas heater glowed red high on the wall, out of the old man's reach.

"I found something new," Khan said. "There will be a revolution."

"Oh yeah?" Agha said without turning his face away from the window. "When?"

"1979."

Agha breathed on the window and wrote the number onto the fogged-up glass. "What's now?"

"1964."

Agha wrote the second number under the first and counted on his fingers. Then he turned to Khan. "Khan."

"Yes."

"You know how I told you we're not going to die, me and you, and Ahmad?" Khan nodded. "I thought a lot about it. And it's going to be all right." Then he remained silent for a little while still looking out. "You know what," he said, "I don't remember the last time I made a snowman."

"You made me one when I was little."

Agha nodded as if reliving the memory in his head. "I want to play."

"You'll catch a cold."

"So what if I do?"

You will die, Khan wanted to say. But he did not. After a long moment, he nodded and Agha's eyes grew big and his face opened with excitement. But when Khan said they had to wait for Pooran to come back and push his wheelbarrow, the sadness in Agha's face hung so heavy that Khan got him dressed: wool long johns and socks, a sweater and a coat, a scarf, knit hat and gloves. Agha hooked his arm around Khan and came down from his chair. He took no more than two steps before he had to stop. Khan was too weak to carry even Agha's disappearing frame. Holding the handle of his walking stick tight in his hand, thumb on the lion, Khan had to let Agha sink onto the floor. Agha crawled to the door and waited until Khan came back from the kitchen with the big tin tray. On the thin layer of snow that had fallen in the walkways since morning, Khan pushed Agha from his door to the area between the hoez and flower bed where the snow was untouched. Sitting in his tray, Agha ruffled the snow with his hands and started to make a small snowman. Khan leaned on his cane and watched him fashion what ended up being little more than a distorted protrusion of compressed snow. When the snowman was done, Agha turned around and threw a snowball at Khan. Both men smiled. Khan dusted the snow from his knee. A second snowball flew past him. "Stop it," Khan said, but a third hit him in the chest. "I said stop it." Agha laughed and then, with the obstinacy of a five-year-old boy, scooped up more snow. Life had sprouted back in his ancient body. Khan stepped back, but the shot got him right in the face. The cold burned his skin. He brushed it from his white mustache. Agha was laughing harder, leaning forward and blowing out clouds. Khan bent down and dug into the snow, but before he could ball up what he had taken, Agha attacked again. Khan raised his hand to throw his snowball, but suddenly froze in place. He received two or three more shots from Agha, but did not seem to mind. He did not remember having seen Agha as happy as he was now. Where had the old man found the force to throw snowballs so hard?

"I'll be back," Khan said hurrying into the house. He picked up the phone and called the doctor. A quarter of an hour passed before the bell rang. Agha was still playing when Khan opened the front door to the fedoraed, big-nosed man holding a brown leather bag in his hand. Standing tall over him in his trench coat, the doctor observed Agha in the large tray, happy in his warm clothes.

"Hello, Doctor?" Agha stretched his hand.

"How are you feeling today?" the doctor asked, shaking Agha's hand, careful not to break the bones.

"Superb. I had forgotten what this was like."

The certainty in Agha's answer did not reassure the man. "Are you feeling any pain?" Agha shook his head. "Anywhere?" The tone of the question made Agha stop fidgeting. The joyous glow in his face faded as he looked up, intently shaking his head. The doctor put his bag down in the snow. "It's okay, Agha," he said as he knelt down. "Just give me your hand."

Khan took a step forward and watched the doctor push up Agha's sleeve and take his pulse. A few seconds passed. The doctor moved the tips of his fingers ever slightly on Agha's wrist and looked up as if he were trying to see a bird that soared high up in the clouds. Finally, he straightened Agha's sleeve and tucked it back into the glove. Then he got to his feet.

"Doctor?" Khan asked.

"I'm sorry, Khan." He picked up his bag. "He giveth life and He taketh it away." He tipped his hat. "Give my condolences to Pooran Khanum."

The doctor left without brushing off the snow from his knees or the bottom of his brown bag. In the tin tray, Agha sat smaller than ever, his head bowed. Khan knelt down with difficulty. A tear dropped from Agha's face onto the front of his coat. "Khan, I'm dead?" His voice was a high-pitched whisper. Khan put his hand on Agha's shoulder. "You are more than alive to me." Pain howled in Khan's left knee like a wounded boar. Gingerly, he sat himself in the empty half of the tray, the two men's legs stretched out over the edge, their heels pressed into the snow. Agha sniffed and wiped his nose with the sleeve of his coat. "This was not supposed to happen." Agha rested his head on Khan's arm. Scattered flakes started to come down softly. Khan put his arm around Agha's small figure and pulled him close.

When Pooran opened the door, the first thing she saw was the two old men sitting in a tray in the yard, the younger holding the older like a father and his son. What Khan told her about how Agha wanted to play in the snow was at odds with the paleness she saw on the small man's face, with his leaden look and downcast eyes. After helping Khan up, she took Agha to his room and brought him hot, herbal tea. Agha's silence was nothing new to her. The refusal to communicate, which she saw as hereditary in the family, left no question or suspicion in her, but only a familiar frustration. The day they went to visit Ahmad in the hospital, when Ahmad asked "is he okay?" she had thrown a sideways look at Khan knowing that Ahmad could not see. Before they left, Khan took advantage of a short time Pooran left the room and whispered his prognostication into Ahmad's ear: "A revolution. In fifteen years."

Will it succeed? Ahmad wrote.

"That's not something I can tell, but the cats are doing their best."

Pooran came back into the room with a big glass of carrot juice in her hand, the traditional remedy for eye maladies. The next night, when Homa slept in the chair beside Ahmad's bed, Pooran put on her olive dress and draped her chador over her head. She sneaked out of the house and stood, twenty minutes later, in the shadows in front of Seyf Zarrabi's shop. Of all the feeble street lights, only the one across from the fabric shop had a broken bulb hanging on a wire. Seyf had flung a piece of stone at it. City officials had replaced it twice but each time Seyf had hurled another rock. Pooran had noticed the patch of dark Seyf had made for her. The blinds were half up. Pooran turned the handle and went in. In the back room, the mattress was already laid. Seyf Zarrabi propped up Pooran's drenched shoes against the oil tank of the Aladdin heater, warmed her cold feet, and smiled at her.

"If you were sick and I brought you carrot juice," Pooran asked, "would you drink it?"

"I'd drink hemlock out of your hands." He planted kisses on her shins one after the other. Then he looked back into her eyes and said, "Be my wife."

Pooran shook her head. "I can't marry."

"You can do whatever you want, dear."

"What would Nosser say?"

Seyf drew himself closer to Pooran. "Nosser is with God now, sweetheart," he said, his face before Pooran's, his lips ready to pout in demand of a kiss.

"Oh, Seyf," Pooran said, not being able to make the fabric seller understand what he would never know. She kissed him, lay on her back, and looked at the yellow light from the bulb hanging from the ceiling reflecting on the glossy scalp of Seyf's bald head.

WHEN THEY BROUGHT SALMAN IN, he saw a new interrogator behind the desk, not much older than himself, rolling his pen between his thumb and forefinger. He had matched his navy-blue tie with his suit. His smart eyes behind the horn-rimmed glasses were the kind Salman had learned during his months in the prison to be the most dangerous: calm and unpredictable. As always, a file was before him.

"Hello," the man said as soon as Salman was seated, his hands cuffed behind his back. "You are now going to tell me about your relationship with a man called Ahmad Torkash-Vand. He is secretly looking for you." With drooping eyes, Salman talked for half an hour of games as innocent boys at the foot of the Alborz mountains in their village of Tajrish, all about Khan, the Orchard, the family's move to Tehran and his irregular contact with Ahmad as a former friend and messenger to his sister. The interrogator listened with a shadow of a smile. When Salman was finished, he paused for a moment and said, "Thank you," and the way he said it, calm and free of emotions, told Salman that he would have to tell those same things again and again.

Two hours later, he was tied to a metal table, shrieking as each blow of the cable left a new bloody line on the soles of his feet. He had been right about the interrogator's type: untrusting, clinical, believing there was always more to wrench out of a man. When the pain in his soles stung so hard that Salman was once again certain that a just God could not exist in this world, the investigator stepped into the torture room and watched a few of the strikes before he nodded to the flogger and left. The flogger untied Salman and helped him sit up. Salman hooked his arm around the man's neck and set his throbbing soles on the cold terrazzo tiles, hobbling out of the room, sharing his weight with his torturer, leaving a trail of bloody footprints behind him along a dimly lit corridor with closed doors, back into the investigation room.

It was like reliving the same scene: the man was sitting at the same place waiting for Salman with the same file before him, rolling his pen between his thumb and forefinger. The click of the cuffs on Salman's wrists echoed in the room. The flogger left. "Now," the interrogator said, "you are going to tell me all that you didn't tell me before." His voice was calm, the look on his face friendly. Salman could not keep his eyes from tearing up. He bowed his head. Rage boiled up somewhere deep within him, but found no way into his tired heart. He talked about the apple buds turning the whole Orchard into a pink paradise and how they went all white like small puffs of clouds floating very close to the ground giving off a dizzying smell that made you want to run. He talked about the Russian that Khan brought to the village, who had an eye for Salman's sister. He told how Ahmad took his sister into his room. Then the Russian took Sara into his room and fed her, the village said, pig's meat and vodka. And Salman did not talk to Ahmad for a long time.

Ahmad moved to Tehran and a few years later Salman did too—"just like I said before"—when he was already a member of the party. He was curious about his friend, so he found Ahmad and stalked him for a few days. After a while Ahmad disappeared. Salman found him again and followed him some more. Then Ahmad disappeared once more, because he got into a fight with his grandfather over a girl named Raana and left his home. All those things Salman had found out later, a few years after he had left the Tudeh Party and worked with groups that would not refrain from pulling the trigger. He told the interrogator about his visit to Ahmad's place some years after when Leyla was born. He had bought the baby red shoes with small Velcro straps.

"Is that all?" the interrogator asked after Salman was finished. For a few moments Salman plowed into the corners of his memory to find anything unsaid about Ahmad. Then he nodded his head and his bound hands started trembling from the thought of what the interrogator might do next. The man got to his feet and buttoned his suit. "Thank you," he said and left the room. Soon the flogger came in. Salman looked for a blindfold in his hands, but the man was empty-handed. That meant he was not going to his cell, but back to the torture room. With the help of the big man, Salman stepped into the short corridor in the opposite direction which the dried blood of his footprints pointed to.

In the torture room, a previous agent, whose arm swings Salman recognized, was mopping the floor. He paused and threw a disgusted look at Salman. Later, Salman learned the interrogator was very meticulous about the cleanliness of the room and corridors. He had ordered "diligence and cleanliness, diligence in cleanliness." Salman's hands were opened. As the man put the handcuffs on a small metal table, Salman stood wondering what it would be this time: the cage, the box, the table, the chair, or the bed. From his metal table, the man took the jug of water and gave the big block of ice in it a swirl before he poured himself some. With the glass to his lips, he looked at Salman and pointed to the table. It was the sole flogging again. Salman sat himself on the table, relieved to get his weight off his feet. He lay down in position, hands where they would be cuffed to the legs of the table, feet where they would be secured with leather straps. The man put the glass down, rolled up his sleeves, and came to the table. He knelt down to put Salman's wrist in the cuff that was permanently attached to the leg of the table. Salman's hand shook violently. The man held it in his hand for a few warm and calm seconds. Then he put the metal around the bruised wrist. The fluorescent light buzzed on the plastered wall.

A FLUORESCENT LIGHT ALSO BUZZED on the plastered wall of Agha's room all night. He had not slept since the day the doctor pronounced him dead. Shortly after the sunset, Khan went to him, the backgammon set under his arm. Agha would not play. Khan sat on the edge of the bed where Agha curled up. "But when did I die, Khan?" he asked. Together, they ruminated on their memories of the crucial incidents in Agha's life. Khan remembered talking to Agha after he pulled the old man out of the hoez water. The night Agha hanged himself, Khan, with the help of Nana Shamsi, had cut the rope first from the ceiling, then from around his neck before laying him on the floor. Agha had taken the glass of water from Nana Shamsi and tried to drink, although he had not been able to. But he had smiled at her. Back they went into Agha's life, but no matter how far they went, they could not find a decisive date. Not long before dawn, Khan lay down on the bed and went to sleep, but Agha sat up awake. If there was one day on which he had died, it was the day a merchant from the city came to his village and took the love of his life as his wife. From the distant wheat field, he had watched her leave on a white horse followed by the people of the village. Agha took his old machete from the corner of the basement, scrubbed it clean, and was sharpening it on the whetstone when his friends came to him to assuage his anger and break the painful news that the merchant's arrangements had met the bride's consent, if not willingness. That night, the young Agha left his village taking only his machete with him for the bandits.

Agha looked out of his window until the sun was in the sky, behind the clouds.

23

AHMAD CAME BACK HOME from the hospital with gauze to remain on his eyes for an extra week, with the feeling that he really had a family that he wanted to be with. It was a few weeks before the New Year, although nobody yet knew they would not have spring for years to come. The girls left for school early in the morning. The little he could do to help with closed eyes, Ahmad would do: he crushed saffron in a small mortar, careful not to waste a speck of the valuable spice; he winnowed beans, lentils, and chickpeas and because he could not pick out the small pebbles, chaff, and husk from the grains, he did the reverse thing: feeling each one individually, he threw the grains one by one into a separate container. Sitting at the dining table with a pile of herbs in front of him, he picked the leaves and put them in a basket, one stem at a time. Homa did the rest: she washed, diced, sautéed, added pinches of spice into the pot like an alchemist, put the lid on, and lowered the flame.

By early afternoon, when the sisters came home from school, the smell of food wafted from the stove across the house. Excited, the girls talked to Ahmad about their day at school, their grades, what a classmate had done, and what their teacher had taught them. Ahmad helped with schoolwork. With the grace of a young lady, Leyla sat on the couch in the living room, one eye on her book and the other on her father as he explained math and science to Lalah. In the evening, the heater warmed the house in the corner of the living room, while it snowed outside. Ahmad listened to the radio. The tension between the clergy and the Shah had been rising. In their public sermons, some notable figures had asked for the freedom of Ayatollah Khomeini who had been put under house arrest nine months before.

Like every year, people cleaned up their houses from ceiling to floor, scoured the walls, scrubbed the kitchens, dusted the furniture, and wiped all the windows. They postponed washing the rugs until summer, which they thought would come in three months. The traditional Haft Seen tables were set for the New Year: nice mirrors were put on them; wheat sprouts were grown in low bowls and ribbons were tied around the stems; and goldfish were placed in bowls. The older bought presents for the younger; some placed brand-new bills inside the Quran to offer as their New Year present, others just fished the money out of their pockets. Shortly before the turn of the year, and dressed in their best clothes, Ahmad and Homa sat at their Haft Seen table with their daughters on their laps, looking at one another in the big mirror flanked by two candles. The goldfish circled in the bowl. The countdown had already started on the radio. In Khan's house, the traditional assemblage was laid not on a table, but on the floor. Agha, Khan, Pooran, and Zeeba looked into their mirror waiting for the moment. Ameer had worn a suit and tie to the New Year Haft Seen. He sat in front of an oval mirror with Sara and Salar. Majeed took photos of his family. Salman and his three cellmates propped up against the wall a tray that did not reflect anything.

A few hours after the turn of the year was announced on the radio with the sound of a cannon fire followed by upbeat music, everyone gathered in Khan's house to pay the elders the New Year visit. In a big basket, fruit came out of the kitchen into the guest room. Nuts were piled in bowls. Cups of steaming tea on saucers passed hands. The children played in the snow in the yard. Pooran moved from the kitchen to the guest room as if she was eighteen again. The kids stood in a row to receive their New Year presents from Khan who kissed them each and handed them an envelope which they opened with excitement to count the money. Embarrassed to confess his death, Agha put on a happy face and feigned life. He did not want to ruin the ceremony. He beat both Majeed and his father at backgammon. Watching him challenge the youth, Khan thought that never in a million years would he have guessed the old man was no longer around.

AT HOMA'S PARENTS' VILLA ON the shores of the Caspian Sea, Colonel Delldaar opened a bottle of his homemade vodka and talked about his plans to make a pool in the garden whose water would come right from the sea. Weeks had passed since the doctor had taken the bandages off of Ahmad's eyes, and now, with his good, wary vision, Ahmad watched Colonel's every action and facial expression closely, careful not to say something he should not. Colonel asked Ahmad about his plans for the upcoming parliamentary elections. The New Iran Party's move toward new faces, although subtle, was neither imperceptible nor unpredictable. Ahmad had started as a voice of the opposition, but had flitted around, distancing himself from his home base, trying to get closer to the conservatives. In the roofed gazebo, Ahmad put coals in the brazier and smacked them level with the back of the coal shovel. Out of a big steel bowl, Colonel Delldaar took marinated chicken wings and impaled them with skewers. "Promisc . . . What's the word? Jumping from one thing to another might work with poetry," said the colonel taking another wing, drenched in orange marinade, out of the bowl, "but certainly not with politics." When the coals were glowing red, Ahmad put the wings on the brazier. *It doesn't matter, Col*, Ahmad wrote in his notepad. *It will be if it's meant to be.*

"If you're talking about the Shah," Colonel said, "he has his own problems."

What Ahmad had meant was his own second term in parliament. He made a vague head movement.

"The army's been on the alert for ten months now, but I don't care anymore," he said, laughing and flipping the skewers with the jovial insouciance of someone who meant what he was saying. "I'll retire next year and then you, my friend, can find me right here knocking back the good stuff, watching the sea in the sun, if these clouds ever clear, that is."

The sauce dripped from the wings and sizzled on the coal. Colonel warmed his hands over the brazier as Ahmad wrote his cautious remark. If he had learned one thing from his catastrophic speech, it was equivocation.

I will remain at the service of His Majesty for now. Then after some time, when he looked at the man who, holding the end of one skewer in his hand, pulled a wing out of the other end and blew at it with such deliberation as if nothing in the world deserved his attention more than a well-cooked wing, he decided that his father-in-law might be trusted with the request about Salman.

Over on the beach, Homa and her mother sat around a fire while the girls ran about in their jackets and red knit hats. A cold breeze blew from the water penetrating the blanket Homa had wound around her. Hugging herself and rocking back and forth, she told her mother about her decision to go to university. "Any help you need," her mother said, turning to her with a smile, "with the kids or with anything else, you just let me know, okay?" Homa nodded and thanked her mom and drew herself closer to her on the driftwood tree trunk they were sitting on.

It was after lunch when Colonel Delldaar made a phone call from his secure line in his room and reported that Ahmad had said he was looking for a leftist friend, by the name of Salman. He had apparently been asking around for a number of weeks now. That information was not new to SAVAK and Ahmad still had some time before he was summoned.

They ate the wings in the gazebo. The kids went inside with their grandparents. Ahmad and Homa walked hand in hand on the beach where calm washed over the fine sand with each wave. Not too far behind them towered mountains covered in oaks, beech, maple, and alder. Behind the mountains was Tehran. They walked until it started raining. That night, with the raindrops rapping at the panes, Ahmad saw happiness in the room, in the bed, and in Homa's face when she brushed her hair. He kissed the nape of her neck. The wind started to pick up in the dark, pouring rain over the house, bending the leafless orange trees in the small garden, drenching the cold coals in the brazier. Winter by the Caspian Sea came in the shape of cold and rains.

"Will you promise me something?"

The rain had calmed to a drizzle. Ahmad's nod could be felt on his pillow.

"Will we always stay together?"

Ahmad nodded, then took her hand and pressed it hard in his.

"Are you sure?" She pressed his hand back.

Ahmad nodded, his head still on the pillow.

"You're like one of those bears that rub their backs to trees." Then she did not say anything as if she was sliding out of the bed into other rooms, on other beaches, but after a few minutes she drew a deep breath and said, "I'm happy," and turned her back to Ahmad.

AFTER THEIR VACATION, HOMA CAME home one afternoon with the girls to a bundle of all the books she needed to study for her university entrance exam. She walked up to the living-room table and read the card taped to the topmost cover: *I'm sure you will make it.* She smiled and in the coming months studied with a dedication that neither Ahmad nor Homa herself had imagined before. Having finished her first batch of books, she bought more. Then she looked at her cluttered desk and, deciding to put away the books she did not need, scooped them in her arms, and put them down on the floor at the foot of the bookcase. She started to empty a separate shelf when a piece of paper fell down from inside a cookbook. She picked it up and unfolded it. It was the prayer she had said for Leyla to open her tongue. All of a sudden, she froze in place. Why had she not asked the prayerwright, Haji, for a line for Ahmad? Incredulous at her stupidity and failure, she paced the room, spending a few minutes dazed, before she ran to her phonebook. Under H she found nothing. She gutted the storage under the staircase, ripped an old box open with a knife, pulled out a small, dog-eared phonebook, and found the number. Coiling the phone cable around her finger. Each tone made her more anxious. There was no answer. She dialed again and waited through the tones. She called after an hour, then again after two hours, and again in the evening and at night.

For a week she tried until she was sure Haji would not answer, so she decided to set out looking for him. The girls were old enough to walk to school together without their mother's company. After they left home, Homa would put on her knee-high, leather snow boots, a raincoat, and a hat and walk carefully to the street in the tracks trodden in the sidewalk by passersby and wait for a taxi. Starting with the neighbor who had condescendingly introduced Haji to her in the first place, she found a trail of addresses and phone numbers. All in vain.

She went farther south into the more crowded neighborhoods of the city; Lalahzar Street with the new movie theaters and several playhouses was brimful with people who went in and came out, stopping to buy steaming food from street carts, taking out their gloves to hold tea glasses in their hands. In an alley adjoining a theater, Homa stopped in front of a brick building and rang the bell. A woman who looked and sounded Armenian opened and shook her head, but took Homa's phone number in case she heard from the prayerwright.

With a dubious hope Homa used the prayer she already had. She whispered the words and blew in Ahmad's direction when his head was hung in his newspaper or when he snored in the bed. Days went by. The prayer was not right; maybe not strong enough or perhaps something in it had expired. She would keep searching for Haji.

AT THE SAVAK HEADQUARTERS, AHMAD stepped into a neat and clean office where the cloudy sky could be seen through the half-open blinds. A major shook hands with him and sat in front of him with a calm smile as he crossed his legs. He started by talking about the weather and then like a friend asked Ahmad how he was doing and nodded with an eager smile as he read the notes. He had been sorry about the incident with Ahmad's eyes and he could barely wait to read Ahmad's new poetry. As far as his duties permitted, he had always been a supporter of "the art of the right word placed at the right place."

"And your speech after the riots," he said, "was a judicious start to your political career. Unlike, unfortunately, your affiliations."

Knowing his presence there could not have been for no reason, even less likely for praise, Ahmad put each word on his notepad with the utmost caution. It would not happen too often that he was happy with his speechlessness, but that was one such day. Words on paper were tamer than the ones that flew off lips.

From a stack of papers on his desk, the major pulled out Ahmad's second book, sat back, and read aloud his favorite poem.

"Provocative, fast-paced, and with epic proportions," he said. "I'm sure you know the Marxist students' march began with this one." Someone had stepped up on a chair and read that poem in the middle of the crowd in front of the university library. Then they had started singing the "My Fellow Classmate" song and stamping their feet. It was those Mosaddegh years when such an association could legally exist at the university.

The major was sending oblique messages, as if opening an imaginary file and showing Ahmad the evidence they had against him, that could be used at any time. The major wished Ahmad good luck. "If you have anything to talk about," he said handing him a card with a number on it, "or if you need help to find something or someone." Ahmad nodded. "You," the major added, "or your wife." Ahmad knew the major meant that he knew about Ahmad's looking for Salman, but did not realize the major was implying that he also knew about Homa's excursions. Instead, he thought of the man's final remarks as a soft threat.

Outside it had started to snow. Ahmad bought a pack of cigarettes. The bitterness grated his throat and sedimented in his lungs as he inhaled his first puff ever. His coughs, white and cloudy, rose in the air. The city was retreating into its evening languor. Two-story brick houses stood shoulder to shoulder in circuitous rows, their roofs no longer a place for mosquito nets. The cries of shovelers echoed along the alleys announcing their service. Heads popped out of windows and doors to call them in and lead them up to the roof. With the snowy spring, the farmers who had come to Tehran for the winter had prolonged their seasonal work. Each passing month brought more villagers to the cities. Careless shovelfuls of snow dropped from over the edge of roofs down into alleys with a muffled thud onto the heap already forming on the ground. Agriculture declined within two years. Farms were left unattended under snow or, in the warmer areas of the south where cold wind was the bane, ravaged by weeds. Minibusfuls of young villagers got stuck on dirt roads, pushed the heavy vehicles out, and arrived in Tehran to shovel snow.

The city population grew. The number of double-decker buses doubled, tripled, then quadrupled, and still sometimes there were no vacant seats. A few stood in the isle, clinging at the bars, inclining toward the driver with each break and retreating toward the back with every acceleration. Lines started to form at the bakeries, bus stops, and grocery stores. A Jewish owner of the first plastic company built the first high-rise in Tehran: the seventeen-story Plasco Building with indoor reflection pools and billiard lounges. The blight of inflation gnawed at the economy. The Communists had their own ideas. The Fadaee Guerillas got armed, got arrested and tortured. In sermons following congregational prayers, with raised fingers pointing upward, the clergy took on the corruption of the government and shouted their opposition of the royal purchase of a Boeing 747 while innumerable families lived in shacks made from tin bins in the expanding slums. The Tehran Cabaret was built in the northern neighborhoods. The city was stretching, pushing against its limits with new buildings that mushroomed between Tehran and the village of Tajrish, where orchards, now frozen for years, had once extended up the foot of the mountains.

It was in this situation that one day a man arrived from abroad with a tape. As he walked out of the airport in his long brown overcoat, hat in hand, he could hear the cassette click against his silver cigarette case in his black leather handbag. The sound was his way of making certain his stash was safe with him. Outside, he put on his hat and sat in a taxi heading for a house at the center of the city in the basement of which Ayatollah Khomeini's speech was played that night out of a Hitachi cassette player. In front of the speaker lay three microphones each connected to separate tape recorders. Now he had three more copies of the speech. He repeated his multiplication process until he had thirty-six copies in his bag. Then the morning after, he set out to five meetings.

Copies of copies were noisy and sounded like the words of a person with a cold. In the third copies, wind blew away whole words and phrases. What remained, though, was enough to be passed from hand to hand in mosques and played in houses and apartments. Years before, the Ayatollah had been arrested and put on an airplane which took off and disappeared into the clouds. His words now appeared on clandestine tapes and flyers. His name was spray-painted among the other slogans that appeared here and there in the alleys and streets on the walls of houses, stores, and sometimes cinemas that still boasted their large posters of bare-legged women and their lovers at whom life had not looked with a favorable eye. It was in those films that Majeed, now in his thirties, still lost himself. He took refuge in the burgundy leather seats that had stopped folding back years before. In the movies nothing had happened to Tehran. The city was immune and calm. Turmoil was only in the hearts and lives of the actors. There was certainty in the love, music, and dance, in the fake world of the screen where the knives of thugs flashed and the skirt of the beloved whirled. It was not until the first cinema was set on fire that Majeed found himself in the Revolution.

Ahmad put the cigarette to his lips and took a second puff. The smoke went down with more ease. He was tired. The joke that was his career in politics now filled him with the dread of being on the list of people especially watched by the Shah's intelligence service. He felt he wanted out. He walked not to his office, but all the way to Khan's house.

In the basement, Ahmad asked his grandfather to show him his calculations again. Khan opened the books on which he had based his theory. He read passages and explicated the gems of ethology in the works of Persian

ALI ARAGHI | 260

thinkers of the tenth to twelfth centuries. He went through the maps and charts with Ahmad and did the math again with a bony finger that shook when he flicked the beads on his abacus. "My knees are weak," he said when he did the final stage of calculations, content with the accuracy of his results, "but this is still working." He knocked on his temple with his finger and then penned down his prophecy on the paper as before: February 1979.

Ahmad sat there for a while, his arms crossed on his chest, eyebrows knotted and face dark with the shadows of wavering thoughts.

"Whatever you decide to do," Khan said, "I will support you. But my predictions have been right. The one with the Coup and the one last year and the smaller ones. In my heart I have no doubt about them." He remained silent for a few seconds. "But the tale," he said, "well, not all of it is true, it seems. Have you seen Agha?"

A smell like that of raw fish had given the air in the Agha's room a bluish tint. Pooran had opened the window and the door and fanned the air with a towel. But the next time she came in, the air was once again blue with the fishy smell. She had gone to Khan, who nodded in response. Pooran had gone back to Agha's room and hugged him so long that the dead man wiggled himself out of her embrace.

Leaning against the wall, Agha sat on his bed in front of the backgammon board, throwing dice and throwing them again. He looked at Ahmad and cast down his eyes as if embarrassed of being dead. A tear dropped on the front of his shirt. Ahmad held the old man in his arms. *Is there anything I can do for you?* he mouthed. Agha's tears slid into and along the creases on his stubbly face.

HIS SERVICE WAS ON A Thursday. Pooran opened the large guest room. Her little granddaughters, Leyla and Lalah, swept the rugs. Maryam took charge of the kitchen and her daughter, Parveen, put the large kettles on. In a neighbor's car, Majeed brought rental dishes. Neighbors had black banners calligraphed with condolences to the family and nailed them outside the house to the walls. Early in the morning, the Quran-reciter arrived, was sat in the guest room, and began his incantation. In the heat of things, when the mourners, dressed in black, streamed in and out, and shook hands with Khan and Ahmad and Majeed, Mr. Zia arrived in a creaseless black suit and pants and sparkling shoes. "I'm sorry for your loss," he said shaking Ahmad's hand. "I'm here for the service," he whispered, "but if you don't want me here, I'll leave right now." From behind the curtained window, Leyla saw Mr. Zia's deliberate walk, as his head turned like a beacon throwing looks around the yard. The service was a pretext, Leyla knew; he had come to see her.

She hurried out of the women's room into the kitchen. Squeezing her way over to the fridge through the women who flitted from steaming kettle to boiling pot, she took the box of dates and dumped some onto a plate and slipped out in time to see Mr. Zia take off his shoes at the door. She adjusted her steps, on her way back to the women's room, to pass him as he was led and accompanied politely toward the men's room. He looked at her with an unmistakable smile in his eyes. Leyla did not look away; she smiled back as she walked into the familiar smell of his bitter cologne. A discreet turn of the head allowed her to watch him enter the men's room. Swiftly, Leyla offered the dates to the women and walked back out. From where Mr. Zia sat, he could see her and he knew he could be seen as she traveled gracefully between the women's room and the kitchen.

Before noon, the guest room was full of mourners dressed in black: older people leaning on poshtis against the walls, the younger sitting cross-legged in rows in the middle. Plates of dates followed trays of tea as a mulla gave a sermon. In a corner, a framed photo of a younger Agha was on a table flanked by lit candles. Agha looked at the picture and remembered the day Khan's father had brought the photographer to the Orchard. It was a few years before he started to go to the bathhouse more often than he went to prayers. Norooz the Gardener came to Agha's tree one day with clean, pressed clothes folded over his arm. Shortly after, dressed in a light-cream suit and pants, a red tie dangling from his neck, Agha was sitting in his wheelbarrow snaking through the trees that swayed in the spring breeze. Norooz was a young man then who spaded around the garden from sunrise to sunset and lifted apple crates two at a time. In front of the building, the whole family was seated on chairs in their best clothes waiting for Agha. Norooz sat him in a chair formed of curved metal and stepped behind the camera to watch with the other maids and servants what the photographer was going to do with his three-legged box. Khan's father sat in the center and looked into the horizon, his wife on his right stared farther away to the right, and Agha on his left looked into the camera. Uncles and aunts filled the periphery sitting straight and uneasy. The five-year-old Khan stood closer than everybody else to the brown wooden box and stared right into its glass. "Now that's *très bien*," said the photographer when he came out from behind the cloth he had stuck his head in. "Portrait time," he then said.

When the mourners stood in lines to say the prayer for the dead, before them was not the dead person's body as was customary, but instead the same framed picture in which Agha's half-turned head, with his thin, white hair combed over to the side and his eyes sparkling in his aging, shaved face, questioned mortality. Unable to join the harmonious moves of the prayer-sayers, the old man himself sat in his chair on the first row, cross-legged and small, and said his own prayer for the dead.

Sofrehs were laid and rental china plates came out of the kitchen. Rice and kebab with grilled tomatoes. Jugs of yogurt drink and water, pieces of sangak bread and plates of basil studded the sofrehs. A cacophony of spoons and forks clinking and clattering against china rose from both rooms over the hum of subdued small talk. The plate in front of Agha remained untouched.

Time came for the guests to leave. At the front door, Khan, Ahmad, Majeed, and his father stood in a row, shaking hands, kissing men, thanking them for coming, and accepting the repeated condolences. From behind the curtain, Leyla watched the long line move ahead and out one by one until Mr. Zia was gone. When Ahmad clanked the doors closed the house fell into a heavy silence. An hour later came the time for departure.

With the dead man on his back, Ahmad walked around the whole house for Agha's farewell tour. They went through the kitchen where Agha opened the fridge, the guest room, the living room, the corridor where he touched the walls, down into the basement, up the elevator onto the roof, into Zeeba's room where Nana Shamsi used to live—Agha wanted to take something of Nana with him, but there was nothing—into Leyla's room where she had never stayed, and up into Lalah's on top of her sister's. On the highest roof, Agha asked Ahmad to linger for a while to look at the snow-covered roofs. The edges of the city stretched far in the distance in all directions. The north was his destination, where the mountains were.

They put Agha in the back of a neighbor's car. Ahmad and Pooran sat on either side of him. Khan held onto his cane in the front seat. Majeed started the engine and they drove through the streets of iced-over asphalt. A row of young trees separated the road from the sidewalk where people strolled in their warm coats. They passed an empty cart pulled by a horse that blew clouds out of its round nostrils. The driver raised his hand and smiled at the strangers in the car. They swerved through buses, bicycles, cars, and people and left the expanding city for Tajrish. When the back wheels started to spin, they parked the car, and up the steep, snowy mountain roads they trudged. Humongous and skeletal, Agha's plane tree towered against the white backdrop of the mountain.

Twenty years had changed the face of the village. New houses with travertine facades replaced the old brick ones. The kids in the alleys looked at the party with curiosity. Some women stepped out to help Pooran up. "Khan's back!" Ahmad heard someone shout and by the time they got to the Orchard, a small crowd was gathered at the door. Mohammad the Carpenter arrived trudging—still fat but old—and hugged Khan. In the Orchard were dead trees half buried in snow. It took Ahmad, Majeed, and the volunteer villagers two hours to clear a path to the tree. Soon Agha was put snug in his home, with fresh blankets under and over him. Mohammad had a young man Khan did not know install a heater inside, its electricity stolen with hook lines from the nearest power post in the alley. One by one, they kissed Agha and held him in their arms. Except for Khan.

"Come, my son," Agha said from inside, "Let me kiss you one last time."

Khan remained outside, his head bowed, his hands resting on his lion. "I am not going in." His turned-up collar fluttered in the mountain wind. "This cannot be my last image of you."

There was no sound for a moment except for the hiss of the wind and Pooran's stifled cries. "You are my children." Agha's sound came from inside the tree. "I have loved you all. I will never forget you." He fell silent for a short time. "But Khan, let me see your face one last time."

Khan shook his head. "I can't," he said before he turned around and crunched away in the snowy trench. After everyone had left, Ahmad hugged Agha once more. Then he stepped out and pulled the tarpaulin curtain. "Ahmad," Agha called out from inside the tree, "don't forget me, my son." From over his shoulder, Ahmad looked at the bluish-gray tarp as he walked away. "Death is frightening, Ahmad."

Down they went followed by neighbors from twenty years before, one unstable foot in front of another, toward the car. When they were saying goodbye to the small crowd, shaking hands and hugging, the voice of Khan came. Khan had not said it, but it was his voice, from the past, words that had lived in those mountains for twenty years now. "These bloods are on your hands, Mulla." Hollow and cold, clear and alive, the voice came sweeping through the alleys and wandered away. If the cemetery had not been covered, like the Orchard, with snow, Khan would have visited Mulla's grave.

Majeed started the car. Men from the village helped push the vehicle out of the snow and a few moments later they were on the road back to Tehran. To Ahmad's left, Agha's absence sat on the backseat bright and buoyant. Majeed turned on the headlights. It was getting dark and there was still a long way until the Revolution. In that situation the opening line of a new poem came to Ahmad. Something told him they were the words to start a great fire.

24

LALAH MADE MOLOTOV COCKTAILS, without her parents knowing. She was a fifteen-year-old beauty and she could see that in the mirror. Her wavy hair was a dark walnut color, like her sister's, but Lalah alone spent a long time in front of the mirror combing. Whatever empty bottles she could lay hands on she wrapped in rags and tucked away at the bottom of her bag. After school, Lalah walked with Shireen to her basement where they stashed their bottles, half-filled them with petrol and engine oil, and ripped wicks off old clothes. That much Lalah could do, but she was not daring enough for the rest. It was Shireen who passed the bottles to the boys.

Shireen's widowed mother had no authority over her. Every month or two Shireen's uncle drove his eighteen-wheeler back to the city, sat her down, tried to talk some sense into her, and then beat her with his belt. After he closed the door behind him, Shireen was back in the basement and then out on the streets passing bottles and spray-painting slogans. "He's kind in the heart," Shireen told Lalah. "He brings me these plants, too, when he comes, but, boy, is he strong." When working in the basement, the girls talked about which boy Shireen would meet. They were a group of four that Lalah had seen from a distance at two rare daytime rendezvous. She liked Ebi, the smaller one with the large ball of curly hair and sideburns that widened down to his earlobes. He could be a singer. "But he's shorter than you," Shireen said the first time Lalah admitted this. Shireen was into the older one in the group, "the man," as Lalah called him. He was much older than the other three, in his fifties maybe. He combed his pepper-salt hair into a side part. His name was Ameer.

The transfer of the explosives had to take place under the cover of the night and that was when Lalah had to be home. Her father wanted her back before dark. "He's become timid since he quit," she told Shireen one day, sitting at her vanity trying on her lipstick. She remembered the day Ahmad resigned from the parliament, when he came home and took his wife and children to the park. "He does that when he feels guilty," she said into the mirror, "he rounds us up and takes us out." Leaning close to the mirror and pressing her cherry lips together, she remembered the day: the park was covered in snow. Flying back and forth on the metal seat of the swing that stung her bottom, Lalah could see her parents talk, her father sitting on a bench, her mother standing, not able to bear the coldness of the green-painted concrete. Leyla was walking around the white playground, kicking snow. Lalah knew something was not right, and her parents were trying to make it seem as if everything was under control. Kicking her feet, she made the swing go faster, but she was not enjoying it. They went to a restaurant and afterward had saffron ice cream with pieces of pistachio and chunks of hard cream. From that day on Ahmad worked at home. Within a year, he finished the collection of poetry he had begun with bloody eyes. He refused a second call from the Ministry of Publications and Information. It was shortly after that when Homa found Haji on a snowy day.

IN HIS MONTH-LONG DETAINMENT, THE prayerwright had cried and begged so much that when his investigator came into the room and said they would let him go provided that he quit his practice, he had accepted with a nonstop expression of his gratitude, right hand on his chest, half-bowing to the investigator and to anyone he talked to or even passed in the corridor. Once out, he had relocated to a new neighborhood in Southern Tehran, where he hoped not many would know him.

Taking care to wrap herself thoroughly in her chador and covering as much of her face as she could, Homa stepped off the bus into snow. Poverty crawled up the walls like ivy. Trying to avoid the stares, she asked for directions from a wizened old woman who sat at her doorstep watching the passersby with a thin layer of snow stuck to her scarfed head. Ahmad would have been mad if he knew she had been walking in those parts alone. Spotting a stranger, bored boys followed her, sniggering all the way. She quickened her steps, trying to ignore them. When she was starting to fear and question her decision, she arrived at Haji's door. The boys threw a snowball at her before they ran away. She rang the bell and waited. The petrol-seller passed by pushing a low cart loaded with black, greasy tin gallons, announcing his arrival at the top of his lungs to the people hidden in their homes.

The door cracked open and Haji's bald head appeared, a Bic pen dangling like a pendulum from his neck by a white string. Homa wanted to hug someone at that moment. "What do you want?" Haji asked without opening the door any farther. He listened and shook his head no. But before Haji could shut the door on her, Homa wedged her foot in the frame.

"I won't go until you talk to me." Haji eyed her for a few seconds, then opened the door after throwing suspicious looks to make sure no one was with her in the alley.

The apartment was dark. The air smelled like sour milk. In the short corridor inside, the stocky man stood before her in his loose, striped pajamas with legs tucked into his socks.

"I don't do that anymore." Homa held out a wad of new, crisp one hundred toman bills. "I can't accept that." Haji shook his head after looking at the money for a few seconds as if shaking a temptation. Homa pulled out a second wad. "How many more are in there?" Haji asked glancing at Homa's bag that hung from her shoulder under her draping chador.

"Enough to take you out of this place."

Haji rubbed his cheek, bearded with short gray hair, took the two wads, and held his hand out for more. By a burning Aladdin heater, they sat on the floor. Homa pressed her leather purse in her lap, her right hand in the bag ready to close around the deer antler handle of a knife. Like years before, Haji sat in front of her, consulted his old books, and took notes in a notebook, but this time he threw glances at the woman who seemed to be in her early thirties. She was trying to put on a serious look by pressing her lips together, which made her dimples show.

"Now give me your hand," Haji said, putting out his hand. Homa paused for a moment, not sure what to do, but looked at the man's thick fingers and the deep-cut lifelines on his palm. "It's for the prayer." She put her left hand in his. The man's knuckles were crooked, but his nails were beautiful: a healthy pink and smooth. He ran his hands on the back of hers one after the other, and then turned it around to examine the palm like fragile glassware from previous centuries. The tips of his forefingers ran deliberately, as if savoring the pattern of the interlocking lines. Then the probing fingers advanced in their path and slid up Homa's forearm. In the future, she would ruminate on that moment more than she wanted to, wondering if she could have done anything differently. Holding Homa's hand in his, the prayerwright's palm pushed up the sleeve of her gray blouse and slithered up and down her forearm. His breathing was the only audible sound in the room. "Oh, pure marble," he said. When he bent over to kiss the soft skin, Homa clasped her hand around the knife in her bag, not the handle, but mistakenly the blade. She felt the warm blood gushing out of her fingers. She took the knife out, pointing it at Haji. Blood dripped on the rug. "That's as far as it goes," she said pulling her sleeve back down. Shocked by the blood, the prayerwright withdrew and looked at her heaving breaths through her nose, her fine nostrils flaring.

Before she left the apartment with the prayer safe in her purse, she accepted the rag that the man brought her at the door. "The man who has you," Haji said as she held out the blue piece of cloth, "I hope he knows what a gem he has. They never do."

Homa felt proud. She had beaten the fate that had tried to hide the prayerwright from her and she had gotten her hands on what she came for. All the way home, Homa pressed the purse to her body and squeezed the rag in her fist.

Homa wrapped up the prayer and cooked Ahmad's favorite dish. After dinner and when the girls were in bed, she did her hair, put on her green dress, and brought the gift to Ahmad with tears in her eyes. She handed him the thin present, but could not wait for him to open it; she threw herself into his arms. "I'm going to hear your voice," she said, crying on his shoulders. Ahmad unwrapped the gift, took the piece of paper out of the envelope behind her back, and looked at the Arabic words written in red ink in a beautiful hand. "Every morning," Homa said, sniffing in a way that let Ahmad know she was smiling, "on an empty stomach." Ahmad patted her on the back.

For the rest of the night, Ahmad looked at the prayer lying flat on his desk and tried to imagine a version of himself who could open his mouth and make meaningful sounds. He could call his daughters instead of walking up to them. He could say Homa's name for the first time. He could read his poems. Of all the voices in his head, he tried to find one that would be his, but it was useless. When he detached himself from himself and looked, like a hovering ghost at an imaginary, vocal Ahmad, he did not recognize himself. He tried to make a new image of himself: an Ahmad who talked like everybody else, but was not frightening or banal. Thoughts slipped out of his mind as easily as water. In bed that night, Ahmad scribbled a line on his notepad and gave it to Homa.

Now tell me how you really cut your hand

A WEEK AFTER HOMA VISITED him, Haji was boiling lamb shank, beans, and potatoes in a pot for his favorite dinner when he heard a knocking. He stopped whistling and tiptoed toward his door. There was a piece of paper on the floor.

Thank you for your prayer. I know it will be worth more than I paid for it. You're despicable, so I will not face you ever again, but the money, I'll leave it in a paper bag in the heap of trash in front of your building.

Haji listened for a sound behind the door in the hallway, any rustling of clothes, soft breathing, or shifting of feet. Then he cracked the curtain to look out with half-squinting eyes. There was a paper bag in the trash. He went back to sit by his Aladdin heater, but no sooner had his behind touched the folded blanket than he got up and checked the window again. The garbage man would soon come and spade the heap from the foot of the wooden power pole into his cart. Haji paced his room and listened to the boiling of broth for a few minutes before he finally pulled his pants over his pajamas, threw on a shirt, and stepped out into the evening dark without doing up his buttons. Orange clouds sprinkled the city with small flakes that glistened in the cones of light the streetlamps shot down into the alley. Haji made sure no one was around before he hastened to the power pole ankle-deep in snow, in his rubber sandals. The bag was wet and reeking with a foul liquid. He turned it over and shook it. It was empty. Furious that the woman had made him rummage in the trash in snow, he strode back to his apartment and slammed the door behind him, but he had barely stepped in when two men jumped on him from behind and pinned him to the floor. A hand pressed over his mouth. When his hands and feet were tied and his lower jaw was on the brink of detaching from his face, they turned him around.

Three men in coats stood above him. He was sure they were SAVAK agents who had finally tracked him down. He wanted to shout, swear to God that he had written only three or four prayers in all those years, but they had stuffed his mouth with cloth. One of the men, who seemed to be the boss, knelt down and looked him in the red face. His eyes were calm and determined. At his gesture, the other two got to work. They brought two small stacks of books from around the apartment and put them down close together on the floor. They untied Haji's hands and stretched his right arm across the two stacks, his elbow resting on one, his wrist on the other. Haji thrashed and yelled against the rag in his mouth, but one man sat on his chest and held his free arm. Haji threw his legs back and forth. His shrill cries did not pass through the rag and spit that stuck to his tongue. The boss knelt down by Haji's extended arm and placed his closed fist in the middle of the forearm that bridged the gap between the two stacks of books. Haji's wrist and elbow were held in place by the other man. The fist came down like a sledgehammer. The sound of snapping bones was audible, louder than any of them expected. Before he got to his feet, the man pulled a piece of paper from his breast pocket and gently put it in Haji's hand, lying limp on the stack of books. They left the apartment without saying a word. If it were not for the prayer they left in his hand, Haji could never have known what had brought the punishment. And he had to move on again.

TWO WEEKS PASSED AND AHMAD had not spoken. Homa asked if he was saying the prayer every morning as it had been prescribed. Ahmad looked her straight in the eye and wrote that he could not change himself beyond recognition. He had to remain who he was. He wrote with such determination that something crumbled in Homa's heart.

"Are you sure this is what you want?" she asked. Ahmad nodded then held her hand in his and mouthed, *Thank you my dear.* The next day, Homa went to Haji's apartment and rang the bell, but no one answered. She slipped in a note under the door. *I want another prayer. Call me. I'll pay for it.* There had to be something she could say without Ahmad realizing it, just like the prayer that had worked on Leyla. Her searches for Haji began again.

It was during this time that Ahmad had to begin writing his poetry on trays. Midway through a particularly bright poem, the paper turned yellow and then brown; it could not stand the heat. Ahmad got up and tore a cardboard box into pieces, but cardboard, too, turned too brown and brittle. He paced his room, worried he might lose his inspiration. From the dish rack he took the tea tray and hastily rummaged in his toolbox for a long nail. Back at his desk, he etched his poem in the tray, scratching each letter with repeating back and forth movements. Once finished, Ahmad could barely hold the hot tray in his hands. In the evening, when all the family was home, Ahmad showed them the new poem. Lalah turned the lights off and, holding the edges of the tray with two folded rags, shone the beam of light that came out of the tray around on the walls and ceiling and into her sister's face. In turn, Leyla placed the tray on the rags on the floor and showed Lalah how to make shapes on the ceiling with the shadows of her hands.

Homa liked the poem so much that she became certain she would continue looking for Haji until she found him. She searched for months with no success. She despaired. She told herself that success comes to those who persevere, and persevere she did until the morning she got dressed, but did not know anymore why she was doing it. Let's just put on my shoes, she told herself, but she stood at the door and stared at the clock and she realized that hope was not strong enough to make her step over the threshold. In her years of solitude later, she would reminisce about her trips around the city, in buses and taxis, and on foot, always carrying a chador and a knife in her shoulder bag. To her closest friends she would confess that neglecting her daughters was the biggest mistake she had made in her life. She had thought them old enough—if not Lalah, without a doubt Leyla—to walk to school and back on their own. She had never suspected a ten-year-old capable of doing what she did.

FROM A TELEPHONE BOOTH ON her way to school or back, Leyla called Mr. Zia. Still too short to reach the receiver, she asked a passerby to insert the coin and dial the number of her "uncle" for her. Then she closed the door and talked until the windows fogged up and Lalah knocked with her gloved hands and shouted that she was cold. The fire that had burned Leyla's heart from the time she saw Mr. Zia had never extinguished. Every morning, she went to school with the excitement of the phone call. "I want to see you," Mr. Zia said, his trembling voice hoarse in the receiver. "I love you," Leyla answered, "but no one can know." After Ahmad had resigned from the parliament, Mr. Zia was gripped by the fear that he would not see Leyla again now that Ahmad would not need him or his uncle in any way. It was the little girl who consoled him, made him certain of her love and the inevitability of union. She asked him to be patient. "I can't wait," Mr. Zia cried into the receiver. Leyla came out of the booth with a racing heart and a face so red that the rowdy Lalah fell silent with the apprehension that something ominous might have happened. After a few more times, Lalah learned that the rose color came with an elated mood that would end up in snow fights for the rest of the way home. Lalah began not only looking forward to the calls, but pushing her sister into the closest telephone booth on their way and waiting patiently for her to open the folding door and step out. The days when there was no call or when Leyla came out prematurely, Lalah knew the walk home would be silent. She loved her sister anyway. Leyla was the center of attention in any gathering because she spoke with long, complicated sentences that were the envy of most adults, but at the end of the day it was with her, Lalah, that Leyla played, it was her homework that she checked every day like a teacher, and it was with her that Leyla talked at night when they were in bed in their room and the lights were off. Such were the bonds of sorority between Lalah and her older sister that when one day Mr. Zia pulled up in his car by the side of the street, in front of the telephone booth, Lalah did not say a word to her mother about the event. She knew Mr. Zia was the man Leyla called from the booth. She was still young and did not know what love was, but she felt and understood the secrecy of the incident. Leyla looked around anxiously, but did not take long to go toward the car and open the front door. Before she closed it, though, she turned to look at Lalah standing by the booth holding the handle of her leather bag in her gloved hand, not knowing what to do, her face showing a fear of being left alone. "Well, what are you waiting for?" Leyla said. "Hop in." This she said with a tone that Lalah liked to read as, Of course I'm not leaving you on your own, silly. Lalah enjoyed the short ride in the back seat and ate the steaming plate of crimson boiled beet cut into irregular chunks that Mr. Zia bought for the two of them. She laughed when the car got stuck in the snow and three other drivers stopped, pushed the car out, and went back to their cars as if pushing was part of driving. At home, Lalah asked Ahmad if they were going to have a car someday. The day after, Mr. Zia asked Leyla for a date.

"Just tell me when?" his voice asked in the receiver. "Even if it's twenty years from now; just tell me when."

"Only two more years. Until I'm in high school."

When Leyla reached high school, Lalah spent her recesses alone in the yard and walked home on her own. She moved to the back of the class and shared a bench with Shireen, whose big eyes wandered off toward the window during class, who was unprepared whenever she was called on by the teacher. Shireen was tall and agile and skipped rope faster than anyone else. She was born in prison, five months after her father and pregnant mother had been arrested in a communal apartment. She lived with her uncle for two years until her mother was released. Although she had never seen her father, Shireen kept a picture of him in her purse. Soon after Lalah switched to the last row of the class, the two girls found such harmony that they could easily cheat on tests without the teacher having the slightest idea.

THE SHAH APPOINTED PRIME MINISTER after Prime Minister to tackle the problems of the country. It had been three years since the beginning of winter. Farmers were almost bankrupt and the population of the villages had dwindled to a third. Prices had shot up in the volatile economy. When more protesting voices started to rise, the Prime Minister had a meeting with the army generals and heads of ministries. It was decided, in spite of most of the generals, that the people had never been actually given a chance to express themselves freely. Venting frustration and anger through verbal channels would prevent unlawful eruptions of violence.

With royal approval, political leniency and tolerance of criticism were adopted and a new age of journalism flourished. Qualifications for starting a newspaper or journal were set as a university degree and thirty years of age. *Iran Illustrated* increased its circulation to eighty thousand and hired a court photographer for exclusive pictures of the royal family. Their rival, *Black and White*, used the freedom to expose the corruption at the core of the government—the way they handled the earthquake, the never-ending construction of the dam, the incurable nepotism, and the unaccounted-for monies—with critical editorials and essays. The journal's editor, Dr. Afshar, a man of words and a believer in stories, paid the highest fees for a good yarn. With dreams of expanding his publication to reach an international readership, he had hired three writers who wrote all the nine stories of each issue. Dr. Afshar published three of the pieces under the writers' names and the remaining six as translations: from the map on his wall, he picked six random countries and penned down fictitious writer names which, because of his basic familiarity with the language, all sounded French.

Three months after the adoption of the policy of leniency, *Iran Illustrated* published a special snow issue. All the photos were of snow with no people in the frame: a line of small, white hills which on a closer look turned out to be buried parked cars, a crow perching on a traffic light—turned red— against a background of a white cloudy sky, a gridlock in a roundabout at the center of which stood an equestrian statue of Father King. They titled the issue *where is this snow coming from?* The next week, *Black and White*'s counterissue came out in white letters on black paper. In it was reports of houses having been damaged by four years of dampness and ceilings that had sagged under the weight of the snow. The headline of the issue became the one question that would repeat itself in the history of Iran and never receive an answer from any government: *where does our oil money go?*

No issue of *Black and White* was published without a poem by Ahmad. Dr. Afshar, the editor, thought he was the one poet alive whose work was worth reading. He visited Ahmad's home in person and, sitting in the living-room armchair with his legs crossed, took out his glasses from a leather case and obsessively cleaned them with a white handkerchief before he read the weekly poem. He accompanied his nods with a few bravos and slid the paper into his cracked leather bag. When the selection committee for the first Shiraz Art Festival was formed, Dr. Afshar made sure Ahmad's name would be among the candidates for poetry, and was not surprised when Ahmad was selected for a reading. With his latest book *Through the Eyes, Blood*, Ahmad had become one of the most well-known poets in the country.

In what would otherwise have been summer, the burial garden of Hafez, a fourteenth-century poet, was shoveled clean. Six concentric steps climbed to a circular platform, upon which a dome, supported by eight high, marble columns, protected the centuries-old gravestone from the snow. Before this monument, seats were lined up in ascending rows. The shovelers kicked the trunks and shook the snow off the branches that arched over the arena. Flags were hoisted up poles and for ten days pioneers of avant-garde art and the paragons of traditional national literature and music stepped onto the stage in front of the audience and the two rickety cameras that sent hesitant pictures to television sets around the country. Ahmad was scheduled on day three. Before him, a traditional music ensemble performed, sitting on the steps of the old poet's tomb and among them, Ahmad recognized Maestro Shahnaz. When, in the middle of a piece, the members of the group turned their heads toward the maestro and he started his solo, Ahmad saw how, like years before at his wedding, the trees budded in knobs of blossoms and shoots. Before the maestro was done, the stage and audience were covered in petals, one of which fell into Ahmad's open book. He picked it up and looked at it: varying shades of pink, delicate, and real. He brought it to his nose, smelled it, and kept it as a souvenir.

After Ahmad's reading came the first of a series of plays that would unfold in the course of seven years by Le Troisième, a French troupe that acted in French. The ménage à trois that the male and the two female actors depicted on the stage for two hours was incomprehensible for those who watched it on flickering screens. It was the first time Ahmad was hearing real French spoken and he understood every word of it. All the entries of Sergey's *dictionnaire* snapped out of their alphabetical order in his head and rearranged themselves into the chagrin of one woman, the ambition of the other, and the whirling emotions on the stage. The three actors kissing one another goodnight in a shared bed was an outlandishly bizarre scene, the tingling guilt of which stoked the fire of religious indignations. Once again, the man who flew in from beyond the clouds with Ayatollah Khomeini's speeches came carrying three new tapes in his bag and took a taxi, bound for the Hitachi tape recorder and the three microphones that awaited him in the basement.

WHEN AHMAD RETURNED HOME FROM the festival, Homa welcomed him with a piece of paper in her hand and a beaming face. She had been accepted to the school of nursing at the University of Tehran. Her first semester would start with the beginning of fall. "Who knows. One day I may become a doctor and set your voice right myself." To celebrate, Ahmad and the girls made her a cake. Homa watched them work in the kitchen. The would-be high schooler, Leyla, was tall enough now to reach the top shelf, her long skirt no longer reached her ankles. Lalah was an inexhaustible hand to Leyla, hurrying to the fridge to fetch things. Her tongue stuck out from between her lips as she concentrated to properly crack eggs or stir the batter. To Homa's surprise, Ahmad looked at home in the apron. He did not even clean his hands with the apron as she would have guessed, but used the proper kitchen towels.

Before school started, they went on another trip to Homa's parents' villa where the trio of bakers made a bigger cake to celebrate. Homa's uncles, aunts, and cousins were all there, along with the cousin who chaperoned Homa on those first days at the café. After lunch, the men sat at a table drinking Colonel Delldaar's homemade vodka and playing cards. "Whatever happened to that friend of yours?" Colonel Delldaar asked Ahmad. "I wish I could have done something for you."

With a sense of premonition in his father-in-law's interest, Ahmad brushed the matter off. He suspected that by asking for news about Salman, he had placed himself in a vulnerable position. If he had stayed in politics, it could have been a threat for his career, but even now he did not want to be on the blacklist of the intelligence service. His poetry was enough to make him fit for any label, from agitator to dissident to leftist. "Wasn't he your good friend?" Colonel asked while pondering what card to play.

WAS, Ahmad mouthed.

"It's an art, finding the right friend," The colonel fingered a card, decided against it. "The true buddy." He slapped a card on the table. "Anyway, if you ever feel like seeing him, they just transferred a bunch to the general section. He could be there."

Ahmad was not certain whether this was a trap. Back in Tehran he went to Sara's house and rang the bell. Her husband opened the door with a smile that was replaced instantly by a look of disgust. The untested but known fact that Ahmad was the father of Ameer, the boy Salar had raised and loved, *his* boy, had eaten his soul for years. Again Salar forwent the formalities and did not invite Ahmad in. He left the door open and went inside.

Sara came to the door in a skirt and blouse, a forty-year-old woman, with forty-year-old creases in the corners of her eyes, who did not seem very excited to see her visitor. Ahmad wrote the news about Salman on his notepad and handed it to Sara. Sara's eyes opened wide, then she quickly regained composure. "Why would they want to trap you?" she asked as if suddenly doubting the veracity of Ahmad's words. The regime had been after the leftists for years, had not stopped hunting, arresting, and imprisoning them even during what they called leniency. They would try to wring more names out of anyone. Ahmad had been a political poet and had run for the parliament backed by a group not known for their conservatism. He asked her not to go to the prison yet.

Sara read the note and looked at Ahmad. Packed with more snow, dark clouds were coming from the western skies to replace the lighter ones. "You are a selfish man, deluded in your ambitions," she said, "and I don't know why I've always loved you." The confession was so abrupt that it took Ahmad a few moments to deliberate on what he had heard. "See, and you never knew that, because nobody else ever matters to you." Halfheartedly, Ahmad started to shake his head, but Sara ignored him: "But the real news is that you loved me and you didn't even know it." Now Ahmad was shaking his head to categorically deny. "No, this is exactly what I'm talking about. When you come to give news about Salman, you make it all about yourself. We can't go look for that poor boy because everything is about you." Not giving Ahmad much time to reply, Sara promised him not to make an inquiry for some time and said goodbye. But once she was back inside, the mere thought of seeing her brother again was strong enough for her to immediately break her promise. She asked Ameer to take her to the prison.

The notorious Evin Prison had been built a few years earlier in the north of the city, far from any existing building. No one came out of it without having confessed whatever it was he had to confess. Sara waited outside as the heavy metal gate cracked for Ameer to go in. A chilly wind swept the dry snow like sand and fluttered the tail of Sara's scarf. Sara went back and sat in the car. Soon the gate opened again and Ameer stepped out. Salman was not there; they had to go to the Palace Prison. Once a Qajar king's dwelling, the Palace Prison was within Tehran and there they found Salman. But, not being an immediate family member, Ameer came back to his mother without having seen him. The snow kept coming down. That was it for Sara. She got out of the car and went in herself.

In the face of the man sitting on the other side of the glass Sara looked for familiar features, but the only thing she found was the wonder in his tired eyes, the disbelief at what he was seeing before him. She had never seen Salman so thin. His cheeks and eyes had sunken into his pale face, his bulging veins snaked up his bony hand. To Sara's questions Salman answered, with an overzealous optimism, that everything was fine. He had been transferred only a week before and there were no problems here. He played volleyball in the yard with new friends and he hoped to be released in the near future. The din of visitors and inmates on both sides of the glass echoed in the hall. Salman had to shout. He was hopeful and he wanted Sara to be too. His words were strong but his eyes betrayed so dark a despair that no matter how earnestly he tried to smile, he could not keep it from Sara. Toward the end of the visit, he was starting to come out of the husk that was sitting behind the glass. She was seeing the familiar hand gestures and movements of his head and in those, Sara found hope: he was still her brother, he was mendable. When the time was called, Salman got to his feet to leave.

"What's outside like?"

"It's been one long winter." She kissed her palm and placed it on the glass. He did not respond.

"Will I see you again?" he asked.

"Every week," Sara said and for the next nine years, she sat every Friday in that hall that was lit only by the snowy sky through three high, barred windows, telling her brother the stories of people they both knew and of those new to him and that was how the story of Leyla made the rounds, passed through the holes in the glass, and reached Salman, the only person who had called her "ladybug."

TOWARD THE END OF HER first year in high school, Leyla disappeared. Homa came home from university late in the afternoon to find Lalah home alone. By evening that day, she had called everyone who might know of her daughter. Ahmad went straight to Mr. Zia's home. Outside the rose garden, he rang the bell and rattled the door by pounding his fist on it, but no matter how long he waited, the metal gate remained shut. When Mr. Zia did not answer his telephone for two days, Ahmad held his notepad before Homa: *Leyla has eloped with Mr. Zia.* Homa could not believe that. First she denied the news, then she questioned Ahmad. "So, that's why you told me to take the kids out of the house?" Ahmad wrote that he had not allowed the two see each other as soon as he suspected. He did not know what else he could have done. She did not know what to think. She felt betrayed, but she was not sure. Hoping for Leyla's return any day, any minute, she skipped classes and stayed home. Noises from the street sounded like the doorbell. "You didn't sell her off to that man, did you?" she shouted at Ahmad. He held her in her arms, but she slapped him on the chest and wiggled free. Every afternoon, at the time the high school was dismissed, Homa was standing out front, scanning the faces of the girls who walked out in groups. At first, she would ask them about Leyla. No one had heard of her lately, but some had seen her weeks ago getting into a car, a beige Peykan. Ahmad went to the Great Zia. He had heard the news, but he did not know where his nephew was.

Ahmad's short political career had taught him not to believe the man readily. He went to some of his influential acquaintances. They promised to do what they could, but two weeks passed and no news came.

Homa cried through the night and frequently during the day, whenever anything reminded her of her daughter. Lalah took up the housework that her mother was neglecting. She reached the top cabinet with a stool. Ahmad cooked when he could, but when he was not around, Lalah turned on the oven and tried simple dishes; she served uncooked lamb for lunch one day and burnt the chicken the next. As soon as school was out, she hurried home. In the evening, she combed her mother's hair as Homa stared into the distance. Lalah wanted to talk to her mother, but was afraid. Instead she made her tea and watched her drink while doing homework. Ahmad decided that things could not go on like this. He had to leave the house to look for Leyla, but worried about leaving Homa alone.

SITTING IN HER ROOM, ZEEBA recognized Lalah's voice approaching in a taxi with her mother and father, so she hurried out and gingerly stepped into the elevator to let Pooran know they were close. A few minutes later, holding Homa's hand and followed by Lalah, Ahmad stepped into Khan's house and let Homa fall into Pooran's open arms. Pooran and Zeeba had already prepared Agha's room for Homa's stay. Zeeba helped carry Lalah's suitcase to her room on the roof which would now be used for the first time. In spite of the pain in his knees, Khan walked out into the yard to make his grandson's family welcome. Mixed with sadness and anguish that he shared with the rest of the family was a satisfaction at the wisdom of building those rooms. "You can stay here as long as you want," he said pressing his hand on his cane, but standing straight, his chest pushed forward.

They waded through into the summer. With sunken eyes and a pale face, Homa was a ghost haunting the house. She got out of the bed in the middle of the night and cranked her way up, then climbed up the metal ladder onto the roof of Leyla's room to crack open Lalah's door and make sure she was in her bed. Both Ahmad and Lalah would wake from the cold drafts that blew in. During the day, Homa went to the high school and waited out-side for her daughter to come out even though the school was closed for the summer. The janitor brought out a folding chair and umbrella, and a hot cup of tea for her. Under a bare plane tree she sat in cold rain or occasional snow. Then she would take the bus back to Khan's going straight to check on Lalah. One day she went up the elevator and did not find Lalah in her room. She hurried down the ladder to Zeeba's room and then down the elevator while shouting Lalah's name, until Pooran rushed into the yard and told her the girl was out to buy bread. Homa ran all the way to the bakery and from that day, Lalah was forbidden to leave the house alone under any pretext. That was how the girl started to grow closer to Zeeba, who taught her how to weave a carpet. Sitting next to one another at the foot of the loom, the two girls tied and cut and combed the colorful yarns one graceful knot at a time. Midsummer snow thawed soft and sloshy, but it did not melt. The search had yielded no results and from that Ahmad concluded that either Colonel Delldaar was not connected to the intelligence service, as Ahmad had sus-pected, or was just a rat, not high on the organizational ladder; otherwise he would have exerted his influence to find his granddaughter.

POORAN WOKE ONE MORNING TO clattering and running water. She shuffled out of her room and found Homa in the kitchen. Homa turned to her with a weak smile. "I'm so hungry." She prepared breakfast for the fam-ily and returned to her room to study and prepare for her second year at the university. Having known this day would come, Pooran was not shocked. She treated Homa's reengagement in her work not as worthy of celebration or even mention, but as the continuation of the normal. When fall came, Pooran suggested she should take Lalah to school and back every day, and Homa accepted. The second year began with promise. Homa had surpassed ev-eryone else in her class and after they taped the midterm exam grades on the wall in the corridor, she found herself answering more hellos and greeting more smiling faces. Soon things appeared to be working like the well-oiled cog wheels of a machine, except that at the heart of them was a hollow. The engine whirred fine but futile; it worked, but it was not going anywhere.

One early winter afternoon, Homa walked over to Ahmad's desk, patted him on the shoulder, and when Ahmad raised his head from his papers said she was leaving. *Where?* Ahmad mouthed.

"Nowhere," she answered, her face empty, "I'm leaving you."

Ahmad shook his head calmly as if answering a question as simple as, Do we have any milk left? When Homa turned away to go, he leaned and grabbed her wrist. *What are you saying? You can't leave,* he mouthed with the certainty of disbelief, looking into her face. Something was dead in Homa's eyes. She tried to wrestle her wrist out of his hand, but she was not strong enough. "Let me go," she said calmly. Ahmad mouthed things that Homa did not understand. Then she reached for the desk lamp and hurled it against the wall. Soon everyone was gathered in Agha's room. Ahmad had gotten up from his desk, without letting go of Homa's wrist. Pooran tried to calm Homa down and make Ahmad let go. She had never seen Ahmad's face so red. He motioned for everyone to leave the room with such fury in his eyes that no one spoke a word. A short while later, he came out too and locked Homa in, ignoring her banging on the door.

In the following days, Ahmad wrote notes apologizing for the troubles he had caused, for his failures and shortcomings, but she refused to read them. To his inevitable question of why she had decided to leave, Homa had unconvincing and unspecific answers: "I just can't anymore"; "I'm tired." Ahmad would kiss her dead face, as if kissing a tree. *I love you,* he mouthed, *Please, stay with me,* he mouthed, but she looked away. Finally Ahmad would grab her lower jaw in his hand, turn her head to face him, and see his mouth form the words *I love you and there is no way I'm letting you leave me.*

Homa stayed locked in Agha's room with the key safe in Ahmad's pocket. In Ahmad's mind was a tempest. Without conjuring them, thoughts appeared of how Homa would try to run away when he was not watching. A week had passed when one morning Ahmad stood on the veranda and imagined an escape path from Agha's window into the yard, up the walls, and down into the alley. The next day, he went out and came back with Oos Abbas and the same welder he had bought some thirteen years before. The passage of time showed in the machine's dents and scratches and flaked paint, just as in the wrinkles on the blacksmith's face and in the slight slouch of his back. They talked as the old man welded bars across the window. Before he left, he shook Ahmad's hand. "I don't know what you're keeping in that room, my boy, but something tells me you're making the wrong decision again."

For a month, Ahmad did not let Homa out of his sight. At night, he locked the door from inside before climbing onto his side of the bed, now with the permanent view of Homa's back. When she had to be out in the yard or the house during the day, Ahmad left the door open to keep a nervous eye on the front door. He could not concentrate. Paper after paper he crumpled up and threw out. He turned his head toward the door and trembled with the cold wind that howled in and the snowflakes that landed on his writing and melted on his face. Soon he would get up and find Homa in the house. He would sit on the floor in the corridor outside of the kitchen, in the living room outside of Pooran's room, outside every door his wife was behind. Homa took all this without resistance or complaint, without showing the slightest intention of flight. When locked in Agha's room, she delved into her textbooks and read as if there was nowhere she wanted to be but inside the heart and kidney and stomach, within the rib cage. Three days a week, she walked with Ahmad to the bus stop and took the double-decker to the university. She would walk with him to her class and come out two hours later to find him standing in the corridor, like a naughty boy who had been expelled by his teacher, awaiting his fate at the principal's office. Sometimes she would find him gesturing to a group of students who had recognized the big poet. But as soon as she stepped out, he cut the conversation and left the eager youths without waving goodbye. Across the snowy campus they walked toward the street that, in ten years, after the Revolution, would be named Revolution Street. A few new bookstores had recently opened next to the older ones.

Then one day, when Homa was deep into her textbook, Ahmad opened the door and came in, dressed in a long, dark raincoat and a black fedora. He stood in front of her and without a word or any significant gesture, pulled the key to the room out of his pocket, put it on the desk, and left. From behind the barred window, Homa watched him cross the yard, open the front door, and step out without turning around to take a second look at the house. The door closed with a clank. No one saw Ahmad leave but Homa. It was a cloudy afternoon.

25

MEER'S HAIR STARTED TO GROW WHITE on the temples when he was twenty-one. He looked into the mirror, turned his head right and then left, and was satisfied with the symmetry. He squeezed a whitehead on his nose with his thumbnails and then laced up his boots, put on his overcoat and wool hat, and stepped out of his room. With his shovel balanced on his shoulder, Ameer stood at the door and shouted to see if his mother wanted him to get anything on his way back. It was over a year now since he had started shoveling.

A few years after the snow had begun, one night the light bulb hanging above the family burnt out when they were sitting around the dinner sofreh. The snow had put extra burden on the city's decrepit infrastructure. Power lines sagged with the weight of snow and mourning doves, and the fluctuation in electricity made appliances burn right and left. In the dark that filled the room, Ameer's father pondered a little and said they had to change their fruit store to an electric shop. People could barely afford fruit and vegetables anymore. The first thing to do in the shop every morning was to throw out the rotten fruit and wilting herbs. Then they had to increase the prices which lowered the sales even more. "You can do without fruit, but you can't live in the dark," Salar said after Ameer had screwed in a new bulb. Even with that change, the family had a hard time making ends meet. The piece of land that Ameer's grandfather had left him had to be sold to pay for his sister's dowry. Ameer had started shoveling after finishing the daily work in the electric shop.

Sara opened the door and she, too, saw the white patches of hair sticking out from under Ameer's wool hat. Her son had grown twice older than his age. Once again, she asked him to see a doctor and once again Ameer declined. He wore his abnormality with pride. Sara thought she knew everything about her son. What she did not know, though, was that every week Ameer rode the bus to the New Town neighborhood, in the far east of Tehran, and from among the two-story brick buildings whose red curtains were closed all evening and night, he entered the one in which he would find his Goli. Each apartment had three bedrooms. On the second floor, three girls lived and worked, each in her room which had to be neat and clean, in a presentable condition at all times. A fourth girl worked downstairs where the madame's office also was. Ameer haggled with the middle-aged woman and slapped on the table less than what they agreed on. Then he stepped out of the first-floor apartment that was Madame's office and climbed up the stairs.

Goli was a petite brunette who often dyed her hair blond and could not stay still for a moment. If Ameer arrived when she was with another customer, he would get mad, grab a lamp and smash it on Madame's desk, throw a stapler at a frame on the wall, or break a window with his shovel before he left. He would return in a week or two, ask Goli about the other man, and watch her explain what kind of person he had been with her head bowed. Then, without putting a finger on her, Ameer went home to digest all he had heard. "Take care of yourself," he would say, slapping a few bills onto the nightstand before he walked out. It was after Ameer learned that the madame appropriated the money that he pulled something like a notepad out of his breast pocket and pressed it into the girl's hand.

"What's this?" she said, not so much looking at the thing in her hand as Ameer's eyes.

He had opened a bank account for her. Ameer was enchanted by her childish smile and half-open, clear eyes as she looked at the passbook. Lying on the bed, he asked her about her men.

"I've already told you," she said with a smile, sitting cross-legged, playing with the lace hem of her red nightgown.

"Tell me again." Ameer ran his palm over her back, every now and then twisting the tips of her long hair that poured down her back in locks.

They were random people. Some were shovelers like Ameer. "You can tell a lot about a man by the way he handles his shovel," Goli said.

Ameer rolled onto his side. "How do I handle my shovel?"

"With grace." She smiled at the ceiling. Ameer wanted to know who else handled his shovel with grace. There had been this one man who was not a shoveler, but had been decent. He had come one night and wrote strange things about cats in the margins of a fashion journal he grabbed from the nightstand. He had not said a word the whole night and took the journal with him when he left. There was something special in the way he wrote that Goli could not explain. She did not say those things to stir Ameer's jealousy, but he was happy the man had not shown up again or given his name, even a fake one. He had been a nobody; there one night, gone the next. Ameer put more money into Goli's account and soon forgot about the man.

AHMAD HAD NEVER THOUGHT ABOUT the girl again either. With his mind less cluttered than an hour before his visit to New Town, he went straight to Sara's house. He was still not sure how to tell Sara or what, for that matter, was most important to tell. He had a cab and a bus ride to decide what to say:

It had taken him three years, but finally he had a poem, the poem. He had started shortly after Homa left him and finally he had written the poem of pure love, and they could use it to free Salman from the prison.

That was a clumsy, meaningless account that confused even Ahmad. The bus stopped and he stepped down onto hardened snow. He walked fast and soon unwound his scarf from around his neck and stuffed it into his pocket. Passing the ice cream shop that marked halfway between the bus stop and Sara's house, he promised himself a bowl of saffron ice cream if it went well.

Sara herself was the consolingly familiar face that opened the door and tilted her head to the side with her arms akimbo as if to say, You again! What do you want now? But her arms fell to her sides and her eyes sparkled with interest and concern when she read Ahmad's note. Anxiously, she asked him in and shook her head as Ahmad told her about his plan, making her gold earrings swing back and forth wildly. With Salman and Sara's father dead, Sara was the only immediate family left, the only person who could visit Salman. But Sara did not want to hear more. She got to her feet and looked down at Ahmad. First, she was afraid; she could not bring herself to convey a message even in the crowded hall where every visitor and inmate tried to shout over the others. Salman had five more years in the general ward and he would be out. Solitary confinement and investigations were behind him. He was a burned wick that no one cared to hold a flame to anymore. What awaited him was boredom, not pain. Ahmad got up from his chair, too.

"You show up after God knows how long, with this? With more danger?" *No one wants to be in there a day more than he has to.* Sara looked at the notepad and said, "We're past our years of adventure." She closed the door behind Ahmad, but she knew he was too obstinate to quit. Her not taking action could be more dangerous for her brother, because now she had given the rein to Ahmad. Sleep evaded her. Yielding to anxiety after only five days, she picked up the phone and called Ahmad's house. No one answered. She called Khan's house. Pooran did not know where Ahmad was and that frightened Sara more. She counted down the three days until the next visiting Thursday and told Salman about Ahmad's visit. Salman fell silent for some time. Then he leaned toward the glass and lowered his voice to an almost inaudible volume. "What was it?"

Sara shook her head.

"You don't trust me?" he said leaning back into his chair.

Within four days after he first broached the idea to Sara, Ahmad had written over two hundred pages of poor-quality poetry in praise of nature and a nebulous ethereal beloved. With the help of Dr. Afshar, he printed and bound the poems into the semblance of a published book and sent it in. The prison inspector leafed through the book in his room. He liked some of them, and making a mental note to buy his own copy, tossed it onto the pile of permitted items.

"I got it," Salman said from behind the glass.

"What? What did you get?"

"It's just a bunch of poems about flowers and whatnot. It's trash. But I think you already know what else it says." Sara shook her head. "You're lying," Salman whispered. "Tell me."

"You'll be out in five years," Sara said, pleading.

"I know that." Salman leaned forward again, resting his elbows on the narrow ledge in front of him. "You think I'm a child? You think this is child's play to me? You think I want to go back in that hell?" he lowered his voice and threw nervous looks around.

"Then what do you want to know it for?"

Salman sat back in his chair and crossed his arms over his chest as if he did not have a good answer for the question. "Curiosity maybe," he said. "I just want to know what on earth can come out of crappy poetry."

Sara fell silent for a long moment. Salman could see the white hairs she had tried to hide by dying her hair, which had started to grow out. She put her little finger to her mouth and chewed on the nail for a few moments until she lifted her face and shook her head. "No, Salman, I can't," she said. "I can't sleep knowing that you even know what you know now." She got up from her chair. "Just throw the book out, please, if you care about me." She left before the visit time was over.

Salman did not throw the book out. That evening he lay down in his bunk and started reading from the beginning. Two thirds into the book he came to a line that caught his attention. He read again. *Two plus two is all I need.* The sentence sounded familiar, fraught with memories of a day in the distant past when he was riding on Ahmad's back, his feet burning with welts from Mulla's cherry branches. Salman sat up. It took him less than two weeks before he could break the code, reading the second words of the second lines.

AHMAD WALKED TO HOMA'S DOOR every other week. She would let him into her rented apartment and make him tea while Ahmad looked around at what seemed like the bare minimum put together: two secondhand chairs and a small wooden table in the living room on an old rug, no photos on the walls, the windows without curtains. Homa brought out the teas. She would ask about Lalah and wait patiently for Ahmad to write, her legs crossed, her hands clasped in her lap, like a doctor waiting for her patient to finish undressing. The telltale signs of impermanence in the sad apartment gave Ahmad hope and brought him back the next time. Every time, Homa saw him to the door and sent him back out.

Months later, Homa's name appeared in Ahmad's poetry for the first time. Homa read the poem in *Black and White*, dabbing at her eyes with a tissue. At his desk in Agha's room, Ahmad wove her into his words for two years. One night, his heart crumpling like paper, in a rare moment of pure and sincere creativity, Ahmad wrote the poem that became the apex of his art. The poem started to emit a strong light by the first line. Midsecond line, a small flame fluttered from under the tip of Ahmad's pen. He slapped the fire out and ran out of Agha's room. The first metallic thing he found in the kitchen was a stainless-steel tea tray in the sink. As he scratched words on the back of the tray, the steel grew warmer and warmer until Ahmad could not hold the needle any longer. He wrapped the tray in a blanket and hurried out into the blowing snow, hugging it and enjoying the warmth it produced. At Oos Abbas's forge, he put on welding glasses and the leather gloves they wore while working with hot metal. Using a nail, he finished the poem on a workbench at the back of the forge and watched how the tray gradually grew red hot on the last word of the poem. The red spot grew brighter. Molten steel dripped onto the table leaving a hole in the tray. He then tried the poem on an unfinished window frame with the same result. It was not a poem to ever be published. To bore a hole in metal, all Salman had to do was etch the words together one after the other.

Salman did not believe it until he saw it with his own eyes. He burned a newspaper page with the sixth word before his suspicion gave way to amazement. Alone in his cell, on his turn to clean, he scratched the poem on the inside of the foot of his bed with a fork. By the time he stood up and straightened the prongs with the handle of another fork, the foot of the bed was already glowing. The corner of the bunk sank as the metal grew soft. After it cooled, the leg was a little shorter than the other three, metal hardened into an amorphous clump at the bottom. His calm was disturbed. He lay in bed at night, listening to his fellow inmates' tossing and turning, Big Boback snoring like a Mack truck, picturing five more years of sleeping in that bunk and staring at the bars above him that kept Big Boback from falling on him and ending his life. Then he would start picturing a break where he would burn all the gates open one after the other, but every time, a failure followed. He would be shot on the spot, or taken away and executed without trial. That would be the blessed way to go. The torture room flashed in his head, dispersing ambitions and inviting sleep into his eyes.

For a month, he was gripped by pangs of temptation. In her perfect glory, the illusion of freedom danced on the walls of his cell, in the putrid squat bathrooms, in the tension and stupor of the yard, and on the high brick walls topped with barbed wire and interrupted here and there with towers on which guards idled with rifles hanging from their backs. For the most part, he used the poem to keep warm. He wrote the first four words on his palms and covered the light with his gloves. Back inside, he spat into his fist and scrubbed the ink off with his thumb.

NEWS FROM OUTSIDE SWEPT THROUGH the prison like plague. Each week would bring an isolated protest in one city, an incident in another. The day the Abadan Refinery workers went on a strike, the government refused to respond at first, but before the end of the third day, the workers were back with doubled wages. They were condemned by the inmates as duplicitous sellouts. The prisoners agreed, though, that the cracks in the edifice of the system were becoming visible.

What crushed the people was the long lines for oil that started to form before the sun came out. In front of small, smelly oil shops with closed shutters and secure padlocks, the old and young kept their twenty-liter tin containers by their feet in the snow until the seller opened. There was always a shortage, no telling how many in the line would get a drop in their containers. "The snow has crippled the country," the Prime Minister announced to reporters. To unblock roads, the officials started to assign shoveling duties to anyone who worked for the government. Clerical employees had to shovel for at least four hours a day. The plan failed soon after it was implemented. Once out on the streets, most stole into cafés and bars and the work of the conscientious few was soon made null by the piles that the shovelers on the roofs dumped down into streets.

The government changed. The new Prime Minister, a four-star general and not a believer in leniency, announced that any civic disruption would be severely confronted. But despite the reinforced police, things did not calm down. Shortly after the general had taken office, many oil shops did not get their expected daily quota. Some of the tankers transferring oil from the south had not reached Tehran. Rumors followed that the general was buying more arms and ammunition for action against the people. The police that were deployed could not dispel the protesting crowd in one of the squares where the equestrian statue of the Shah's father stood on a tall pedestal. People hurled rocks and broke Jeep windshields and a nose. Shots were fired into the air. The protesters escaped into the streets that veined off of the square, but not before a Molotov cocktail flew through the broken window of a bank.

"Banks are not safe anymore," Ameer told Goli. "You should close your account." Goli put her finger on her lips. The madame could be listening. Goli had no place to keep anything safe.

"Can you take me away from here?" she asked as she knelt in front of Ameer to unbuckle his belt.

"No." Ameer caressed her hair, dyed yellow as he liked it, and tied in a ponytail.

"Leave that other girl," Goli asked in a playful way, as if it might turn Ameer on.

"You know I love you," Ameer said into her deep brown eyes that looked up into his, "but I can't leave any of you. I don't have time for fidelity." Ameer's marriage had been planned for later that year. His fiancée was beautiful, already divorced once. The youngest daughter of a well-off family, she had never gone to school but was a masterful cook and dexterous on the sewing machine.

"What if I told the girl's family about me and ruined your life?" Goli asked, her eyes locked into his, a smile on her thin lips. "What if I bit this off?"

Ameer ran his palm on her cheek and neck. "You won't do either," he said. "Because you love me. And because you pity me."

Goli pulled his pants all the way down. Creaseless and clean, his clothes smelled of fresh laundry. The smell of his cologne always entered the room before him. Ameer was a lover of good food and good women, which he told Goli once were the best medicine to delay the senility that was already catching up with him.

He had grown a mustache soon after starting middle school. In the morning, clutching his leather bag in his hand, he had stood in the bathroom as his father shaved off the fine hairs for him. He sat in the back row, and the women teachers felt uncomfortable calling him up to the front. The first day of high school, a new math teacher mistook him for the district inspector. With meticulous care, Ameer had looked at himself in the mirror and pulled at the skin on the corner of his eyes with the tips of his fingers to examine the few creases. He pulled his hair back to see if his hairline had receded. It was during one of these examinations that he had found his first white strand. He buried his face in his hands and cried until his father needed to use the bathroom. That was the day he realized that his time passed twice as fast as other people's.

Accepting the inevitable, he was emancipated from the responsibility of preserving life and decided that if he had half the time to live, he had to live twice as hard. That was the only way for him to take revenge on his fate. He poured his pills into the squat toilet, stepped out of the bathroom, and told his father he would not go to school anymore. He worked hard first at his father's shop, and then as a shoveler. He watched all the movies in the city, tried food from every street vendor's cart, went to cabarets, was present when a protest was underway, and treated himself to a big meal afterward. The day the bank caught fire, he was so close to the Molotov-cocktail boy that he saw him blow at his cold hands before he could strike the match. A thin boy no older than eighteen, with brown hair, swift as a gazelle, shouting, "The imperialist monsters. The militarist bastards," before hurling the bottle.

THE ANNOUNCED REASON FOR THE shortage of oil was the tankers' accidents. The general ordered an urgent allocation of extra funds for securing and plowing the roads. "The snow is crippling," he said to the reporters unapologetically, "but we'll beat it." Ahmad learned the real cause of the accidents one afternoon when he went to the *Black and White* office with a new poem. A reporter had interviewed one of the drivers at the hospital. Some hours after midnight, he had drawn close to the big city, listening to music from the cassette player he had screwed to the dashboard. The road was nothing but a small stretch of snow lit by the headlights. The rest was absolute dark. The wipers lashed back and forth cleaning the occasional flakes that melted instantly as they hit the windshield. He leaned ahead to take out the tape and put another on, but when he looked back at the road, he saw dozens of shining eyes in front of him, like a constellation of phosphorous-green stars, on that border of dark and light beyond which his head-lights could not shine. In a moment of panic, he jerked the wheel, but lost control. The tanker skidded and slid on the ice before it flipped onto its side.

Other drivers had told similar stories. A hoard of beasts jumping in front of their trucks out of the black of the night. *Black and White*'s headline, in the largest font possible, read: *wolves on their way*. Below it was a black sil-houette of a wolf's face looking with menacing white eyes at the reader. But the general consensus was that the government had spun the tale to dodge criticism and scrutiny into its squandering and corruption. In the next tape that came in from outside of winter, Ayatollah Khomeini said, "They say wolves. They think they can mislead the people with children's stories. If there is a wolf, it's the one with the crown."

The sentence caught on, was soon sprayed across the city, and entered hushed daily conversations as "the Wolf with the Crown." But Ahmad knew it was not true. Khan knew that, too, but he had long lost his interest in cats. With an obstinacy and anxiousness characteristic of old age, he worried about his body. Clutching at his walking stick or anything else at hand—a table, a chair, or the door—he pushed himself to his shaking legs early every morning. Staying still meant death. His freckled hands showed aged bones and bulging veins. He tried to eat more, but his throat closed off after a few bites. Nevertheless, he would get to his feet and head to the kitchen. He of-fered to help Zeeba, who did her work with such ease that everyone had forgotten she was blind. Pooran was worried Khan would spill hot water on himself, lop his finger in half, or fall off the chair. Out of the kitchen she drove him. In the yard, Khan took the shovel from where it leaned against the wall and tried to scrape clean the path from the house to the front door. Then he would sit, alone on the veranda, or in Agha's room with Ahmad, or inside with Pooran, his thoughts meandering into the past that was nowhere anymore but in his head. Before long, he snapped out of it and scrambled to his feet again. In the street, he walked from store to store, his agate beads in his hand, a nonfunctioning remnant of a lost passion, an expired quest. He had learned the truth up to the point beyond which no knowledge would help him. The day Ahmad opened the door with the *Black and White* weekly in his hand, Khan was catching his breath, both hands clutched around the handle of the shovel. He could no longer read without his glasses. Sitting by the oil heater in the corner of his black room, Khan listened to Pooran read the news out loud.

"They are shrewder than I thought," Khan said.

"The wolves are hungry, too," Pooran said.

"They're not wolves," Khan said. "They're cats."

"I'll die before I see a grown-up man in my life," Pooran said, tucking her salt-and-pepper hair under her scarf. She had worn one since the beginning of the long winter. She had worn scarves before, too, in those early days of her marriage with Nosser. Although there was no religious restriction then, she felt more comfortable wearing one. The color was very important to her at first. From her large wardrobe, she would pick the one that matched her clothes, or sometimes the colors of the Orchard: green, red, or pink, depending on the season. A month or two after her marriage, she stopped wearing headscarves and started to style her hair instead. When Leyla left, she put a black scarf on and did not take it off. In the wardrobe, she had set aside clothes for the day Leyla would come back, both the dress and the quince scarf.

"I told you not to do politics. You didn't listen to me," she said to Ahmad as she got up, "You saw what happened. You lost your beautiful wife and daughter. Now I'm telling you, Ahmad, put your feet on the ground. Be a father for Lalah, mend things with your wife, put your life back together. Or you'll unravel. Stop wandering. Look at yourself. Have you seen yourself? You're already forty."

He was forty-one.

Ahmad stood in front of the mirror that night. He looked no younger than his age. Short tufts of hair stuck out of his nostrils. His eyes had lost that buoyant glow that is in the eyes from birth. *Am I wasting my life?* He held his notepad before Khan who was polishing his shoes in his room. Khan stopped the brush midair and squinted to read the big letters. He asked for his reading spectacles. Ahmad pulled the glasses from a leather pouch and put them on Khan's face. Khan looked at the paper, then turned back to his work, one hand inside the shoe, the other running the brush back and forth along the length of it.

"You're not asking to know," he finally said. "What you want is denial." The swishing of the brush was the only sound in the room. "You have done good things. You have done stupid things." Ahmad got up to leave. "But the world is too complicated a place," Khan said. "We're all losers. You know that better than me."

Before he left, Ahmad scribbled on his notepad.

YOU'RE WRONG. I WROTE THE POEM OF FREEDOM.

WITH THE POKER FACE OF a veteran politician, the Great Zia told Ahmad again that he did not know where Mr. Zia was.

"Don't worry yourself, son," he said with a smile, patting Ahmad on the shoulder. "Your daughter is in good hands. You're probably already a grandfather."

Ahmad said goodbye and left the man's house. The next morning, as he had the past sixty years, Great Zia woke at five o'clock. He stirred a teaspoon of honey into his tea and drank with the radio on before he stepped out for his morning walk, which he had not stopped even with the winter. The chills of the past few days had abated. Rolls of dark-blue clouds in the eastern sky promised the beginning of the day, a good day with the snow coming down in big flakes of cotton, much better than the small, dry ones. The neighborhood windows were lighting up as parents woke to prepare breakfast for their kids before school. At the end of the alley, he turned onto the street that lead to the park, which was quiet and dark, with yellow streetlights shining over snow. In front of the park, before he crossed, he took careful looks both ways. There were no cars in sight. When he reached the middle of the street, he turned his head and saw a car coming toward him with its lights off, like a bolt of lightning from another world. The next moment, the car was speeding away down the street, leaving behind Great Zia's body to twitch on a blanket of snow for a short while before coming to rest. Later they had a hard time taking his walking stick out of his frozen hand. When they found him, he was already covered in a thin layer of snow.

Three days later, Great Zia was lowered into his grave under the black umbrellas that throngs of friends, family, and politicians held above their heads, amidst the wailing of women and the recitation of the Quran. His nephew, Mr. Zia, was not among the mourners, but he showed up for the Seventh-night service at the mosque. He could not bring himself to go in among the people who crowded the main hall and corridors, hugging and offering condolences. Hands deep in his jacket pockets, he bowed his head on the sidewalk across from the mosque. After a while, he walked back to the bus stop, rode for four stops, got off, wound through quiet streets, took another bus, and finally stepped into his parked car and drove back to his apartment, keeping a vigilant eye on the rearview mirror the whole way.

Later that night, Ahmad was parked in front of his door, looking at the second-floor window of the two-story brick building from the passenger seat. He motioned for the driver and the two men in the back to wait. Ahmad rang the doorbell and heard it echo inside. Hands tucked in the pockets of his long raincoat, Ahmad kicked the snow and looked down the quiet street: only two men were walking in the distance; two shadows in the shadows. The rest was white. Footsteps climbing down the stairs sounded through the door, and soon Leyla opened, with a chador draped over her head. She looked at Ahmad, first trying to make out the details of the face silhouetted against the streetlight and then with eyes blurred with tears.

"I'm sorry, I'm sorry." She buried herself in her father's arms. The last time she had done that, she reached no higher than Ahmad's chest; now she rested her head on his shoulder.

"Who is it?" Mr. Zia's voice came down the stairwell. Ahmad took Leyla's hand and went up. In his pajama bottoms and undershirt, Mr. Zia froze in place like a tree as the father and daughter stepped up. He was not sure if he should be ready to defend himself, to plead, or to run away.

"Father, he's been very nice to me," Leyla said, turning to Ahmad and grabbing his arm, anxiety in her voice. Her voice had changed, too, almost imperceptibly deeper. She was a young woman now.

Ahmad turned his menacingly calm face to Leyla and mouthed, *Are you married?* She nodded, holding up her ringed left hand. While Leyla packed her suitcase, Mr. Zia dressed himself and found nothing to say to Ahmad beyond repeated apology. He had grown bald but he was still good-looking. It was only when Ahmad and Leyla were leaving that he asked, "Will I see her again?"

Ahmad eyed him for a few seconds, but turned his back to him without saying anything. He walked out of the door, holding his daughter's hand in one hand and her suitcase in the other.

On their way home, Ahmad and Leyla sat in the back, while two of the men shared the passenger seat. The driver broke into song. Snapping their fingers to the rhythm of the tune, the two-man chorus sang the refrain along the slippery roads.

Ahmad turned to Leyla and mouthed, *You're not pregnant, are you?*

In the yellow lights that flashed into the car from the streetlamps, Ahmad saw her cast down her eyes. He held her face in his hand and turned it toward himself.

When?

Holding her hand down so the driver would not see in the rearview mirror, Leyla showed Ahmad two fingers. In the front, the driver rolled down the window and screamed his song into the cold.

The next day, when Homa stepped out of the hospital at the end of her shift, she saw Ahmad, Lalah, and Leyla standing side by side on the sidewalk with smiles. The girls had red roses in their hands which Homa knew had been Ahmad's idea. If they had not been in public, she would have hugged them all, planted kisses on Ahmad's face. Instead, she ran down the steps and held her long-lost daughter tight in her arms, oblivious of the gazes of the passersby. Feeling elated and supported by the obstinacy and determination of her husband, which she had seen as steel coldness, she celebrated the reunion of her family. But contrary to Ahmad's expectation, when he asked her at night to unite as a family, she said, "I need more time on my own, Ahmad." Stubbornness of that sort was not something Ahmad had known in Homa. He had thought that if he could find Leyla, Homa would have no reason not to mend the family back into its previous completeness. He felt indignant.

"Give her some time," Pooran told Ahmad.

Until the baby is born, Ahmad mouthed.

26

NTIL THE BABY WAS BORN, Ahmad decreed that Leyla had to be in Khan's house where Pooran and Lalah could tend to her. Any talk about what had happened in the past and what would come about in the future was postponed. Leyla's husband could come and see her anytime he wanted, and Homa was welcome to visit her daughters as often as she wished. Zeeba opened Leyla's room, swept the rugs, and dusted the furniture. Life came to the house once again. Khan brought in a mason to plan a new room for the baby. The two men stood on the snow-covered roof and looked at the three rooms already crowning the building. The mason rubbed his chin. He was not sure if it was a good idea to add any more weight on top of a house that had seen so many years. Khan said, "Some mason's making me a room. It's either you or someone else," and so it was that before the baby was born, the fourth room was ready, on top of Zeeba's. Its travertine facade, cemented over the brick walls, was visible from both ends of the alley. The first two rooms stood side by side, with a space between them wide enough only for two people to pass, but the ones on top faced one another. Each was accessed by a metal staircase. Of the previous three, only two rooms had been put to real use, one by Nana Shamsi and her granddaughter and the other by Lalah. The four-cube arrangement seemed to Ahmad unnecessary, only the realization of Khan's age-old hunger to reach higher. The pregnant Leyla never stayed in her room either, since Pooran would not allow her to take the rickety elevator. "That kind of work will turn the baby around," she said. "Plus, as long as I live, my granddaughter won't be trudging the snow between her bed and dinner." She gave Leyla her own bedroom and slept on a mattress in the living room.

"Why don't you take Ahmad's old room, at least?" Leyla asked.

"No dear," Pooran answered. "There should be a woman seven steps or closer to a pregnant woman at night."

And so it was that Pooran slept close to Leyla's door and pulled the covers up to her nose. Five days had passed when she woke in the middle of the night with her body tense with cold. She stepped out of the bed and found the door that opened to the veranda left ajar. She closed it and went back to bed hugging herself. The shivers that ran up and down her spine refused to abate for a few hours as she stared at the ceiling trying to stop the involuntary rattle of her teeth. In the morning, her head felt heavy. She found cat prints outside on the veranda and decided to lock that door from then on. The animals were looking for food at night. They pawed at doors and smelled their way into kitchens. Pooran developed a headache which was replaced at night by a fever and a cough that kept her awake. After three delirious days in bed, the fever relented. The cough persisted. Khan said, and Ahmad nodded, that the cat had not been looking for food, but had opened the door on purpose. Pooran thought cats were innocent creations of God, less harmful than most people. Ahmad called the doctor and after two weeks of intermittent fevers, Pooran stepped out of the bed and started to arrange for spring cleaning, although spring had not come for the past nine years and would not return until six years later.

"With or without spring," she said, "the year will turn. The new will replace the old."

THE TIME-OLD TRADITIONS WERE STILL observed, in spite of—or perhaps because of—the general misery of the failing economy and harsh weather. As a New Year present, Third Lieutenant Akbari, the mail inspector of the Palace Prison, a small man who loved his uniform and dreamed of climbing up the ladder, decided to give his niece a book. He had not forgotten an incoming collection of poetry for a prisoner by the name of Salman something a few months before. He had liked most of the lines he read as he leafed through. After his shift, Third Lieutenant Akbari left the prison for the street that had the University of Tehran on one side and the bookstores on the other, the street that after the Revolution was renamed Revolution Street. For two hours, he came out of one bookstore and entered another, but the book could not be found. No one had even heard of it. The next afternoon, a soldier came to the ward and took Salman with him. After a short but emotionally turbulent walk, Salman was in the inspection room with four officers sitting at their heaped-up desks. Salman's heart was racing so hard that he thought he would have a heart attack any minute. "So it's you," said Lieutenant Akbari from behind his desk, "you got a book, some time ago, right?" The four officers were looking at Salman now and the soldier that brought him in was standing behind him at attention. "With poems and stuff, right?" For a second he felt he was going to wet his pants. He nodded his head, his arms stiff by his sides, as if he, too, was standing at attention in compliance with an unheard order. "Do you know where I can find a copy?" Salman paused, unable to imagine what would happen if they found out that the book was fake. Fortunately, it took little insisting to persuade the officer to accept his own copy as a present.

Back behind the bars, Salman flopped on his bed and started shaking from head to toe. Big Boback's round face appeared upside down from the top bunk and asked him what the hell the problem was with him, but Salman was unable to open his mouth. "Put your feet up." Big Boback jumped down shaking the bed with his weight. He put his pillow under Salman's feet and stirred a dash of salt in a glass of water and made him drink a few gulps. For a week Salman thought anyone in uniform was coming to take him. Any footstep in the corridors was the promise of leather straps and electric shocks, blood and sweat, blows in the stomach that curled him up on cold concrete, small, weak, and filthy. His fear was so great that finally he told Big Boback he could not take it anymore and they planned the escape: Salman, Big Boback, and two of their closest friends, Esi Goldfingers and Mamad Cucumber.

One early evening, before lights out and after the sun had set behind the western houses of the city, the quartet snuck into the bathroom. Standing on the shoulders of Big Boback, Salman scratched the poem on the thick bars of the window high in the wall. In a few seconds the bars fell clattering onto the concrete terrazzo floor still red hot on the ends. "Get out of here!" Big Boback said in a hushed voice, his large eyes wide in amazement, his large hands holding Salman's ankels. "This can't be real."

Outside the window they found themselves in a narrow backyard scattered with trash and covered halfway in snow. Esi Goldfingers led the way. He had been there for twenty years and there was no nook or cranny of the prison he did not know. They army-crawled toward the end of the backyard where a sizable door opened into a storage room. Drawing heavy breaths, Salman got to his feet and etched the poem onto the rusty shackle of the padlock and lay back down on his stomach. The lock fell into the snow with a sizzle. In they went, Salman with Boback and Mamad behind him, but a few seconds passed and Esi did not follow. They looked at each other with questioning eyes until Mamad crawled back on all fours and stuck his head out to look. Esi Goldfingers was lying in the snow in his army-crawl position, hands knotted into fists, lips pressed together, eyes fixed ahead. Mamad Cucumber motioned for him to hurry, but Esi did not move. Even petrified, he was charming and handsome, his face fit, as they said, for the large screen.

Esi's lips quivered as he whispered something Mamad did not hear. "I want to go back," Esi whispered, this time louder. Mamad put his finger on his lips and shushed him, looking around. Salman, too, crawled over to the door. He saw and heard Esi's teeth rattling. Then the two men retreated to clear the way for Big Boback who crawled out the door—his abundant bottom wiggling like a black bear's—reached out, and grabbed Esi's wrists in his fat hands, then pulled him in like a frozen carcass. Once inside, they closed the door and tried to calm Esi down. Mamad Cucumber hugged him from behind, lay straight on his back to warm him, and whispered quiet words in his ear. The storage room was used partly as the prison arsenal and partly as repository for oil heaters, Jeep tires, toolboxes, ropes, and kitchen utensils. Located behind the sergeant officer's room, it had three doors: one that the sergeant officer on duty had access to, one to the courtyard through which they had entered, and one that had fallen into disuse. That third door led to a short corridor at the end of which was the room to the sewage. The sewage was where they were going.

Mamad Cucumber had changed from "short and fat" to "short and thin"—from Mamad Gourd to Mamad Cucumber—the first week they had brought him into the prison and that was why he lay on Esi's back not as a heavy weight, but as a consoling embrace, like a quilt. Big Boback's face opened in a smile when he saw Esi finally nodding to something Mamad told him. Salman breathed a silent sigh of relief and motioned for everybody to hurry up. Mamad Cucumber rolled off of Esi and they got back to work.

Two padlocks, one from inside the storage room, and one on the other side, secured the disused door. They took off their shirts and piled them up on the floor to muffle the clatter of the falling padlock. Salman and Esi Goldfingers dumped handfuls of snow on the glowing lock as soon as it dropped from the door. The bigger problem was the lock on the other side of the door. They crawled back into the small yard. A barred window opened into the corridor behind the door through which Esi Goldfingers and Mamad Cucumber went to the other side; Esi because Mamad had told him he would be the first of the four to leave the place, and Mamad because he had promised Esi not to leave his side until the end. Salman and Big Boback went back to the storage room and waited. The minutes passed slowly. Behind the other door, Salman could hear two officers laughing. Big Boback wheezed as he looked nervously at Salman. They could barely hear the weak sound of scratching on the other side, but nothing happened. Salman tapped lightly on the door to transfer the anxiety and make them hurry. Then came some clanking. They were fidgeting with the lock. When he could not stand it anymore, Salman tiptoed to the backyard and army-crawled to the narrow window. The two had forgotten the last line of the poem. Esi Goldfingers had scratched his version on the shackle but it had only warmed up the lock and created a strong light. Mamad Cucumber had crossed out Esi's last line and scratched his reworded version, which had proven wrong, too. Through the window, Salman handed them fistfuls of snow to soothe their blistering hands, and whispered the right order of words. But there were already too many wrong words and scratch marks on the shackle and the poem would not form.

"Write it on the body," Salman whispered.

Esi and Mamad took turns scribbling the poem onto the rusted body of the padlock with a nail. A few minutes later there was a hole in the middle of the lock, but still it would not open. Big Boback came to the window, panting from exertion, with a fine screwdriver from a toolbox on a top shelf. With his directions whispered through the window, Mamad Cucumber pried the lock open after nervously running his hand across the crew cut on his round scalp a few times. Down the corridor and into another room they went until they reached the grate that covered the sewage. Drenched in slimy waste in the putrid dark, Salman, Esi Goldfingers, and Mamad Cucumber inched their way through the narrow tunnel toward the street. Big Boback got stuck and no matter how hard Salman pulled, he could not free the big boy. Big Boback was arrested in the morning and a week later, as the protests unfolded in the streets, he was suffocated in a tub full of excrement with his wrists handcuffed behind his back, the investigator's gloved hand pushing his large head all the way down until his nose was crushed against the bottom of the tub.

THE PRISON BREAK WAS A slap in the face of the new Prime Minister, a challenge to his inflated authority. The secret service raided the prison and confiscated all the belongings of the prisoners. Yard time was cut in half and the amount of meals was reduced. The few that raised their voices in protest were immediately taken away.

Published in newspapers and circulating from mouth to mouth as one of the three fugitives, Salman's name warmed Ahmad's heart. He felt like he had made up for the speech that they said had started the crackdown. He threw the newspaper into Khan's lap. By the headline he had penned, in large letters, *I DID THAT.*

Khan put his glasses on and read without haste. "You're helping those cats then," he said.

I helped my friend.

"You're wreaking havoc."

Ahmad found in himself no remorse for what he had done. Was it not Khan himself who had blamed the havoc on the cats? Had it not been he who had drawn the charts and marked the maps and done such persuasive calculations? He had predicted things and they had come true. The old man was now contradicting himself. His mental astuteness had begun to decline. His body was already worn out, his limbs were weak, and his hair had fallen out of his crest, leaving a band of sparse, white bristles around his head. The only remnant of the vigor, charisma, and power he had exuded years before was his mustache. He had not stopped waxing and twirling up the ends of his whiskers.

"Come to think of it," Khan said slowly, as if finding words had become a tax his body could not afford, "it was you who was for the law and against disrupting the order, no?" Khan's sarcasm referred to Ahmad's speech.

I was, but how long can you bend your head?

Khan held the paper close to his face and moved his glasses. "I can't read this," he said. "Write bigger."

I WAS, BUT HOW LONG CAN YOU BEND YOUR HEAD?

Khan looked at Ahmad for a moment. "Did you see what the cats did to your mother?" he said. "She could have caught pneumonia."

You said the cats were doing all this and I believed you. If toppling the regime is what they're after, I'm with the cats, then.

Khan looked closely at the words jammed into the margin of the newspaper. "I can't read this."

Ahmad took his notebook out of his inside breast pocket and started writing.

"Why don't you sit down? You can take that by the desk"—Khan pointed to a chair that leaned against the black, tarred wall—"or sit here on the bed. Do you want me to bring you the chair?"

Ahmad shook his head as he wrote. Khan looked out the window. A sparrow landed in the persimmon three, shaking the snow off the branch. It jerked its small head to both sides for a few seconds before taking flight again. The naked branch quivered, but soon calmed back into the graceful stillness of the tree.

You say the cats want to pull the Shah down, I say let them. I'm going to help them if I can. You say they wanted to kill my mother, I say I don't know. Why would they want to do that? And even if so, what can I do? What did you do to prevent the cat attack, to hinder the catastrophe?

Khan took the note. His eyes squinted behind his glasses.

"I can't read this." He gave the paper back to Ahmad. "You know what, do what you want. I'm tired. Agha told us about all of this in his own way. I denied it. Then I saw it myself. I've been trying to make you see it too. You told me once you did, but you don't. You go and do what you want."

IN THE PROTESTS THAT FOLLOWED the raid of the prison, Lalah was busy making Molotov cocktails in her friend's basement. She had taken up Zeeba's responsibility of filling the heaters, so she could steal oil and have a reason to reek of it when she came back home. The second day after the prison break, she and Shireen made fourteen bottles. When Shireen brought the baskets, Lalah said, "I'm going with you."

"Don't get your hopes up," Shireen said. "Ebi might not come today."

"We'll see," Lalah answered putting the first bottle in the basket. They topped the bottles with armfuls of parsley that Lalah had bought at the neighborhood fruit and herbs shop. When the sun had just set, they draped chadors over their heads to look unobtrusive and set off. They walked for half an hour eastward, along sidewalks, across a number of streets, through a snowy park, out onto other sidewalks, checking out passersby, looking into grocery stores, electric shops, confectionary stores, clothes shops, and a defunct ice stand, and finally turned into the narrow street where the bottles were to be transferred to the boys. It was rather quiet, but there was no guarantee that eyes were not spying on them from the flanking houses. The boys were sitting in a parked Peykan. The girls walked past them, checking the car from the corners of their eyes. Lalah saw the older man, Ameer, at the wheel and another one of the guys, perhaps Comrade Bijan, beside him blowing into his hands. A little way ahead, they walked between two parked cars and swiftly put their baskets down on the ground, then walked away.

"He was there, he was there," Shireen said, pinching Lalah on the arm as she often did when her passion for Ameer was too much for her to bear. "What do I do? What do I do? What do I do?"

Although the man had never shown anything but politeness and appropriate behavior, Shireen thought she spotted a desire in his eyes. At Lalah's suggestion, the girls rushed to the end of the street, turned into the next, and swiftly pulled their chadors off their heads, crumpling them quickly into their shoulder bags. Then they hurried back to where the boys were parked. But the car was gone. So were the shopping baskets.

There was no visible sign of distress or frustration in Shireen's face, but as they crunched the snow back home, now a little slower, hands in jacket pockets, she pinched Lalah on the arm and said, "I'm going to whatever's happening tomorrow. I'm calling the guys tonight to ask. Are you coming?"

By noon the next day, Lalah and Shireen were taking shelter behind parked cars with other people, almost all men, watching the protesters from a short distance, running here and there. The gathering had blocked a small roundabout. Cars soon turned around and left the arena to people. The slogans were about the Prime Minister, and the corruption in the government. They asked for the release of the political prisoners and for food and warmth. Soon the police arrived. The crowd dispersed but did not go away. The stores had closed as soon as the protesters started gathering. Ignoring the men who told them this was not a suitable place for girls, Shireen and Lalah drew farther forward until Shireen spotted one of the four boys. Soon an army truck brought reinforcement. Soldiers jumped out of the tarpaulin-covered back of the vehicle with rifles in their hands. After the shots that were fired into the air proved as futile as the warnings a colonel barked into a megaphone, a high school student was shot dead. His head tilted back as he collapsed to the ground with open arms, his blood spilled out of his chest and ran into the slush on the asphalt. Three young men sprinted to him with backs and knees bent to make smaller targets of themselves. When they picked up the boy's body to carry him back, they saw a red tulip had grown where his chest had touched the ground. After the Revolution, that roundabout was renamed Tulip Square, the day celebrated as Student's Day.

The Fortieth-day service for the boy was held at a mosque full of people clad in black who, moved by the tragic death, took to the streets after the service. The police and army were deployed. In her heart, Lalah found an affinity with the movement, with the young men who, ebullient with gracious rage, stamped their determined feet into the snow and punched their fists into the air. At their next rendezvous, this time with Comrade Bijan and Jamsheed, a few weeks later, she found an opportune moment and said, "I want to be in the streets with you guys."

"That's what we're fighting for," Comrade Bijan said as he closed the trunk. He had said a good thing, but in a bad way. And he had not gotten the point. And he had not combed his hair again. Lalah watched the red taillights fade away into the snow.

A few weeks later when another protest was brewing in the city, she showed up in Shireen's basement with a pair of scissors. "What are you doing?" Shireen asked, curious and a little anxious. Lalah grabbed her own braid in her fist and by the time Shireen stifled her short shriek and got to her feet, Lalah had snipped it off with a few quick strokes. She rolled the yellow hair band off and tossed the long tress into the trash can. "You idiot, are you out of your mind?" Shireen cried, her hand over her mouth. Lalah's small face looked even smaller now with one braid sprouting on one side of her head and dangling over her breast. Lalah cut the second braid and rolled the band off onto her wrist. Shireen went to the trash can and took the braids out. "Look at this lovely hair," she said. "Just look at it. Now what the hell was that about? What will your father say?"

"Oh, he won't say anything," Lalah answered with a narrow smile and Shireen wondered for a moment what it would be like to kiss those thin, beautiful lips.

A FEW DAYS LATER, WITH her short hair comfortably tucked under a wool hat, Lalah's face looked like a big hazelnut. Zipping up her loose, army-green overcoat, Lalah watched Shireen pull up the pants that were loose enough, but also a bit too short for her. Shireen could not bring herself to cut her hair. If examined closely, her hat would betray the fullness of the bun underneath it. With heads bowed to avoid looks, and collars turned up, they walked up and down the streets until enough people were gathered. As the crowd walked past them chanting slogans, Lalah jumped from the sidewalk, over the ditch, into the street and the next moment she was walking among them. Her heart was pounding. She could not hear what the men cried. All she knew was that she was surrounded by them, one with the current and none of them had the faintest idea she was a girl. No one was even looking at her. She closed her hand and threw her fist up in the air and soon found Shireen by her side.

"I'm going to go find my man," she said, joking about Ameer's age.

By the time the crowd was dispersed by the warning shots, Shireen had found Ameer. She had to introduce herself to him as they ran away into a back street. "You're a changed girl I'll have to admit," Ameer said and Shireen became the third girl in his life at that moment. In her he admired a brazenness that the other two lacked. In the rather long interval of calm political atmosphere after that day, Ameer juggled the three. He postponed the wedding once. He found himself unable to detach from any of those women, but he knew the day would come when things could not go on like that anymore.

To Shireen, he remained the fifty-year-old man that she thought he was. He made up a new backstory for her: a man with a history of resistance as far back as the Coup. He had had a difficult past and never enough time to think about women. He told her his memories of that historic day, how he had yanked the picture of the Shah out of the hands of a goon with a club and ran off. Shireen listened with credulity and curious questions that made Ameer's story flourish with spontaneous details. "I wish you could be the mother of my child," he told her one day at a cheap restaurant. Shireen blushed. The feeling in her heart told her she had found, if not the man of her dreams, a good man, a reliable and honest man, someone alongside whom she could fight and with whom she could eat cheap sausage sandwiches.

"Only if he was younger," she told Lalah pinching her arm. "Even just ten years."

"I want you to be the mother of my child," Ameer breathed into Goli's ear the next time he was on top of her in her room. At that moment, Goli was not thinking about how she would manage the costs of raising a baby or what the madame would do if she found out she was pregnant. She felt all she wanted was to swing a crib, sing lullabies, and nag about how the little thing would not let her sleep.

IN SPITE OF POORAN, LEYLA gave birth at a hospital. "Babies shouldn't be born where the sick go to die," Pooran said. She had been born at home and she herself had borne many babies at home. "Both of you were born in my room," she told Ahmad and Maryam, standing in front of her children in the waiting area, not able to stop talking, coughing from time to time, "and you're fine." Her cold had lingered as a persistent cough. She did not sit for the whole time, but walked to talk to the nurses at the reception desk, and strike up conversations with the others also waiting for something to happen. "She was not half as anxious," Maryam said to Ahmad, "when my kids were coming." She raised her eyebrows. "Well, we know she likes boys better than girls."

Leyla's baby was a boy who cried a little upside down, but started smiling as soon as the nurse held him in her arms. Leyla held the receiver to the baby's mouth so Mr. Zia could hear his son. "Don't cry," she said into the phone, her voice weak. "Come in three, four hours. I'll make sure Father is gone by then."

One hour after the baby was born, the whole family was gathered around Leyla's bed. Pooran, Khan, Maryam and her family, Lalah, Zeeba, Ahmad, Homa, her mother, and Colonel Delldaar. The baby was so sweet that anyone who held him broke an involuntarily, honest smile looking at his naturally happy face. They called him Behrooz, "the fortunate." When the nurse came in and asked them to let Leyla rest, Majeed asked for a second, took out his camera, and put everyone together in the tight space between the bed and the window. What the photo did not show was that behind Lalah, in the short time while Majeed looked into his camera with one eye closed, instructing everyone to huddle more closely, Homa touched Ahmad's pinkie with the tip of her forefinger as if cautiously testing a pot handle, until the camera clicked and saved that moment from oblivion.

THE NEXT AFTERNOON HOMA GINGERLY entered the room where Leyla was sleeping and bent over to watch the swaddled newborn in a calm sleep by his mother, trying to figure out who he had taken after. His eyebrows were high and his face open and inviting. He had Ahmad's eyes and lips; in his forehead she saw traces of herself. She kissed Leyla on the forehead and turned up the heater before she left the room. Slipping into Pooran's black galoshes, Homa crossed the yard and knocked on Ahmad's door, turning the handle knowing that she would not hear a "come in." Standing by the barred window, through which came a soft, white light, Ahmad was plucking dead leaves from his begonia on the sill. He had started to keep plants indoors in the years after Homa had left him, which Homa had learned from the girls who went to visit her in her apartment. Ahmad turned to her with a calm in his face that made Homa wish someone could snap a photo of him at that moment, so she could keep that frame on the table in her room.

"Ahmad, I want us to get back together," she said, as if making a plea, as if it was the only thing that would warm her heart in that cold world.

Ahmad looked at her: brimming with a mature beauty, her cheeks rosy from the winds, and her tied hair tucked under her short-brimmed hat. Then he looked within himself and found a cornucopia of memories with that woman, the most vivid from the beginning when she came to that café with her chaperone to hear Ahmad's poems. Bad memories were in his heart, like from the days when Leyla was gone, and Homa was a ghost, looking at him as if he was the devil incarnate. He went from memory to memory and from feeling to feeling, but no matter how deep he plowed, he was unable to find passion for her, even remnants of a lost one. He was surprised. He had not expected that moment would come. For the last years, every time he had gone to her door to silently plead her to come back, he had expected she would finally say yes, or something vague that would be a ray of hope for him. But she had so determinedly rejected him every time. Now his heart was empty. He shook his head.

The way Homa's lips trembled for a few seconds, unable to utter a word, keeping her dark eyes fixed on Ahmad, with the door half-open behind her, with her galoshes still on, chunks of the ice and snow that clung to them starting to melt and slide down onto the doormat, that was how Ahmad would remember Homa in the future when years later, he asked himself, *Did I make a mistake somewhere along the way?*

27

I N THE MONTH THAT IT TOOK the mason and his workers to make the new room for Behrooz, Ahmad readied himself for the Shiraz Art Festival which during the past seven years had turned into one of the most important summer arts events in the world. As well as the vanguards of performing and literary arts, tourists came for skiing. With the snow amassed for years, they had made slopes at the edge of the city, the core of which was hardened ice. With the hope of boosting the economy, the government had equipped the resorts with chair lifts and restaurants to attract worldwide tourists who looked to escape the summer heat. But the routes to get there were mainly closed. Roads were icy if not blocked, trains got stuck on the way for hours and days, and flying was limited to a handful of days in the year when black clouds were not rumbling and storms of infernal powers were not shaking the skies.

When the festival season came, though, the thousand-kilometer road from Tehran to Shiraz was plowed for the transportation of the guests and the queen, who supported and supervised the ceremony in person. The year before, Maestro Shahnaz had, for the sixth year in a row, made the frozen trees bloom with his music, and received the National Medal for Excellence in Art and that made Ahmad wonder: Why was Maestro's music a whiff of life but his own poetry a flash of raging fire? He concluded that the same form of energy flowed within both forms of art; the difference was the medium. Through sound, the energy was directly issued from the instrument and enveloped all that was around it. It penetrated and warmed in a way that excited life into things. With writing, all the energy was concentrated in the words, on the page, and through the eyes into the reader who was already alive. It was the concentration that heated the words, made them burn things. If he could read his poems himself, he would have read the ones he could not write down on anything. Then he would have done more than make trees blossom, and the National Medal would be his. Since that was not possible, Ahmad suspected that there must be a way to make words themselves into sound. A machine to extract the hidden sounds of the words directly off the page? Something analogous to a cassette player.

Occupied with his new passion, he bought a gramophone and started to work. First, he wrote his poems in circles and glued the paper onto a record, then he scratched words into the record with a needle, but to no avail. He penned his poems in small letters on the tape of a new cassette. Once rewound and played, nothing came out of the speakers but some faint clicking and cracking. Using two large magnifying glasses, he repeated the experiment, this time putting extremely tiny letters on the tape. The broken hiss and fizz was meaningless and fleeting and Ahmad knew it was not a question of size. Next, he spread out the words on the whole length of the tape, but nothing came out and at that point he realized that the available machinery would not suffice for what he had in mind. He took his cassettes and tape recorder in his arms and walked down into the basement and in a short while surrounded himself with tools and apparatuses: several models of cassette players and recorders, gramophones, screwdrivers, hammers, pliers, small motors, batteries, and soldering irons.

After his daily attempt at shoveling, Khan walked over to the top of the basement steps and climbed down with the help of Ahmad to sit in the chair and watch his grandson work. When Ahmad came to the conclusion that he had to better understand the relationship between each word and its inherent sound, Khan's memory was keen enough to point to the philosophers of the past, to Miskawayh, Mulla Sadra, Avicenna, and others whose books he had gathered through years in the large wooden bookcases against the wall. Ahmad read the books and thought and came to the conclusion that the key missing piece was *sight*. If the gramophone and tape recorder had failed to speak his poetry, it was because those machines were bereft of a reading eye. His nephew, Majeed, had the eyes. Down in the basement, Majeed showed Ahmad the features of a handheld video camera that you had to hold and point at the subject like a gun. After Ahmad gave a confirming nod that he knew what he needed to know about the machine, Majeed went up to shovel the roof, as it was around that time that Pooran made Khan stop shoveling. One early morning Khan had gotten up from his bed and pulled a second pair of wool leg warmers on in spite of the electrifying pain in his knees. Once on the veranda, he looked for his shovel in the dim light of the cloudy dawn, but it was not leaning against the dead cherry tree where he had left it the day before.

"As long as I'm alive," Pooran had said a few hours later when Khan knocked on her door and went in, "you won't shovel anymore. If something happens, I can't take care of you. I'm not strong anymore, Khan, and neither are you."

Khan turned around and closed the door behind him, but the disappearance of the shovel did not make him sit in a corner like an old man. He began getting up in the dark and shuffling his way to the oil line with an empty can swinging in his hand which later, if he was lucky enough to get oil, Zeeba or Ahmad would carry back home. He sat in the kitchen with a tray full of lentils to be winnowed from chaff and small pebbles. He would wipe at the windows with a rag. All that, he did while fighting pain and drowsiness. Sleep came to him as erratically as a leopard pouncing over its prey. He hung his head and fell asleep in the oil line, sitting on his tin can until someone tapped him on the shoulder and told him to move ahead. He fell asleep at the kitchen table, the lentils unready, the lunch delayed. He left the windows dirtier, with spots of dust smudged across in curves. On his bed, in his room, he cried himself to sleep under the blanket. He spent much of his time in the basement, on a wicker chair padded with thin mats, warming his hands over the oil heater and watching Ahmad fidget with things. Soon he would doze off.

It was during one of Khan's naps that Ahmad finally attached the camera to the cassette player, but his expectation turned to exasperation when he held a page of his poetry in front of the lens, yet nothing came out of the player except persistent silence. He experimented with other texts: a newspaper, a page from a book, and different handwritten notes before he replaced the video with a photo camera. After the picture was snapped, the film would roll into the cassette player to be processed like an audio tape. To no avail. Ahmad held his head between his hands and rethought his process. In front of him, sitting in the wicker chair in suit and tie, Khan's head hung over his chest, his freckled scalp reflecting the yellow light bulb hanging from the ceiling. Ahmad had the eye. He had the mouth. What was missing was the brain, something with which to translate image to sound. Reluctantly accepting that it would not be ready for the festival that year, Ahmad left his mindless machine on the table and promised himself that he would go back the following year with his machine complete. He packed his suitcase and took the train to the city of Shiraz, ten hours across a white landscape, sometimes circumscribed with distant hills or low mountains and other times free and unending like the ocean.

On the second day of the festival, the troupe Le Troisième performed a new piece, a dance and play combination with two men and two women, including choreographed abstractions of repeated sex. The actresses' dresses, thin as fog and barely covering anything underneath, attracted more attention than anything else: the minimalist set, the lighting, the actors in leather pants, or the two cats dyed crimson red that played so harmoniously one had to wonder how they had been trained. Ahmad knew that was no negligible matter. An uneasy feeling told him that the cats were not only there as part of the show but rather, for the first time, he was seeing them make a mark on history. What those two little red animals could achieve by lithely placing one paw in front of the other, weaving between the legs of the actors, and leaping from one shoulder to the branches of the makeshift tree was something Ahmad could not fathom as he watched. Indignant, and offended by the indecency of the show, a group of protesters, clad in shrouds, set off from the religious city of Qom for Tehran. It was a three-day walk in snow, but they had set out with rage.

The festival was canceled and Ahmad boarded the train for Tehran without even having his poems read by someone else. In his compartment, the man sitting in front of him put his transistor radio on the shaky folding tray, and they heard that the Shiraz Art Festival was canceled not for that year only, but for good. When he arrived home, before he went to his room, Ahmad left his suitcase in the snow and went down to the basement. Khan was there, sleeping on the chair as if he had not woken since Ahmad left. Ahmad picked up the hammer and smashed his apparatuses to bits that could be held between a thumb and forefinger. Khan was startled awake and looked around for a few moments. Ahmad wanted to tell him something, but the old man's eyes were too bad to read in the dim light of that basement. *From now on*, he wrote on a piece of paper at the *Black and White* editor's office, *I'll stick with literature only. That's where I belong.* He sent Dr. Afshar a poem a day, too many to publish in the weekly journal.

"The good thing is," Dr. Afshar said, pulling his reading glasses down over the tip of his nose and looking above them at Ahmad, "I'll have enough for the next century."

When Ahmad told him he wanted to start his own magazine, Dr. Afshar took his glasses off and shook his head. "Publishing is the most dangerous job in this country," he said tapping his hand on his desk to accentuate his point. "Do anything you want, anything else, but not that." *I'm not here to ask for help or advice*, Ahmad wrote, *I'm just telling a friend.* When Dr. Afshar saw he could not make Ahmad change his mind, he said, "At least wait a little longer until we see what happens with this government. Until things are more stable." But instability was nothing to discourage Ahmad. The next day, he went to the Ministry of Publications and Information to apply for a permit. The bank rejected his loan application, but he decided to be optimistic and believe that the money problem would somehow solve itself. At the Ferdowsi Bookstore in front of the University of Tehran, a meeting place of writers and poets, he broached the idea and found the interested writers. The money came one night when Lalah knocked and came in hiding something behind her back. Ahmad squinted expectantly, a faint smile on his lips as his daughter, in loose sweatpants and a T-shirt, walked across the room. When Lalah put the passbook on his desk, a questioning frown knotted Ahmad's eyebrows.

"I'm sure you'll be successful." The passbook belonged to the account they had opened years before to set aside money for her dowry. "Go get it all. It's not like I need it now."

Ahmad stood up and hugged her. He borrowed the other half that he needed and in two months he started to put together his first issue.

THE CANCELATION OF THE SHIRAZ Art Festival did not placate the shroud-bearers. Three days after their departure, so many people joined them in the streets that the shrouds were barely visible. That Wednesday a number of government buildings were set on fire, telephone booth panes smashed and street signs were uprooted. Bloody and warm, thirty-seven bodies were carried away in people's hands. Lalah was one of the carriers.

After two shots toppled two men, she sprinted from behind a car to help take the bodies back. She held the wrist of a boy who could not be more than twenty. There was no blood on his chest, only a small hole in his overcoat breast pocket. Panting, she carried the boy with two other men back to where more people huddled. Someone stopped a passing car. They jammed the boy into the back seat and someone else slammed the door closed. The image of the boy's head, hanging loose as she carried him, was too much for Lalah to bear. She had touched a dead person for the first time and that was enough fighting for her on a day that was later hailed as Blood Wednesday. Without trying to find Shireen, she detached herself from the crowd and walked away from the center of the conflict. Hands in her jacket pockets and head down, she went home.

Early the next morning, a curfew was announced for the first time. Six p.m., until further notice. She did not mind, at least that day. Going out was not on her mind. She picked up her nephew and held him in her arms. Since he was born, he had brought peace and happiness to the house. His plump cheeks jutted out of his rosy face like two small tomatoes. His eyes had taken after Ahmad's and Khan's. His eyebrows were from his father's side, high up on his forehead. With the way he looked into everyone's eyes and smiled, Behrooz had become everybody's favorite in the house. Together with Zeeba, Lalah took care of him almost all the time, until the day Leyla left with her husband. Lalah had heard the couple argue in Leyla's room, the second room on the roof and the largest of the four. That was where they were when Mr. Zia was first permitted to come see her. Lalah had not been able to make out most of the words, but she had heard her sister say, "Not now. I can't."

"I say we all stay here," Lalah said to Leyla one day. "There's room for everyone."

"Once you're married," Leyla answered, "you belong where your husband is. But I'll try to stay with you as long as I can."

With her first baby born and her mother gone, Leyla felt the responsibility of motherhood on her shoulders as if Behrooz, the baby, was her second child, her first, the teenage girl who was also her sister. She knew Lalah was out in the streets, and when Lalah came home with her short hair, Leyla told everyone it was she who suggested that Lalah cut it for a change. She also knew Lalah did not tell her everything. One night, when Behrooz was still inside her, she had woken up parched and seen, from behind the kitchen door left ajar, Lalah funneling oil from the twenty-liter can into an empty Rika bottle. After so many years away, Leyla needed more time to regain her sister's confidence, and that was why when, up on the roof in her room, Mr. Zia told her it was time for them to leave, she shook her head.

"Not until the baby is a little older. I can't do it all alone." On top of that, the difficult conversation with Ahmad was coming.

"All that man cares about," Mr. Zia said, "is himself. I want to live with you again."

"It's not a good time," she said. "I have to ask my father's permission."

"We are married. You need no one's permission. That's what law and tradition say."

"The law says I need your permission."

"Stop it," Mr. Zia said. "You know I'd never pull such a thing on you."

"Will you allow me stay here longer?" Leyla pulled herself closer to him, running her hand on his arm.

"I said stop it." He held her in his arms. "I don't want you to ask my permission."

Mr. Zia went back to his rented room and called old friends. He had been away for too long and the times were not favorable for returning to politics with a smeared reputation. After Mr. Zia had disappeared, his wife was the first one to spread word that he had eloped with a lover. Great Zia had to send a lawyer to negotiate with her, and it was not without considerable money, including the rose garden, that the woman consented to a divorce. On top of that, a bill had been proposed by the Shah to annul all political parties. In their place the Resurrection Party, the party of people, the party of the country, would be founded in which everyone could and should register as a member. Mr. Zia brought Leyla a small pot of violets and said, "I lost everything to be with you. This house is everything we wanted to leave behind. Both of us."

Leyla dusted the windowsill before putting the pot on it. "Please," she said tilting her head, "a little longer." When the baby was asleep she went up to her own room on the roof. The first day she opened the door, everything was so clean and bright that she knelt and smelled the rug. Woven by Zeeba years before, it still smelled new. The bundle of mattresses, blankets, and pillows was neatly stacked in a corner of the room. Two curtained windows faced each other, one with a view of the outside of Zeeba's room and the other of East Tehran, where the sun used to rise before the clouds had amassed in the skies. She was soon integrated in the flow of the house, taking up some of Pooran's responsibilities so her grandmother could rest, since she spent most of her nights up coughing. Rocking Behrooz in her arms, Leyla made decisions about lunch and dinner and saw to it that Khan put on enough clothes before he stepped into the yard.

One evening she went down to the basement and like always, Ahmad broke into a smile at the sight of her and put aside the tape recorder he was opening with a screwdriver. But when Leyla suggested her parents get back together, he shook his head, picked up the machine, and motioned for her to leave the basement. From that day, she started to act like her mother. She began by bringing Ahmad tea, right after he came back home, after each meal, and a few times in between. Little by little she replaced the details of the house with ones from the past: first she changed the cups for the small tea glasses her mother used at home, then she removed the saucer which her mother hated, and then she changed the tray and sugar bowl. Finally, she began to change herself. She combed down her bangs and tied her hair into a neat bun and carefully plucked the right hairs from her eyebrows to create a curve that was her mother's. One day, Ahmad walked past the kitchen and, for a moment, thought he saw a young Homa standing at the oven stirring the pot. He went in, looked at Leyla for a little while, and then nodded his consent, his face beaming with a hopeful smile. The girl smiled and kissed him, her arms clasped behind her father's neck, before she ran out to tell her grandmother.

"We should clean up the house," Pooran said, flinging the comforter away and stepping out of her bed. "My Homa is coming back."

Pooran dyed her hair, cut her nails with scissors, and gave orders to the girls and Ahmad on how to go about the chores. Ahmad scrubbed the floors. Lalah wiped the windows from inside and out. Zeeba dusted and did the laundry and dishes. With her old obsession triggered, this time by happiness rather than distress, Pooran thanked Ahmad every time she passed him for bringing the family back together and had the girls rewash the clean dishes and rewipe the sparkling windows. From the wardrobe she took out Khan's suit and had Leyla iron his red striped tie.

On Friday, after Zeeba took the laundry from the lines tied to nails above the heater in the living room, Pooran told Leyla, "It's time." The girl hurried up the creaking elevator and came down in her sandy-brown hat, chocolate coat, and sumac boots. It was two hours before noon. As Leyla strode off down the street, Ahmad kicked snow off the trees in the flower bed, tidied up his basement, took the lid of the pot to smell saffron in the food—Homa liked saffron, he added some more—and went to Khan. In suits and ties, the two men sat in chairs by the radio and listened to the news, handing Behrooz back and forth from lap to lap. A light snow started an hour after noon. It fell without haste. Lalah took the baby and changed him. When the day was almost over, but some light was still left in the skies, the doorbell rang. Everybody hurried to the yard to welcome Homa. Lalah opened the door. Leyla was back, alone.

28

T WAS A DOMINO EFFECT: the anniversary of the thirty-seven killed on Blood Wednesday was held in the city of Tabriz; the Fortieth-night service of the five killed in Tabriz was held in the city of Isfahan; and the anniversary of the twenty-two killed in Isfahan was held in Tehran. Expecting these gatherings, the new government announced a curfew in Tehran for the first time in two years, starting at six o'clock in the evening, according to the radio news, then, after the intelligence officials opined, four in the afternoon.

A cassette came in through the clouds that said, in a husky voice, "Don't heed the curfew. The curfew is a ruse, to silence the movement of our people. Take to the streets and put your trust in God."

Around noon, the rallies were in full swing on Reza-Shah Street in front of the University of Tehran. Shortly after, the confrontations began.

Since his escape, Salman had kept himself away from trouble. He read and heard the news, but didn't dare to be anywhere near a gathering of people. He grew out his beard and found work as a loang man at a bathhouse in the southern parts of the city, mopping floors, cleaning the private showers, and buying supplies. He lived in the part of the city where roofs, old as God, had given in to the weight of years of snow and people were so poor they had forgotten the names of foods. Women had learned to cook a lukewarm soup with snow and turnip and when turnip was out of season, they compressed and sliced snow which they seasoned with salt and served on dried flat bread. Salman panicked the first evening he found a hand sticking out of a snow pile. He cried at the passersby for help as he dug out the little girl with his empty hands. Horrified at the indifference of those who looked at him in passing, he pulled out the frozen girl, her face livid and her eyes still open. He found more bodies later, young and old, so many he had to stop his morbid excavation. The day he found a customer's ID on the bathhouse floor, Salman slid it in his pants pocket and did not raise his head from his mop when the man came asking after it the next day.

"I'll keep an eye out," he said to the bathhouse master.

He sheared his beard to stubble and a mustache, glancing in turn at the card and his forty-five-year-old face in the bathhouse mirror. The document gave him the courage to venture north toward the center, where the city was more familiar and where the protests happened. He watched from afar the young men running like gazelles, while whispering the slogans to himself. Then he went for a tea and hookah.

At the chai house, men, many of them workers, sat in two facing rows, against the walls, with hookahs erect in front of them on metal tables, sucking at the ends of hoses and breathing out gray smoke. If there was a sign of the outside world, it was in their conversations about the government, the prices going up, how a friend had lost his land to the new land reform policies, and in their jokes. Other than that, there was warmth, burning coal, and hot tea. Among those men, one day, with the mouthpiece between his lips, Salman saw Mamad Cucumber for the first time after the escape. His hollow cheeks had been replaced by a full face and his long, black hair had been combed to one side. He was thirty-two and he looked thirty-two, ten years younger than the ghost Salman had known in prison.

Turning to say a few words to the middle-aged man by his side, Mamad threw knowing glances at Salman. Soon he left the chai house. Salman paid for his tea and hookah and followed him out. In a quiet alley, they took their gloves off, shook hands, and hugged like brothers reuniting after a long separation. Mamad Cucumber had recovered his ties with the Fadaee Guerrillas and was starting to ramp up opposition and resistance. On the anniversary of the twenty-two killed in Isfahan, Mamad picked up Salman at his door and drove him to the rally. Salman shook his head and sat in the parked car to watch with the windshield wipers on. Mamad nodded and closed the door. After an hour, he came back.

"They say people are going to the air force base," he said with the excitement of a child, putting the car into first gear. "Ah, the guns." Driving through the busy streets, which people crossed at whim, was slow and the heavy snow had just started. Swerving ahead as fast as he could and stopping once to push another car out of snow, they arrived half an hour later. "Come on, let's go," Mamad Cucumber said as he parked and pulled the hand break. "This is big." But Salman preferred to stay.

From where they parked, Salman did not have a view of the base. He could only hear the commotion rise and fall and see the people who ran past the car to join whatever was happening. Soon his patience ran out. He would not get into anything, just stand near enough to take a closer look. He killed the car and locked the door. The wind howled in his ears. Snow came down in slanted lines. On the only guard tower of the base, three soldiers stood behind the curtains of snow with G-3s in their gloved hands and the olive domes of smooth helmets on their heads. Even topped with coils of barbed wire, the metal-bar fence that enclosed the base did not seem to reassure the major, who came out of the main buildings with a megaphone in his hand, eyeing the crowd behind the fence all singing slogans and punching the air. He raised his megaphone to his mouth and cried, "This is a military facility! Any violators will be subject to arrest. We are asking you to disperse immediately."

The few soldiers the major had at his disposition were positioned across the white yard, facing the crowd that grew in numbers by the minute. At that moment Salman saw Mamad Cucumber approaching him fast through the crowd. "You were supposed to be in the car," he said agitated, almost shouting. "Good thing I found you. What was the name of that girl in the poem?" Together with three other young men, Mamad Cucumber had been trying to penetrate the facility by removing a few bars in the fence. Relying on the inadequate number of guards and a tall tree that blocked the view, Mamad had scratched the poem as he remembered it, but he had paused on the last word; he had forgotten the name of the girl. He removed his welding goggles. One of his friends urged him to hurry up. The light from the metal bar was strong. Between "Rosa," "Ayda," and "Saba," Mamad picked "Ayda." When the name did not work, he took off his heat-resistant gloves and sent for Salman, who had already left the car. The four of them scattered in the crowd to find him. It was at that time when the major saw the light from his office window and made a phone call. The tanks and trucks were deployed a minute later. He ordered three of the guards to watch the spot in the fence and shouted into his megaphone, "The guards have orders to fire at anyone who sets foot inside."

"What was the name of that girl in the poem?" Salman went with Mamad Cucumber, nudging his way through the crowd. His return to the action was sudden and without question, as if somewhere inside him he always knew the right moment would come, and now was that moment. At a different spot, with fewer guards, they etched Homa's name at the end of the poem on three of the bars. Cucumber was the first to step inside, and following him, an avalanche of people. The base fell. By the time the two tanks arrived, the arsenal was empty of guns and ammunitions, the raiders gone.

"I can't help you with any kind of transfer," Salman said in Mamad's car, in whose trunk clanked thirty-six automatic rifles, seventeen handguns, and a case of cartridges.

"You have already done more than your share, my friend," Mamad slapped him on the shoulder. "The movement is armed."

Alarmed, the government promised on the radio news that the perpetrators would be sought and punished. A daily four-o'clock curfew was announced which unlike the previous one would last for two years, until the day the Revolution came to its culmination. The previous curfew had lasted less than a month.

"Thank God it's over, Khan," Pooran had said, "I was nervous the girl might do something stupid." Although Lalah had never broken the curfew and Leyla and Behrooz were still with them, Pooran would go to the yard and call out to Lalah every once in a while to make sure she was home. The girl would crank down the elevator to do the chores Pooran asked of her or just accompany her to the store, to a neighbor's house for an afternoon tea, or to women's religious gatherings. She knew Pooran was worried about her. She also knew that Pooran wanted to show her off to other women who were looking for wives for their sons. Although she was aware of this plot, when the first suitor actually arrived at the house, Lalah was shocked, then amused.

He came in a navy suit and tie, a fedora, and a pocket square and was so impolite as to step in through the front door before his parents. From the kitchen, Lalah listened to the two families exchanging regular pleasantries, comments about the snow and storms, and Khan talking to the boy's father about the issues of the country, before the suitor's aunt changed the subject. The boy was twenty-three and worked with his father in a confectionary shop. They had brought a box of sweets that he had specifically baked for Lalah. When it was time for her to bring the tea, Lalah's heart pounded not from love, but from the excitement of the new. She straightened her dress and lifted the heavy tray laden with steaming tea cups and the silver sugar bowl. When she entered the guest room, all eyes turned to her and she felt for a moment a trembling build up in her. She offered tea to everyone, starting with the eldest of the guests, then Khan and Pooran, and then the groom. She glanced at the boy's face as he took a cup from the tray. His eyes were olive and for a brief moment she thought she could find calm and adventure in that color at the same time. But after the guests were gone, she shook her head when Pooran asked her what she thought. She had seen little in him aside from that elusive color. The suitor's aunt had not liked it that Lalah had shown up without covering herself either.

"The audacity," Leyla told her sister, pacing the room. Lalah's room was her favorite part of the house. Plants of different sorts, in colored pots, were everywhere: all along the windowsill, across a wooden table by the window, at the foot of the bed on the floor, on top of the radio that Lalah never turned on, and along the foot of the wall. She had asked some of the names and forgotten later—there were so many—but she knew Lalah got them from her friend, Shireen, whose uncle was a truck driver and brought her the plants from beyond the reach of winter. Shireen was too lazy to keep a living thing alive.

Lalah shrugged, indifferent as God about the misfortunes of his people. On the armchair by her bed, she was painting her toenails cherry red, one bent knee under her, the other up against her chest.

"Aren't you upset?" Leyla asked. "What is it to them to talk about what you wear?"

"It's kind of obvious, isn't it?" Lalah answered. "They want a girl for their boy who dresses in such and such a way, I'm not doing that and it's fine if they don't like it." She started on her other foot. "I'm only doing this for Grandma."

Leyla sat cross-legged on the bed, holding her ankles in her hands as if ready to hear an amusing story. "Is there someone else?" she asked.

"Always," Lalah said without lifting her head from her toes.

His name was Ebrahim. Ameer and the other two boys called him Ebi. He was the brain of the group: he decided the number of the Molotov cocktails for the week and determined the pickup times and places. Although Ebi had not shown any particular interest in her, when Lalah learned that the group had put him in charge of communication, she immediately requested the responsibility on the girls' side which Shireen gracefully gave her. She called Ebi from public telephones.

After sliding the coin into the slot, her finger still hovering over the rotary dial, she felt she was nearly fitting into a memory of Leyla's. In those days, she had only waited for Leyla to step out of the booth and hoped she would be in a good mood so they would play on the way home. But her sister had called someone who was madly in love with her, who left his life behind to be with her. Lalah was a nobody to Ebi. Still, when the coin dropped with a metallic sound, something surged in her blood with the dial tone, something with a taste of fear and expectation. Before she dialed, she would say "hi," a few times out loud, testing for any trembling, putting more power behind her voice. She listened and talked to Ebi with heavy breaths. Through the panes, her eyes slid over the cold life of the street, but she did not see the cars that went down the road with tire chains clattering, the men who walked with overcoat collars turned up, the women who sheltered their shopping baskets under their chadors, and the kids who threw snowballs.

The day she cut her hair and dressed in Shireen's father's old clothes to hit the streets, she kept her eyes peeled for Ebi's hair that hovered above his head like a fuzzy black cloud topped with a layer of white. It was not difficult to find him; a dozen marchers ahead, his hair bobbed as he punched the air with the slogans. Lalah was not sure what she would tell him, but she elbowed her way through men. As opposed to Ameer, who had not recognized Shireen in her boy's clothes, Ebi called her by the name the moment he saw her. "Lalah, what are you doing here?" he said. "It's dangerous."

"If you think I can't run, try me," Lalah said, then turned her face ahead and chanted the antigovernment slogan, checking Ebi from the corner of her eye. Her heart was on fire from Ebi's lingering look on her. After a few moments, Ebi said, with the poise becoming of a leader, "When the running begins, don't leave my side." And it was thus that the Revolution became synonymous with passion and excitement for both Lalah and Shireen, a meeting place with destiny, a rendezvous with fervor and danger. During telephone calls, in back-alley meetings, and while taking determined steps in the streets, Lalah felt the gradual change in Ebi, as if he had actually come to believe in her existence. The running that Ebi had mentioned the first day happened a few weeks later, after shots were heard somewhere in the front. The crowd started to scatter. Ebi and Lalah ran onto a smaller street and it was in the course of that run that Ebi took Lalah's gloved hand for the first time, pulling her after him amazingly fast, faster than Lalah had thought he could run. After a few turns right and left into streets and alleys, they slowed to a stroll, but Ebi refused to let go. Encouraged, Lalah participated in every protest Ebi went to. She pulled her hat down over her forehead and hiked her neck scarf up to cover her lips when she rode the bus or as they stopped at the beet-seller's hand cart, to buy steaming lentil soup.

One afternoon Ebi asked her on the phone if she wanted to go out to dinner on Friday, and she said yes, and he said, "You know you won't need to hide yourself, right?" When she stepped out of the telephone booth, she wished she had a little sister waiting for her, someone to run and shout and laugh with, someone to throw snowballs at.

On Friday, she neatly packed her clothes in her bag and told Pooran she was going to Shireen's. She changed in the basement, balanced her hand mirror on top of an oil tin to make up her face. When she was ready, she stepped back and looked at herself in the small mirror, turning right and left to check how she looked. Shireen came in with a plant in a pot the size of a cup. A cluster of leaves—almost oval—grew out like a loose, opened cabbage. The green leaves had grayish fur and dark-red edges. "I bet this one is meat eater," Lalah said.

"You've got to give the boy something." Shireen held out the pot ignoring Lalah's joke.

Out in the street, Lalah saw Ebi's car already parked in front of the newsstand. He never made anyone wait. She walked a little slower than normal, keeping her head down at the slippery path in the snow, giving Ebi enough time to look at her green dress with red and orange plaid. Inside the car, she pulled the panda plant out of her purse and gave it to Ebi.

Over the next months, Lalah saw Ebi in cafés and restaurants as the girl she was, and a few times among the crowds as the boy she was not. But each time, she felt the bonds that attached them together grow stronger and tauter. Courteous and polite, Ebi remained within the bounds of social decorum and moral propriety, until the day they were walking in a park when he said, "I think it's time for us to take the next step." With cans in their coat pockets, they were waiting for the dark to spray-paint slogans. Lalah agreed; without armed resistance, the movement would be doomed to defeat.

"That's not what I'm saying," Ebi said, a smile on his face. His next words created so much joy in Lalah that no matter how much she tried later, she could not remember the rest of the night, where they went and what slogans they spray-painted. In six months, he would have his family make the arrangements and ask her hand for marriage. Lalah could not wait to see Ebi and his parents in Khan's house, like the five other men she had rejected. He would sit in the armchair in the living room with his knees pressed together and hands in his lap, all quiet, not knowing what to do. It was the restless excitement of the promised day that gave her the strength to bear her sister's departure after Mr. Zia took Leyla and his son with him.

With the little Behrooz gone, Pooran was back to her routines, the blandness of which Lalah could taste in the foods she cooked. Her grandmother's dry coughs, once less noticeable over the laughs and cries of the baby, now reverberated in the house, day and night, ticking off time like an irregular clock.

"My last wish is to see you in a bride's gown," she told Lalah and two weeks later a new suitor knocked on the door. From behind the lace curtain of her room, Lalah spied on the family as they stepped out of a blue Chevrolet into the yard. There was nothing special in that one either, except that he was the tallest who had come to propose. In a beige suit and red tie, he walked behind his parents, his black hair slicked back, a box of sweets and a bouquet of flowers in his hands. But something about him felt good, maybe the look he took around at the dry trees, as if appreciating the beauty they once had brought to the yard.

When the two families had talked for some time and before Lalah was asked to bring in the tea, she threw a furtive glance at the man through the half-open door and was disturbed about the amiable charm she saw in the stranger's face and the disinterest she sought, but failed to find, in her heart. On the contrary, she wanted to learn more about him. She did not reject him right after they left.

"I need time to think," she told Pooran, who hurried to her after seeing off the guests.

The next day in the booth, Lalah asked Ebi if he could start the ceremonies sooner. "Like any act of resistance," he said on his end, "a marriage has to be approached cautiously. Or it'll blow."

LIKE HIS POLITICAL CAREER, AHMAD'S endeavors in publishing were doomed to fail. Shortly after the third issue of his magazine was out, the government cracked down on the publications that it deemed detrimental to the social order. Twenty-seven newspapers and journals were shuttered, including Ahmad's and *Black and White*. At the ministry, Ahmad did not succeed in meeting with the colonel in charge of publications, the post he was offered in his hospital bed years before. He walked home with snow on his hair and shoulders, in debt to his daughter and others. His brown leather bag in his hand and his head bent, he opened the front door, shuffled across the yard, and went into his room. A mourning dove landed on a persimmon branch shaking a flutter of snow down into the hoez that was now a large mound of white.

Soon, Pooran opened the house door and stepped onto the veranda in the dark-green coat she wore for quick trips around the garden. She descended the steps carefully and went toward Agha's room on the pathways Majeed shoveled every morning in the knee-high snow. She opened the door and saw Ahmad lying on his back on the floor, arms and legs sprawled. He had not taken any of his clothes off. His neck scarf lay on the rug like it had frozen while fluttering in the wind. Ahmad did not open his eyes at the sound of the door opening, nor at the chill that blew in over his face, nor even when Pooran called his name. He just mouthed.

"You're not a failure," Pooran answered. "You just failed in this. You will try again." He could hear that special rasp that age gives to an old voice. Ahmad mouthed.

"Yes, you will," she said, now fully a captain, ready to bark orders. "You are a good poet. Now look at me."

So exhausted was his soul that Ahmad felt even opening his eyes was too taxing.

"I said look at me," Pooran said, this time louder. Ahmad opened his eyes. "You made mistakes in the past, but there is time to set things right." Pooran coughed between her sentences. She was starting to shrink the way old women did. Her gray hair had lost its luster. She kept it short now. He saw the beginning of her end in the dark-green bulge of the veins in her hands. And yet she stood above him, urging him to his feet, reassuring him that what lay ahead was not only attainable, but worthwhile.

Pooran was not surprised when Ahmad stayed in his room for three days. "They all do that," she told Lalah after the girl came back from Ahmad's room with the tray of food untouched. "When we first came to the city, Khan disappeared for ages. I'll tell you that story some time." She paused for a moment. "So, should I cut fabric for my beautiful bride?"

Bearing the burden of her irreconcilable feelings for the two young men was difficult enough for Lalah. Pooran's high hopes made things even harder. That evening, she went to Shireen's.

Lalah thought she could smell the alcohol from behind the door, before Shireen's mother opened it. The woman's eyes looked past Lalah into distant worlds as she put her finger on her lips and told Lalah, in a whisper, that Shireen was asleep. "But come on in," she said motioning with two hands as if inviting her in on a secret. In her small room, Shireen was lying under the blanket. The open curtains revealed a broken pane covered with cardboard and taped over with wide, opaque khaki tape. "Hey," Lalah whispered lest Shireen was really sleeping. Shireen stuck her head out with a helpless look on her face, eyes swollen and red like two ripe cherries.

"What's wrong?" Lalah seated herself on the edge of the bed.

"I want to keep it," Shireen said in as low a whisper as she could. Then she buried her face into her pillow and stifled her cry.

Lalah put her hand on Shireen's head, bent over, and asked in a hushed voice, "Keep what?" When Shireen's whole body convulsed with sobs, Lalah got her answer. She could hear Shireen's mother snore outside. After another fight with Shireen a few days earlier, the woman had threatened to call Uncle if Shireen stayed out even a minute after the curfew. "I'll leave you forever if he touches me one more time," Shireen had yelled in her mother's face before she stormed out. Not sure what else to do, Shireen's mother had picked up the phone and dialed her brother's number. He was on his way.

"Is it Ameer's?" Lalah asked.

Shireen could not answer. Lalah hugged her friend from behind, resting her head on Shireen's back, her hand caressing the long curly hair that cascaded over her shoulders onto the pillow. "Waves of ecstasy and euphoria," Ameer had called them. Shireen was mature enough not to fall for vacuous praise. Some other essence of youth was in the man that contradicted his appearance. Beneath his sixty-year-old creases, a thirty-year-old vigor was trapped, but still palpable, and compatible with his own childlike account of being a prince under a spell. Shireen had asked more than a few times how old he was. Every time, he told his story of a witch who had expanded the neck of the hourglass that measured his life. The grains of sand trickled down not one by one, but two at a time. Only true love could save him from his ever-nearing end. And love was what he demanded of her.

"Amusing," Shireen had said the first time Ameer told her the story. "But this is not how you approach girls these days, grandpa."

A short while later, when the opportunity had arisen for her to steal a look at Ameer's driver's license in his absence, she found that the date of birth printed on the card confirmed his story. She decided that was a ruse, a false document. But she could not ignore the vitality with which he lived either: the way he ran as fast as any twenty-year-old when the warning shots were fired, the way he treated himself with caviar, lamb kebab, and sheep's brain and tongue, and the way he sweated through the heavy shoveling work. One early afternoon, at the famous Naderi Café, where big writers and wrestlers and sometimes actors and actresses had hung out for years, Ameer had finished his rice and stew and sat back with his hands crossed on his chest.

"What kind of a princess are you, tell me," Ameer asked, "who doesn't care about her prince being trapped in the claws of death?"

Unlike the previous times when she ignored his buffoonery with a smile, Shireen leaned toward him, put her elbows on the table, and said in a soft, low voice, "May you find the elixir of life in your quest for love."

Two hours after the dark, Ameer had bought a ticket from the small booth at the bus stop and got on the bus after leaving his shovel at home. The door buzzed open soon after he rang the bell. Inside candle flames outlined a path through the dark of the apartment into a room that smelled of Shireen.

"Where is your mother?" Four candles burning on a ledge in the wall above the bed shed a dim but warm light on Shireen. Lying on her side under the blanket, she was watching Ameer.

"How many demons did you slay," she whispered, "to get to this chamber, Prince Ameer?"

"Oh, I've come a long a way, your highness," he answered. "Allow me to tell you my dark tale." He closed the door behind him and invited the darkness.

When, a few weeks later, she told him she was pregnant, Ameer took the news without surprise.

"Good," he said, "His name should be Ameer."

THAT WAS WHAT HE SAID to the other women, too: to his fiancée, to Goli, and to another girl he got to know later. Only Shireen and Goli were pregnant. With the other two, he had only fantasized about a child of his own name. He stopped seeing Shireen. She had been a nice girl, but would not have understood what it meant to have two days of one's life go by with each day. He planned to send her money and other things she, or in the coming years, the child, could use, for as long as he lived.

Of the girls he had been with, Goli was the only one he had not left yet. When her baby was born, the madame held the little pink creature in her arms and said, "This is the first baby this home has seen," smiling a golden-toothed smile at the newborn. She gave Goli three months to rest and recuperate. The madame had the small storage room downstairs cleaned and prepared for Goli and exempted her from work. Although friendly and helpful to her face, the other girls in the house were jealous of the way Madame treated Goli without trying to hide or justify her discrimination. A pregnant girl dies in the street, that was the number one rule of the house. With those extra three months, Madame would be paying for Goli for a whole year without work. Some of the girls said it was not the madame paying, but the old man, Ameer, who put his hand into his pocket. He visited the mother and son every week, and never empty-handed. He scooped the boy into his arms and rocked him, patting his small back, listening to his gurgling and murmuring. Goli would watch the father of her child walk into the room with snow on his shoulders, step out and come back with the fruit washed, open the box of sweets, or unfold a blouse he had bought for her.

"Once a week," she said with genuine calm, "we're like a family. We're all together. We're happy." She smiled.

Although temporary and fleeting, although evanescent and untrustworthy, the presence of that man warmed her heart. What never left her mind were her mother's words when she taught little Goli to accept and appreciate the little, imperfect happinesses of her life and not lust for what she could not have. She wanted Ameer, but she did not take him for granted. "Will you come again?" she would ask at the door, brushing his hair with her hand and making sure his collar was straight. After he assured her that he would, she told herself she would never see him again. She asked him to leave his other girls and take her with him, but she never said it as if she really meant it, rather as a passing remark when Ameer was playing with the baby or with her, and many times when he was putting on his shoes to leave. Hope was her deadliest enemy and she was wary not to fall for its temptations.

One evening, after she pinched a piece of thread off of Ameer's coat and saw him off, Goli knocked on the madame's door. "Will you let me leave?" she asked standing in front of the large desk. "I want to raise my boy in a home. I want to make him a home."

"With what money, honey?" the madame asked.

"I'll work."

"That's what you are doing here, my flower." The madame got up from her chair and patted Goli on the cheek. "After all I did for you, this is how you treat me? Without you, this house will be without a rose." The madame said that with the authority of someone who had Goli's birth certificate locked up in a safe, but with such honesty that Goli believed she actually liked her.

"Will you marry me?" she asked Ameer the next time she saw him. Ameer's response was the promise of more money in her bank account. "Will you help me run away, then?"

Ameer looked up from the baby at Goli on the loveseat pulling up her knee-high red stockings to prepare for the night. "There's snow and wretch-edness outside," Ameer answered. "Either will kill a baby. Plus if you are not here, how can I find you?"

Although he did not take Goli very seriously, when he left that night, Ameer went to the madame. He drank the tea that she poured him and paid extra for the night. He slapped a few more bills into the woman's hand before saying goodbye. "This is for keeping an eye on the both of them," he said. When Ameer came back the next week, Goli had escaped with her baby. Ameer was sure she would soon be back. The madame's men would find her wandering in the streets nearby or in some park as she tried to find a place for the night. But Goli never returned.

THE LAST THING KHAN DID on his own feet was to take out the wheelbarrow and leave it in the trash. Rusted and with its purple paint flaking off, it had sat in a corner of the garden since Agha passed. It dripped on the rare days that the winds and snow relented and the city warmed under the clouds, but soon turned back into a white cone. Sometimes at the end of his painful, slow shoveling in the veranda and yard, Khan had tried to scrape the ice and snow off its sides, as if to make sure it was still there. After Pooran confiscated the shovel, he resorted to wiping some of the snow away with his gloved hands before going back in. One night that was not unlike any other night, Khan went to bed and pulled the comforter up to his chest, but midnight came and sleep was not even in the room yet.

He grabbed his cane, got up from the bed, and put his coat on. But before he could open the door to the veranda, a light went on behind him. It was Pooran standing with a flashlight, a tacit question in her face.

"I'm not going to be put in that thing," Khan told her, pointing through the veranda door at the white heap in the yard.

Pooran looked at Khan, who was holding a trembling grip on his cane and a second on the doorframe. "I'll go with you."

In the yard, they scooped out the snow from inside the wheelbarrow. When Pooran stepped forward to grab the handles, Khan raised his hand.

"Let me."

He handed Pooran his walking stick and out into the night they went. With her flashlight, Pooran swept the sidewalk where the streetlamps failed to reach as Khan took a few slow, arduous steps before he dropped the handle to catch his breath. His raspy panting played over the background of the wobbly, creaking wheel all the way to the pile of trash at end of the alley. He parked the wheelbarrow by the heap and watched it for a moment in the circle of light Pooran cast: its handle touched the concrete power pole. Snowflakes quickly bespeckled the purple. Before morning, the wheelbarrow would be indistinguishable from the white heap of the trash. They returned along the winding line the wheel had left in the snow, tracing their own footsteps, the aging woman's hand fastened around the old man's arm.

The next morning, Pooran woke with the feeling of absence. Khan was not in the kitchen making tea or preparing breakfast, or trying to wash the dishes. The house was silent. As she rushed to his room, she wondered what she would do if he had left like he had once before. But Khan was in his bed. His eyes were open and his lips pressed together as if in terror of something that would not let him cry, something that was not in the room, though Khan could see it.

"What's wrong, Khan?"

Power had left his knees. No matter how hard he tried, he could not muster the strength to get to his feet on his own.

"This is what I feared most," he said to Ahmad later when the two were alone together, his voice trembling. "But I won't end up like Agha." Ahmad held his hand and pulled the blankets over him. Khan clutched at his wrist. "My arms are still strong," he said, eager as in those past times when he had found a new secret about the cats, having struck upon some truth that others had to know. "Get me a wheelchair."

AFTER HIS JOURNAL WAS SHUT down, Ahmad lay in his room for three days thinking of the debts he still owed, then emerged and went to the Ministry of Education. Soon he started as a high school teacher. After school, he worked as the editor of a tabloid that published photos of actresses and soccer players on its covers. He did not like it, but it was an easy job. It paid.

Ahmad and Zeeba put Khan into his wheelchair every morning before dawn according to his instructions. With the knocking of the girl on his door, Ahmad woke up and dragged his feet in the snow to Khan's room, eyes barely open, nodding to Zeeba's "good morning!" and admiring her punctuality and perseverance. They would roll Khan first to his side and then to a sitting position. Hugging him tight, chest to chest, Ahmad lifted Khan and put him in the chair before going back to bed. Like a child on a bike, gliding out of one room and into the other, smiling at everyone, the old man rolled around the house until late in the evening. He had regained his freedom to move without depending on others, and the joy was too great to harness. Ahmad found a broken door in the trash and made a ramp from the veranda down into the yard. On days when no one was home to push him back up the door, Ahmad would return from teaching to find Khan stuck in the yard. He brushed the snow from his grandfather's lap and Astrakhan hat and then took him in, waiting for someone to return before he left for the tabloid office.

Three weeks before the end of calendar winter, Khan heard the honking of a car horn from behind the front door. Horns blasted every day in the alley to warn the children who played outside and the men who threw shovelfuls down from the roofs. But the car honked a second time, a third. Khan called Zeeba, but Pooran came out of the house and crossed the yard. In the street, Ahmad stuck his head out the window of a new beige Peykan with a smile that she'd last seen on his face the day when he expected Homa's return. The car's wipers scraped clean the flakes that landed on the windshield. Shortly thereafter, Khan was in the front seat and the rest of the house in the back: Lalah and Zeeba flanking Pooran on either side. They rode along the streets and watched the excitement of the new year: cars crowding the streets, people shopping for new clothes, women wiping windows, men on ladders hanging clean curtains, and red tubs of goldfish in store windows for the Haft Seen tables. They drove by the police cars and army Jeeps parked in major squares. They went to the Sawee Park and watched the animals in its small public zoo. Lalah and Zeeba took turns pushing Khan's wheelchair up and down the pathways. With a sisterly patience, Lalah described the park to the blind girl, the tall pine trees white with snow, the peacock with barely any feathers on his tail, the sickly bear sitting on its hind quarters in his dark and small cage, the handful of ducks waddling and quacking in a modest pond frozen solid, but for a small hole the keeper cracked open every morning, and the one rabbit chomping on a lettuce leaf. On their way back, Lalah hugged her father's neck from the back seat.

The car was an investment, a tool Ahmad needed for his third job. After he left the tabloid office, he worked as an unofficial taxi driver, driving around the city to pick up passengers who waited on the side of the street. He worked until minutes before the curfew, and so he was not home the day his mother found the kittens.

The spring cleaning had started two weeks before the New Year. Anything not washable had to be swept or scoured or wiped or rinsed, from top to bottom: first the four rooms on the roof, then the house proper, then Agha's room in the yard, and finally, the basement. Pooran heard the weak meowing before she saw them in a corner by the bookcase: three black-and-white kittens that could barely walk. One with a white tail was more adventurous; it braved a few wobbly steps ahead looking around and glancing at the big woman standing with her arms akimbo. The other two looked up as if not sure whether to be afraid. The white tail took a few steps toward Pooran. Ahmad must have left the door ajar, she thought. She had seen that many times, since she was a child, cats delivering their kittens in the warmth of basements, sheds, and stables. The only way to get rid of them was to sweep them with a broom into a bag, take the bag outside of the city, and let the creatures out in the barren lands. Otherwise they would find their way back. She hesitated, thinking back on Khan's obsession. She had had no interest in him keeping a dirty street cat in a cage and working through the night down there, but the intensity with which Khan had engaged with that work made Pooran feel she had to tell him, lest the three kittens held any significance. She closed the door and locked it.

Khan wanted to see them for himself. Pooran said he had to wait for Ahmad. "No, he's on their side," Khan said and tossed his blanket aside. Pooran sighed and shook her head. Once in his wheelchair, Khan had Zeeba push him out to the veranda and down into the yard. The two women tried to work the wheelchair down the four steps into the basement, but when Khan got stuck sideways, Pooran called the tabloid office for Ahmad.

"They are here," Khan said when he was finally dislodged and alone with his grandson. The kittens had crawled out of the corner and now were meowing under the table. Ahmad squatted down and picked them up, two in one hand and one in the other. The trio of meows grew into a crescendo of short and shrieky but feeble cries. Ahmad put the squirming things on the table. The brave kitten paddled its paws to the edges and looked over at the abyss that was the floor. The other two busied themselves with the bits and pieces of broken camera and other tools scattered on the tabletop.

"They are in this very house. Ah, the Revolution." Like the other things that Khan had predicted, it was already happening, even though no one called it a revolution yet. Whatever it was, those small furry things were standing up against two and a half millennia of monarchy. But Ahmad struggled to see any malice or ambition in those balls of fluff. The one that had ventured to the edges of their square world was now back with the other two kittens in the middle of the table, trying to grab his sister's tail with its uncertain paws. The third one was rolling on its back, slender paws in the air. Maybe cuteness was their natural defense, with which they camouflaged their true intentions. He took out his notepad and wrote big, a word a page.

"The eyes can be blind to the truth sometimes," Khan said.

The sister kitten pawed at the film that lay on the table in coils, gleaming in the light.

"Agha was right; we should have killed them. I should not have kept my research a secret. I should have shouted it out, showed people how you can track these feral things and tell when something will blow up. If everyone had gotten rid of one or two of them, this country would not be on the verge of civil war."

But was it not a good thing that the cats were causing a revolution? The cats would be content at overthrowing the regime; so would Ahmad, and so would many others. The political prisoners would be freed. People could publish a journal without fear of it being shut down for criticizing the government. Those who ran the country would no longer sit on thrones of jewel and don gold on their heads. Perhaps, one day, the factory worker who toiled from sunup to sundown could afford to send his children to school; there would be doctors to treat the feverish daughter of the farmer who broke his back working the field in such and such remote village in the South; or that at least there might be pipes everywhere—not only in big cities—that spat out clean water. Once the Shah was killed, maybe the cats would go back to their country. Maybe that was the end of Agha's myth: a revenge equal to the original crime. A king for a king.

"You're disillusioned if you think this country will be anything without the Shah," Khan said with unwavering conviction. "All of the misfortune is because of them. It's the Shah who is keeping this land from harm. Who is going to run this country after him? A bunch of Communists who come for your money at the end of the month? Would you work for free? Would you give them your house and live in a matchbox-size apartment? Or those turban-heads who make you stand to prayer ten times a day and not eat or drink for a whole month? You think they know how to run a country?" The sister kitten, which was black on the top and white on her face and stomach, had rested her head on White Tail's back. The two had curled into a black-and-white ball of fur. It was the second brother's turn to travel to the edge of the table. Unlike White Tail, this one leaned forward imprudently, lost his balance for a second, managed to pull himself back, but leaned forward again as if not sure whether or not to jump. The skin below his fur gave his paws a pinkish tint. Ahmad scooped him up in his hand and put him down. It looked around for a while, then took unsteady pink steps toward Ahmad, stopped at his foot, and stared at his shoestring. He raised his front paw and held it in the air for a moment before cautiously clawing at the string. Then he curled up and closed his eyes as if safe and cozy by the side of Ahmad's shoe.

Ahmad picked up the kitten and looked at him face-to-face. Pink paws hanging, gently paddling in the air, as if in a relaxed flight, the kitten looked into Ahmad's eyes and meowed. He wrote.

I'm keeping these for a little. I'm sure they're very dangerous.

POORAN WOULD NOT HAVE ANY animals in the house or in the yard. Ahmad put the kittens in a large cage in his room. When he came home at night, he would let them out to play around. No longer so weak as to fall back down as soon as they rose to their trembling feet, they now walked and ran around the room, pawing at everything. They hid under the bed. They balled up on top of the pillow. White Tail sat on the windowsill by the begonia and looked at the yard. The sister kitten walked up to Ahmad, leapt up to hug his pant leg, and tried to climb. Ahmad took her and put her on the desk, only to brush her off his papers later; he petted the three of them entangled into a furry mass in his lap. "You'll get sick," Pooran told him. "Those things belong on the streets." She would not even set foot in Ahmad's room, but the kittens attracted Lalah and Zeeba, who fed them, cleaned them, and played with them. Ahmad was starting to like his room, now that the girls liked to be there; it was not just a space for solitary moping.

ANOTHER SPRING CAME, MORE WINTERY than the winter. Nature was unheeding of people's yearly celebration of the vernal equinox with wheat sprouts and hyacinths on the New Year's Haft Seen tables. As a fourth job, Ahmad brought home editing work. He wielded his red pen until late at night when he placed his forehead on his forearm and fell asleep at his desk. The weight of something soft and warm perched on the back of his neck woke him in the morning. Hurriedly he would get dressed, and, repeatedly checking his watch, give his kittens as long as he could to play before he put them in the cage and headed for the school.

The shenanigans that the teenage boys pulled in their other classes were absent from Ahmad's. He was not just a teacher, but a famous poet. On top of that, Ahmad sat silently at his desk and supervised as his class abandoned the school's usual lecture setting in favor of cooperative discussion. The boys felt engaged and responsible, and when Ahmad turned his back to them to write on the board, there was little tomfoolery. But even the haven of Ahmad's class was not impervious to what was stirring outside in the city. From time to time, he caught a glimpse of a folded paper passing hands, a cassette poorly hidden inside a book, or a rolled picture of Ayatollah Khomeini in an open bag. Four of his students took part in everything that happened at the University of Tehran. When their seats were empty, everyone knew the university students were protesting. In a tacit shared understanding, Ahmad's aide would not read their names during roll call and Ahmad himself would not mark them absent. The next day they would be back at their bench-desks, unless another protest was underway.

By midspring, Ahmad had saved enough to pay back half of Lalah's dowry savings. He wanted her to continue her studies and go to college before she got married and was bogged down with babies, but he saw that she had taken a liking to the last suitor. Remembering the painful days when he stood in front of Khan, tongue-tied and fearing the prospect of being sent to Paris—away from his mother, the Orchard, Agha, Sara—Ahmad promised himself not to impose anything on Lalah. Lalah had let her hair grow long again, and although she postponed giving a final answer, she had not said no yet. The suitor had shown an unconventional patience facing Lalah's repeated deferrals, but every time the young man's mother called Pooran to ask if there was an answer, Pooran became certain there would not be a next time.

"That's it," she scolded Lalah. "I don't know what else you want. The boy is handsome. He has a good family. He has money. He can have any girl he wants and he's been waiting for you, how long it is, God knows. When I was your age, I already had your aunt Maryam. And what do you do? Hide in Ahmad's room playing with those cats. You're on your own. Don't come to me crying when he's gone."

She then opened the china cabinet in the hall and hauled the dishes, six at time, into the kitchen sink to wash. A few weeks later, the phone rang again. Lalah hoped time would solve everything, that by putting off making a decision, the dilemma she found herself in would vanish and she would not have to bear the responsibility of her future. If the suitor's family stopped calling, she would content herself with the thought that the boy was not meant for her, that he had not persisted long and hard enough in wanting her. She wished Ebi would propose already. Every call from the suitor's mother brought worry and pride. Someone wanted her and was waiting for her to want him back, and by that he was ripping her to pieces.

His name was Reza. He was twenty-five years old and he sold and repaired bicycles and motorbikes. He had started working in the summer of the year he turned twelve, first at a bus garage, then at a bicycle and motorbike repair shop, helping out the mechanics. Four summers later, he was working on his own. In an empty piece of land between two buildings in his neighborhood, he sat with a screwdriver and an adjustable wrench. The screwdriver he had stolen from the repair shop and the wrench from the bus garage. He fixed bikes for free for a month and when he had enough customers, by the end of the summer, not only had he returned the screwdriver and the wrench, but he had a full toolbox and a canopy over his head to keep the snow away. After he finished high school, Reza opened his own shop and before he turned twenty-three, he had three mechanics working for him. The day of the proposal ceremony, Reza had come in a blue Chevrolet Nova and smelled of good perfume. After her third equivocal reply, Lalah told Pooran she could not decide unless she spent some more time with him.

"That's what engagement is for," Pooran answered. Nonetheless she went ahead and invited the suitor's family over for lunch. She had Lalah make the main stew, but did not leave the kitchen herself the whole time to ensure it was perfect, down to the last grain of salt. Pooran did not fail to laud Lalah's cooking at the sofreh before everyone started. The little time that Reza and Lalah had to talk, Reza spent with polite gentility and genuine attention, his hands in his pockets. He cranked the two of them up to the roof and got excited explaining the principles of pulleys, taking his hands out to gesticulate. He gave the whole structure of the elevator a shake and said, "This needs a good fixing." From up on the roof, the clouds looked so low that it seemed to Lalah Reza could reach them.

"I'm starting to forget the last time it wasn't cloudy," Reza said, looking at the sky. "I hope the winter ends someday."

Lalah nodded.

"And I hope you will accept my hand." He said that without taking his eyes from the sky, as if it was a prayer he directed to the heavens. Lalah was scared by how her heart raced at the sincerity in Reza's words. She decided not to see him when he came to tend to the elevator the next week. She stayed in her room and spied from behind her lace curtains as he installed a motor on the parapet.

She called Ebi from the booth more often and held his hand tighter when they were together. "Are you not going to the demonstrations with me anymore?" Ebi asked her one day.

"Of course I am. Why?"

"Your hair."

Lalah touched her bangs. "Of course I am," she replied. "I'll cut them off as soon as something big turns up. I thought I'd make myself pretty in between."

Ebi smiled but did not believe her. Change was what he feared most, although it was also what he was fighting for. To him, a change on the outside was, without an exception, a manifestation of a change within. He himself had let his hair grow out after high school, once there was no longer a principal to check that the students' hair was not long enough to be pinched between a thumb and forefinger. Ebi's curly hair had become as big as a football, and he had kept it that way ever since, for the past four years. Impatiently, he looked forward to the next rally to see if he would find the old Lalah by his side, chanting the slogans, mimicking a deep, man's voice. The opportunity arose when a university professor passed away of old age, peacefully in his bed. As his body was carried over the shoulders of his admirers out the gates of the University of Tehran, the gendarmes arrived and tried to disperse the crowd. In response, antigovernment slogans were chanted and soon two of the mourners lay lifeless on the street, not too far from the body of the professor. Word got around and the Seventh-night service was announced as the day of the next march, in front of the university gates.

Without too much of a surprise for Ebi, Lalah decided not to go to that one. Afraid of what this change in her meant, Ebi delegated his coordinating responsibilities to a friend and suggested to Lalah that they go out instead. As time went on, he offered her more and more anxious dates. They ate at restaurants and cafés, looked at art in museums, and walked the streets and neighborhoods which were so close to where people demonstrated and yet so far. Lalah saw how Ebi grew ever more eager about going places, how he talked about the movie they just walked out of, or a painting they were standing before. He told her about the books he read. He took her to one expensive restaurant after another. Lalah tried to engage, but felt unable to pass an invisible barrier. She knew she was not a good actor, that Ebi saw her hesitation. How easy things would have been if she did not love that football-haired boy.

At the end of spring, Lalah graduated from high school. With her mornings suddenly free, Ebi thought they would have more time to be together. But she did not call him for a whole week. He took the phone to his bed and waited all afternoon and evening. He picked up the receiver and even called her number a few times, but hung up before Pooran answered.

"I'm sorry, I was very ill," Lalah lied when she called at last.

"Can we meet?" he asked.

"I'm still weak."

That afternoon, Ebi walked up to his parents in the kitchen. They turned their heads to look at their son standing in the door.

"There's a girl," Ebi said, trying to hold his hands still by his side. "I'm going to ask for her hand. With or without you." His father glanced at his son's feet and saw that he kept shifting his weight from heel to toe, rocking ever so slightly, as he did when he was nervous.

Lalah did not call him for another week. She could find no resolution in her soul. If she was at first only doubtful, her heart now held two loves in equal proportion. She could not understand why the more Ebi approached her, the farther her heart wandered away from him. She felt guilty for not having told him about the suitors her grandmother had brought home from the beginning, while he had nearly abandoned his political activities in the past months to be with her. It was too late now. After he motorized the elevator, Reza had come to the house a few more times. He was the first person Pooran called the day Khan's wheelchair broke, when the left back wheel locked one morning and refused to budge at Zeeba's pushing.

The next week Pooran called again and two hours later, Reza opened the trunk of his Nova to take out the tricycle Pooran had wanted, a gift for Leyla's son, Behrooz. Never, from the very beginning, had Reza paid a visit without a tiny bouquet of flowers, even though fourteen years of winter had turned roses into items of luxury. Pooran made him stay for lunch or dinner. Ahmad drank tea with him and Khan found in him a backgammon rival. Reza had become part of the family even before Lalah could make any decisions. Everything had dragged on longer than its ideal course: Ebi had waited too long to propose; Lalah herself had failed to know her heart's desire in time; the winter had lingered and lingered and lingered.

"I talked to my parents," Ebi said on the other end of the receiver the next time in the booth. "My mother will call your grandmother as soon as I ask her. When do you think is best?"

At that moment, Lalah felt how lucky she had been years before when she stood on the other side of the door. She was never alone, she was free of concern, unfamiliar with the pain inside that yellow cubicle of iron and glass. She missed her sister. She missed her childhood. Overwhelmed, she did the thing she thought herself incapable of doing and told Ebi she had a suitor, someone her family approved of, someone well-off. A long silence fell. Seconds became minutes, minutes as long as hours.

"Are they making you marry him?" Ebi was confused.

Once again she had taken too long to hang up and now she was facing an even more difficult question: how could she be such a two-timing fraud? After she walked out of the telephone booth that snowy summer, Lalah never heard Ebi's voice again. But even when there was not a strand of black hair left on her head, images of protests on TV or in the papers, anywhere in the world, reminded her of the boy who had held her hand and lead her panting along Tehran's alleys, away from arrest and bullets. She could never again bear to take part in a demonstration herself, even during the last months of the Revolution when things happened that no one could have foreseen, when seven columns of smoke rose up from the city to the sky. Not even when the Shah flew away and Ayatollah Khomeini returned: the day the winter ended.

Years later, her own daughter graduated from high school and went, without her knowing, to a fortune-teller to see if she would pass the university entrance test. Lalah scolded her daughter, but later visited the old woman herself to find out whether she knew how to take love out of one's heart. "Just whisper his name into this." The fortune-teller held out an old tin can, dented on the side, like the ones canned tomato paste came in. "I can hold my ears if you want, but I already know his name." Lalah looked into the can, but decided she wanted that small love in the corner of her heart to remain.

LALAH'S ENGAGEMENT TO REZA was arranged for the fall and the wedding for a year after. It was during that year that the Air Force Arsenal was conquered. Intelligence had not been able to determine what kind of tool was used to melt the fence, but speculated it had to be some kind of oxy-fuel torch. The unending curfew that was announced did not help the government. Soon, *Down with the Shah!* appeared among the spray-painted slogans on the walls. Until then no one had dared say anything about the king himself.

Even when the power cuts began, Khan defended the royalty with more and more conviction. Focused on Lalah's imminent wedding, Ahmad would not answer the sarcastic remarks and bitter words that Khan threw at him from his wheelchair. With his thick glasses on, Khan shook the newspaper in Ahmad's direction when he came home from work. There was not a day that the country was calm.

"Look what your felines have done this time? And you keep them warm in your room. In *my* house. I'll kill them myself. I should have killed them from the start. Look what they have done."

Ahmad brushed the snow from the man's hat and coat and wheeled him back inside. Knowing the hardheadedness in her family, Pooran was worried about Khan and Ahmad's growing divergence toward the opposite ends of the political fight. She wanted the wedding to take place soon, before a catastrophe broke out. When the groom's mother suggested postponing the wedding until the end of the curfew, Pooran replied that even if it rained stones, the wedding had to happen on its designated day. She hung up the phone and crossed the yard to Ahmad's door.

"My last wish in this world is to see my granddaughter in that white gown," she told him from the doorway. She would not step into Ahmad's room with all the cat hair. "I beg you, don't let whatever is between you and Khan ruin the girl's day." Ahmad came to the door. Pooran bent over to kiss his hand, but Ahmad yanked it away and held his mother in his arms.

I'll let the cats go tomorrow.

When he came back from the school the next afternoon, Ahmad did not see Khan in the yard. He went to his room to leave his bag and change, but he found the door left ajar. Inside, the cage was open. The cats were gone. Pooran rushed out of the kitchen at the noise and found Ahmad in the basement wildly throwing things around.

"What is it?"

Unheeding, Ahmad went out and ran up into the house. He flung Khan's door open and stood in front of his wheelchair, panting, his mouth open as if in an inaudible cry. Khan said nothing. Arms on the armrests, smaller and older than ever, he had fixed his cold, unapologetic look on Ahmad. Pooran arrived.

"What is going on?"

Ahmad ran out of the room without answering.

"What is going on, Khan?" Pooran asked again.

On the veranda, Ahmad took a look at the snow and then he easily saw it: a new path half-heartedly plowed from Agha's room to the hoez. He sprang down the steps and grabbed the first usable thing he could find: a frozen broom. With the long, wooden handle, he poked into the years-old mountain of snow in the hoez until he dug out a gunnysack, its mouth tied with a rope into puckering lips. Inside were hard, irregularly shaped objects clanking against each other. Ahmad knew what he would face before he untied the rope. He thought of burying the sack without opening it, but he had to see his kittens one last time. Frozen stiff, White Tail had his eyes open wide as if to an unimaginable horror. His brother looked as if he was lying on his back holding his pink paws up. Their sister had curled up the way she liked to do under Ahmad's desk or, on the nights he forgot to put them in the cage, on Ahmad's chest. It was as though at the last moments of her life, she decided against fighting. She had closed her eyes without hope and let the cold devour her.

Contrary to what Pooran expected, Ahmad did not disappear or lock himself in his room. Instead, he put on his jacket and pulled a knit hat over his head and clicked the door behind him, his sack of frozen cats in his hand. He came back two hours after the curfew and never mentioned them again. In the gray hours before the dark, Pooran heard a loud continuous howling from the yard. Once on the veranda, she saw the lights in Ahmad's room were on. By the time she reached to open the door, Zeeba was there, too, to see where the noise came from. Ahmad did not hear the door open. With his back to the two women, he was vacuuming the floor, holding the pipe in his hands, pushing and pulling, the blue-and-white cube roaring behind him on the ground. By the door was the box the new machine had come out of. Ahmad vacuumed all the cat hair and washed everything that could be washed so Pooran felt comfortable to come into his room again, after more than a year. Without visible remorse or bitterness, he went to Khan and wrote on his notepad, *Would you help me throw a decent wedding for my girl, please?*

IT HAD BECOME THE TRADITION not to leave the pride of the family to whim or luck. So against the custom that expected the groom's side to throw the wedding, Khan and Ahmad took charge. The groom suggested an orchard in the country as the venue. "There are a hundred guests from my side alone," he said. But he soon realized he had little say. Khan's workers arrived with sledgehammers on their shoulders. The three men tore down a section of the wall that separated Khan's yard from the neighbor's and built an archway in its place. Soon metal poles were planted in the ground and a tarp ceiling stretched over the two yards. The snow was wheelbarrowed out and the hardened ice cracked with pickaxes.

In the midst of the work Pooran went to Khan and Ahmad, anxiously slapped one hand on the back of her other hand, and said, "We forgot about the power cuts." Fuel shortage had been announced by the regime as the cause of power outages that began shortly after the curfew. They happened without a regular pattern in stretches of two to four hours after dark. Word circulated that it was during the outages that the secret service made its arrests of dissidents. "How can I look into that girl's eyes again if her wedding is ruined?" Pooran said.

When the night came, the whole area was lit by the glowing pieces of paper pinned to the underside of the tarp. Parveen's children had cut up small squares with scissors and copied one of Ahmad's poems 1,037 times. Later at school, they would do it as a trick, and soon their classmates would learn the words and write them out at home for their parents to see. Uncle Majeed stood on a stepladder and pinned the papers to the tarp. Then he went into the house and taped them to the walls.

Together with Leyla and Mr. Zia, holding Behrooz's hand in hers, Homa arrived in the morning when preparations were still underway. Her black hair, now dyed blond and tied up in a chignon, made her a new person, like a familiar old friend one is not sure would welcome a pat on the shoulder. She was in a skirt and blouse; her wedding clothes, Ahmad knew, were in the bag she held in her hand. They had agreed to be there together for their daughter. Once on the veranda, she looked around the yard and spotted Ahmad. He smiled at her and thought he saw on Homa's face, before she led the little boy in, the shadow of a smile—one that said, *that pat on the shoulder is really okay.*

The guests started arriving around noon and were seated at tables laden with large dishes of fruit and sweets. Pooran would shortly appear at the table to welcome the new guests, beaming, talkative, and happy, her lips painted a red too vivid for the younger girls, her hair now short and dyed hazel. Glass cups of tea circulated on trays over the hands of the women servants hired for the night. Pooran had not allowed any alcohol in the house. Anyone thirsty for more than tea or sweet drinks had to step through the arch into the neighbor's yard where the bottles had been laid on a large wooden table.

The pop band set up a keyboard and a percussion set, and when they started to play, Ahmad missed Maestro Shahnaz's traditional music at his own wedding. He had persuaded Khan to allow the couple to select their own music. The guests danced, but only those drunk on vodka and youth; there was agitation and excitement in the music, but it wanted life. Half a dozen children packed themselves on the planks that formed the floor of the elevator and flicked the switch on and off, climbing up to the roof and back down to the yard, sometimes hanging in the middle, making loud noises as they watched the bride and groom step out of the building into the yard.

Hand in hand, the couple went around the tables and offered their greetings to the guests before the next round of dance began. Walking next to Reza, reaching no higher than his shoulder, Lalah had to balance a confusion of feelings within her with the difficulty of walking in high heels as an uncontrollable avalanche of white lace skirt hung from her waist. She looked at her family, her father handsome in a coffee suit and pants with a tawny tie, walking straight with a hand in his pants pocket and smiling at the guests, her mother more beautiful than ever in a light-ocher dress, walking with Ahmad as if they had planned the color harmony; her sister unable to hold back her happy tears; her grandmother walking proud; Khan, sitting in armchairs with the elders from Reza's family; and all the new faces, smiling at her, congratulating, shaking hands with Reza, putting their hands on their chests and half-bowing to her. Beside her, Reza seemed in control of his feelings.

He shook hands with everyone smiling an elegant smile, neither too eager nor too brief. He did not seem nervous. That gave Lalah relief and reassurance; she could follow him and she would be fine.

When the time came, Ahmad and Homa stood beside one another behind Lalah, next to the groom's parents, wearing smiles that made them look like a happy couple. Ahmad found himself flooded by memories revived by Homa's perfume. When the mulla prepared the marriage contract and read it out loud to the couple and friends and family standing in silence, Ahmad did what Homa had done in that small postpartum room: he slipped his hand into hers. Homa did not pull her hand away. Ahmad felt her fingers close around his, tight like in those early years. He could see Lalah behind the white veil in the mirror, her large mascaraed eyes, her slender nose, her beautiful face, although a little hazy, as if through a fog, and he knew that she had not seen her parents' hands.

Just over the heads of the seated couple, Ahmad looked at Homa in the mirror, stared at her until she turned her eyes and looked back at him without shying away, and it was at that moment when Ahmad told himself, That's my wife. After the mulla pronounced the couple man and wife, Ahmad took out his notepad and wrote.

I have kept our home like it was.

Homa looked at the paper for a few moments. She took a tissue from a nearby table and dabbed at her eyes before tears slid down her mascaraed eyelashes. Then she lifted her face and looked at Ahmad, unable to say a word. Ahmad could not interpret the look on her face. Finally Homa's lips quivered and a tear came down, leaving a dark trail on her cheek. "I found someone else, Ahmad."

Ahmad turned around and strode outside to lose himself in the craze of the wedding. In the neighbor's yard, he filled cup after cup with the bitter fluid. He danced with his daughters in the circle of guests and the few tears that fell on his tie everyone thought were of happiness. Then he held his son-in-law's hand and motioned for more upbeat music. Although banal and sloppily put together, the words of the song churned in his head, seeking but failing to find a way out. He danced with Reza and cajoled some of the other guests onto the floor. Fingers snapped, hips gyrated, foreheads beaded with sweat. Ahmad pushed through the circle of dancers to Khan and careened his wheelchair into the middle, whirling the old man around on the back wheels. Khan waved his cane in the air and twitched his mustache by pouting his lips. He whooped and clapped his hands and when Ahmad turned to take him back, he threw his hand up and shouted, "No, no! More, more!"

When his wet shirt stuck to his body, Ahmad sat at an empty table, wiped his neck and forehead, and watched: a young man danced as if he was doing jumping jacks, boys and girls kept bouncing up and down on the floor, people were in conversation across the garden, a lascivious, old man tried to flirt with a girl in her twenties, and two naughty little boys plucked from the walls the little bright poems and shoved them into their pockets, from which rays of light shone. He felt a tap on his shoulder and turned around to find a man standing by his side. It took Ahmad's tired eyes a few seconds to focus on the bearded face and recognize his old friend in a smart, white suit and trimmed hair combed back.

"The whole neighborhood has been talking about the wedding of the poet's daughter," Salman said in answer to Ahmad's questioning looks. "Word gets around, my friend." He pulled out a chair and sat down. "I missed you, brother."

Ahmad slung his arm around Salman's neck. Sitting at that metal table, surrounded by oohs and aahs from the dance floor, the two men scoured at the rust on their friendship, trying to find the person they once knew under the changed skin and sharp face bones. *Should I ask about those years?* Ahmad wrote. "It's a happy day today," Salman said sitting back, smiling a cheerful smile. "Why waste it on sad things?" Ahmad drank from his cup and nodded. "Let me tell you about the good things." It was then that Ahmad found out the Air Force Arsenal attack had been carried out with his poem.

"If the movement ever gets anywhere," Salman said, "you can claim being no small part of it."

Ahmad pulled his arm away. *And if it doesn't?* Ahmad wrote on his notepad. *And if they find out it was me?*

"You don't trust me," Salman said, "and you have all the right. I messed up once. But you saved me from that hell. This time, they won't get their hands even on my dead body."

Does anyone else know?

"Two or three comrades, yes, but I'd trust them with my life. And they don't know who wrote it."

Ahmad stared at Salman for some time, as if pondering something that could be written in a book with the word sorrow in its title. Then he wrote on his notepad. *I'm a terrible person. I put you in prison.* "That's water under the bridge, Ahmad." Salman tried to console him. He put his hand on Ahmad's thigh, but Ahmad was now crying. *I put you in prison*, he wrote again. *I took your youth.* He lifted his head and stared into Salman's face as if he was not seeing him. Then he wrote again. *I'm despicable.* "What happened would have happened without you, too. You were an excuse, you were nothing." Salman did not know if his words meant anything to Ahmad, who looked at him with his lips pressed together and his head sorrowfully shaking. After long moments filled with music and happy sounds, Ahmad nodded his head and wrote: *I think you're right.* Salman was relieved, but Ahmad continued: *I'm nothing.* His shoulders shook with a new bout of crying. "That's not what I mean," Salman drew closer and threw an arm around Ahmad's neck, but before he could say anything else, Ahmad lifted his head, with a look that showed he had found a great answer to an unsolvable problem. *I know*, he wrote, *you have to slap me.* "What?" Salman read with a frown. Ahmad got to his feet and held his face out, leaning forward a little. "Sit down," Salman said. With his hand mimicking a slap in the air, Ahmad urged Salman to hit him. "I'm not slapping you, Ahmad." Ahmad took a step toward Salman and leaned forward. His red tie hung from his head as if his head was caught in an upside-down noose. Salman rose from his chair and took a step backward. "I'm not slapping you, Ahmad," he said a little louder. He was getting nervous. *Slap me*, Ahmad mouthed as if shouting, taking another step forward and making Salman retreat, then he bowed his head and started crying again. This time Salman did not comfort him. He took another step back and buttoned his suit. "I'm sorry, my friend," he said, his voice calm again. "You can't have everything you want." He turned around and walked toward the dance floor. Pulling two wads from his pocket, he showered the couple with crisp ten-toman bills and left.

A HEAVY SADNESS DESCENDED UPON the house after the wedding. For a few days, there was some activity as the workers tore down the arch with sledgehammers and fixed the wall where they had ripped it open. Then they took down the tarps and the scaffolding. Pooran looked at the yard and found it smaller. Soon a fine layer of snow covered the hoez, the yard, and the flower beds. Even without going up to Lalah's room on the roof, Pooran felt the weight of that emptiness. "Come sit with me?" Pooran asked Khan who was resting in his bed. She helped him to his side and into his wheelchair. She pushed him to the living room and parked him by an armchair. Then she turned the radio on and sat. A light music played.

"What would we do, Khan, if Ahmad left us?"

"He won't. He's not that kind of a son. I know him."

Pooran reached out and placed her hand on Khan's arm. Khan smiled.

THREE MONTHS AFTER LALAH'S WEDDING, they came for Ahmad. When he opened his locker in the morning, a note fell onto the floor. He picked it up. It was bad handwriting, not naturally so, but as if intentionally.

The principal found out about the absences you've been ignoring. He ratted you out last evening. They're coming today.

Ahmad looked around to see if anyone in the teacher's room had noticed him. He tried to close his locker. Books and papers fell and made a loud echoing noise. Throwing hasty looks to his right and left, he picked them up and stuffed them into the locker and tried to close the door, but something else was keeping it from closing. He stopped trying, picked up his bag, and walked out of the teacher's room. The books and papers fell again behind him. He rushed across the yard and motioned to the janitor, who guarded the gate, that he would be back shortly. A few minutes later, he sat in the Peykan. His hand was shaking. He fumbled with the bunch of keys before he could turn on the engine, and became a fugitive until the end of the Revolution.

Later he heard that agents had raided three classes and taken the teachers with them. He withdrew from his account what was left of his salary and drove toward Oos Abbas's forge. The neighborhood had changed. New shops had opened: a pharmacy, an electric shop, a bank. Some buildings had been renovated, others had popped up where before there was nothing. The street was crowded. When he got to where the forge had been, Ahmad found instead a dairy shop. Inside were large fridge display counters with white buckets of yogurt, yellow lumps of butter, and small containers of cream. He thought he had made a mistake. He walked up and down the sidewalk and looked into the shops again, but the forge was gone. Finally, he entered the dairy shop, his note ready in his hand. The man behind the counter told him Oos Abbas had died two years earlier. His family had sold the shop and returned to their hometown, Isfahan, to buy a house. Ahmad nodded a thank you and left. He spent a few nights at a cheap inn in East Tehran and looked for work, but found none. At the end of a week, he bought a shovel.

With the little that he earned, he found a basement room that belonged to a mechanic. Oos Saeed the Mechanic was short, wore his belt under his hanging belly, and looked for his cracked glasses on his tools table to read Ahmad's notes. The stairs down to Ahmad's room were at the back of the mechanic's shop, the greasy black floor and walls of which reminded Ahmad of the forge. Every morning, Oos Saeed offered Ahmad tea before he set off for the streets. In the evening, if Oos Saeed had gone home already, Ahmad would open the small door installed in the larger metal gate and step alone into the dark garage. The days he was back earlier, he would sit and watch the mechanic work. "Pass the seven-inch wrench," Oos Saeed would sometimes ask. "It seems like you'd have a lot to say if you had a tongue," he said once, his head invisible in the engine of a car. "By the way," he said another day, "why don't you leave that nice car of yours inside when we're free. And we're free many nights. You'll delay the rust and keep cats away." Ahmad motioned for him to say more. "They crawl under cars, and into the engine. It's warm after you kill the engine. They curl up there for the night."

When a short while later General Akbar Oveisi, the chief of the gendarmerie, died in the mountains of the North, Ahmad asked the mechanic if the cats could tamper with the engine or some other part. The general's car had veered off the road and tumbled down a valley. The mechanic was not sure. "What I know is you don't want cat's blood on your car when you start it in the morning," he said. "It's a bad omen." The government blamed the event on the saboteurs and the announcement was made on the radio: the assembly of more than ten people was forbidden. Two days later Ahmad found a flyer in the garage. Ayatollah Khomeini had made a speech. The flyer was poorly made, the smudgy letters ran into one another.

They want to scare us. They want to separate us. They want to stifle the people's movement. They want us at home so they can do their arresting and killing without a concern. I tell you that is what they want. I say this is a ploy. This is a plot. Heed not to the plot. Take to the streets. The regime has no legitimacy. The people have the legitimacy.

AND THEY DID. IT STARTED from the square that later was called the Square of the Eight. Within two hours a police station was attacked. The noncommissioned officers escaped. Rocks shattered the windows, a car was set on fire, and the three guns and some ammunition were snatched from the cabinets and drawers before army reinforcement arrived. Someone from among the protesters fired a shot and the commander ordered the soldiers to fire back. Everyone scattered; everyone except eight young bodies left with holes in them.

At a safe distance Ahmad jumped up into the back of a pickup truck by the street and witnessed the commotion. For the first time in thirteen years, he found himself at a rally. Fear of losing his legislative seat and dread of the intelligence system even after his resignation had kept him away from the streets. Now he was a runaway with no job and a shovel in his hand.

He would not be able to read his poetry in front of people again. His name would not be published at the bottom of a magazine page, but on blacklists.

Ahmad looked around for cats. If they were helping the movement, or if they, and not people, were the cause of the movement, as Khan thought, they would be near. At first, Ahmad saw them here and there, apparently not doing anything helpful: sitting in trees, walking on top of walls, lying under parked cars, and running in less crowded patches of the streets. Busy barricading the streets, filling sacks with dirt, and breaking into government buildings, people did not seem to heed those everyday appearances and Ahmad, too, did not intend to be a bystander and only watch anymore. He jumped down from the truck and joined the crowd. Although he did not walk too far ahead, he chanted the slogans with the people in his head and felt he understood the occasional need to pick up a rock from the flower bed and hurl it at those khaki uniforms in the distance.

At some point, as he was walking ahead among the crowd, Ahmad heard noises from behind and saw that heads turned back and people hurried aside, as if to clear the way for something coming from behind. "Move over, move over," a voice shouted. Ahmad turned and saw a wheel of fire rolling toward him in the middle of the street, shooting red flames that raged so high the snow could not put them out. He ran to the sidewalk. There were shouts and cries from all over. It was a tire, not a small one, but that of an eighteen-wheeler or a lorry. As it rolled past him, Ahmad saw for an instant an orange cat inside, running as if for its life and rolling the tire forward toward the rows of soldiers. Together with the crowd, Ahmad returned to the street in the wake of the tire and watched how the cat split open the uniform-wearers, too, with that hellish fire. It was then that he opened his mouth to shout the slogans with everyone, even though no sound came out.

"HELLO?" POORAN SAID HALTINGLY INTO the phone. "Hello?"

Knock.

"Ahmad, is that you?"

Knock.

"How are you, my son?"

Knock.

"Are you taking care of yourself?"

Knock.

"Do you have enough money?"

Knock.

"We are good, too. Majeed was here this morning. He brought bread and some fruit. He's a good boy. I haven't been to Leyla's in a week. I'm going this Friday. I don't know what to bring for Behrooz. The other day he called and said, 'Grandma, come play with me.' I said, 'I'll come this Friday.' He said, 'Bring Aunt Zeeba, too.' He's such a sweet boy. I'm taking Khan, too. Otherwise Zeeba has to stay home to take care of him. Poor girl. She never complains. I said, 'Khan, you need to come, you need to get out, it's good for you and Zeeba.' He grunted and growled, but it wasn't like he meant it. He nags a little, you know, but I'll take him . . . Ahmad . . . Are you there?"

Knock.

"Are you going to be at this number for a little while?"

Knock knock.

"Will you send me a new number again when you can?"

Knock . . .

"Ahmad."

Knock . . .

"Are you coming home? . . ."

"Are you?"

Knock knock.

SO OLD AND WEARY WAS the sound of Pooran's voice over the phone that if it were not for the news that came out toward the end of summer, Ahmad would have returned home to care for her. A fuel train heading for Tehran from the refineries in the South had been derailed. The tank cars blazed for three days before the snowstorm came to help. A week after the fire was out, some newspapers reported that the investigators had found poetic scrawls on the remnants of the tracks. They had no doubt that the incident had been an act of sabotage. A passenger train was derailed a week later, killing twenty people. A bank was robbed, the bars melted off security doors, the hinges on the vault an amorphous lump of metal on the floor.

Ahmad's poem was going around in the hands of how many people, he did not know. His only hope was that the regime would not learn his name and Salman would be safe from danger. Whatever it was, it would end. It was less than a year and half until the day Khan had predicted as the culmination of the Revolution. That was not a long time. Ahmad could lay low in the dark and damp basement of Oos Saeed waiting for the cats and people to do whatever they were doing. Or he could take shelter among the people who filled the streets, the unnamed thousands bound by their shared desire for things to be otherwise. In that havoc of bodies running replete with hope and fear, Ahmad was a nobody. He had already made his choice. The day they wrapped ropes and cables around the equestrian statue of the Shah and pulled it down, Ahmad was among the people yanking.

31

AKING UP FOR HER LOSS OF EYESIGHT, Zeeba's ears had
grown so keen she could hear what lovers whispered to each other
in bed three houses away. Soon after Nana Shamsi brought her to
Khan's house, she learned to recognize the footsteps of each member of the
family. From the sound of breathing in the room below, Zeeba could tell if
Pooran was sleeping on her back or her side. If someone was eating downstairs, she could tell who it was and what they were chewing. So the night
she heard the footsteps on the roof, crunching on the blanket of snow, she
did not panic. It was Ahmad coming back. Zeeba heard him climb up a short
parapet and jump lightly onto the roof of the adjoining building. She had
missed the sound of his breathing, the way he put his feet on the ground
with determination, heel first, even now that he was sneaking on the roofs

of houses in the dead of the night. She listened to the alarm clock ticking by the side of her mattress on the floor. It sounded like a quarter to three. Finally the footsteps reached Khan's house, jumping over onto the new room, Behrooz's room, then creaking down the metal stairs to the roof of the main building. Then came the creaking of the elevator, the hum of the motor, and shortly after, Ahmad stood in the veranda, opened the door, and went in.

He sat at the telephone table in the hall and waited for the morning. A faint light came in from the yard; the snow had light in it as if saved from its descent through the sky. In fourteen years no night had passed in absolute dark. Hours went by in silence until a dampened call for prayer sounded from a mosque somewhere in the night. Not long after, a door creaked open and Ahmad saw his mother step out of her room. Halfway toward the kitchen, she stopped, paused for a second, and turned on the light.

"I'll make you some breakfast," she said to Ahmad as if she had been expecting to find her son sitting in the hall at that early hour. "You look hungry."

The lines in her face were more pronounced than Ahmad remembered. She walked slowly, and it seemed she exerted herself to stay standing. The slouch in her back had grown more pronounced, making her a smaller mother than the he had last seen, as if she was starting to shrink to nothing.

Khan had lost the power in his arms. Lying in his bed, he turned to Ahmad and smiled. "Now that the family is together again," he said, sitting up, "we can have a good breakfast." When Ahmad pulled the wheelchair close to the bed and threw back the sheets, a sour whiff of urine rose to his nostrils from a large, wet spot that darkened the front of Khan's pajamas. Khan looked down and his face turned with the force of a suppressed sob. He pressed his palms over his face and pulled the sheets back over him. From his wardrobe Ahmad took out fresh pajamas and put a hand on Khan's frail shoulder, but Khan hid under the sheets and refused to come out until Zeeba walked in.

"I'm going to make you an egg," she said, "the way you like it."

"Ahmad," Khan said from under the blanket, "you go out."

Ahmad walked out of the room and let Zeeba change him.

"Last time they came for you was two months ago," Pooran said in the kitchen. "Maybe they stopped looking."

Ahmad gave her the phone number of the mechanic's shop and emphasized that she should never call from the home line.

Two hours past midnight, Zeeba and Ahmad helped Pooran and Khan onto the elevator. The moon shone from behind a thin screen of clouds. Ahmad kissed his mother and held her in a long hug. Then he put an imaginary telephone handset to his ears. "From the booth," Pooran said, nodding calmly to assure Ahmad again that she would be prudent. Ahmad turned to Khan. "When will you come next?" Khan asked. Ahmad shrugged his shoulders. "Okay, go now." Khan was too proud to show his feelings. He turned his head to look out over the white city where yellow lights shone in a haze that hovered lightly above burdened roofs. Ahmad drew closer, stepped around to be in front of Khan, but, like a stubborn little boy, he turned his head the other way. "Khan!" Pooran scolded. "I'm not looking at him until he says when he is coming." Ahmad held up two fingers. In his peripheral vision, Khan saw them, forming a V. "Weeks?" he asked, a little doubtful of his optimism. Ahmad shook his head. "Months?" He still was not free of the fear he would be wrong. But Ahmad nodded. Khan looked relaxed and satisfied. He opened his arms. Ahmad leaned forward and hugged him, then turned to the girl whose blue eyes were unmoving. He wanted to thank her and tell her she was what held the house together. He looked at her for a moment, not knowing what to do. At last, he put his hand on her arm and gave a gentle squeeze. Zeeba put her hand on his. "It will feel quiet without you," she said. Ahmad gave another gentle squeeze to her arm, but Zeeba also heard him nod slightly, then she heard his footsteps as he jumped over onto the neighbor's roof. She also heard the footsteps of a cat walking on the edge of the roof of a nearby building, but did not notice when the cat stopped walking and sat on her hinds. Paws pressed together in front of her, and tail curved behind her on the snow, she looked up, with green eyes, at the sky where the pale light from a full moon sifted through thin clouds to shine on her shimmering, black fur.

Zeeba took Khan downstairs and put him in his bed, then she washed the dishes and went up to her own bed. She tried to close her ears to the sounds of the night and banish Majeed from her mind. He would come in the morning to shovel the yard and roof and sneak into Zeeba's room, which was now easily done, with everyone gone from the house and with the Railways Company in a state of inactivity. Following the latest sabotage of the tracks, the government ordered a temporary cancellation of all train transit until the tracks were inspected and secured, but soon after, a new cassette had flown in and the Railways workers had gone on strike. So Majeed spent half of his days at work not working and the other half with his camera in the streets. He had taken hundreds of photographs of the protests and succeeded in selling a dozen to journals and newspapers. When a year later Cinema Rex was set on fire, he told Short Poet there was now no going back. From then until the end of the Revolution, Majeed stole nine feature films from movie theaters. In one of the fires, he came out with a blistering arm, sprinting away from the theater doorman into the protesting crowds. He screened the films in his private theater, for himself alone, for his friends, and twice for Zeeba. He put a chair for her right in front of the screen at equal distance from the two speakers and watched her smiles, her frowns, and the raising and lowering of her eyebrows. He sat behind her and whispered into her ears the actions of the film when there was no dialog. When the actors talked, he hugged her neck from behind, and slipped his hand down her dress. She pushed her feet into the floor and tilted the chair back, certain that there was someone to catch her from behind. Majeed went to each new film with his portable tape recorder. The next day, on Khan's roof, he would pass the tape to Zeeba.

"This one is wrapped in green," he said. "The ribbon is green too, only a little lighter, say pistachio."

Years later, when Majeed was at work, Zeeba would play the tapes over and over again and watch the films in her head. Her daughter liked to look at her father's photo albums. "Tell Mommy which one you are looking at now, Anna?" Zeeba asked. With a lisp, saying the S by putting the tip of her tongue between her teeth, Anna described those in the photo and told her mother about the people running and shouting and about the cars and buildings, but she quickly turned the pages to the pictures she liked best, from the week before the Shah flew away. "Are you looking at the kitties?" Zeeba asked, even though she knew. "Under the Jeep," Anna started, putting her little finger on the felines she found in each photo, "there is a kitty that is green because he has played with the paint and turned over the bucket and the tire is green and the kitty is green." She turned the page. "Two kitties in the trash can. One is like looking at the other and she says, 'Why is your hair standing up?' And he says, 'Why, don't you see there is fire in the trash can behind you?' And she says, 'It's okay, we can jump out and go swim in a pool and eat strawberries.'"

She turned the pages. Anna always ended with her favorite image, taken on the very last day. It showed an army soldier with a helmet on, his hands clutching his G-3, surrounded by a group of boys who could not be over twelve. Standing in front of the soldier, a woman was inserting the stem of a rose into the barrel of the rifle. The boys were smiling. No one seemed to have noticed the camera or the orange cat that stood on top of three rows of sandbags behind the group, holding up its tail straight. It was not the only photo of people giving roses to the soldiers, but it was the only one in which a cat was looking directly into the camera. "Mrs. JeeJee says, 'Oh, no, boys, don't pick the flowers.' And the boys say, 'We picked the flower because this gun needs flowers.' Mrs. JeeJee says, 'Okay, but next time buy from the shop.'" "Where did the boys pick the flowers, Anna?" Zeeba asked. "From the park." Majeed had knelt down and zoomed in on the scene. It was a simple shot. Right before he pressed the button, the cat had jumped up from behind the makeshift bunker and peered deep into the lens.

Ahmad had seen them everywhere, too. The cat in the blazing tire was only the beginning; from then until the day the Revolution claimed victory, he saw so many that he stopped counting. He saw two cats shot out of an open door holding burning sticks in their mouths and galloping across the sloshy street. On the other side, they snuck into the basement window of a building which Ahmad later learned was the court archives where prisoners' records were kept, and minutes later the flames roared through the windows of the basement that turned into a furnace. He saw two cats dragging two punctured gunnysacks with their teeth while a third played around, rolling in the snow, like it had lost its mind, only to later realize that the salt they scattered had melted enough ice for throngs of protesting feet. He saw a cat with a red-hot screwdriver in his mouth run under an army Jeep and poke a hole in a front tire making it unusable. But nothing compared to the last day of the monarchy.

All through the city—and across the country—people were out. At any major square Ahmad would have seen the fall of the regime firsthand, but that last day he came out of the mechanic's shop and walked toward the University of Tehran. Some shops were still open, but as Ahmad drew closer, there were more closed blinds. The streets became crowded with people apparently wandering around, hurrying toward indistinct destinations. Cars tried to veer past the unpredictable human flow. People talked to each other, passed on news that no one could confirm as true or false. "Look at that, look at that," Ahmad heard a young man say to his friend with amused, short laughter, and when he looked, Ahmad saw somewhere around ten cats on top of a car, clinging low to the bars of the cargo rack as if headed for the battlefield.

An ambulance wailed past, in the opposite direction of the university. Ahmad walked on. Now there were some women, too, both those in chadors and others in pants and coats. A group of young boys and girls a little ways ahead in the street walked hand in hand as a sign of unity. A blue pickup passed and the back of it, too, was full of cats. Before Ahmad lost sight of it, the taillights went red, and the vehicle stopped at a barricade in the street. The hitchhikers leapt off and disappeared among the parked cars.

Past the barricade—a heap of trash: broken chairs and furniture, crumpled plastic cans, a piece of metal railing—the farthest person was two steps away and there was certainly no driving in those streets. Slogans rose from various corners and swept through the proceeding crowd. Fists went up and shouts rang out. Shots echoed across the city, but no one knew in which direction the bullets were flying.

When they were close, Ahmad realized that from what later became Revolution Square to the closed gates of the university was a no man's land. To the east of the gates, the soldiers stood in rows with rifles in hands. To the west and south were throngs of shouting people. In between, the bravest charged at the soldiers. Feeling less vulnerable behind fences and bold with the no-uniform-on-campus law, the university students shouted out slogans, threw rocks, and shook the bars.

There was barely any snow left on the ground, all melted by salt or soles. People punched the air and stamped their feet. If the officers in the distance had anything to say into their megaphones, it was impossible to hear over the din. Ahmad squeezed through the crowd toward the front line. Warm blood surged in his veins. White smoke from fires in the middle of the street blurred the view and separated the people from the soldiers. Then, more tires on fire, this time three, came rolling through the crowd. Near the gates of the university, the cats dashed out and let the tires drop to their sides making a barrier between the people and the army Jeeps ready to ram through the people. Farther ahead, behind a few stacked sand bags, a young man sheltered, lying on his stomach in a flower bed and pointing his rifle toward the soldiers.

Tear gas was fired. Ahmad ran back. Holding rags to their mouths and noses, two boys sprinted toward the fuming cans, grabbed them, and threw them back. More than once, a cat leaping out of the street ditch snatched the bellowing can faster than anyone and zoomed toward the soldiers in a zigzag to dodge bullets. Ahmad threw a few stones as hard as he could and immediately lost track of them in the air. He walked ahead, ran back. He saw young people melting to the ground, blood-red circles growing on their chests from the bullets that came out of the white curtain of smoke, past which one could not see. He saw a rifle fixed in place in the railing of a small first-floor balcony, its barrel aimed at the soldiers and two cats operating it. One had an eye closed, and looked, with the other, through the front and back sights. The cats could not move their weapon; instead they waited for a target to position himself in front of the rifle. The second cat was ready to fire: he was lying by the side of the rifle like the Sphinx, resting his black paw on the trigger. Ahmad lingered to see them at work when they fired a shot. The cat taking aim was brown, had his paws slung on the stock like a gambler at the tracks leaning against the railing following his horse. He held his tail up straight. The other was tricolor, lying on his stomach, relaxed except for the paw on the trigger. It happened in a fraction of a second: the brown tail came down and the black paw pulled the trigger and a loud bang rang out with from the muzzle. Kicked back to their feet, the two cats lay back in place, ready for their next shot.

News came by the hour: the people occupied the national television stations, soldiers joined the people ten at a time, waiting for the opportune moment to detach themselves and taking off their uniforms as they ran to the opposite side in undershirts.

Two hours after noon, the soldiers in front of the university were still resisting. After a round of bullets was fired, Ahmad ran back and turned onto one of the branching streets, and it was there that he saw a company of cats of all colors running into the open door of the six-story building on the corner, last in a row of buildings of more or less the same size that formed the southern edge of the main street. There was something about those cats, their lean, lithe build, the way they ran strong and confident, that made Ahmad follow them. None of them turned a head to check anything in the street: they were a focused line, hurrying to do something they knew well.

The corridors were dark but for weak streams of light from small windows. Ahmad ran up the stairs following the soft footsteps of the agile felines, until he went through a metal door onto the roof. The cats jumped over the short parapet that separated the roofs of the adjacent buildings. Ahmad ran after them, and a few roofs ahead came to a stop. He could see what the cats were planning to do, one roof ahead from where he stood. About twenty cats stood in a line, sitting on their hind legs, tails slowly swaying. On their turn each cat stepped forward and stood still on all fours to get strapped with a pair of black plastic wings. At that moment, Ahmad realized: those cats were going to fly. Or at least try.

A three-legged black-and-white and a fat tabby carried the wings from piles on either side of the installing station. The pilot cats stepped into the straps of the right wing, which the black-and-white fastened with the help of the tabby. Trying with difficulty not to lose his balance on one hind leg, the black-and-white pushed on the velcros to make sure they were secure. Then the tabby got a left wing from the pile on the left and installed it with the help of the black-and-white.

Ahmad hurried to the edge of the roof, bending over so as not to be seen, and looked down. They were very close to the line of soldiers, almost on top of them. He dashed back to the separating parapet to watch. In that moment, several cats in line noticed his presence, turned their heads, and watched him for a few seconds, but then turned back to their work, perhaps deciding Ahmad would not be a problem. When all the pilots had their wings on, the tabby opened the lid of a wooden case. Inside were guns, small handguns no bigger than half of Ahmad's palm; he recognized a semiautomatic Beretta among the different kinds. The winged cats stood in line again and Ahmad realized that the strapping on the right side had something like a holster where the tabby and the black-and-white fit the guns in place. A miniature string and pulley system made it possible for the pilots to pull the trigger by yanking one end of the string in their mouths.

A siren wailed in the distance. The cats were ready, their guns pointing straight down, the ends of strings in their mouths. Ahmad ran to the edge of the roof, again keeping his head low. He wanted to see it all. The cats stood in rows of four—Ahmad could count them now: there were sixteen—bodies lowered, ears flat, and the tips of their wings almost touching. Then as if by a silent order, the first row began running toward the edge of the roof. Behind them, the second row broke to a gallop, and behind them the other two rows. The cats ran the length of the roof, gaining momentum, and at the end sprang up on the short parapet and took a long leap into the air. With four paws hanging, and no control over the plastic wings, they flew off in different directions, ready to pull on the string as soon as the breeze and luck positioned them on top of the soldiers. The soldiers looked up. The officers stood in shock for a few seconds and then gave orders to fire at the flying objects.

The air raid was not very successful. Three of the pilots glided smoothly into the dry plane trees that lined the street and a fourth was unlucky enough to get caught in the power lines, the pilot stuck hanging in the air. The rest were blown by the breeze toward the protestors and the campus. They slowly circled and floated in the air, gradually losing altitude until they landed within the crowd or among the students who, excited and amused, caught them and confiscated the guns. A few cats ran away before people set their hands on them. They could not run too fast, though, or else they would start to take off again, what with the wings still on their backs. There was one pilot—a gray Persian—whose wings took him toward the target, over the line of soldiers. Bullets whizzed past his ears. When he decided his position was right, he jerked the string without taking aim, as if scared. The soldiers fired bullets at him above their heads and moments later, he drifted softly to the ground, lifeless, his long fur drenched in blood, his eyes closed, the string hanging from the holster. A soldier picked him up and turned to his officer. The Persian had killed a soldier.

Ahmad went back down into the street where everything was on the verge of sliding into a whirlpool. Banks were destroyed. Flowers were offered. The picture of the Shah was cut out of the bills; the picture of the Ayatollah taped in its place. It was the last day.

He later heard how, to purge the city from the filth of the regime, a group of revolutionaries got in cars, revved the engines, and set off for New Town, the neighborhood in East Tehran where the brothels had been built. Madame started to take things seriously only after she heard the news of the Shah's departure. She had heard muffled shots in the distance, more frequently than the days before. It was about two in the afternoon when she called her girls.

"Everybody get dressed and come down pronto," she shouted from the bottom of the stairs. She kept their birth certificates but opened her vault, gave them cash, and sent them away. Before the last one left Madame's room, the front door was smashed. Men poured in carrying guns and hoisting sticks and pipes. Someone swung a shovel handle at a lamp on the small table in the entrance. A middle-aged man grabbed the girl by the arm and took her away. Glued to her chair, Madame watched as three men came for her, two striding around the desk and one leaping onto it. As they dragged her out, she saw a fourth man emptying a canteen of gasoline all over her office. Years later, Goli turned the pages of *The Journal Future,* looked closely at the page, and recognized the bloody face of Madame lying on the asphalt, her mouth open and her face streaked with blood. She threw only passing looks at the photos of the storming of the Evin Prison, and so she did not recognize the profile of Ameer in one photo pointing an outstretched arm toward the large metal gates, like an old commander ordering his men to assail the lines of enemy, for those souls behind brutal walls and in underground cells who had been the vanguards of a movement now so close to victory.

Goli would never see Ameer again; she contented herself with what she had left of him: a boy she called Ameer, as Ameer had once wanted. Neither would she ever see the other women Ameer had been with. She had asked Ameer about them, and knew their names. She knew there could be another Ameer boy somewhere by a mother called Shireen, who once had told her friend, when her son was accepted to college, "I should keep an eye on him. His father was one of those animals who scattered his seeds far and wide. His real grandfather was not much better either. It's in their blood. You won't believe me if I told you who he was. You just won't. I'll give you a hint: he's a famous poet."

AHMAD CELEBRATED THE REVOLUTION WITH everyone else, as a simple man amid the happy honking of horns and dancing and shouting. He went straight to Khan's house, and hugged his mother free from fear. Within days, many of the generals and top officials of the previous regime were arrested. The revolutionaries were helped by the markings of an unknown group who left distinguishable scratches on the doors of traitors: the agents of SAVAK, the top brass.

Within two weeks, Pooran invited the whole family to reunite and celebrate. She walked with difficulty, but she could not sit still. With her children and grandchildren taking care of everything, there was not much for her to do. She walked around the house and watched them at work. Leyla,

Maryam, and Parveen did most of the cooking. Lalah was pregnant, but strongheaded as she was, she refused to sit and rest. Parveen's children and Behrooz kicked at a ball in the garden. It would not be too long before they too would have their own babies. Time went fast. Sitting in his wheelchair, with a blanket spread over his lap, Khan watched them from the veranda. Pooran rested her hands on Khan's shoulders. Fluttering from branch to branch, sparrows chirped in the persimmon tree. Pooran felt a numbing calm settle within her and make her believe that everything was in its place now, and that all the rest could be peaceful. Life did not have to be defined by calamities. It could be uneventful. It could be just like when Khan and Agha sat by the hoez doing nothing. She had her winter. Now she deserved her spring.

When the guests were gone and the last rays of a bright sunset had turned the sky purple and orange, Pooran took one last look at the garden to make sure everything was in order and saw the ball the children were playing with in the lantanas. She put her slippers on and went down into the garden to pick it up. Walking back toward the house, with the ball in her hands, she saw from the corner of her eyes a metallic flash in the basement. For an instant, she was filled with a paralyzing horror as she made out the dark figure of a man lurking down there, but soon she recognized him. The whole time it took her to descend the four steps and open the narrow doors of the basement, she kept her eyes on him, although her weak vision showed her little of the uniform and the rifle. When she flicked the switch on, Nosser was standing in the middle of the basement, his left arm straight by his side, his right hand clasping the strap of the rusty rifle slung on his shoulder, pointing toward the low ceiling. The mud on his boots had dried into thick clumps, his uniform was dusty, and his young, bony face was dark with a few days' stubble. He looked at her with hollow eyes in a face void of emotions. "I stopped hoping to see you again," Pooran said with tears in her eyes.

"I'm happy," Nosser said, though he did not seem happy. "Everyone was happy today."

Pooran took a step ahead. "Can I hug you?" she asked. Nosser did not answer. Pooran put the ball down on the walnut table and slowly went to her husband, put her hand on his chest as if to make sure there really was someone under that dusty uniform, and then locked her hands behind him. "Am I going to be alone? Do I need a guard again?" Nosser did not answer. The basement felt outside of time. Finally, Pooran detached herself from her husband and said, "Let's go up and get you cleaned." She held his hand, but Nosser did not move.

"Not now," he said, "but maybe later."

The ball had rolled very slowly toward the edge of the table, and now fell and bounced a few times. Pooran and Nosser watched it roll on the floor and come to a rest.

LIKE EVERYTHING ELSE, THE HIGH school Ahmad had taught in was overcome by revolutionary dizziness. The old principal and deputy had fled and half of the students were absent from the classes that met irregularly. One of the teachers who had taken up the responsibilities of the principal nodded and Ahmad returned to work. But before the first real spring came to an end, he was arrested by the Revolutionary Committee on an afternoon that boasted its brilliant sun in a blue sky. It was the same day General Babapoor, the head of SAVAK, was tied to an antenna pole and executed by a firing squad. Two young revolutionary guards, in boots and olive overcoats, approached Ahmad as he walked toward his car after school.

"Ahmad Torkash-Vand?" the young man asked.

Ahmad nodded his head.

"Were you a member of the twenty-first parliament?"

Ahmad nodded his head.

"Would you come with us, please, sir?"

In his confessions after his arrest, General Babapoor had mentioned Ahmad's speech that preceded a crackdown on revolutionary violence. Ahmad was tried in court and convicted of collusion in the death, torture, and persecution of many civilians and fighters of the Revolution. Ahmad tried, but could not offer counterproof of having written the poem that enabled the Air Force Arsenal occupation, the derailment of trains, and many more acts that harmed the regime.

"Even if you did write that, sir," the judge said, "you wrote it for a woman, not the Revolution."

Because Ahmad had left the parliament and because his name was found on a SAVAK blacklist, he received a clement sentence of nine years.

32

ZEEBA THOUGHT POORAN was going crazy because she heard her spend long hours in the basement talking to her dead husband. She heard Pooran shuffle down the steps and say things like, "Do you want anything besides water?" or "At least have a seat, dear." She saved her longer conversations for nighttime. Up on the roof, Zeeba heard Pooran sit in the creaking chair and talk about her day before drifting into memories. Zeeba was worried Pooran would deteriorate into madness, but a few months passed and, besides talking to herself in the basement, Pooran was the same astute woman she had always known, and so Zeeba came to ignore the sounds she heard from the basement and sleep with peace of mind.

For a year and a half, Nosser did not sit down, except at night when Pooran came and insisted. Then one night, he still would not sit when she arrived, only shook his head, and she knew it was important. "You are leaving, aren't you." She did not ask, she knew it. Nosser did not answer, but in his concrete-cold face there was a look of sadness, of tears unable to flow. "Can you sit with me this one last time?" Pooran asked.

Nosser rearranged the strap of his rifle on his shoulder. "The Iraqis are coming." He walked toward the door, stopped before going out, and turned back to Pooran. "Can I take the ball?" He glanced at the plastic ball that had sat in the bookshelf since the first night. "War is dreary."

Pooran nodded softly, then got to her feet and took the ball from the shelf. She put her hands on his chest and strong arms, hugged him, and breathed the dusty smell of his uniform. Then she detached herself and waited for him to leave. Nosser opened the door and stepped out. He turned and said, "I love you," then climbed the stairs, one hand on the strap, one hand holding the ball.

THE FIRST YEAR, THE WAR was only in the west. The second year, Pooran went to the store and bought rolls of protective tape.

"I want to help," Khan said from his wheelchair.

Pooran gave him the scissors to hold and cut the tape for her. The old house had many windows and panes. They took their time. Khan put the scissors down in his lap and picked them up when Pooran unrolled the tape before him with a screech. Within three days there were X's on all the glass panes of the house, except for the ones Pooran could not reach. The red siren alert sounded over the radio and the two TV channels, but Pooran relied on Zeeba whose ears were more reliable than the alerts. When she heard the bombers in the sky, the girl would hurry down the elevator and put Khan in his wheelchair long before the alarms went off. Panting, the two women took the wheelchair down the stairs and through the narrow door of the basement. The top of the walnut table was the storage space for canned beans, boxes of crackers, a radio, two flashlights, extra batteries, two blankets, three rosewater bottles refilled with drinking water, and clean sheets. One night, Zeeba heard the fighter planes once again whistling in the distance and sprang to her feet as usual. When she rode the elevator down to the yard, though, she heard Khan refusing to get out of bed. Pooran was trying to persuade him.

"Who are they to scare me in my own home?" Khan's voice was calm and determined. "I'm lying right here."

Pooran took Zeeba's hand and consulted with her out in the hall. Back in Khan's room, they threw the sheets off of the old man. Zeeba held his arms and Pooran grabbed his legs. The frail figure thrashed with unbelievable strength, as if his life depended on his resistance. He fought all the way down to the basement, until they laid him on the walnut table. The next morning, Pooran found Khan's room locked from the inside.

"This is my house and I'm staying where I want," he called out. Pooran picked up the phone and called the locksmith. When they opened the door, Khan was sitting on the floor leaning against the wall, legs stretched and spread, polishing his shoes. "Leave me alone," he said, his head down to his work. "I'm not going to die. Agha's not dead either. These doctors don't know their heads from their asses."

Pooran stepped forward and stood over him. "Khan," she said, "I'm not young anymore." Khan looked up. "It's hard enough to deal with things as they are. If you don't go to the basement with us the next time, I'll take you there and lock you up." She said that with such certitude that Khan dropped his eyes and resumed brushing his cracked shoe. Pooran took the door key away, and for a week things were normal.

Majeed came and took the three of them to the park. He pushed Khan's chair and described to Zeeba the small Ferris wheel—red rings with two blue and two yellow seats—on which the children were riding. He reminded her about the first day they both rode a Ferris wheel, but he did not tell her about his jealousy of the new baby, Leyla, who had attracted all of his mother's attention at the time. He told Zeeba that there was a moment on that ride when he saw her from behind, sitting by the side of his sister, Parveen, and wondered how could her hair be so yellow? The four of them sat in the shade of an elm tree, Majeed, Zeeba, Pooran on the wooden bench and Khan in his chair, and bought ice cream cones from a man who walked around the park with an ice box strapped over his shoulder. Only three cones; Khan had already dozed off.

A week later, Zeeba came down shortly after dark to announce another raid. She went with Pooran to Khan's room, but he was not there. With anxious voices they called his name and searched the house until Zeeba heard a faint rustle from under the bed. When Pooran ducked down to look, he was grasping the legs tight with both hands. After they finally pulled him out and took him down onto the walnut desk, Pooran was almost crying from the pain that throbbed in her back and knees. That was the night that Pooran locked Khan in the basement for two years until the chemical attacks began and it was no longer clear whether the basement was the safest place or the roof. Then she gave up and had Zeeba and Majeed take Khan back to his room.

"From now on, you can do whatever you want," she told him.

Khan looked at her from his bed and said, "I want to see my grandson."

AT HER NEXT VISIT, POORAN tried to talk to someone in charge at the prison, but the young soldiers barely listened to her. "Immediate family only," they repeated. She came back home with no answer. Khan looked at her as if he did not quite understand her. "I'm his grandfather. Almost his father."

One day, he picked up the small bell from his nightstand and gave it a shake. Pooran rushed in. "I want to ride the Ferris wheel in the park."

That weekend, Majeed scooped him from his wheelchair into the crude metal seat and Khan smiled with the laughing children who were amused at seeing the old man. When the wheel stopped at the end of the round and Majeed came forward to pick him up, Khan tilted his head. "Can I go again?" He rode in the sun that sifted through the green leaves of trees and smiled even more. Late that evening, he rang his bell again.

"I want to see my grandson," he said to Pooran. The red alert sounded and the whole time the two women waited in the basement, Zeeba could hear Khan through the walls, ringing the bell in his bed.

AHMAD WAS WATCHING A GAME of soccer between young inmates when thunder rumbled in the east. Nothing was in the sky but the yellow disk of the sun pinned to the interminable blue. For a moment, they thought a new type of air raid was underway. Someone said the enemy had bought invisible bombers. Someone else said the new bombers flew so high the eye could not see them. But a few minutes later, a tiny patch of cloud appeared, flying very low, barely higher than the coils of barbed wire along the walls. The game stopped. The guards in the towers and the inmates in the yard watched the cloud slow when it approached the spot where Ahmad was squatting against the wall with Comrade Comrade, a friend in his forties, about ten years younger than Ahmad, with a Stalin mustache. Then it rained. First a few drops and then a shower poured on the two men like a vertical river. Drained into water that puddled on the asphalt, the cloud vanished. Ahmad turned to Comrade Comrade, equally drenched by his side, and mouthed something the man failed to understand.

"What is it, old man?"

Ahmad put his dripping forehead on his friend's wet shoulder and sobbed a silent sob.

"What is it?" Comrade asked again. Ahmad walked to the nearest dry wall, and wrote with his wet finger,

Khan has died.

33

AHMAD WAS RELEASED one year before the end of the war that took eight years to come to no result other than hundreds of thousands of new Iranian and Iraqi graves. Half the faces of the family that waited to welcome him in front of the prison gates were unfamiliar. Those he had known had developed an alien air, the others were new but had the looks of the people who used to come to his readings with a smile that said, *I know you so you should know me.* The women and girls wore long-sleeve, dark manteaux that came down to their ankles. Pooran was in her usual black chador. Ahmad's grandson, Behrooz, was a tall thirteen-year old boy. Maryam's husband had white hair on his temples. A little girl stood by Majeed and Zeeba's side who looked like a round hazelnut in head cover.

Ahmad sat in the front seat of Mr. Zia's car, his mother, Pooran; his daughter Leyla; and his grandson Behrooz in the back. The rest of the cars followed and the convoy passed through streets that were also now alien. There were cars everywhere, and only a rare, single bicycle dodging between. All women were covered from head to toe. Horns honked. Windows were crossed with wide tape, some with X's, others with a + as well as an X. All of that sparkled, a strange new city under a generous sun.

It took Ahmad five years before he managed to start work at a publication house as the poetry editor. In prison he had tried to write, lying in his bed in the dark, but the light that came from the page was so dim that it could not lead him anywhere. He thought he was losing it. Two years before his release, the light died: he wrote a word, there was a flutter, and then darkness. At the publishing house he could barely stand the trends among young poets, the play on words, poetry that pointed to its own poemness, language for the sake of language. His own books were still in the bookstores, selling more than any other poet, but not as many as the years before the Revolution. Fewer people bought books. Fewer people read poetry. Ahmad wanted to create something urgent, something that burned. He wanted to see the light again. He went to his old wardrobe and took out the poems that he had etched on trays. He unwrapped the towels and put his finger on the metal. They were still warm, but in a dull way. He copied the poems out on cardboard. They did not burn. He copied the poems on paper. The words sat on the page, inert.

At his seventieth birthday, the University of Tehran celebrated Ahmad Torkash-Vand's fifty-five years of literary accomplishment in a hall with a lit stage and rows of seats upholstered with red velvet. Four guests talked about his work and life, then Ahmad stepped onto the stage and mouthed as someone read from his most recent work. Ahmad looked out at the audience, his daughters and Maryam with their families in the front rows; colleagues, men and women of words here and there; and many he did not know, whose faces in the unlit back rows he could not make out without his eyeglasses. Men were in suit and pants, the younger ones in shirts, and the students in T-shirts and jeans. Women, still covered in manteaux, with scarves or shawls covering their hair, wore less dreary colors than when Ahmad had first come out of the prison: brown, olive, cream, navy. All sat in their seats listening carefully and clapping enthusiastically. As his eyes flit from face to face, he thought he saw someone familiar. He took his glasses out of his breast pocket and looked again. But he was mistaken. It was not Homa.

Ahmad lived for six more years and died two autumns before unrest broke out once more in the country. I don't know if he would have blamed the cats for the batons that went up and came down again, for the clicks of handcuffs, or for the young bodies that were dragged on the asphalt by their legs. He scooped spoonfuls of his lunch on scrap paper and stepped outside of the publisher's building to feed Rosie, the furry, gray street cat with a pink nose who reclined on the concrete edge of the flower bed in the sun. The cats were no longer fighting. They shared the streets and alleys with people. They ate trash without fear. They took naps on park benches. They traipsed around, the flaneurs of the city. Never did Ahmad ever see them fly again, or use their fangs and claws for a purpose.

When Ahmad wrote to his secretary about his decision to publish his previously unpublishable poems, she was more than eager to type them up for him. In the evening, she opened Ahmad's wardrobe and stood with arms akimbo in front of stacks of old trays before she started hauling them by the armful down the elevator and dropping them into the trunk of her car with a loud clatter. Three days later, the bell rang and there at the door, she pulled a bunch of papers out of her purse. When the sun was setting behind Ahmad's windows, as the orange stretched over the city with no ends, Ahmad sat at his desk and looked at the neat stack of poems in front of him that once set fire to any paper. Outside, the crows cawed misery as they circled in the sky.

Sitting in his chair, fingers drumming nonstop on the armrest, Ahmad looked for a long time. There were only three crows left flying in the sky when Ahmad's fingers stopped their unrestful rhythm. He pulled the drawer open and took out a piece of paper. He uncapped his pen and started to copy out his poem of the Revolution. Curve after graceful curve formed, word after slow word. No flame sputtered from the tip of his pen. The paper did not turn brown. Not even a faint light blinked under the letters. Then he came to the last word. He paused for a few seconds before he put the pen back on the paper and wrote.

In the last of the daylight Ahmad looked at the poem. Homa's name, which had burned holes in steel, sat on his desk drab and docile. Twirling his pen between his thumb and forefinger, Ahmad realized that the words were of the past, impotent, extinguished, and nullified. Once true and fiery at the core, they were now just lore.